WAR: DISRUPTION

ALSO BY VANESSA KIER

<u>The Surgical Strike Unit (SSU) Series</u>

Vengeance

Betrayal

Retribution

Payback

Aftermath

Undercover (Prequel Novella)

<u>The WAR Series</u>

WAR: Disruption

WAR: Intrusion

WAR: Opposition

WAR: DISRUPTION

WAR
BOOK ONE

VANESSA KIER

FIFTEEN YEARS AGO

As the clock moved from 1999 to 2000, many of the democratic countries of West Africa started a period of internal dissent. People rose up against corrupt, inefficient politicians. Civil wars broke out and spread throughout the region. In the aftermath, a new geopolitical structure emerged. In the east of the region Nigeria merged with Niger to form the Greater Niger Republic. Burkina Faso and the northern-most regions of Ghana, Togo, and Benin formed the United African Republic (UAR). The remainder of Benin and a bit of Togo became the Republic of Dahomey. The rest of Ghana and Togo became the Republic of the Volta. Côte d'Ivoire separated into the Ivory Republic (north) and the Democratic Republic of the Ivory Coast (south). Mali, Senegal, and Gambia became the New Mali Federation. Guinea-Bissau, Guinea, Liberia, and Sierra Leone became the Republic of West Guinea.

Now, however, the democratic societies have once again become overrun with corruption. The people are dissatisfied with their governments and with seeing multi-national corporations get rich off West African resources while the people remain in poverty. The African Freedom Army (AFA) promises to give power back to the West African people and offers hope for a better life. Yet their brutal tactics against both foreigners and any Africans who disagree with their strict doctrine and animist religion has begun to turn public opinion against them.

That's where the West African Rangers come in. An underground military and political group, WAR is dedicated to stopping AFA and returning true and honest democracy to the people.

This is the environment in which our story begins...

CHAPTER ONE

Day One
The United African Republic
West Africa

PEERING BENEATH HIS BLINDFOLD, Max Lansing saw Ansgar Ziegler's hand moving toward him holding a long, thin needle. Max braced himself against the wooden chair and tried once again to break his rawhide bonds. But he was trussed too tightly.

Sweat trickled down his spine as the needle touched the skin at the base of his neck. Max clenched his teeth and vowed not to scream this time, no matter how much pain the acupuncture needle inflicted as it triggered his nerves. He—

The door slammed open. Ziegler dropped his hand and spun toward the sound.

"Herr Ziegler, the scout reports that the boss's helicopter is fast approaching," one of the guards said in African accented English.

Ziegler cursed in German. "Rest up, Max," he muttered. "We shall finish this later."

"Can't...wait," Max said.

"Remove him," Ziegler ordered as he braced his case of needles with his deformed, scarred left hand and zipped it closed with his undamaged right hand.

Max felt a spurt of satisfaction knowing Ziegler had received those burns in a fight against him and his team. Of course, if Ziegler hadn't been injured, he wouldn't be torturing Max out of revenge. Instead, Max would have been turned over to Ziegler's boss, Dietrich, who had his own axe to grind with Max.

One of the guards untied Max from the chair, then two sets of hands captured his arms and dragged him into the hallway. A moment later they threw him into the tiny room that served as his cell. Pain rocketed through him as he hit the packed dirt floor and he almost blacked out. In addition to using needles, Ziegler had viciously kicked Max's torso and legs with the steel-reinforced toes on his loafers, damaging one of Max's ribs and leaving his whole body aching.

By the time Max's senses stopped swimming, the guards had tied his feet to a stake in the ground and left.

Max spat a hunk of his long blond hair out of his mouth and took a shallow breath, trying not to jar his ribs. Then he waited for the sound of footsteps in the hallway to disappear. This was the first moment in two...three... Hell, he'd lost track. The first time since he'd been captured that he didn't feel groggy from drugs.

He had to escape. Now.

He rubbed his cheek on the small piece of wood sticking up out of the dirt floor until his blindfold slid down his face. Not that he could see much more without the filthy rag covering his eyes. A trickle of light slipped through a crack up by the ceiling to reveal a room approximately six feet by six feet. The walls were standard for this part of West Africa, plastered concrete with a corrugated metal roof.

The most important detail? He was alone.

He exhaled in relief.

His hands were bound behind him, but not staked. He raised them to his waist and fumbled with his belt until he was able to slip the buckle around to the back. Then he pressed the mechanism to release the spring-activated knife. Sloppy of Ziegler's men not to do a thorough body search. Just because Max had quit Unit 3 and gone off on his own didn't mean that he hadn't brought some of the team's toys with him to Africa.

The blade sprung free. He rubbed his bindings across the blade's edge, keeping an ear out for approaching footsteps.

But all he heard was the approach of a helicopter.

Good. It would keep Ziegler and company distracted.

The rawhide gave slightly and Max increased the pressure until the bindings snapped. He made quick work of the bonds at his ankles, then gingerly moved his body—yeah, definitely at least one cracked or severely bruised rib—biting back groans of pain. Once he made it to his feet, he stepped around the congealed pool of vomit that marked the spot where he'd been sick the first night they brought him here and walked a few times along the exterior of the room to get circulation back in his arms and legs. Then he removed his belt and knelt down. Using the buckle as a trowel, he traced the outline of the trap door underneath the dirt.

If Ziegler had checked with the locals before choosing this building as a holding cell, he would have learned that this was a smuggler's storeroom. Max had figured it out the first time they threw him into the room. He'd hit the dirt and the corner of the trap door had poked into his cheek. Lucky for him, the trap door was on the far side of the room. The guards had tossed Max in, then advanced only far enough to tie his feet to the stake. They'd never stepped far enough in to feel the trap door beneath their feet.

Max's hands hurt from being stomped on and slashed at, but nothing was broken, so he kept scraping the dirt away with the belt buckle. It took him several more agonizing minutes to completely uncover the door.

"Herr Ziegler, you were not supposed to damage the prisoner. He is mine to hurt. To kill. Mine alone. Do you understand?"

Max froze at the angry voice speaking German with a faint Austrian accent. So familiar. So hated that his pain vanished under a wash of sheer fury.

Dietrich *was* alive.

Every instinct in Max urged him to race to the door. Break out and confront the man who'd been responsible for the attack that took his brother's lower legs and killed dozens.

His heart pounded. His hands shook with the need to bring Dietrich to justice.

So. Close.

This was the first time in a year that he'd been in the same location as the international arms dealer. His superiors back at Unit 3 had continued to insist that Dietrich died two years ago during a crash en route to a holding facility after being captured in a raid by Max and his team. None of the evidence Max and his teammates had gathered to prove that Dietrich had survived the crash had convinced their superiors otherwise. In fact, they'd ordered his team to drop the matter, then assigned them to other missions.

But Max and his teammates had known the truth. Although his co-leader Kris and many of the others had eventually quit Unit 3, Max had stayed. And he'd never given up searching for Dietrich.

He strained to hear more of the conversation, but they moved out of earshot. All he could tell was that Ziegler's response sounded defensive, never a good choice given Dietrich's insistence on absolute loyalty. Then another voice interrupted, sounding urgent and worried. Dietrich cursed. Their footsteps hurried away.

Good. Whatever emergency had come up, it had distracted Dietrich from paying Max an immediate visit.

He stared blindly at the trap door. God, he wanted Dietrich's head with such ferocity that he could barely think over the pounding of his blood through his veins. He wanted to make Dietrich pay for all the lives he'd destroyed. Wanted to discover the name of whoever in the U.S. military had been protecting Dietrich.

Max's vision pulsed in and out. Shit. He was in no shape to tackle Dietrich now. He'd come across the border chasing rumors that Dietrich had a major arms deal going down in just over two weeks. Less than that now, depending on how long he'd been held here.

The deal supposedly would result in an attack on American military or diplomatic facilities in the region. An attack that might impact Wil, who was stationed at the U.S. compound in the capital of the Greater Niger Republic. His younger brother had already lost his lower legs due to weapons Dietrich had supplied to terrorists in Afghanistan. Max wasn't going to let Wil be hurt again.

Christ. It killed him to leave, but what choice did he have? If he stuck around, he'd end up at the receiving end of Ziegler's needles again. Or Dietrich's knife. It was damn sure they weren't going to hold an entire conversation about the upcoming deal where Max could hear it.

He squared his shoulders then continued digging. He had to stick to his original plan. Find a safe place to hole up and recover. Then figure out where the deal was going down and stop it.

Piece of cake.

Yeah, right.

He slipped his battered, bloody fingers under the edge of the trap door and lifted. Because it was too dangerous to use his hidden flashlight to show him how deep the smuggler's hole was, he lay down on his belly, reached his arm into the hole, and dropped the buckle end of the belt down. When it brushed dirt, he knew he didn't have a very long drop. Good, because the fall might cause him to black out.

Knowing he wouldn't have much of a head start once someone entered the room and saw the hole, he took the dirt he'd removed from the hatch and piled it against the base of the door, hoping it would block Ziegler's men from entering long enough to give him a few extra minutes of lead time. Then he lowered himself into the hole, pulled the trap door closed, and used the small flashlight hidden in the sole of his boot to guide him through the rough, crawling-room-only tunnel to freedom.

Day Two
The Republic of the Volta
West Africa

THE TRO-TRO JERKED TO A STOP, yanking Emily Iwasaki out of a light doze. Blinking sleepily against the overhead light, she saw that the mate—the teenage boy who collected the money and announced the stops—had opened his door and hopped out. Lifting her head from the window of the battered minivan that served as a public bus, she peered outside, trying to figure out why they'd stopped. But she saw only her own reflection wavering against the darkness. Her hand rose reflexively to cover the scars on her neck and she deliberately let it drop. Part of her reason for coming to Africa was to learn how to be less self-conscious about the acid burn scars that stretched from the edge of her jaw down to the top of her right shoulder. For a moment she stared at the reflection of the shiny patches of damaged and grafted skin. After their initial curiosity, the people in her home-stay village had quickly ignored her imperfection. Yet Emily found it impossible to forget that she was no longer the elegant, beautiful dancer fit to play queens on stage. That she was now unemployed. Adrift in a world that no longer revolved around ballet.

The woman next to Emily let out a loud, coughing snort and jolted awake. As she rearranged her position, she jabbed Emily in the side several times with her elbow. Emily accepted the woman's murmured apology and shifted sideways on the cracked vinyl seat to give the woman more room. Pressed closer to the window, Emily focused past her reflection to the night beyond, trying to understand why they'd stopped. The road was too far from major population centers to have streetlights. No light shone from the jungle. No irrigation canals lined the dirt road. There were no nearby buildings or intersecting roads or other signs of nearby habitation. So this wasn't the way station where she was supposed to get off and meet the rest of her tour group. Not even a regularly scheduled stop.

Unease slithered through her. Her heart gave a few flutters, a warning that she needed to be careful or she'd end up with one of the panic attacks she now occasionally suffered from. She glanced across the aisle at Masaud, the tour company's guard who'd been sent to fetch her from the village. He met her eyes and gave a little shrug and a head shake. Still, he didn't seem alarmed, so some of her tension eased.

Okay. So maybe they weren't in danger. Most of the other passengers remained asleep. The few who were awake didn't seem concerned by their unexpected stop. Probably the teenager had simply gone to relieve himself. Or there was something blocking the road. After taking several deep breaths, Emily slowly moved her neck through a series of rolls to loosen muscles stiff from dozing with the side of her head against the window.

Yet she kept her attention on the open passenger door, unable to completely shake her unease. As far as she knew, the rebels who'd been slowly taking over West Africa hadn't entered this country yet, but then, she'd spent the last week on a homestay in a village with no electricity and so hadn't heard any recent news reports.

Outside, the teenager raised his voice in a sharp question. Emily leaned forward, straining to hear. A deep male voice with an American accent answered, "Yes, I can pay."

All vestiges of sleep gone, Emily straightened in her seat. This section of the country wasn't popular with foreign tourists. In fact, some of the children in her homestay village had never met a white person before. Of the six women in the dance tour group, Emily and two others had been placed with homestay families scattered across this upper east region. The other three had been sent to villages in the southeast region. According to the local grapevine, Emily was the only foreigner for miles.

So what was an American doing on a deserted road in the middle of the night?

The side door to the tro-tro slid open and a white guy climbed inside. She couldn't see much of him as the people nearest the door shifted to give him room, but he appeared to be a fit man not that much older than her. Maybe in his late twenties or early thirties. He wore a light-colored, sweat-stained t-shirt underneath an unbuttoned, untucked khaki shirt over khaki pants. The road's thick red dust clung to his body and clothes in a fine film and dulled the long, blond ponytail that snaked out from underneath his baseball cap. Several days' worth of stubble covered his jaw.

As he ducked inside he surveyed the passengers. She couldn't see the color of his eyes beneath the shadow of his ball cap, but his attention sharpened when it reached Masaud. A moment later, his gaze moved on to her. She sensed that her presence startled him, and that he was assessing her. As what? A threat? A potential ally? An unimportant freak because of the ruined skin on her neck? Keeping her shoulders back and her chin up, she waited while he finished his scrutiny, fighting the urge to once again put her hand over her scars. Aware that since local custom had the other female passengers fashionably dressed in traditional blouses and skirts, her own t-shirt and cargo pants made her appear grubby in comparison. Finally, the stranger dipped his chin in a nod and turned away.

Emily let out a breath. Who was this man? Even the ballet company's assistant director, known for intimidating dancers with his critical gaze during performance reviews, hadn't watched her with such intensity. And how had he picked Masaud out as being dangerous? Out of courtesy to the driver, the guard's pistol wasn't visible.

As the door slammed shut, the stranger placed his worn backpack on the floor and settled into the one available seat without giving her a second glance. His shoulders jerked toward his ears as he sat, and he held his elbows close to his body, carefully avoiding contact with his neighbors. Quite a feat in these cramped quarters, but Emily recognized the protective action. One of her dance partners had cracked a rib in an auto accident and he'd held himself in just such a way for days afterward. Wondering how the stranger been injured, Emily's unease returned.

Several of the passengers whispered amongst themselves. She heard the word *obruni*, which meant foreigner. A few eyes glanced her way.

Emily dropped her gaze, twisting her hands together on a sudden burst of fear. Were some of the passengers rebel sympathizers? Was she in danger? So far, she'd received only a warm welcome from the locals. She'd seen no evidence that the people here subscribed to the vicious, nationalistic rhetoric of the African Freedom Army that had resulted in many foreigners being kidnapped or killed in neighboring countries. Emily would never have joined this tour if the rebels had been active here.

The tro-tro started up again. Emily's heart stuttered as the overhead light shut off, plunging the interior into darkness. But when the other passengers settled quietly back into sleep, she gradually relaxed. The tour company had guaranteed that no harm would come to her or the other women on the tour. In the weeks leading up to their arrival, the rebels had been busy fighting government forces next door in the Democratic Republic of the Ivory Coast. The government of the Republic of the Volta had backed up the tour company's promise. They'd assured Emily and the other women that should the rebels approach the border, their armed forces were strong enough to fight off any attack. The government wanted the tour to go ahead, to show the rest of the world that the country was safe for tourists. Plus, both the tour company and the government had explained that the men guarding the women were highly skilled former soldiers. Emily trusted that Masaud would protect her.

Even with tonight's hint of danger, she didn't regret turning down her father's offer to hire an additional, private bodyguard. She had to learn how to navigate the non-ballet world on her own. Danger and all.

Besides, she just wanted to blend into the world as much as her scars allowed. Having a private bodyguard would have set her apart from the others on the tour and prevented her from making the friendships that had already developed between her and the other women.

The homestays were the only point at which the women were on their own, allowing them to learn local dances and customs that they'd later incorporate into a dance program with the orphans. The tour company had offered strong assurances that all the villages were located in very calm, pro-foreigner regions of the country. Emily was supposed to have been picked up by the tour this morning, but instead Masaud had shown up on foot and explained that the group's Land Cruiser had two flat tires and was holed up at a regional way station, the equivalent to an American rest stop. The way station didn't have appropriate replacement tires, so their driver had borrowed a vehicle and headed to the regional capital. Masaud had taken the morning tro-tro and then walked to Emily's village after being dropped off on the main road.

The tro-tro picked up speed, zigging and zagging as it avoided the worst of the potholes on this unpaved road. Emily had the distinct sensation that her life was similarly moving out of her control. Nerves coiled in her belly, different from what she used to experience before going on stage. Then, her success had depended on her own ability to perform the complicated choreography. Now, her safety rested on the skill of the tro-tro driver, the good will of her fellow passengers, and Masaud.

She stole one more glance at the stranger. She should feel sympathy for him, since he'd been walking all alone in the dark. Yet she couldn't figure out where he'd come from. She knew from experience that navigating a dirt road in the pitch dark was hazardous. On the first night of her homestay, she'd decided to find a place to watch the thick blanket of stars without overhanging branches blocking her view. She hadn't taken a lantern. After walking only a few yards, she'd stumbled on the uneven ground and nearly ended up facedown in a ditch.

So what had caused the stranger to walk for miles along this road in the dark? And why couldn't she shake the sensation that something was wrong?

Biting her lip, Emily watched the night pass. Her nerves would probably settle once she reached the way station. Kofi, their tour guide, acted like a good-natured big brother to her and the other women in the group. He'd laugh off her concerns, make a joke, and she'd feel better. Tomorrow they'd head south, join up with the other three women, their tour guide and guard, then continue on to the orphanage where they'd begin dance rehearsals with a group of children and teens displaced by the rebels' violence.

Yes, all would be well. She had no reason to be so uneasy.

Day Three

THE NEXT MORNING, AFTER A FEW HOURS' rest in one of the way station's guest rooms, Max stood over the pit toilet out back and finished sawing at his ponytail with a sturdy knife he'd borrowed from the kitchen. Having long blond hair had aided his cover of being a hippie college professor gathering research for a book. Now that he had Dietrich's men after him, he couldn't afford to stand out as more than just another white adventurer too reckless to avoid this dangerous section of Africa. Although Volta and its neighbors to the east continued to insist that they were stable and safe for foreigners, people who'd been traveling the region, like Max, knew that the rebels had their sights set on taking over all of West Africa and had already begun laying the foundation for a full out assault.

The hair broke free. Max watched the bright strands sink into the watery sludge far below, then stuck his baseball cap over his shortened hair and headed back toward the main building. A quick glance toward the far corner of the lorry park—the dirt square where the tro-tros and buses dropped off passengers— showed that the American tour group's Land Cruiser was still there, so he continued up the outside stairs to his room.

After escaping Ziegler's cell through the smuggler's tunnel, Max had retrieved his stuff from its hiding place and snuck across the border. He'd caught a few hours' sleep before hitching a ride with a farmer early the next morning, but after the man left him at the northern crossroads, Max's luck had run out. There'd been no other vehicles on the road and he'd been forced to walk south, aiming for his contact Sulaiman's village. He'd been stumbling along in the dark, searching for a safe place to sleep, when the tro-tro had shocked the hell out of him by stopping when he'd waved it down. He'd figured there'd been a good chance the driver would consider a lone white man too dangerous to pick up given the region's slide toward anti-foreigner violence. Too many people were already avoiding all contact with foreigners, afraid of being targeted as foreign sympathizers when the rebels moved in.

Yet the tro-tro had braked for Max and the driver had offered him a ride as long as he could pay.

He'd received another surprise when the mate told him they had an American lady on board. The wariness in the woman's almond shaped brown eyes when she spotted him had hit like a punch to the gut. He'd quickly catalogued her delicate Asian features, her black hair pulled back in a tight bun, and the river of scars that started at the edge of her jaw and ran down her neck to disappear beneath her t-shirt, then dismissed her as non-threatening. An African man with the erect bearing and sharp-eyed gaze of a soldier had shared a few looks with the woman from his seat across the aisle. Probably her bodyguard. So the woman hadn't been completely stupid and traveling alone.

Still, she had a right to be wary. Being around Max could be dangerous. But he'd been in too much pain to ignore the ride. Plus, he hadn't seen any signs that he'd been followed.

When he'd learned that the tro-tro was dropping the American woman off at this way station to meet her tour group, Max had figured he'd be safer blending with a group of other foreigners than standing out because he was the only white person left on the tro-tro. So he'd had the driver leave him here, feeling confident he'd be able to convince the tour's leader to give him a ride.

Yeah, so much for that. When he'd spoken to the man first thing this morning, the tour guide said he'd gladly give Max a ride. Unfortunately, their Land Cruiser had two flat tires and his driver had gone to the capital to find replacements. Now the clock was edging toward noon and the driver still hadn't returned. Max couldn't hang around any longer. He needed to get to Sulaiman's village so he could rest and heal. Then he'd resume his search for details on Dietrich's deal.

The bad news just kept coming, though. When Max had

asked Madame Eunice, the woman who owned the way station, about renting a car she'd just shrugged sympathetically and told him that the tour group's driver had taken the only available vehicle. So Max was once again going to have to hoof it.

He grabbed his backpack out of his room. After checking that no evidence of his stay remained, he headed downstairs.

As he was about to round the corner into the lorry park, he heard the roar of an engine and an authoritative shout in the local language. He put his back against the building and peered around the corner in time to see a rebel Jeep turn off the main road.

He spotted a familiar white man in the passenger seat and froze.

Dammit to hell, how had Ziegler found him so quickly? Max could have taken any one of three directions at the crossroads. How had Ziegler managed to track him here? He quickly patted himself down. Did he have a tracking device on him? Had Ziegler deliberately left him alone in that room expecting him to escape? If so, why?

Not feeling any unexpected lumps, Max decided that when he caught some real down time, he'd have to check every inch of his skin and clothing to make sure he wasn't bugged. For the moment, he'd have to assume he wasn't being tracked. It was more likely that Ziegler had several teams out looking for him and it was just his bad luck that Ziegler had shown up here.

Time to disappear.

He turned smoothly away, keeping to the shadows until he reached the open space to the side of the main building. The Jeep screeched to a halt back in the lorry park. Max hesitated, checking behind him for any sign he'd been spotted. At the far end, where the alley opened into the lorry park, he could just barely make out Ziegler and his rebel cohort getting out of the Jeep and being accosted by Madame Eunice. The bodyguard from the tro-tro last night stood off to one side.

Max wanted to tell Madame Eunice that arguing with Ziegler was a bad idea, but the distraction allowed him to slip unnoticed across the exposed area between the building and the tall Guinea grass that formed the border between the way station and the jungle.

He'd just reached the concealment of the vegetation when the rebel shouted at the woman. A second later, the rat-tat-tat of an AK-47 shattered the morning's peace. Max dared another glance back. From this position, he had a better angle of sight into the lorry park. He was relieved to see that the rebel had only shot into the air.

Then another Jeep full of rebels pulled in behind the first vehicle. Interesting. Ziegler was here without his standard group of mostly white, Germanic guards. Dietrich and Ziegler were usually all about rigid control and adherence to a rather old-fashioned code of honor. They normally wouldn't trust their business to the unruly rebels. So what was Ziegler up to?

If it doesn't involve the upcoming deal, it's not my concern. Ignoring the pain in his ribs, Max slung his backpack onto his shoulders and headed at a fast walk through the man-height grass toward the additional protection of the tree line.

Then he paused, remembering the Asian American woman. He'd spotted her walking into the jungle over an hour ago.

Dammit, he didn't have time to find her and warn her. And yet...

He knew what the rebels did to women.

Cursing under his breath, he turned and walked toward where he'd last seen her.

CHAPTER TWO

From her prone position on the jungle floor, elbows propped in front of her on the tarp she'd borrowed from Madame Eunice, Emily held her breath, her finger hovering over the shutter-release button on her camera. The warthog baby snuffled in the dirt a few feet away, searching for grubs. Emily waited for it to raise its head. She ignored the press of the thick jungle air that turned her skin damp with perspiration. She ignored the buzz of the occasional fly around her ears and face, and shoved away thoughts of what insects or other critters might be crawling toward her. This little fellow was so ugly he was adorable. She wanted a series of photos of him before she went back to the States.

The warthog jerked its head up.

Emily took a series of rapid shots as the warthog stared fixedly into the jungle, then spun and bolted. A second later, a series of loud pops sounded from the direction of the way station. Emily startled and almost dropped her camera. Were those gunshots?

She froze, straining to hear more. But the jungle had fallen eerily silent.

O-kay. Maybe it had just been the locals out hunting.

Or maybe the rebels had invaded.

She shivered. Suddenly she understood why Masaud had told her not to venture too far into the jungle. She slapped the cover onto the camera's lens, then pushed to her feet. A bird called out in annoyance, then the rest of the jungle sounds—birds, insects, and the occasional grunt from an animal—returned. Telling herself that this was a good sign, she decided that she'd better return to the way station. At the very least, she needed to check if there was any word from the driver. Or maybe Kofi and the other women had returned from their walking tour of the nearby palm oil plantation.

Emily massaged the tight muscles in her neck and shoulder, gathered up her things, and set off. A few minutes later, she'd almost reached the way station when she heard angry voices ahead. She slowed, reluctant to step out of the relative safety of the thick vegetation into the middle of a violent disagreement. Instead, she inched forward until the broad leaves of a banana tree partially hid her, then peeked out.

An African man in an army green uniform with a yellow and black insignia sewn above the pocket and on the shirt sleeves was arguing with Madam Eunice. Masaud stood in the shadows off to one side.

"No!" The soldier punctuated his furious shout by firing his rifle into the air. Emily flinched.

At the far corner of the lorry park, two figures stepped out from an alley between the buildings. They saw the altercation and halted.

Oh, God, Crystal and Sue. The other women in her group. Kofi moved into view, placing himself between the women and the soldier. Gun in hand, Masaud jerked his head back toward the alley, indicating for the women to get out of sight as he too, positioned himself in front of them.

Crystal turned to flee, pushing Sue, who was shorter, in front of her. But in her panic, Crystal moved out from behind the protection of Masaud and Kofi. As she spun to leave, the fan of her long blonde hair caught the sun. With a speed Emily hadn't believed possible, the white man standing with the soldier pulled out a pistol and fired at Crystal.

Emily screamed. The scene in front of her slowed down, like a movie reel that had been switched to frame by frame view.

Red bloomed on Crystal's upper back. She stumbled into Sue. For a moment it seemed the women would regain their balance and reach the safety of the alley. But then the white man fired again and she fell. Sue half-turned to see what had happened to Crystal. The soldier open fired. Masaud fell first. Then Kofi. Then Sue.

Emily opened her to mouth to scream again, only to have the sound muffled by a large hand covering her mouth. An arm circled her waist, yanking her against a hard body.

She struggled, even as she was unable to take her eyes off the sight before her. Her friends lay on the ground, their bodies crumpled in unnatural poses. The white man raced over to the fallen women. He yanked on Crystal's hair, turning her face toward him. Lips curling in fury, he looked up and snarled something at the soldier.

The soldier turned to Madam Eunice and gestured angrily. The woman shook her head. The white man stood up and loomed over the woman. After a brief exchange, she pointed toward the guest rooms. The white man nodded to one of the soldiers and headed toward the building.

"I hope you didn't leave behind anything you care about," the man holding Emily said in American English.

"N-no. I brought my b-backpack with me."

"Good. Did anyone see you head out this way? If not, that might buy us some time."

"Yes," she whispered. Her heart pounded and her vision

swam as panic flooded her. "M-my guard. B-but h-he's...h-he's d-dead." She choked back a sob. "A-and the woman—"

Her stomach plummeted as another soldier entered the lorry park, dragging Madam Attipoe, the woman who ran the restaurant. She'd provided Emily the information on the best places to take photos. One of the soldiers asked Madam Attipoe some questions. After a lot of frightened head shaking, she motioned toward the place where Emily had initially entered the jungle. Another soldier raised his rifle and started firing at the spot, moving left as he shot.

"Down!" the American behind her said.

Not waiting for her response, he pulled her off her feet seconds before bullets shredded the tree above her. His body covered her once they hit the ground, shielding her from the bits of leaf and bark that rained down.

"Death to foreigners!" one of the men shouted.

She heard a squeal of tires from the road leading to the lorry park. Oh, God. More soldiers?

A man barked out an order in the local language. Another man answered, his tone pleading. The reply was two shots. A woman screamed. Then there were several more shots.

The man who'd pulled her down cursed softly. He rolled away and Emily got her first look at him. It was the American from the tro-tro.

He tugged on her hand. "Let's go."

She glanced toward the way station, but couldn't see anything through the dense grass.

An ululating cry of triumph rolled through the air. More gunfire sounded, although this time it seemed celebratory.

The American grabbed her wrist, pulled her to her feet and dragged her toward the trees. "We've got to get out of here."

"But—"

Women wailed. Men protested in the local language and were met with angry words.

Emily glanced behind her and saw two rows of soldiers moving toward them. Panic froze her limbs. She couldn't take a full breath.

"No buts," the American barked out. "Those are AFA rebels, lady. Haven't you heard? They're purging West Africa of all foreigners." He tightened his grip on her wrist and hauled her forward. "Run!"

She stumbled after him.

Don't panic. Focus. Stay alive. Repeating the mantra in her head, Emily followed the man through the jungle until she thought her lungs were going to burst. Fear gave her legs strength. Eventually she pushed past the pain in her body and lungs and entered that sweet spot where her body moved in a sort of autonomous harmony.

Behind them, shouts continued to mix with gunfire. In the intermittent spells of quiet, she heard men crashing through the jungle. Oh, God. This was real. The rebels were really chasing them.

The image of Crystal and Sue falling flashed across her mind. She stumbled.

"Easy, there." Her rescuer reached back and steadied her.

"Thanks." She shot him a shaky smile.

He gave a nod of acknowledgment, then turned around and resumed running. Sweat trickled into Emily's eyes, burning. She swiped angrily at it, but kept her focus on the stranger's backpack as he easily navigated the jungle's obstacles. God, she'd thought she was in good shape. But even hours of rigorous training since the accident hadn't prepared her for running full-out while carrying a backpack across rough terrain in heat over ninety degrees with equal humidity. Who was this man who ran through the jungle so easily, even suffering from what she suspected was a cracked rib? Despite her best attempts, her pace had already slowed.

No. Can't slow down. The rebels will catch me. Kill me. Like... Like...

Oh, God. How could this be real? How could she have gone from taking photos to running for her life?

Why did Crystal and Sue have to die? What had they ever done to—

Her rescuer cursed and stopped so abruptly, Emily nearly plowed into his back.

"Why are you stopping?" she demanded, glancing back over her shoulder. "Those men are going to find us. They're going to kill us. They're—"

The man slapped his hand over her mouth and pulled her back against his body with his other arm. "Quiet. Panicking isn't going to help. Look." He turned them around so that she could see that the ground in front of them dropped into a wide ditch clogged with grass and densely packed bushes.

"We almost fell in. Now, if I let you go, will you promise to stop screeching? Because even though the sounds of pursuit have faded, more hysterical shouting will act as a beacon to the rebels."

She nodded and he dropped his hand. "I'm sorry," she whispered. "I didn't realize... I just..." She bit back a sob. "I don't want to die."

"Yeah, well, that's not exactly high on my agenda, either. Help me find another path so we can get the hell out of here."

"Okay." She held her breath a moment to listen and realized that he was right. She couldn't hear the sound of men crashing through the jungle. Did that mean their pursuers had given up? Or had they simply switched tactics?

"Lady? Are you just going to stand there?"

"Sorry." She looked around for an easy path through the tangle of vegetation. Having something to do steadied her and she could almost hear her father's voice as he explained during their emergency training that the key to survival was to stay calm at all costs.

Stop. Assess. Plan.

Easier said than done, father.

"Here. This way." The man gestured toward a faint break in the bushes to his right.

Emily froze, staring at his hand. It had scabs on the fingertips and a partially healed cut across the back. She slowly dragged her gaze up his body as her heart tripped in panic. His t-shirt was soaked with sweat and clung to the lean muscles of his torso. About six foot two, he carried himself with a focused confidence that screamed danger as much as the myriad bruises and scrapes hiding underneath his few days' growth of beard. A cut split his lower lip. The tail of a partially scabbed over scrape peeked out from beneath the collar of his shirt.

Her stomach twisted at these signs of violence. Had he been in a fight? Or maybe a car accident?

Was she really any safer with this stranger than on her own?

Instead of his ponytail, short, bluntly cut hair peeked out from underneath his baseball cap. Why had he cut his hair? The heat? Or to hide such a distinctive feature?

Was he the reason the men had attacked? Was he some kind of fugitive?

Had Crystal died because her hair had resembled his?

Her breath started coming in shallow pants as panic raised its head. Oh, God. He... Crystal...

"Hey. Are you okay?" His light blue eyes met hers with such fierce focus that she shivered.

Emily took a step back, shaking her head. Feeling the start of one of the panic attacks she'd developed after Agatha had thrown acid on her, she tried to focus on her breathing to calm herself down.

The man shifted, and she noticed that he held a matte black, semi-automatic pistol alongside his leg. Her breath caught and she took another step back. "You're armed."

Oh, God. She'd been right. He *was* dangerous.

He glanced down. "Yep." With a casualness that spoke of long use, he slid the gun into a holster attached to his belt and twitched the tail of his shirt to hide it. Her father had drilled the family in emergency preparedness, including firearms, and she was pretty sure this man's gun was military issue only.

"Who the hell are you?" she demanded. "Are you CIA or—"

The man held a finger to his lips. "Shh. Someone's coming."

Emily listened. The white noise of birds, insects and other small, daytime critters had fallen silent. She didn't hear any footsteps, but the hair on the back of her neck stood up.

A radio crackled nearby and Emily almost jumped out of her skin. Her companion put his arm around her and eased her carefully between the giant, buttressed roots of two ofram trees.

A man's voice spoke in one of the local dialects, answering whoever had contacted him on the radio. Her rescuer stood slightly in front of her, blocking her view, his body tense, his gun out again and held at the ready.

Emily's heart beat as fast as if she'd just performed a whirlwind set of pirouettes. Yet not being able to see the threat only frightened her more, so she peeked around her companion's shoulder. Through the trees she could just make out the side of a man's head and the black and yellow patch on his uniform. Was this the man who'd shot her friends?

Please let him walk on by. I don't want to die. Please let him walk on by.

She held her breath and pressed closer to her rescuer.

The rebel listened to the response from the other end of his walkie talkie, then grumbled a reply. He stomped around a bit, poked at the vegetation with the tip of his rifle, then walked off.

Emily sagged against her companion. Inhaled the scent of

male sweat and bug repellent and accepted that once again they'd escaped death.

Her rescuer remained on alert for several more minutes. When he finally turned to her his face was set in a cold, hard expression that sent chills down her spine. She pulled back and he blinked, his light blue eyes warming with startling suddenness. "You okay?" he said quietly.

She nodded, then shook her head. For a brief moment she had the urge to lean her head on his chest. Wanted to feel his strong arms around her and hear him tell her everything was going to be all right. But it wasn't. It couldn't be. Crystal and Sue...

Wait. What if he'd been wrong? What if those shots hadn't killed them? Clinging to hope, she met his eyes. "Isn't there a chance one of the women is still alive?" she whispered.

He shook his head. "Those were fatal shots. Even if they hadn't died instantly, the rebels would have killed them. I'm sorry. They really do hate all foreigners and they wouldn't waste energy keeping injured ones alive."

Emily turned her head so he wouldn't see her tears. She hadn't known either woman well. Sue had been a retired kindergarten teacher and lifelong folk dancer, eager to branch out and learn West African dance. Crystal had been a college student trying to decide whether to major in dance or sociology. She'd also been a huge ballet fan and had oohed and ahed over Emily, treating her as if she were still an active ballerina, instead of an unemployed dancer with no future.

Thinking about the bullets hitting the women, how their bodies had slumped to the ground, made her want to scream at fate for being so unfair. The images of the white man—middle-aged, medium height and build, honey blond hair styled like a bank executive—and the rebel soldiers were forever burned into her mind. "They—" She cleared her throat and glanced back at him. "They have families. We have to tell someone so they...so they..."

The man flinched slightly, then said, "As soon as we reach the capital, we can report their deaths to the embassy. Make certain someone goes back to retrieve their bodies."

Oh, God, he was right. She hadn't thought that far ahead. "I..." She swallowed heavily. "Thank you." She crossed her arms over her chest. "What's your name?"

"Max."

She waited. When he didn't elaborate, she said, "Just Max?"

"Yep. And you are?"

"Emily Iwasaki." Years of ingrained manners had her last name popping out of her mouth before she could stop it.

"Okay, Emily." Max nodded, checked his watch, then glanced around the jungle. "If we continue that way," he pointed to their right, "then angle back toward the road, we should make it to the next village by nightfall." He turned and started walking.

Emily followed, fighting back her sudden anger. She didn't want to be stuck here in the jungle on the run from rebels with a man she didn't fully trust. This was supposed to have been a safe place to visit. Not someplace that would demand the sacrifice of two wonderful women. Tired of being afraid, she embraced and nursed her anger for over an hour.

"The rebels aren't even supposed to be in this country," she finally snapped, but only loudly enough for Max to hear her. "We were told it was safe."

Max gave a disbelieving laugh and shoved aside a hanging vine. "Who told you that? The tour company? Because if they did, they were trying to make a buck at the risk of your lives. The rebels might not have started a major offensive in this country yet, but they've been hopping back and forth across the western border for weeks now. And each time they do, they kill or capture whatever foreigners they find."

No wonder Masaud had seemed particularly tense when he'd come to pick her up. He must have known the danger had increased, yet been ordered not to say anything. "Is that what happened to you?"

His body stiffened and she wished she could see his face. "No. My condition is the result of a personal disagreement."

"That must have been some disagreement," she muttered. Yeah, right. She bet he really was a spy. "You never did answer my question. Are you CIA?"

"Why do people assume that every American carrying a weapon is with the damn CIA?"

"That's not an answer. Besides, you didn't give me a last name, exactly the sort of thing a CIA agent would do."

He snorted. "And you know so much about the CIA?"

She felt her cheeks heat. But before she could respond, he said, "Think whatever you want."

"Well," she huffed. "Who are you then?"

"A history and folklore professor who likes his privacy and is just in the area gathering data for his next book."

This time she snorted. She might not have attended college, but no way could she picture this man with his barely contained energy and his military-grade weapon confining himself to a classroom or a stuffy office all day. "Don't think I believe that for a minute. No history professor is going to carry such a—" No, better not let him know that she'd recognized his gun. "Such a... um...lethal looking weapon."

"With the unrest and the violence against foreigners, anyone in this area had better damn well be armed," Max retorted.

Okay, he had a point.

"As an American woman, you shouldn't even have come to this region," Max continued. "What are you anyway, a college student or something?"

It wasn't the first time she'd been asked the question, but still her breath caught on the pain of what she'd lost. "I was a ballet dancer."

"Was?" He turned his head and nailed her with those probing eyes.

She gestured to her neck. "There was an...incident." Somehow she couldn't use the word attack. Not with this stranger. Attack made her feel too much like a victim. Too much like the naïve woman who hadn't recognized that Agatha's jealousy had spilled over into virulent hatred. "Acid..." Her hand jerked toward her scars, but she stopped herself from covering them. They were part of who she was now and she had to accept that. Like it or not.

She cleared her throat. "I...ah...am no longer considered employable as a professional dancer." The wrenching pain in her chest as she confessed the truth hadn't lessened with time and she stared at the floor of the jungle. Everyone told her how lucky she'd been that the acid Agatha used had been weak. That her scars would have been much deeper if there hadn't been water immediately at hand to quickly rinse the acid off. She should be grateful, they said, that she'd only suffered a minimal loss of range of motion on the right side of her neck and shoulder.

What did they know? It wasn't fair. Even though Agatha had been arrested instead of taking over Emily's job as she'd intended, the woman had still succeeded in ruining Emily's career. Once it had become clear that Emily's damaged shoulder could no longer sustain the demanding positions required of a principal ballet dancer, she'd lost her job.

Leaving her adrift in the world. What was she supposed to do with her life if she couldn't dance? She'd never wanted anything else.

"I'm sorry," Max said. "That sucks." To her surprise, he seemed to mean it. His expression softened, making him look younger. Less harsh. More approachable.

But he carried a gun and bore signs of having survived physical violence. Even if the shooting back at the way station had nothing to do with him, he was dangerous. So she just gave a curt "Thanks."

Max returned his attention to the path he was forging. A few minutes later he said, "So what the hell were you thinking, coming to West Africa?"

Scowling at his back, Emily rubbed her hands up and down her bare forearms. She'd been thinking that her best friend JoAnn was right. That she needed to get over her depression about not being able to dance professionally again. That a change of scenery might pull her out of the funk she'd fallen into.

JoAnn had wanted to visit Africa and explore her family's roots since she'd been a teenager. So when she heard about the month-long dance tour of West Africa that would raise awareness for the plight of war orphans, she'd bullied and cajoled Emily into going. Only, at the last minute a family emergency had kept JoAnn at home. Emily had cursed her friend out and nearly withdrawn from the trip, but JoAnn had made her promise to carry on for both of their sakes. And Emily's therapist had told her that helping others would give her the sense of purpose she'd been lacking.

Now Emily was grateful JoAnn had stayed at home. While she felt sick over the deaths of Crystal and Sue, losing her best friend would have been worse.

"Hello? Emily?"

"Sorry. I—" She shook her head. He didn't need to know where her thoughts had gone. "We each learned the local dances. We were supposed to meet up and visit an orphanage that uses art and dance to heal children damaged by the war." How naïve they'd been. "Then we'd go on tour to raise money and awareness for the orphans. And now—" Her throat tightened on a wave of grief. "It's not fair! They didn't do anything wrong, yet Crystal and Sue were shot down like...like..." She brushed away a tear.

Max halted, put his hand on her shoulder, and squeezed gently. "I know it's hard to stop thinking about what happened, but you have to stay focused. Our primary job is to keep ourselves alive. We have to find our way out of the jungle and to safety before the rebels find us. Okay?"

She nodded.

"Good." Giving her shoulder one last squeeze, he resumed walking.

Biting her lip, Emily turned and followed him deeper into the jungle.

CHAPTER THREE

As the light under the trees faded to dusk, Max checked the compass on his watch again. Sulaiman's village should be just around the next bend. He and Emily had been walking inside the jungle along the edge of the red dirt road for the past hour and a half and not a single vehicle had passed them. Not even a person on a bicycle. Odd. Last time he'd been in the area there'd at least been occasional foot traffic along the road. Maybe that had been a market day?

"Almost there," he announced. Emily muttered in what he thought was Japanese. The corner of his mouth lifted in reluctant admiration. She'd impressed him. Despite standing about five eight or five nine, her slender frame made her look fragile enough to knock over with a feather. It fit that she'd been a dancer, because even while carrying her backpack she appeared to be floating on air. As if gravity made an exception when it came to her.

That impression of being delicate had made him worry about her stamina. But once they'd settled into a rhythm, she'd lost her uneven, panicked breathing and kept up with him without a word of complaint.

Not that he was at peak performance. His ribs hurt like a mother and a bulge in his backpack that he hadn't been able to fix kept bumping against the knife slice across his lower back. So his pace wasn't nearly as rapid as he wanted.

He slapped at a mosquito on his forearm, then winced as the smear of blood reminded him of the woman Ziegler had shot. It hadn't escaped Max that she'd been targeted because her long, light blonde hair had been remarkably similar to his. And once Ziegler had turned on her, the rebels had shot her companions.

A stab of guilt nearly took his breath away. His steps faltered. The women had families back in the States. People who didn't know their loved ones were dead.

Just like your family wouldn't have known about your death if Ziegler had killed you.

He clenched his teeth and shoved the guilt down deep, to be dealt with later.

Yet his mind couldn't completely leave it alone. Why the hell had Ziegler shot the girl so quickly? He was normally more controlled than that. Too cool-headed to indulge in the split-second decision to kill that he'd exhibited back at the lorry park. In fact, Max wondered what Dietrich would say if he knew that his second-in-command planned to kill Max and had involved the rebels in the hunt.

Max walked around the bend and spotted a mud hut sitting quiet and dark behind a fenced-in garden. If he remembered correctly, the village proper was just beyond the row of banana trees on the far side of the garden.

Emily gave a quiet but heartfelt cheer and walked up beside him. He put his arm out to stop her from moving past him. "Hold up."

She glanced at him in surprise. "What's wrong?"

"Let me investigate. Make certain the rebels aren't there. You wait here."

"No." She crossed her arms over her chest. "Not on your life. I'm going with you."

"Emily—"

"Don't. I am *not* going to wait in the jungle where there's almost no light. I'm a city girl. I'm not used to being in the woods, let alone the freaking jungle where there are predators that I have no way of fighting off." Her voice held an edge of hysteria.

O-kay. Again with the panic. "Emily, calm down. What if the rebels have taken over the village? We could be walking into a trap." He didn't really think the rebels were here. It was far too quiet and they weren't known for stealth. However, if they had already been through here and left behind their usual destruction, he didn't want her seeing more dead bodies.

"Don't you tell me to calm down." She lifted her chin. "I will go absolutely bonkers if you leave me, Max. I'm not kidding. I will stay behind you as you approach the village. Be as quiet as I possibly can. But there is no way in hell I'm staying out in the jungle all by myself."

Her chest rose quickly and he saw the fear in her eyes. Too bad. He wasn't exposing her to more danger. "No."

He took her hand and placed it on the trunk of a nearby tree, then moved her body so she was well hidden. "Stay. Here. You're out of sight. Don't make any sound and you'll be fine. I'll return once I know the village is safe."

Emily once again opened her mouth as if to protest.

"Do I need to tie you to the tree?"

Her head rocked back in shock. "N-no."

"Good." Not giving her time to protest again, he walked away, removing his pistol from its holster as he moved.

Once he cleared the trees, the shadowy outlines of other houses took shape along the side of the road. But the glow of lanterns and cooking fires was missing. He didn't hear any conversation. Didn't scent food, even though it was dinnertime.

He counted houses. When he was near Sulaiman's place, he

walked across the narrow concrete slab that spanned the open sewage ditch running parallel to the road. On the other side, a path led between Sulaiman's house and its neighbor. There was still no sign of other people. Max picked his way through the deep shadows between the houses, hoping that his friend was safe.

On the concrete rear patios, cooking pots hung over charcoal braziers, the coals thankfully cold. Bikes and stools lay on their sides in yards or on the dirt walkways, as if the villagers had left in a hurry. But Max didn't see any signs of violence. He figured the villagers must have been warned that the rebels were coming and fled into the jungle. Because if the rebels had found them, there'd be corpses.

Sulaiman's gate was ajar and the front door was open. Max moved cautiously into the yard and up the two concrete steps to the narrow porch. He pushed the door wider and swept the room beyond with his weapon.

Empty.

He carefully picked his way through the house. Toys littered the concrete floor in the kids' room. Flies buzzed over plates of partially eaten food left on the dining table. Max touched a bowl of stew. Cold. So, they'd left a while ago.

Reassured that his friend and his family weren't lying injured or dead in one of the four rooms, he headed outside. To be safe, he conducted a house-to-house search, pulling the night vision goggles out of his backpack once the light failed completely. It was unsettling to see the deserted yards and hear nothing, not even a stray chicken. But at least the absence of bodies meant both that the rebels hadn't attacked and that sudden disease hadn't swept through, killing everyone.

When he returned to Emily forty-five minutes later, he found her standing exactly where he'd left her. Her fingernails had sunk deep into the bark of the tree where he'd placed her hand. Her eyes stared fixedly into space.

Christ. She really *had* been terrified. Had she even blinked in the entire time he'd been gone?

He stopped before he got too close, not wanting to scare her. "Emily?" he called quietly. "You okay?"

She didn't answer. He took off his night vision goggles, knowing they made him look like a freaky bug, and inched forward. "It's okay, Emily. The village is safe. You can come in now."

Still no answer.

"Emily!" He waved his hand in front of her face. "Snap out of it."

She shuddered and blinked several times, then turned her head toward him. "M-Max?"

"Yeah."

"You c-came back."

Oh, hell. "Of course I did. I told you I would." He reached out and pried her fingers away from the tree. Jesus, her skin was freezing.

"B-but... The rebels... Might have killed you... A-and... You have no reason to take me with you..."

Great. Now he felt like a complete asshole for leaving her. Even though it had been the right decision. "I'm not going to abandon you, okay? I promise." He rubbed her hand with his, trying to warm her up. "I'm going to deliver you safe and sound to the embassy."

"O-okay." But he could tell she didn't believe him.

"You're doing great, Emily. Just hang on a little longer."

She gave him a weak smile and shrugged, which only increased his sense of having failed her.

Wait. Failed her? He barely knew her. He didn't owe her anything except the safe passage he'd promised her. He cleared his throat. "C'mon, there's a car at the chief's house we can borrow. We'll pick up some supplies, as well." He took her hand

and placed it on his backpack. "Hold onto me. I've got night vision goggles, so I can see where we're going."

Once he felt her grab tightly onto the pack, he moved out.

"Are we going to spend the night here?" she asked as they walked into the village.

"No. Too dangerous." Sulaiman wouldn't mind if Max used his house, but the empty village would be an obvious place for Ziegler and the rebels to search.

It didn't take long to reach the chief's house. Underneath the corrugated metal roof of the attached carport, the grill of the old Cadillac gleamed faintly in a sideways beam of moonlight.

"I'll check if the car runs. Why don't you see if they have any food that we can eat on the go?" People in this region cooked most of their meals, so there probably wouldn't be much that they could eat raw. "Just enough to get us through tomorrow, when we should reach the capital." Max slipped off his rucksack and placed it by the back door of the car. "Here, take the night vision goggles. I can see pretty well in the dark." He passed her the goggles and showed her how to adjust them to her smaller head.

After removing her own pack, Emily gave him a nod. She peeked into the storeroom, then cautiously stepped inside.

Max found the keys to the Caddy hanging on a peg inside the side door of the chief's house. The engine started right up and he grinned. Finally, a lucky break. The tank was even three-quarters full. He poured in enough gas to top it off, then grabbed a couple of full jerry cans from the carport just in case they were on the road long enough to need to refuel. As he placed the last one in the trunk, he heard the rumble of a vehicle on the road.

He slammed the trunk closed and ran for the storeroom. "Company's coming," he called softly. "We've got to go."

Emily shoved a box of supplies into his arms and picked up a bulging nylon sack of the type that the locals used to haul everything from groceries to clothes. They ran to the Cadillac and shoved everything into the back seat.

He'd just reached for the door handle when two rebels holding AK-47's stepped out from the trees behind the house. They froze in surprise when they noticed Max and Emily. Emily gasped. The rebels yelled a warning and raised their rifles.

Max pulled his pistol and shot them each in the chest. Twice. Emily screamed.

"Get in the car!" He jumped behind the wheel. When Emily didn't open her door, he looked over and saw that she was staring in shock at the dead rebels.

Cursing, he reached across the console and pushed open her door. "Emily. Get in the damn car. Now. Before the rest of the rebels arrive."

She shook her head slightly, as if waking from a trance. Glanced warily at him. "T-they're dead. You k-killed them."

"What the hell did you expect? They're rebels. They were going to shoot us. Get in the car or I'm leaving you here."

"B-but—" She took a step back. "Y-you didn't even think about it. Y-you just shot them."

Christ. "Yes. It's us or them." What was her problem? He'd seen a threat and eliminated it. "I saved your life. If you want to stay alive, get in the fucking car."

With one more frightened glance at the bodies, Emily slid into the passenger seat.

Max slammed his foot on the accelerator and drove out the back of the village.

With a squeak of protest, Emily lunged for her swinging door and pulled it shut.

He glanced in the rearview mirror and saw headlights turn toward the village.

"Give me the goggles." He held out his hand.

With a small sob, Emily yanked the night vision goggles off her head and slapped them into his palm. He fitted them in place one handed. Ah, much better. Now he could see the worn earth where the villagers walked to the fields.

Keeping the Cadillac's headlights off, he turned right. A patch of waist-high cassava plants flanked them on the left, while on their right the houses shielded them from detection by anyone on the road.

Emily sat tensely in the passenger seat, her breathing choppy again. "Easy, Em. We're going to be okay. Just take deep breaths."

"I—" Her panicked breathing was loud enough to hear over the grumble of the Caddy's engine. She crossed her arms tightly over her chest. Took several deep, shuddering breaths before snapping, "Maybe you're used to seeing people die. For all I know, you kill people every day. But I don't. I'm sorry, but I'm not okay with watching anyone get gunned down in front of me." She shook her head and added, "It's not normal."

"Normal?" Spotting the main road up ahead, he turned left before reaching it, staying within the tall mix of grasses and bushes that ran alongside the road. "Emily, for this part of the world, that *was* normal." By her definition, his life hadn't been normal since the day he'd joined the Marines. "You should be glad I handled it the way I did, or you'd be lying dead back there."

She flinched and scooted closer to the door.

Great. Now he'd scared her.

"Listen, I'm not a threat to you, okay? I promised that I'd keep you safe. That's what I'm doing, whether you approve or not."

She didn't answer, but at least her panicked breathing quieted. He could live with that.

After several minutes, the road cut sharply across the jungle in front of him. Since the bend would hide them from any pursuers, Max eased the Cadillac onto the road, turned south, and increased their speed.

"Are we safe now?" Emily asked a few minutes later.

Max glanced in the rearview mirror. No sign of other vehicles.

"Yeah—" A Jeep rounded the bend behind them. "Shit. No." It wouldn't take long before the other vehicle's headlights caught the Caddy.

He saw the muzzle flashes as someone in the Jeep opened fire. "Max!"

"I know." In a normal race on a flat, smooth surface, the Cadillac would leave the Jeep far behind. But the potholes and ruts in the dirt road gave the Jeep the advantage. Max searched his memory for someplace they could pull off and ditch the Caddy. Dammit, he couldn't remember. He'd only spent one night at Sulaiman's house before moving on. That had been months ago. And while he always mapped emergency exit routes wherever he was, he couldn't recall the lay of the land in this direction. He thought there were only a handful of villages along this route before a side road intersected. But that was miles away.

The rebels fired off a long volley of shots.

Emily screamed, then slapped her hand over her mouth. "Sorry."

He shook his head, then rubbed his ear. Damn, but the woman had a pair of lungs on her. "Don't panic. They're too far away to be dangerous. The idiots are just wasting ammunition."

They reached a patch of smooth, hard-packed dirt and Max stomped hard on the accelerator. The needle inched up on the speedometer and the rebels dropped farther behind. By the time they hit the next spot of rough road, the rebels had disappeared from view. "Keep your eyes open for another village."

She threw a startled glance at him from wide eyes. "What? Why?"

"They've seen this vehicle. We need to swap it for something different." He kept an eye on the rearview mirror and saw the headlights of their pursuers appear about a mile behind.

"Scratch that. Help me find a place where we can get off the road and hide until they pass by."

"But... Won't they see our tire tracks? Or our dust?"

"We're not kicking up that much dust. And the road's surface is too hard to show our tire tracks. Plus, it's dark. We just need to find a place to pull off where we won't leave an obvious trail of flattened grass."

"I... Okay."

A few minutes later, she pointed to a dirt trail heading into the tall Guinea grass along the right side of the road. Max drove along the trail until it met the edge of the jungle, then continued inside the edge of the jungle for several minutes, before finally parking behind a cluster of banana trees. "Wait here. I'll be right back." He hopped out and walked quickly back to the road to reduce the signs of their passage. He waited just out of sight until he saw the rebel Jeep roar past, then he returned to the vehicle

"Are we safe *now*?" Emily asked after he'd closed his door.

He shrugged. "The rebels have passed. We'll wait half an hour to give them time to get far ahead of us and to make sure there's not another truck coming. Then we'll drive along the edge of the road until we find another village. Hopefully they'll have a vehicle we can exchange for the Cadillac. We'll drive to the capital, I'll take you to the embassy, and you'll be on your way home before you know it. In the meantime, you should grab something to eat and drink. Sleep a bit. I'll keep watch."

She gave him a dubious look, but he stared her down. He was used to going without rest. Besides, with the pain he was in, he doubted he had any chance of sleeping.

Finally, she shrugged. She undid her seatbelt and eased into the back seat. "Okay, what can I get you to eat?"

"I don't care. Anything." His mind wasn't on food, although he knew he needed the fuel.

Taking Emily to the embassy was the opposite of what he'd had planned. He'd expected to be able to find someone at Sulaiman's village to take her the rest of the way while he healed. The clock in his head was ticking down the days until Dietrich's big deal. Before he'd been captured the deal had been scheduled to take place in about sixteen days. He'd spent one day of that time chasing down leads. Then he'd been captured. Escaped on the third day. That left twelve days until the deal. It had taken him one day to reach the point where the tro-tro had picked him up last night. As of today, he had roughly ten days to figure out where the deal was going to be and find a way to stop it. Assuming the initial timing had been correct.

Shit. He didn't have *time* to play white knight.

He closed his eyes and gave a deep sigh. Like he had any choice. He couldn't leave Emily to make her own way to the capital. With the rebels on patrol and Ziegler acting more aggressively than usual, Max would have to take her all the way to the embassy gates.

And hope that no one on duty had been warned about him.

"WHAT DO YOU MEAN, you lost track of Maximilian?" Such incompetence belonged to the rebels, which is why Dietrich had not given them sole responsibility for finding Max. "I expected better of you, Herr Ziegler."

His second-in-command winced at his formality. Good. The man had shown a distressing tendency lately to put his personal vendetta against Max ahead of Dietrich's instructions. "Not only did you capture Max and fail to inform me, but you allowed him to escape."

"I did not allow it, sir. He should have been too damaged to move."

Dietrich steepled his fingers on the desk top. The sun coming through the concrete building's barred windows threw a grid pattern on Ziegler's face. "That is another unpleasant surprise. Did I, or did I not make it clear that should Max be found no one except for me was to hurt him? That the only force to be directed against him was that which was needed to restrain him. Yet when I arrived—after being told by a confidential source that you had captured Max without reporting such to me—I discovered that you had been using your needles on the man for days. Can you give me a reason for your disobedience, Herr Ziegler?"

"I did what needed to be done. The man knows about the deal. I had to make certain that he had not told anyone else."

"Hmm..." Dietrich did not entirely believe the smooth retort. It sounded rehearsed. And yet, he had no direct evidence that Ziegler had tortured Max for personal reasons. "For now we shall set aside your treatment of Max. The fact remains that he escaped because you failed to learn pertinent details about the location where you held him. If you had done your research, you would have discovered that the spot had been a smuggler's hideout. You would have known that putting Max in that room—without adequately securing him so that his bonds were unbreakable—would give him access to the escape tunnels underneath." Dietrich took a deep breath, trying to quell his anger. He had been so close to confronting Max. To making the man pay for the harm he had done over the years. But Ziegler had ruined it.

"Do I need to remind you, Herr Ziegler, that a free Max is a threat to our upcoming deal? We need him back in our custody. And yet, while you tracked him to the way station, he once again eluded capture. A dozen rebels were not enough to find him and bring him in. Which makes me wonder, did you deliberately fail to take our personal guards with you because you secretly hoped Max would escape again? Or were you simply too arrogant to believe that Max could outsmart you a second time?"

He watched his second-in-command carefully. While Ziegler had perfected the art of keeping his face expressionless and his body still during questioning, Dietrich saw the man's pupils dilate slightly. That slight signal of unease gave Dietrich the patience to wait for the reply, which he was certain would be a lie.

"With the urgency to find the missing plane, I thought it more efficient if I pursued Max on my own."

Ah, yes. The plane. Dietrich had hired one of the most experienced pilots in the international smuggling arena to fly his courier here from South Africa with the items for the upcoming deal. It should have been a simple matter. Yet, the tracking beacon in the courier's briefcase had stopped transmitting halfway through the journey. Then, although the pilot had radioed in to confirm that he was approaching the hidden airfield in the Republic of the Volta, the plane never arrived. They assumed it had crashed somewhere in the nearby jungle. Dietrich had indeed put high priority on the search for the plane and for the recovery of the secure briefcase containing both the plans for the weapon and a small prototype. However, choosing to pursue Max on his own was not a decision Ziegler had the right to make.

"Ah," Dietrich said. "So you expected to be able to return Max to me without taking resources away from the search for the crash site?" His small cadre of personal guards would not be able to scour the entire area, so Dietrich had ordered a platoon of his private soldiers to aid in the search. They were expected to arrive tomorrow morning.

Ziegler dipped his chin in assent.

"That, then, is why you used the rebels in your hunt?"

Another slight nod.

"Yet you have failed, Herr Ziegler. Not only has Max once again eluded you, but the rebels delighted in informing me that you shot an American girl without provocation." Such a rash act was not typical for Ziegler. "Do you not realize that this will draw attention to the very area of the country where we do not wish others to look? Do you *want* the government to discover that we are searching for our missing plane here?"

Ziegler's shoulders remained back and his head remained high, but there was the briefest flicker of remorse across his features. Otherwise, he gave no other sign that he regretted his action. Dietrich wondered if this insubordination had been building for some time and he had simply been too busy to notice it, or if something had happened recently to provoke Ziegler.

"Do you not have anything to say in your defense?" Dietrich asked. "Or do you fail to realize that by killing an American, you have also exposed us to inquiry by the United States government? They have so far kept their distance from us as promised, but the agreement was that we would not directly harm Americans. Our protector will not be able to shield us now that you've killed the girl in front of witnesses."

"The rebels will not dare to say anything. They killed the other American woman."

"Fool. The rebels will do anything to purge the continent of foreign devils such as ourselves. The only reason they have not already informed on us is because the weapons we sell them are their very lifeblood. Once they feel secure in their power, they will attempt to destroy us, too. In the meantime, my sources tell me that someone has sent cell phone video to the local media showing the killing. You should have done a better job of cleaning up your mess, Herr Ziegler. To have missed that the way station had an Internet connection was very sloppy. Whether it was the rebels who uploaded the video, hoping to undermine our position so that they can negotiate more beneficial terms for their weapons, or a concerned citizen who turned in the evidence, you are now a highly wanted man."

Ziegler only shrugged. "Many governments have tried to apprehend me before. They failed. This also will disappear from their priority list as more of their citizens are captured and killed."

Dietrich barely refrained from shaking his head. Once, Ziegler would have weighed all the repercussions before pulling his weapon. And if by some chance he had been overtaken by madness and killed without foresight, he would have provided a full apology and given steps he would take to reduce the impact of the fallout. This careless disregard for both their overall mission—to remain covert so that none of the larger nations would bother to hunt them down and destroy their organization —and their current mission to find the missing plane without alerting others to their search, was not like him.

Inwardly, Dietrich sighed. He had been working with Ziegler for over twenty years. They had, until recently, worked together impeccably. It was unforgivable that Ziegler saw no need to apologize for his mistake. Instead, Dietrich saw only the fanatical zeal of a crazy man.

Ziegler's need for revenge against Max had apparently veered so far into obsession that he no longer cared what Dietrich wanted. All this because Ziegler's hand had been burned into uselessness during a raid by Max's team. Such an inconsequential matter. Ziegler had lived. Prospered. He ought to be focused on furthering their business interests, rather than punishing Max.

Regardless of the cause of Ziegler's strange transformation, he could no longer be trusted. Yet he knew too much to simply be allowed to walk away. This matter would require more drastic measures. Because Ziegler could not be allowed to go unpunished for such actions. Dietrich's men must understand that his authority was absolute.

Unfortunately, for the moment Dietrich needed Ziegler's help. "The buyer will arrive in ten days. You will tell our contact with the rebels that Max is most likely heading to the capital. If they spot him, they should apprehend him and return him to us. In the meantime, you will coordinate the search with the leader of our soldiers when they arrive tomorrow. And I want to know why the tracking beacon stopped transmitting."

"Yes, Herr Dietrich."

"Good. Oh, and Herr Ziegler, you will report to me every day. If I do not hear from you, and do not hear that you are making progress, then I will tell the squad to eliminate you. Is that clear?"

The man stiffened, then gave a curt nod.

"Dismissed."

Dietrich stared into space for a long while after Ziegler's exit. This was the most important deal of his career. Not only because of the money, but because the experimental weapon had the potential to change the balance of power in West Africa. Success here would also prove to the international community that he remained one of the elite weapons dealers. Max and his team had already ruined too many of his previous deals, damaging his reputation in ways that had taken years to repair.

Now only Max continued to pursue him, but the man's persistence and intelligence were a constant threat. Dietrich could not afford to have Max running around, searching for ways to disrupt this deal. He must die before then.

CHAPTER FOUR

Day Four

EMILY WOKE up with her head leaning against the passenger side window of the old Toyota pickup truck Max had stolen to replace the Cadillac. She rubbed the sleep out of her eyes and blinked against the late afternoon sun. Man, she'd really gone down for the count.

Staring groggily out the window at the low concrete buildings lining the paved road, she asked, "Where are we?"

"Outskirts of the capital, New Accra."

She nodded toward the line of vehicles stopped in front of them. "What's going on?"

"Checkpoint."

Nerves danced awake in her belly. "Why?"

Max shrugged. "The rebels are in the country. This is probably just a precautionary measure." His hands were relaxed on the steering wheel and he didn't appear alarmed. She took a deep breath and her muscles lost most of their tension.

"Do you have your passport?" he asked.

"What? Oh. Yes. It's in my money belt." She patted her stomach.

He nodded in approval. "Good. Let me do the talking."

"Um…" She shot him a sidelong glance, then flinched in sympathy. Deep circles ringed his eyes. The bruises underneath his unshaven cheeks looked stark against the unnatural paleness of his skin. Lines of pain drew his mouth into a grimace. He looked like he was barely staying conscious. "Ah, Max, have you looked in the mirror lately? Because if I was a checkpoint guard, I'd definitely think you looked suspicious."

Max swore and tilted his head so he could see his reflection in the rearview mirror. Then he gave a gruff laugh. "Hell, I'll just tell them a version of the truth. That we were at a way station that was attacked by rebels and barely escaped with our lives. Maybe they'll take pity on us and we'll get an armed escort to the embassy."

Emily perked up. "You think so?"

He shook his head, then winced. "No. Sorry, I was just being flip. I doubt they have the manpower to spare."

"Oh." She tried to hold back her disappointment.

He motioned toward the glove box. "I stuck the map in there. Since I've only been to the capital once before, I'm not sure where the embassy is. Why don't you plot us the best route?"

The neon blue bus in front of them lurched forward in line. It might once have been a school bus, but had since been fitted with a roof luggage rack that was jammed with suitcases, bags of yams, and live goats and chickens. As their pickup followed, Emily pulled out the map. She only half focused on deciphering the streets and symbols, keeping the majority of her attention on the checkpoint. But as they drew nearer, she saw that Max was right. The soldiers, wearing government patches of red and black on their uniforms, were basically just waving people through after a cursory glance inside.

When it was their turn, Max cranked down the window.

The round faced soldier peeked inside. "*Obruni*, why you coming here? There is great danger now for your people. You should leave."

Max nodded. "We're trying to get to the embassy."

The man shrugged. "You best hurry, then." He straightened and waved them through.

When they were out of earshot, Emily let out a shaky laugh. "Well. That was anticlimactic."

"Yeah." Max slowly brought the truck up to speed and followed the other vehicles along the paved road. "I see a stoplight up ahead. Which way do we go?"

Emily returned her attention to the map. "Ah... Keep going straight."

Twenty minutes later, they pulled onto a wide street and spotted the walled compound that housed the United States Embassy. Max pulled over to the side of the road half a block from the gates. "You go on from here."

"Wait. What? Aren't you coming with me?"

He shook his head. "No. I've got unfinished business here in the country." His hand pulled the brim of his baseball cap down farther, shielding his eyes.

She glanced nervously toward the embassy's gate. "Max, are you in some sort of trouble? Are you..." She swallowed heavily. "Are you afraid of being arrested?" Did his reluctance to approach the embassy have anything to do with the reason Crystal had been killed?

He only shrugged, which made her heart sink. "I've got a bit of...explaining to do. This isn't the time. But don't worry. I'll watch from here to make sure you get inside okay."

"Oh." She glanced down at her hands. "Well, then. Thanks for saving my life, Max." Fighting back a surprising wave of disappointment, Emily opened the door, then reached into the back seat for her pack.

"You take care of yourself, Emily Iwasaki," Max said through the rolled down window after she'd closed the door.

Tears pricked the back of her eyes. Oh, no. She widened her eyes, tried not to blink and willed herself not to cry, afraid that if she let the tears fall all of her dammed-up emotions from the past day would come pouring out and she wouldn't stop sobbing for hours. "I don't even know your last name."

He hesitated. "It's Lansing. Max Lansing."

"Thank you." She stared at him, memorizing the planes of his face, the stubborn set to his jaw. The long fingers dotted with scabbed-over cuts. The way his light blue eyes watched her without giving any hint of emotion.

Right. He didn't want or need her company. It was time to get on with her life. Still, a lump formed in her throat as she said, "Good-bye, Max Lansing. I hope things work out for you." Turning on her heel, she walked down the road, feeling the weight of Max's gaze. She didn't understand this sadness at leaving him. She barely knew him. He was dangerous. He was probably the reason Crystal and the others had been killed. And yet, whether he was a spy or someone on the wrong side of the law, he'd saved her life. He'd been nothing but kind to her. More, he'd been a symbol of strength and security in the midst of the frightening chaos of the past twenty-four hours.

Keeping her back straight, she approached the gate, making sure she didn't limp. Her thin tennis shoes had long ago rubbed off the skin on her heels, but she was accustomed to ignoring physical pain. Forgetting Max? For some reason she thought that would be much, much harder.

She reached the gate and found that the guard box on the other side was empty. That was strange. She pushed on the gate, but it was locked. "Hello?" She rattled the gate. "Hello?"

Noticing a buzzer set into the wall, she pressed it over and over again, resisting the urge to look back down the street to see if Max had left.

Finally, a local man wearing a tunic and slacks hurried toward her across the courtyard. "What do you want?" he called out. "We're closed."

"I—" She glanced up at the sign. "Isn't this the United States embassy?"

"Yes, yes."

She gave him a puzzled glance. "I'm an American. My tour group was attacked by rebels and I need help getting out of the country."

The man drew close enough for her to see that he had gray hair interspersed with his dark curls. "I'm sorry, child. Your ambassador withdrew all the staff yesterday at the request of our president."

"What?" She gripped the bars. "You mean everyone is gone? But—"

The man shrugged. "Without foreigners in the capital, the rebels have less reason to attack us."

"But what am I going to do?"

"I suggest you go to the airport. There should be one more flight out today, but you best hurry. Once night falls there will be no more flights until curfew is lifted in the morning."

Emily couldn't help it. She turned her head to check down the street. To her relief, the truck still sat where she'd left it. She sighed. "Okay then, which way is the airport?"

The man gave her directions. After she'd repeated them back, she thanked him.

"God be with you, child," he said, then walked back toward the main building.

Emily stood rooted in place, unable to fight back her disappointment. Trying hard to battle tears now that the promise of safety had once again been shattered. God, she couldn't wait to get out of this country. Get back to her normal, boring world. Even if she still didn't know what to do with her life, at least she wouldn't be in constant danger.

She blew out a breath. Well, there was no use in wallowing in pity. She just had to hope that Max would be willing to help her a little longer.

"What's up?" he asked when she returned to the truck.

She explained. "I'm sorry. I know you have other things to do, but would you please give me a ride to the airport?"

"Of course."

She hadn't realized how much she'd feared that Max would reject her until her shoulders sagged.

"Hey," Max said. "I'm not going to just abandon you, okay? I promise I won't leave until you're safe."

"Thank you." She stowed her pack then climbed into the passenger seat.

EMILY DASHED up to the line of scared, angry foreigners waiting on the tarmac just as the last flight of the day taxied toward the end of the runway. Her stomach sank and her fists clenched—she'd been so close to being free of this horrible place—but she refused to give in to emotion in front of all these strangers.

"You can't just leave us here!" the man next to her shouted to the male airline representative who indicated that the crowd should return to the terminal. The man's wife briefly met Emily's gaze with frightened eyes before she bent down to comfort their two young children. The young woman's fear struck a chord inside Emily, threatening to destroy her façade of calm.

No. She wouldn't panic. Max had promised to stay until she was safe. He'd help her figure out her next step. Protect her.

"I'm sorry," the airline representative said, adjusting his tie. "Come back in the morning and try your luck then."

"No. I waited hours to get this far," the man replied. "We're not leaving. We're going to stay right here so that my family and I are first on the plane tomorrow."

The airline representative shook his head. "No one is allowed to stay. There's a curfew. You have to go away."

"Screw your curfew!" The man took a threatening step forward.

Taking their cue from him, other people surged toward the airline representative. "We want to go home!"

The airline representative bolted toward the stairs leading into the terminal as security vehicles sped toward the crowd with sirens blaring. Wanting no part of a fight, Emily turned away, moving against the tide of angry people. She was jostled and shoved so hard she barely managed to keep her balance. The fear that she might go down under the mob threatened to bring on a full-blown panic attack. She tried to suck in air, but it felt as if iron hands had seized her lungs. Oh God, if she panicked now, she might fall and be trampled to death. She might—

Strong hands clasped her arms and pulled her free. She found herself pressed against a familiar chest covered in a sweaty, dirty t-shirt. "C'mon, Em," Max said. "Let's get out of here before this turns nasty."

Emily briefly let herself enjoy the sense of safety of being in Max's arms, then pushed away as her panic receded. "So now what?" She bit her lip. "I don't have money to pay for a hotel. The tour company took care of the big expenses, so we were told to just bring a little spending cash."

He escorted her through the nearly empty terminal. "Never mind, a hotel isn't safe."

"Then what are we going to do?"

He stopped and looked down at her. "Do you trust me?"

"Sure."

One corner of his mouth quirked up, as if he didn't quite believe her. Then he gently removed her hand from her scars. The protective gesture was so instinctive, she hadn't even realized that she'd covered them.

He didn't release her hand and the warmth of his touch slid

up her arm and chased away the chill of panic she'd felt out on the tarmac. The muted shouting from the angry crowd faded as she stared into his eyes.

"Don't hide, Emily. Particularly not from me."

Her whole body stilled. Not in fear, but with the sense that something had just changed between them. "Do you have a plan?" she finally found the breath to ask, breaking the weird tension.

Some deep emotion passed over his face, gone before she could fully identify it. "We're going to find someplace quiet, then I'll call for help." His smile was strained. "Don't worry, I'll find us a safe place to spend the night. Tomorrow morning, you'll be on the first flight home."

HALF AN HOUR LATER, Max glanced back to where Emily waited inside the truck in the deepening twilight. He'd navigated away from the airport without incident, then driven along the coastal road until he'd found this quiet strip of beach where his satellite phone's antenna would have an unobstructed view of the sky. Thankfully, Emily hadn't protested when he told her to stay put. He needed privacy for what he was about to do.

He stared at the phone in his hands as if it had fangs. Such a simple thing, making a phone call. There'd been a time when he wouldn't have hesitated to do this. When Kris and the others had been as close to him as brothers. When he'd known without a doubt that his teammates had his back and vice versa.

That was before everything at Unit 3 had deteriorated. Before Kris and the others had one by one given up fighting against the inept, hostile leadership and struck out on their own. Before Max had discovered proof that their suspicions were correct, that Dietrich was alive and someone in the U.S. military didn't want him found. Before Max had quit and been branded a rogue for going after Dietrich.

His fingers started to lose feeling from clutching the phone so hard and he eased back on his grip. He didn't want to do this. Didn't want to risk Kris and the others being hit by the political shit that was going to fly when Max took Dietrich down.

But Max didn't know this city. He didn't have any contacts here. Didn't have any place he knew was safe to keep Emily until tomorrow's flight.

Kris would know. He and half a dozen of Max's former Unit 3 teammates had formed their own private special operations group. They'd originally been based in the U.S., but had relocated to West Africa about a year ago, joining forces with an infant counterinsurgency movement calling itself the West African Rangers, or WAR. Kris had been after Max for months to join them.

Max kept saying no. And would continue to say no until he'd put Dietrich away. If he survived the confrontation with Dietrich and if he wasn't taken down by the traitor within the military, only then would Max consider joining his old team.

Which was why making this call was so damn hard. He didn't want to field the usual questions. To deal with the regret that always hit him, making him wish he could say yes. Because he missed the camaraderie. Missed knowing that if he failed, others would step in to finish the job.

His eyes cut over to the truck. He had to suck it up. Emily needed help.

Taking a deep breath, he dialed.

"Montgomery Enterprises," Kristoff said, giving the name of his front company.

"Hey, Kris, it's me. Ah...Max."

"Max, you motherfucker, where the hell have you been? I've been trying to get ahold of you for days. Or have we degenerated to the point where you're ignoring my calls?"

Max winced at the bite behind his friend's words. Yeah, now that he thought about it, he had been particularly rude during his last refusal. He cleared his throat. "I'm sorry. I was...indisposed. This is my backup phone." Christ. How hard would it be to admit that he'd been captured? Yet he couldn't say the words. Didn't want Kris's pity.

Not allowing his friend to comment, he rushed on, "I'm in New Accra, trying to get an American girl out of the country, but the last flight of the day was full. We need a safe place to spend the night."

Kris huffed out a breath. "You surprise me, Max. I thought nothing mattered but your hunt for Dietrich."

"I'm not a complete bastard," Max muttered.

"No, you're too much the white knight. Which is why you've been turning me down all these months, Mr. I'll-Go-It-Alone-To-Protect-You."

Max rubbed between his eyes, feeling a headache starting. "Can we forget all that for the moment? The girl's tour group was attacked and she's the only survivor. I just need a safe place for us to spend the night."

"A safe place and some medical treatment for you, am I right?"

"Kris," Max warned.

"Am. I. Right."

Max sighed. "Yes, damn you. How'd you know?"

"We were partners for six years. I know what you mean when you use a word like 'indisposed' for Christ's sake. Besides, don't you think I know how you sound when you're at the end of your reserves? Wouldn't you recognize the same if it were me?"

He was right, but Max wasn't going to admit it. Because if he did, he'd be closer to giving in and saying yes to the job offer. "So, a safe house?"

There was a hint of disappointment in his voice when Kris responded. "I'll give you an address, but I need a promise from you first."

"Are you fucking kidding me? A woman's life is on the line here."

"Max, you and I both know that you'll do whatever it takes to keep her alive. Finding a safe house is just the easiest option."

"Easy my ass," Max muttered, earning a chuckle from Kris. "So what's this promise?"

"I've got a mission that's right up your alley."

"Kris—"

"Max, trust me. You're gonna want to hear this. It involves Dietrich."

"Son of a bitch, Kris. Don't mess with me."

"I swear this is real. Accept the mission and I'll give you the address."

"Give me details."

"Uh-uh. If you agree, I'll fill you in once you reach the safe house. Do we have a deal?"

Bottom line, did he trust Kris? Always. He blew out a breath. "Yeah, deal."

"Excellent. I'll call you back in five."

Max stared at the phone after Kris disconnected. Well, that had been...interesting. Dammit, what did Kris expect from him? Two excellent commanders had been killed when separate operations had gone horribly wrong at the last minute. A number of men had been injured. All because someone kept tipping Dietrich off.

Someone with that type of power could ruin Kris and his new team. Better that only Max have his career ruined.

The phone rang. Kris rattled off the address and the security code, then hung up before Max could thank him.

Emily was dozing with her head back against the seat when he returned to the truck. Damn, but he admired her ability to sleep any place, any time. He'd once been able to do that, having been trained to take cat naps when he could. But since he'd been hunting Dietrich, it seemed that every time he closed his eyes he ended up in the middle of a nightmare.

When Max opened the truck's door, Emily blinked sleepily at him and his body stirred. Christ. Not now. He had too much to deal with to add a sudden attraction to Emily.

Yet although she wasn't his usual type—he preferred sturdy, outdoorsy women rather than fragile city dwellers—he had to admit that her hazel, almond shaped eyes and delicate face were stunning, even covered with red dust and sweat.

She gave him a puzzled smile and he caught his breath. Her wide, bold mouth changed her face from dainty and prim into one with character, hinting at her surprising stubborn streak. Her mouth revealed the strength behind her fragile appearance. A strength only reinforced by the melted skin that ran down her neck and disappeared beneath the collar of her shirt. Anyone who'd survived that kind of damage had grit. And courage.

"Max?"

Realizing that he'd been staring at her, he blinked and refocused.

"Everything okay?" she asked.

Not by half. "Yeah," he said. "I found us a safe house."

She raised her brows at his surly tone, but thankfully didn't ask any questions. Still, he felt her curiosity pressing against him as they headed out.

To his surprise, the safe house was in a swank neighborhood that rivaled a Beverly Hills suburb. Huge, multi-storied houses sat behind tall security fences. Emily whistled appreciatively, echoing Max's thoughts. Damn, WAR must have some high-ranking supporters, because just keeping the well-manicured lawns so green would cost more than most locals made in a year.

Following Kris's instructions, he turned down a back lane until he reached the rear entrance to the safe house. Max punched in the security code and a moment later, the gates swung open on well-oiled hinges. Sensors turned on the outside lights as he parked in the attached garage to the two-story, hacienda style house.

Max climbed out of the truck. Emily opened her door and started to stand, then sank back onto her seat with a low curse.

"Em? What's wrong?"

"My feet hurt. Just...give me a second."

"Do you require assistance, my friend?" a voice called from the back door.

"Rene." Max whipped his head around in surprise. "What the hell are you doing here?"

"Always a pleasure to meet you again, *mon ami*." Dr. Rene LaSalle's accent, a mix of Cameroonian and Parisian French, smoothed the bite in his comment as he walked down the stairs from the back door.

"Sorry. That came out wrong. Good to see you, man. I thought you were working in The Democratic Republic of the Ivory Coast." With his tight, short cornrows and his light brown skin, Rene could have passed for a reggae star. In reality, he was a traveling doctor who moved from conflict to conflict. Sort of like Doctors Without Borders, only Rene worked independently. He'd saved Max's life a couple of times.

"I was," Rene said. "However, I just attended a conference here in New Accra that was an excellent opportunity to increase my knowledge of infectious diseases while also gathering information."

Right. As Max's foggy brain finally remembered, in addition to offering medical treatment to its operatives, Rene often assisted WAR by providing intelligence.

"So. Kristoff tells me you need a safe place to stay." Rene moved in to embrace Max in greeting, but Max instinctively stepped back to protect his ribs. His friend gave him a knowing look, then glanced into the truck.

"Who is this?"

"Ah, Emily Iwasaki, meet Dr. Rene La Salle. He's a friend."

Rene's eyes narrowed as he noticed Emily raise her hand to cover her scars, but otherwise he showed no reaction as he took her free hand and placed a kiss on the back, European style. "My pleasure, Mademoiselle."

"Hello." Emily grimaced. "I apologize for not standing to greet you, but my feet are a bit...sore."

"Allow me to assist you, then." Rene reached inside and slipped his arms underneath Emily. Ignoring her cry of protest, he lifted her out of the truck with ease. "Hush, Mademoiselle. Your friend Max would do this himself, but I fear he is too injured, yes?" He glanced over Emily's head to meet Max's eyes. "What is it? Ribs?"

"Goddamn Kris and his big mouth."

Rene's answering smile was only slightly mocking. "I am a skilled doctor, my friend. I recognize the signs without any prompting from Kristoff."

Emily snorted in amusement and Max narrowed his eyes at her.

"This way, please," Rene said.

Max scowled at Rene's back as he followed his friend up the stairs. The spurt of anger he'd felt when Rene touched Emily surprised him. He barely knew the woman. Why should he care if Rene was the one to carry her? It wasn't as if she were in any danger of being dropped. Rene might look like an average businessman in his kente cloth tunic and western trousers, but as a traveling doctor who worked in some of the most remote, most dangerous locations in the region, he often had to carry patients out of threatening situations before treating them. Hell, he'd even carried Max to safety once while dodging trigger-happy rebel patrols.

Rene moved easily through the house until he reached one of the upstairs guest rooms. "Here you go, Mademoiselle." He set her on top of the covers. "Now, shall we see what is causing you such pain?"

Emily's eyes widened in panic. "Um...no need. I can... I'll..."

Max could have told her to hold her breath. Nothing derailed Rene once he set his mind to it. He bent and removed Emily's sneakers before she could stop him. As he slid off her socks, he hissed in surprise, then said, "Mademoiselle, I think you and Max must have quite a story to tell."

"What?" Max moved forward. Emily's feet were covered with blisters, most broken and bloody but a few still pregnant with liquid. "What the hell, Em? Have you been walking with blisters since the beginning?"

She just shrugged.

"Why didn't you say something?" He ran a hand over his face. "Dammit, how was I supposed to know you were hurting? You didn't even limp."

Face red, Emily wiggled her toes. "Take a good look at the state of my feet, Max."

Rene pointed to a thick callus on her big toe that was partially covered with blood. Emily nodded. "I'm—" The misery that filled her eyes made his chest ache. She quickly glanced away, cleared her throat, then started again. "I was a ballet dancer. Calluses, blisters, and broken toes are par for the course. I didn't limp or complain because I'm used to pain in my feet."

"Then why'd you need Rene to carry you inside?"

She gave a rueful smile. "Because I'd been sitting funny in the truck and my feet had fallen asleep." She shrugged. "You know. Pins and needles."

Rene's mouth curled into a smile. "I am relieved that it is not worse. Would you like to bathe? Afterwards, I will bandage your feet."

Emily nodded so violently, Max snorted. She pushed hesitantly to her feet, but her balance was good. She took one step, then halted. "Do you have a phone that can make international calls? I need to let my family know I'm okay. And—" Her voice caught and she glanced down.

"Don't worry about it," Max said. "We'll make sure word gets to your family and to the families of the women who were killed."

She nodded without looking up at him. "Thanks. The tour company needs to be notified as well. Also, there were three other women who were part of the tour. They were in the southeast region. Would it be possible for you to check that they're okay?"

"Of course we'll check on the women. But it's safer if the tour company thinks you're dead."

Her head snapped up.

"Don't worry, we'll make certain your family learns the truth. But until we know if anyone on the tour company's staff was involved in sending the rebels to the way station, it's better that they not know you're a witness."

"Oh."

That one word made her sound very young and very scared. She searched his eyes. He had no idea what she saw, but she gave him a tentative nod.

"Mademoiselle, I promise that we will take care of the notifications for you," Rene said. "For now, if you will please come with me." He turned and stepped into the hall.

Max kept an eye on Emily as she followed Rene, just in case her feet gave out.

"Mademoiselle, the bathroom is just there." Rene pointed toward an open door. "You should find all that you need inside."

"Thank you." Emily glanced at Max. "Uh... Good night, Max. Thanks for sticking with me."

He shrugged. "Nite."

Emily disappeared into the bathroom and shut the door behind her.

"That is your room." Rene nodded toward the guest suite across the hall. "Are you able to undress yourself? Because quite frankly, my friend, you stink. You should wash before you call Kristoff."

Max frowned. "I'm good to go. The ribs are just bruised."

When Rene raised one brow, Max rolled his eyes. "Okay, Dr. Dad. My ribs hurt like hell, but I'll manage on my own." Even if he had to cut his t-shirt off.

"Ah, you Americans. So afraid to ask for help."

"Yeah, well, I didn't tell Kris I needed medical care."

"Yet he knows you better than that, does he not?" Rene shook his head and jerked his chin toward the door.

Max threw Rene an irreverent salute, then walked into the suite. Compared to the outside of the house, the bedroom was simple. A gleaming wooden armoire for clothes. A plain wooden headboard for the bed and a matching bedside table.

What really proclaimed the wealth of the owner, aside from the quality of the wood, was the attached bathroom. Max dumped his pack on the bed, removed his spare set of clothes, then headed into the bathroom. Okay, truth? He could have used some help with the shirt if he didn't want to aggravate his ribs, but goddammit, he was sick of being helpless. He managed to wrestle his shirt off without causing too much pain.

Max groaned as he stood under hot, steady water for the first time since his capture. Most of his cuts and scrapes had started to scab over, but a few had been irritated raw by his backpack. Yet it felt so good to be clean, he barely noticed the small stings. He was free. And alive.

Tremors wracked his body and he steadied himself against the wall. Damn. He'd come too close to dying. He'd been completely helpless against Ziegler. Known that Ziegler was going to kill him. How ironic that Dietrich's arrival had saved him, because the arms dealer wanted Max dead by his own hand.

Yet if he hadn't escaped, Emily's friends would be alive.

The memory of the women's deaths brought Max's guilt bubbling up in a scalding froth that threatened to send him to his knees.

It should have been me that died. Not those innocent women.

Max leaned his head on his folded arms and let the wall hold him up. For a long while he stood like that with his eyes closed, letting the water sluice over him and carry his tears away. Letting the heat ease the tension in his muscles as he shoved the guilt back into its cage. He couldn't go back and save them. All he could do was make certain Emily got safely out of the country, then make damn sure that Ziegler went down with Dietrich.

CHAPTER FIVE

An hour later, Max sat alone at the safe house's dining room table, staring into space. His hands were clasped around an empty bowl, trying to absorb the lingering warmth from the tomato and onion stew over rice that Rene had prepared for him. Without the mechanical motions of eating to distract him, and with Rene down the hall in the office, Max couldn't stop his mind from replaying the moment when Ziegler shot that girl.

"Max?" Rene asked from the doorway. "Is everything okay?"

Max startled, then shrugged. "Ah. Yeah. Just thinking."

"Hmm." Rene gathered Max's dishes and carried them over to the sink.

Max pushed to his feet. "Hey, I got that, man."

Rene waved him down. "No. Sit. It is my pleasure. Once I have tended to your wounds and you have had a decent night's rest, then I will allow you to help." He quickly washed the dishes and stacked them on the drying rack. Then he nodded toward the hallway. "Come, let me—"

Max's satellite phone vibrated, then the networked house phone rang as the incoming call was transferred. Max glared at it before answering. "Yeah."

"You at the safe house yet?" Kristoff said without preamble.

Max sighed. "Yeah."

"Good. Is Rene there?"

"Yes."

"Put me on speaker phone."

Max hit the button. "All right, Kris, Rene can hear you now. What's up?"

Rene leaned back against the sink and crossed his arms.

"Rene already knows some of this, but I want him to be aware of the latest developments. Long story short, on the twenty-seventh—that's nine days from now—Dietrich has an unknown buyer coming in to take possession of a highly lethal, experimental weapon gone missing from a South African military research facility."

"I knew Dietrich had a deal coming up," Max acknowledged, "but I haven't been able to find out where."

"We don't know where either, only when it's taking place. Unfortunately for Dietrich, the plane containing the briefcase with the weapon's plans and a prototype went down in the north of the country. Our source said that even after the plane disappeared from radar, Dietrich waited until the courier failed to make his scheduled check-in before sending teams into the jungle. As far as we know, he hasn't found it yet."

"Good luck with that," Max said. "With some of that deeply forested terrain, you'd have to be right on top of the plane in order to find it. Didn't Dietrich have a beacon or other tracking device on the plane?"

"Apparently it malfunctioned. Or it might have been disabled by the pilot. You know how smugglers are. They don't want anything on board that could be used by the authorities or by their clients to track them."

"Yeah."

"We've managed to sneak access to a satellite image of the area, but there's no sign of the plane."

Max got a sinking feeling. "You want me to go after it."

"Yes."

"Dammit, Kris. That's like looking for a needle in a haystack."

"I know. I'm sorry. We tried to contact you as soon as we learned the plane had gone down, but you didn't answer."

All too aware that Rene was listening intently, Max said, "That's because I was captured and spent a few days at the mercy of Ziegler's temper before I managed to escape."

"Christ, Max. Rene, is he even up for the challenge?"

Rene gave Max his Serious Doctor look. "I have not yet had time to examine him. At best guess, he has at least one cracked or severely bruised rib. And from what I can see on his face and hands, he has been beaten extensively."

"Max?" Kris asked. "I know I made this mission a condition of using the safe house, but if you're seriously injured, I take it back."

"I'm fine," Max growled. "I just don't know what you expect me to do. If Dietrich's men can't find it, how do you expect me to? It's not like I have access to satellite photos and computer analysis software." Even if he were back in his office at Unit 3 with his full arsenal of analytic tools, finding the plane would be difficult. Jungle vegetation grew fast and would have started to obliterate any obvious signs of the crash within days. "Has there been any intel from the locals?"

"No. That's the problem. Our source was the only contact we had in the area. With him dead—shot in the back of the head yesterday—we have no one to investigate for us."

Max snorted. "In case you haven't noticed, I'm a white guy. Not exactly inconspicuous. I go up there and start asking questions, Dietrich will hear about it."

"Dude, give me some credit for not being a moron. I know you'll stick out, but we don't have a choice here."

Max winced. "Sorry."

"No, you're not. You're just being your usual arrogant self."

Despite himself, Max felt the corners of his lips curl in amusement. Damn, but he'd missed Kris.

"At the very least, I need you to monitor Dietrich's progress," Kris continued. "Either steal the briefcase once his men have found it, or call us in so we can take care of it."

Max ran his hand over his face. "Why aren't you sending a team in right now? Or one of the guys?"

"Because you're there. And because the rebels are on the move and WAR's busy putting out fires. We can't spare a team unless we have a specific target."

Max blew out a breath. "Fine. I'll do it. But before I start, I have to get Emily on the first plane out of here tomorrow morning."

"Rene can do that. I need you to head back north. In the general vicinity of a village called Bamasi."

Max closed his eyes and gave a disbelieving laugh.

"What?"

"That's not far from where I hitched a ride south. I have to warn you, the rebels are working with Ziegler and Dietrich and have already done some killing in that area."

There was a long pause. "I know. Rene, you didn't tell him?"

"I have not had the opportunity."

Max glanced at Rene. "What?"

Rene's lips tightened before he spoke. "A cell phone video showing Ziegler shooting an American girl, and the rebels killing her companion and several locals was sent to the local media and passed on to WAR."

The memory hit Max with such force he bowed his head, clenching his fists to fight back the pain.

"Max?" Rene put his hand on Max's head. "What's wrong?"

Keeping his head lowered—dammit he did *not* want Rene's pity—Max spat out, "Ziegler shot the girl because he thought she was me. I'd just cut my hair that morning. So when the girl turned to run and her blonde hair fanned out behind her, Ziegler shot her."

"You were there?" Kris asked.

"Yeah. The women belonged to Emily's tour group. Lucky for her, Emily had gone off alone into the jungle to take photos. She was on her way back when I grabbed her." He swallowed back guilt. "I stopped Em from getting killed, but wasn't fast enough to save the other women."

"Max," Kris said. "I've seen the video. Ziegler drew and fired too fast. The rebel standing next to him fired seconds later. If you were in the jungle, there's no way you could've stopped them."

"Dietrich wants me alive," Max said, ignoring Kris's attempt to relieve his guilt. "He wants to kill me personally. He's made that perfectly clear. So I never expected Ziegler to react with deadly force in response to someone who might have been me. That puts him in direct violation of Dietrich's orders."

"I'm sorry, Max," Rene said.

"The hell of it is, I don't know how Ziegler ended up at the way station." Max wished that Rene would step away and give him some damn breathing room. "I saw no sign of pursuit. I even checked my clothing and belongings for tracking devices and found nothing." He rubbed his face in his palms. "I suppose it's possible that a rebel sympathizer was on the tro-tro and had already reported to the rebels that there was a white girl on board before I joined them. Or maybe someone sent a text after I was picked up."

"Was there enough time for someone at the way station to place a landline call?" Kris asked.

"Yeah. But Ziegler had to have already been on the road in order to arrive when he did. We reached the way station around dawn. I'm estimating that the trip from where I was held prisoner would be a good eight or nine hours by car. But Ziegler showed up roughly five hours after us."

"It doesn't really matter how he found you," Kris pointed out.

"The fact is, you didn't race into the way station yards ahead of Ziegler, leading him to the tour group. You didn't point Ziegler at that girl as a way to protect yourself."

"Of course not!"

"Exactly. So stop taking the blame. Ziegler pulled the trigger. Ziegler. Not you. Get over it."

"She's still dead because she looked like me," Max snarled, raising his head to glare at the phone. Couldn't they see? This was precisely the type of situation he'd been trying to avoid by staying away from Kris and the others.

"Fine, you want another damn incident to add to that load of guilt you're carrying around, have at it." Kris's voice offered no mercy. "Just pull yourself out of your pity party long enough to carry out this mission. Then you can go back to playing Mr. Martyr Man and be miserable all by your lonesome, you stubborn bastard."

"Ouch."

"Yeah, well, when are you going to get it through your thick head that we care about you? You're family, whether you want to admit it or not. *We* don't abandon family."

"I—"

"Shut it. I'm not in the mood to hear your protestations that you've locked us out for our own protection. For the last damn time, we're a team. That means we've got each other's backs. Through thick and thin. No matter what."

Emotion lodged in Max's throat. It was *because* the team was family that he'd gone solo. Why couldn't they accept that the level of danger they'd be in was unacceptable? "How many times do I fucking have to tell you? I'm not going to let Dietrich's sponsor put you on some damn black list so that everyone in the U.S. military or law enforcement is after you. Or—"

"I said, shut it. I'm not arguing with you over this any more. Rene, work your doctor's magic on Max. Then make sure he gets a good night's sleep if you have to knock him out with a hammer. Max, check in before you leave tomorrow."

"Yes, sir!" Max snapped.

"That's more like it," Kris said. "Good—"

"Wait! Kris...those women..." He cleared his throat. "God, their families need to be notified before the video goes public. Emily's family needs to know she's alive. And she's worried about the safety of the other three women who were part of the group. They were stationed in the southeast region."

"Don't worry, we're on it. The video was received by one of WAR's informants. She knew better than to air it. She passed it on to us and then to a contact in the regional police that we trust. We'll make sure the families are notified in an appropriate manner and look into the status of the other women."

"Thank you. That will mean a lot to Emily."

"You're welcome." With that, Kris disconnected.

"You heard the man," Rene said, offering Max his hand. "Come down to the bathroom and I will examine your injuries. The sooner we get you patched up and tucked into bed, the better."

"Thank you, Dr. Dad." With a heartfelt groan, Max let his friend pull him to his feet. Damn. His muscles had frozen up after sitting too long and each step was agony.

I can barely walk and I'm supposed to go after Dietrich and this weapon tomorrow? Some superhero I am.

Day Five

"MADEMOISELLE. MADEMOISELLE IWASAKI!"

Emily tried to ignore the unfamiliar voice and snuggle down into the pillow, but an insistent hand shook her shoulder. "G'way."

"Mademoiselle Iwasaki, you must wake up. The line will be forming soon at the airport."

Emily cracked open one eye. "Huh?" The man bending toward her had light brown skin, black hair arranged in neat, short cornrows, and heavy lidded, bedroom eyes. It took her a moment to recognize Max's friend. "You're the doctor."

"Yes. I will drive you to the airport so you can go home."

Home.

That jolted her into full alertness. She sat up. Glanced around the small room that contained a twin bed, a wooden armoire, and a bedside table. But no clock. Purple batik cloth covered the louvered glass window, yet she saw no light filtering through. "What time is it?"

"About five in the morning. We must leave soon if you wish to arrive at the airport in time."

That's right, she wanted to be one of the first people in line. She swung her feet over the side then froze, staring at her bare, bandaged feet. Her clean toes stuck out from beneath pristine white bandages. Once again, the humiliation of having the doctor and Max see her mangled feet made her face burn. Yes, nasty, gnarly feet were a badge of honor among some dancers, but Emily had always found them just plain ugly. To the extent that she never wore sandals or open toed shoes.

"How are your feet this morning?"

Emily shrugged, then winced as her bad shoulder flared with pain. She'd spent too many hours in the car with her shoulder hitched up toward her ear. She began kneading the muscles as she replied, "They're fine."

He raised an eyebrow and her hand rose to cover the scars on her neck, even though she knew it was too late to hide them.

Why does it bother you so much that someone recently saw your scars and your ugly feet when Crystal and Sue are dead?

Tears filled her eyes and she blinked them back. To distract herself, she glanced around the room. There, in the corner by the armoire, was her backpack. Her sneakers—cleaned of dirt—sat next to it on the floor, but there was no sign of her socks.

The doctor noticed the direction of her gaze. "There were too many holes in your socks. Since you had an extra pair in your pack, I threw them away."

She turned to stare at him. "You went through my things?" Had she fallen that deeply asleep?

He shrugged, unrepentant. "I would have kept the socks for you otherwise."

Deciding it wasn't worth arguing over, she glanced at her watch. "How long until we leave?"

"Twenty minutes. We had longer, but you were quite determined to stay asleep."

She felt herself blush again. "Okay. Let me use the bathroom and I'll be right with you."

She waited for him to leave. When he didn't, she raised a brow. "Dr. LaSalle, may I have some privacy?"

"Show me that you can stand on your own and I will go. And please, call me Rene."

Rolling her eyes at his bossiness, Emily carefully stood up. Yesterday, even the soles of her feet had been sore. The bit about the pins and needles had been true, but the bottoms of her feet had also felt bruised from walking over such rough terrain with only a thin layer of rubber to protect her. But today there was just a mild stiffness from overexertion. She nodded at the doctor.

He gave her a short bow. "Be downstairs in fifteen minutes, please. Oh, and word came in this morning. The other three women made it safely over the border to the neighboring embassy."

"Thank God!"

The doctor smiled and reached for the doorknob.

"Wait!"

"Yes?"

"Where's Max?"

"Ah. Max is still asleep. Last night, he asked me to see you safely on your way."

"Oh." She glanced down to hide her disappointment. Well, what had she expected? That Max would put his life on hold for her?

No. But at least she'd thought he'd be around to say good-bye. She lifted her head and put on her expressionless pre-performance face. "Okay. I don't think Max slept much while we traveled, so I bet he was exhausted."

"Indeed." After giving her another courteous nod, the doctor let himself out of the room.

Sighing, she made her way down the hall to use the facilities. With her remaining time, she gently worked her feet and body through a short series of stretches. Then, seeing that her time was almost up, she shouldered her backpack and headed out.

Along the hallway to the left, a staircase with an elaborately carved wooden balustrade led down to a sunken living room. The furnishings were all glistening, dark wood and bright silken fabrics. This was by far the fanciest house she'd seen in the country since her arrival.

Just how rich were Max's friends?

Following the low murmur of voices, she found Dr. LaSalle in the kitchen talking to Max. Max flicked her a glance over the cup of coffee in his hands, but immediately returned his attention to the doctor.

Despite the lack of warmth in Max's eyes, Emily's heart still leapt at the sight of him. He looked one hundred percent better than when she'd last seen him. His skin had lost that grayish cast and he wasn't holding his body so stiffly.

Continuing to ignore Emily, he yawned, then took a big sip of coffee.

Annoyed by his aloofness, Emily cleared her throat. "Dr. LaSalle, don't we need to be going?"

"She is right," the doctor said. "Max, we will finish this

conversation when I return. Mademoiselle, if you will follow me out to the car."

Emily intended to walk right past Max, but found herself stopping next to him. "Thanks again for all of your help, Max," she said with icy politeness. "I hope you have a nice life."

He met her eyes, some emotion burning there that she couldn't identify. "Why are you mad at me?" he snapped. "I did what I promised. You're safe. Rene will get you to the airport and then you'll be on your way home."

She shook her head. "I don't know." Somehow, the thought of leaving him here in this dangerous city didn't feel right. She couldn't help remember how easily that man had killed Crystal. How he'd probably meant to kill Max, instead. "Never mind, it's probably just the stress of the past few days. Forget it."

He held her eyes a moment longer.

Don't stay, she almost said. *Come with me. Be safe.* But with his freshly shaved cheeks revealing several bruises and cuts, she knew this was a man who never took the safer route. Fighting back a stab of grief that he might die here, all alone, she glanced away. "So. I've got to go now. Good-bye."

"Good-bye, Emily Iwasaki. Safe journey. I know you'll be fine. You've got grit."

"Thank you." Wondering why she felt the urge to run her hand along his cheek and press a kiss to his mouth, she tightened her grip on the straps of her backpack and headed into the garage. She'd heard that life-threatening events could create strong emotional bonds between strangers, but surely she hadn't fallen for Max already. That was ridiculous.

But then why did she feel this wrenching sadness over leaving him behind? Shaking her head, she placed her backpack on the rear seat of the doctor's small, four-door sedan.

"You have to go!" A skinny teenage boy with dark skin raced across the back yard and dashed into the garage. "You must leave now!" The boy waved his arms.

"Emily, get back." Max bolted out of the house, shoved her behind him, and leveled his pistol at the boy. "Stop!"

The boy froze, the look of horror on his face almost comical.

"Easy, Max." Dr. LaSalle put his hand on Max's shoulder. "This is a friend. One of the boys who keeps the house clean."

Max lowered his gun, but the tension didn't leave his body.

"Abdullah, calm down." The doctor walked over to the boy. "What has happened?"

"The rebels have arrived. They attacked the government buildings not two hours ago, and those they did not kill have now fled. Patrols are already marching through the street, looking for foreigners." He removed a piece of paper from the pocket of his ragged khaki shorts and held it up so they could see it was a flyer with a bad photograph of Max under the word WANTED. "Looking for this man in particular."

Emily sucked in a breath.

"Let me see that." Max took the flyer from Abdullah and scanned it quickly. "No charges. It just says that I'm armed and dangerous and to report me to the nearest rebel patrol."

"Wait," Emily said. "The nearest *rebel* patrol? Not the police? Max, why do the *rebels* have a price on your head? What have you done?"

"Max has done the same as many of us," the doctor said. "He has tried to stop the rebels from tearing this region apart." He flicked his finger against the paper. "Very slick. I doubt the rebels prepared this on their own," he murmured, sharing a tense glance with Max. "So, it appears that certain players are aware of your presence here."

Max just shrugged.

"The reward for your capture is quite high. It is a good thing you are leaving."

"Who—" She shook her head as Max ducked back inside the house. They wouldn't tell her even if she did ask again what was going on.

Dr. LaSalle turned to the boy. "How close are they, Abdullah? Can we still reach the airport to get Mademoiselle Emily safely away?"

The boy shook his head. "No. The rebels have blocked off the streets to the airport and the government tanks are approaching. No planes will be leaving." He bounced on his feet with excitement. "I have borrowed my cousin's Jeep. Very good condition. Excellent for traveling over rough roads. Plenty of gas and oil." Pride shone from his eyes. "I will take the lady over the border. The rebels entered from the west, so we shall leave on the northern road."

The doctor hesitated, then shook his head. "It is the duty of you and I to help those injured by the fighting. I need you to serve as my eyes and ears here in the capital."

Abdullah's excitement dimmed. He opened his mouth to protest, but the doctor held up his hand. "However, we accept the gift of your cousin's vehicle. Where is it?"

The boy pointed to the lane on the other side of the wall.

"Very good. For the moment, let us quickly gather supplies for our friends." The two turned around just as Max ran out of the house carrying his rucksack and tugging his baseball cap down over his forehead. The boy tossed a set of keys to Max, then he and the doctor disappeared into the house.

Max handed a second baseball cap to Emily. "Put this on. It will provide a little bit of camouflage against anyone looking for us."

She swallowed nervously, but did as he said. Then she pulled her backpack out of the doctor's car.

Max met her eyes. "Ready?"

No. Never. This was too unreal. Too frightening to be her life. She didn't want to have to run from the rebels with this mysterious, dangerous man. She just wanted to go home. But she nodded. What else could she do?

He gave her an encouraging smile. "All right, let's go."

Max grabbed her hand and ran toward the gate, which swung open as they approached to reveal a slightly battered Jeep with a bunch of jerry cans strapped under a cargo net on the roof. They threw their packs into the back seat. Max slid behind the wheel and tossed a phone onto the console as Emily strapped herself into the passenger seat. Max had just started the engine when the doctor and Abdullah raced up. They shoved several bags into the cargo compartment.

Max rolled his window down.

"Supplies and a first aid kit," the doctor said. "Including antibiotics." He met Emily's eyes. "Please make certain that Max takes one pill every day for the next ten days and that he is careful of his damaged ribs."

She nodded, then flicked a glance at Max. Just how badly had he been hurt?

"Head north," Abdullah advised. "That is the safest way."

Max held his hand out to the doctor. "Thanks, man," he said as they shook. The doctor just nodded in return, then jerked his head to indicate they should leave.

As they drove down the concrete lane running behind the houses, the doctor called after them "God be with you, my friends."

"Yeah," Max muttered. "We're going to need it."

CHAPTER SIX

As Max drove toward the intersection with the main road north, an explosion rocked the neighborhood.

Emily squealed in alarm. "That felt really close."

"Yeah." Max gave the Jeep more gas. So much for the government's declaration that they would never let the rebels over the border.

"Is Dr. LaSalle going to be all right?"

Max sure as hell hoped so. With light brown skin and slightly Caucasian features, it was clear Rene was mixed race despite his cornrows. But his friend was also smart and resourceful. Not to mention stubbornly determined to help those in need. "Rene knows how to take care of himself. He's been providing medical care in conflict areas for years."

Hearing a high pitched whistling, Max glanced over his shoulder. "Incoming. Hold on!"

He gunned the engine, swerving to the left as the rocket-propelled grenade exploded in the spot where they'd been a moment ago. The Jeep rocked under the force of the blast, but stayed upright. Max straightened the wheels and sped down the road.

"Oh, God," Emily said. She turned in her seat, craning her neck to see out the back window. "Where are they? How did they find us so quickly?"

He glanced in the rearview mirror, but didn't see any rebel vehicles or soldiers. "I think that was just a lucky shot on their part. Probably one of rebels fired at random in order to intimidate people and we just happened to be in the wrong place at the wrong time."

"That's not particularly reassuring."

He shrugged. "What do you want me to say? The rebels don't care who they hurt. Violence terrorizes people and the resulting fear helps them control the population."

"You say that as if it's normal."

"For this part of the world, it is."

Emily crossed her arms over her chest, settled deeper into her seat, then lapsed into an uneasy silence.

Ten minutes later, they reached the crossroads and found it heavy with traffic. Battered taxis vied with tro-tros, commercial trucks, and private vehicles to get out of town. Max joined the stream of vehicles as it inched across a bridge spanning a large irrigation canal. He drummed his fingers against the steering wheel. He didn't like this slow pace. It made them too vulnerable.

"Looks like everyone is trying to outrun the rebels," Emily said.

"Yeah." Max's impatience grew. His sixth sense warned him they needed to leave the group in order to stay safe.

Then the crowd's forward momentum stopped.

"Max? What's going on?"

"I don't know." He craned his neck, but couldn't see past the small bus in front of him.

"Let me look." Emily cranked down her window and climbed through to stand gracefully with one foot balanced on the open window as she peered over the crowd. Max's heart skipped a beat. "Dammit, Emily."

She shimmied back inside. "There are a couple of Jeeps blocking the road, along with one of those big army trucks with the canvas arching over the back."

"Troop transport."

She nodded.

Max steered the Jeep over to the side of the road, earning the ire of the other drivers who honked and shouted at him. But he didn't care.

"Max?"

"We've got to get to that small side road up ahead before the rebels spot us. I'm on a wanted poster, remember?"

Max nudged the Jeep the last few feet, turned onto the unpaved side road, and slowly increased their speed so as not to draw additional attention. He killed the headlights, too, not needing them in the growing morning light.

"Did the white man at the way station work with the rebels to create the wanted poster? I know he shot Crystal because he thought she was you."

Christ. How long ago had she figured it out? Recognizing the hint of panic in her voice, he looked at her out of the corner of his eye. She watched him warily, her back pressed against the passenger door.

"You've cut your hair, but you had a long blond ponytail when you got on the tro-tro. That man saw Crystal's hair and thought he was killing you. Who *are* you?"

The fear and accusation in her voice cut to the heart of him. "I'm one of the good guys."

"So you say!"

He shot a quick, hard glance at her before returning his attention to the road. "Listen, can you put the hysterics on hold until we get safely away?"

"Hysterics? I am *not* having hysterics. I'm furious that an innocent woman was killed because she resembled you, you bastard!

And I'm terrified because instead of being safe, traveling with you has put me in the sights of a killer!"

She took a deep breath and Max hoped she was done. Because, damn, his ears were ringing.

"What kind of trouble are you in?" she demanded. "And don't you dare give me that crap about being a history professor working on some dry treatise."

He rubbed his right ear. "I'm sorry about your friends, okay? I had no idea Ziegler was so unstable. He's usually more careful than that."

"See! You admit that it's all your fault."

He winced. "Yes. All right, yes. Ziegler killed her because of me. Are you happy now?"

"No. You're too dangerous. Sue was killed because she had the bad luck to be standing next to your double, Crystal. I'm not going to sit here and suffer the same fate. Stop the car. I want out."

Dammit, did she think he'd wanted Ziegler to kill that girl? That he didn't care? "You want me to drop you at one of these houses?" He jerked his chin toward the window. "With the rebels demanding that all foreigners be turned over to them, do you really think you'll be safer depending on the kindness of strangers than with me? Haven't I kept you safe so far? If you don't trust me, at least trust Rene. He thought I could protect you."

"He didn't know about your friend Ziegfried."

"Ziegler. And yes, he did. Rene knows that if I could have stopped Ziegler from killing your friend, I would have."

"Whatever. Just let me out."

"No." He sped up. "Believe it or not, you're safe with me. I *will* protect you. From both the rebels and Ziegler."

"I hate you."

"Yeah, well, welcome to the club," he muttered under his breath.

With a frustrated growl, Emily subsided into silence.

Great. Just what he needed. To spend hours trapped in a car with a woman who hated and feared him.

Emily shifted in her seat, trying to get comfortable. Watching her, Max was hit by a surprising wave of compassion that cut straight through his self-righteous anger. Dammit, she hadn't asked for any of this. All she'd wanted was to draw attention to the plight of war orphans. It wasn't her fault she got mixed up with him, or that trouble seemed to be all he knew lately.

Failure. You're always failing the ones you care about. You failed to stop Dietrich before the attack that hurt Wil. You failed to hold the team together, letting them go off and form their own band under Kristoff. You failed to stop Ziegler from killing that girl.

Face it. Emily would be better off without you.

Max clenched his teeth and wrenched his mind onto the task at hand. He couldn't afford to get stuck in self-pity or self-recrimination. He had a job to do. Get Emily safely to the border. Find the plane. Retrieve or steal the briefcase with the weapon prototype. Ruin Dietrich's deal.

Right. No problem.

A check of the rearview mirror confirmed that no one had followed them, but Max didn't relax. This road headed east, toward the rising sun. Any pursuers would see their Jeep silhouetted against the pink and blue sky.

Five minutes later, a massive explosion shook the ground, sending the vehicle into a skid. Max fought the wheel and managed to bring it back under control.

Emily stared in horror out the back window. "That was the bridge, wasn't it?"

"Probably."

"Max, all those cars. People will be hurt. Dying!"

"I know. If we'd stayed, we'd be dead, too." He picked up his phone from the console where he'd been charging it via the cigarette lighter and handed it to her. "Text Rene about the bridge being hit. He'll make sure the victims get help."

Emily's terrified eyes met his. "You're sure Dr. LaSalle and Abdullah will be okay?"

"Yeah." He said the word with more confidence than he felt. "Rene's a survivor. Besides, he's a doctor. Even the rebels might hesitate to kill a doctor."

Emily's lips tightened, showing that she'd picked up on his use of the word might. What could he say? The rebels were comprised of a lot of hot-headed, angry young men who were often hyped up on drugs, making them unpredictable. A rebel leader might see the advantage to keeping a doctor alive, but a trigger-happy boy who saw a light-skinned, well-dressed man was more likely to shoot on sight.

Even worse, if Ziegler and the rebels learned that Rene had helped Max escape, his friend would become a target.

But as he'd said, Rene was a survivor.

After a moment of scrutinizing him, Emily turned back in her seat and began to type. "Will the text message go through?"

"You'll need to take the antenna out—it's in the small, round case—and stick it to the roof. The antenna is magnetic, so you might as well leave it on the roof until we receive a response." He peered up at the sky, then stopped in the middle of the road. "There aren't any trees overhanging this part of the road, so we should have a clear line of sight to the satellites." A satellite phone had become a necessity once the rebels started destroying cell phone towers and cutting landline phone cables in each area they conquered. All part of their push to purge West Africa of foreign technology they blamed for the region's continued lack of economic prosperity. They claimed that Africans should create their own communications network, but Max knew that their words were just a smoke screen. Cutting means of communication made the local population less able to send and receive information that wasn't approved by the rebels.

Emily followed his instructions as he opened his door.

"Where are you going?"

"I've got to disable the taillights so they won't be a beacon to anyone following us."

She shot him a startled glance. "But... Abdullah's cousin—"

He sighed. "I'll make sure he's reimbursed for the damage." Hell, the way his luck was going, Max expected he'd be financing an entirely new vehicle for the man once this was over.

Emily nodded then returned her attention to the phone.

Max climbed out of the driver's seat, then used the butt of his pistol to break the glass over the tail and brake lights.

When he returned to his seat, Emily said, "Okay, text sent."

"Thanks." He drove forward. At least the explosion seemed to have made her forget that she was afraid of him.

"So," she said wearily. "Where are we going?"

"I don't know. The Greater New Accra Region is pretty suburbanized. We should have several options for roads out of here." He tilted his head toward his rucksack in the back seat. "The maps and a small flashlight are in the front pocket of my pack. It's not safe to use the overhead light." He reached up and turned the light to the permanent off position. "Check to see where this road ends up."

"Can't your phone tell us where to go?"

"No. It's a satellite phone. It's pretty basic and doesn't run apps."

"Well, darn."

His bag was close enough that Emily simply reached into the back seat to retrieve the maps. Then she settled back in her seat, spread a map over her lap and clicked on the flashlight. Even with the sun coming up, the interior of the Jeep was still dim. "Where are we?" she asked. "Can you give me a reference point?"

He gave her the name of the main road north and the street the safe house had been on. "Look for a bridge north of that.

We're on the first side road on the right, heading roughly due east."

Out of the corner of his eye he saw her moving her finger across the map. "Okay. I've got it."

"Where does this dead end?"

"Hmm... It looks like there's a T-junction with a smaller north-south road coming up."

"Good. Can we reach the border on that road? You might need to grab the national or regional map for that."

Emily flipped through the other maps until she found the one she needed. While she figured out which one to use, he kept an eye on the road behind them. He thought he'd seen a flash of light on a windshield a minute ago when they'd been on a long, straight stretch of road, but then the road had turned and he'd lost visual contact. If he'd actually seen something. He might have just caught a glimpse of someone turning their house lights on.

Or maybe he wasn't being paranoid and the rebels really were following them.

"The north-south road twists and turns," Emily said, "but eventually it runs northwest and joins the main road not too far from the way station."

"Okay." His eyes flicked to the rearview mirror again. Damn. That was definitely another vehicle behind them.

WAR Headquarters
The Democratic Republic of the Ivory Coast
West Africa

"Dɪᴅ Max get out of the capital ahead of the rebels?"

Kristoff Wren turned away from his desk at WAR's headquarters to see Wil Lansing wheeling his chair into the room. "Just barely," Kris said. "According to Rene, Max and the girl left minutes before the rebels took over the block the safe house is on."

"Is Rene okay?" Wil asked, pushing his wheelchair forward with a powerful thrust of his arms. Lines of strain marked his face and Kris clenched his fist in order not to reach out and offer the man comfort. The fact that Wil had resorted to his wheelchair meant that something wasn't right with his new prostheses.

"Yeah, Rene's fine," Kris answered. "He called me from a triage center in town."

Wil nodded. "Figures. He always manages to end up wherever the wounded need him."

Kris glanced at the phone on his desk, then realized his mistake when Wil paused halfway across the room. "What's wrong?" Wil demanded.

Wishing he could avoid this conversation, Kris gave him a tired smile. "Ziegler got hold of Max for a couple of days."

Wil sucked in a breath. "He's okay?"

Kris shrugged. "You know Max. Always downplaying his injuries. Rene said the worst of Max's injuries are a couple of damaged ribs and a shallow knife slice across his lower back that only required a few stitches. He cleared Max for duty, so it can't have been that bad."

"Dammit." Wil slammed his hands down on the chair's armrests. "You know as well as I do the agony Ziegler can inflict with those fucking needles of his."

Once again Kris had to stop himself from touching Wil. He wanted to let the other man know that he wasn't alone in worrying about Max. *Dammit, Max why'd you have to go rogue, you selfish bastard?* It was hard enough watching his best friend put himself at such risk while refusing all of Kris's offers to help bring Dietrich down. Kris would have eventually forgiven Max that, because he didn't expect anything else from his stubbornly protective friend.

However, Kris couldn't so easily forgive the worry Max was

causing Wil. Max's brother was still adjusting both to life without his lower legs and to being back with the now decimated counterterrorism group that had been the target of the attack. With the U.S. focused on events in Iraq and Afghanistan, there'd been little political will or funding to restore the West African counterterrorism group. The remaining members of the group barely had the resources to take care of their first order of business, revamping security at U.S. military and diplomatic facilities in West Africa. Chasing down and neutralizing potential terrorist threats had become a secondary mission. The last thing Wil needed was the added stress of wondering if Dietrich was finally going to kill his brother. Or if the U.S. government was going to haul Max in and put him on trial for insubordination or treason.

Max's superiors at Unit 3 had ignored his resignation, instead declaring him AWOL. That only solidified Kris's belief that Dietrich's sponsor planned to sacrifice Max in order to protect Dietrich. Yet despite his team's best efforts, Kris still hadn't been able to discover the traitor's identity.

With Wil determined to protect Max, Kris feared that Wil would become the traitor's next target. So Kris had told his team to keep an additional ear out for any chatter regarding moves against Wil. Because Wil could be even more stubborn than Max when it came to ignoring threats to his life.

He'd have done the same for any friend or teammate. The fact that his world would be a darker place without Wil in it hadn't influenced his decision at all.

Knowing he was lying to himself, Kris crossed his arms over his chest. The only thing about the situation he felt grateful for was that he'd been spending a lot more time with Wil. Not that the other man had given any sign that he felt even the slightest bit attracted to Kris. Understandable. Wil hadn't just lost his lower legs in the explosion. His lover had been one of the first men killed by the blast. But even if Wil never returned his affection, Kris would at least be able to look back on these days and remember the mix of anticipation and respect that swamped him every time he was in Wil's presence.

Kris shook his head. Shit. He had it bad. The hell of it was that even if Wil did reciprocate the attraction, there wasn't much they could do about it. Homosexuality was not acceptable in Africa. While the guys from Unit 3 knew Kris was gay, none of the other members of WAR did. Kris had no idea how the African members would react if they found out. Even Azumah, the leader and founder of WAR, who Kris considered to be a very open-minded guy, might not be able to handle the news.

Things were only marginally better at the U.S. compound. Because there were so many locals working with the Americans, Wil mostly kept his sexual orientation a secret. And no matter the loosening of restrictions, being gay in the military still wasn't safe.

Logically, Kris understood all this. Emotionally? It killed him. He hadn't come to Africa expecting to fall for someone. Hell, all the guys in his group had pretty much given up any hope of a social life by signing up with WAR. Hard to date when you weren't even technically supposed to be on the continent.

But once Kris had met Wil, well...

He rubbed the back of his neck. He was willing to wait until Wil showed signs of easing back from his total dedication to his job enough to notice Kris's interest. But then what? Even if Wil did eventually return his affection, they'd have to sneak around if they wanted any romantic alone time.

Suck it up. At least you're alive.

"Yeah," he muttered, aware that it was a sad state of affairs that he was talking to himself. *Where there's life, there's hope, right?*

"Who do we have in the area that can help him?" Wil demanded, cutting into Kris's thoughts.

It always surprised Kris how thoroughly Wil had embraced WAR and Kris's special unit within it when Max, who'd been their teammate for years, still insisted on shoving them away.

"At the moment? No one," Kris said. "With the fighting in

Ivory Republic nearing the northeast border with Volta, we might have a team in place in a few days that could offer support."

"So, Max is on his own?"

"Yeah. I'm sorry."

Wil cut his hand through the air. "Don't be. Maybe it will push him into realizing that he can't do this all alone. That—God forbid—he actually needs help."

Kris knew that despite the tough love attitude, it would devastate Wil if anything happened to his brother. "I'm looking into our current assignments to see if there's anyone we can move into place sooner."

"Thanks." Wil's voice was gruff. He wheeled over to the map on the wall. After staring at it for a long moment, he picked up a red push pin and set it in place. "The embassy in New Accra has been evacuated. According to the ambassador, the Voltan president ordered all foreigners, including the diplomats, to leave or be thrown out by the military."

"Why?"

"The president thought it might buy time if the rebels knew there were no more foreigners in the capital."

Kris rolled his eyes. "That didn't work out so well."

"Yeah." Wil shook his head. "No one expected the city to be attacked so quickly."

Kris heard the frustration in Wil's voice. Like his brother, Wil assumed more responsibility than was due him. "What about civilians?" Kris asked "Any casualties?"

"Not yet. Unfortunately, rumor has it there are foreign nationals trapped at the airport while the rebels and the government forces fight on the perimeter. We're working on an evac plan."

"That confirms what Max said. Emily just missed the last plane out yesterday."

"That's when Max called you."

"Yeah. They were going to try to get her on a plane this morning, but the rebels attacked." Kris nodded at the map. "What about the embassy's tech?" One of the weird characteristics of the rebel movement was that despite their public statements condemning all technology as a form of Western oppression, the rebels had been stealing computers, servers, and other forms of technology and storing them in an unknown location.

"The security team trucked out as much stuff as possible on the day the ambassador called for the evacuation. They did their best to destroy the rest of it." Wil shrugged. "Is it enough to screw up whatever plans the rebels have for the technology? I haven't got a clue." He glared at the map, as if by force of will he could stop the rebels' path of destruction.

Kris wondered if he'd ever get the chance to be the target of Wil's fierce concentration, then mentally chided himself for being so easily distracted.

"No word yet on who the buyer is in Dietrich's upcoming deal?" Kris asked, standing up and walking over to stand next to Wil.

"No. We've only got eight days. If Dietrich finds the plane and retrieves the weapon in time, then we've got maybe two to three weeks after that to figure out the target for the attack." Wil gestured angrily toward the map. "Thanks to bureaucratic red tape and contractor delays, we've only upgraded the security at three of the smaller diplomatic missions. There's not enough time." He rubbed his hand over his face, then sighed. "I have another meeting with the head brass in the morning to urge them to speed things up, but they're starting to look at me like I'm as crazy as Max. I seriously think that Dietrich's protector is working against me." He sighed. "Or maybe I really am as obsessed and delusional as my brother."

Kris put a hand on Wil's shoulder. "You're doing the best you can. And we both know that Max isn't nuts." Underneath his hand, Wil's shoulders rose, then fell dejectedly.

"More good men are going to die or be critically wounded if

this attack goes forward," Wil said bitterly. "But we're no closer to finding out the target now than we were a month ago!"

Kris hated to see Wil in so much emotional pain. As the suspected date of the attack grew nearer, Wil had become increasingly grim and driven. So determined to protect other U.S. soldiers from suffering his fate, no matter the cost to himself, that he reminded Kris strongly of Max.

Kris cleared his throat. "You look tired, Wil. Why don't you call it a night?"

Wil shook his head. "I'm too wound up to sleep."

Something else Kris could lay at Max's door. "What time are you heading out in the morning?" Wil had to be careful not to be followed when he came and went from WAR's headquarters. Kwame Azumah, the former Côte d'Ivoire prime minister before the country split into the Ivory Republic and the Democratic Republic of the Ivory Coast, had founded WAR to be an underground movement to counteract the growing rebel presence across West Africa. Part of WAR's strength depended on it being shrouded in secrecy. The citizens of West Africa might whisper of mysterious troops that helped fight back the rebels, or unidentified saviors who broke people out of jail and delivered crucial payments that kept hospitals and charities alive, but no one knew the name of the organization except for a few key allies.

Most of the foreign military and diplomatic missions were also not privy to the secret. Only a few select individuals who'd proven they could be trusted.

Wil glanced at his watch. "I leave at oh-four-hundred."

Kris winced. "There's not much more we can do tonight. If you really don't think you can sleep, how about a game of poker?"

Wil raised his eyebrows. "Trying to earn back the money you lost last time?"

"That was a total fluke and you know it."

Wil snorted. "In your dreams. But if you want to delude yourself that you're a better player than me, then you're on."

CHAPTER SEVEN

The Republic of the Volta
West Africa

MAX SPED UP.

Emily picked up on his tension and glanced over. "Max?"

"I think we're being followed." It could just be a local leaving for an early morning job or heading home after a late night. But his gut didn't like having an unknown entity trailing behind them. "Can you tell how far it is to the intersection?"

"I'm not sure. Maybe the same distance as from the bridge back to the safe house."

"Okay." This Jeep, despite having a beat-up exterior, had a smooth, powerful engine, so they should be able to give the rebels a run for their money. If that was who pursued them.

Keeping watch via the rearview mirror, he inched the speed up until he felt balanced on the edge of control. But the other vehicle—he thought it was another Jeep—kept advancing.

Shit.

Max took the next turn too fast and almost overbalanced. Emily yelped and braced herself against her door.

"Hold on," he said as he straightened out the wheels. A few minutes later he jerked the Jeep around another turn and finally spotted the illumination from the streetlights on the north-south feeder road. Max glanced behind him. That last turn had blocked them from view of whoever followed them. Taking advantage of the moment of anonymity, Max raced toward the intersection. Traffic wasn't quite as dense here as on the other road and was moving faster. He merged aggressively into the stream of traffic, barely reducing speed. Ignoring the angry honks of the drivers around him, he steered sideways until the Jeep was on the far side of the road. Only then did he slow to match the pace of the other vehicles.

The sun cleared the horizon and the streetlights went out.

Seconds later, an open-topped Jeep screeched to a halt at the place where the side road emptied into this one. A rebel stood on the passenger's seat. He scanned the passing traffic, then scowled down at someone behind him that Max couldn't see. Shaking his head, the rebel soldier fired his AK-47 into the crowd of vehicles.

Emily jumped in her seat. "Not again!" He heard the anger and fear in her voice and wished he could soothe her. But this was how it went with the rebels. With luck, you got away from them. Without it, you ended up shot for being in the wrong place at the wrong time.

He glanced in the rearview mirror in time to see a rickety bus ram the rebels' Jeep.

Both vehicles tipped over. Other vehicles tried to swerve out of the way, but many of them crashed into the overturned vehicles. Then the AK fired. People screamed.

Max lost sight of the crash as he drove away. "Can't we—?" Emily cut herself off with a choked sob and a shake of her head. "I know we can't go back and help, that we're targets because of the color of our skin, but I hate this. It's not fair. These people are just trying to get to safety. They're fleeing their homes. Yet that rebel shot at them like they were wild animals."

Turning in her seat, Emily stared out the back window for a long while before facing front again. "I never had much time to watch TV," she said quietly. "For years, my days were pretty much ballet from the moment I woke up to the moment I went to sleep. But every once in a while I'd catch a glimpse of the TV news." She waved toward the other vehicles. "We see images like this, of people fleeing their homes, and while we feel sympathy, as soon as the newscast changes to the next story, most of us forget all about it. We never stop to think about the mothers forced to wake their children and pile them into the car." She nodded at a battered Toyota 4Runner with three young faces pressed to the rear window. "Or everyone else forced to drop whatever they were doing in order to run for their lives." She smacked her hand against the dashboard. "I hate being helpless to stop the rebels from killing people." She threw a glare over her shoulder toward the rebel Jeep. "I swear, I'm normally a pretty even-tempered lady, but if you gave me one of those weapons, I'd be tempted to shoot the rebels myself!"

Max clamped his lips together so he wouldn't laugh. But she cracked him up. She sat so primly in her seat, her posture perfect thanks to her ballet training. Her voice was cultured. Yet her words were so fierce. Revealing the heart and passion of a warrior.

The contrast delighted him.

Damn. He couldn't remember the last time he'd felt like laughing. How pathetic was that? Shoving aside the sadness that thought caused, he watched Emily. More than just angry over the situation, she genuinely wanted to help. And once she focused her attention on a subject, he bet she wouldn't stop until she'd accomplished her goals.

His humor fled, replaced by admiration. And that was quickly followed by a jolt of arousal that had him shifting in his seat as he imagined being the focus of Emily's sensual attention.

"I'm sorry you have to be here for this," he said, when he

thought the danger of him laughing or reaching over and kissing her had passed.

Emily shook her head. "I'm not. It's time I woke up to what's going on in the rest of the world." With a hiss of anger, she twisted and reached behind her. "Ugh. Too far." She unfastened her seat belt and crawled into the back seat.

Max did his best not to react to first her breast, then her butt sliding past his cheek, but it was damn hard not to give in to the temptation to turn his face and place his mouth on her. Didn't matter which part. He just wanted a little nibble.

Ah, hell. The last thing Emily needed was his adrenaline-fueled lust.

He tried to focus his attention on the road. But Emily's sounds of exertion just made him think about what she'd sound like in bed. Great. This was a first. Not the sudden desire for sex. Adrenaline tended to have that effect on a guy. In fact, he was surprised it had taken him this long. But he usually just felt the urge for a quick roll in the sheets. Thinking that he'd like to take his companion to bed and not let her out for a week or so? *That* was new.

Yeah. He was Mr. Smooth for sure. Uh-huh. He'd been in the wild for so damn long, he'd lost any traces of civilization. And people used to think his brother, the career military man, was the barbarian.

Ha.

Max waited for Emily to reappear. Instead, he heard her moving deeper into the cargo compartment. "Emily, what are you doing?"

"I can't just sit here and do nothing, so I'm taking photos."

"Can you even see enough to get decent shots?" Dawn's deep shadows still blanketed the road.

"Yeah, I've changed the settings to adjust for the low light."

"All right. Go for it." He was just relieved that she'd focused her attention on something positive, rather than holding on to her fear of him.

About fifteen minutes later, Emily returned to her seat, camera in hand. She alternated between checking the images she'd already taken, and pointing the camera out the window. But eventually, her hands dropped to her lap. He glanced over and found that her head was tipped back against the headrest. He shook his head. She was asleep.

Damn. He was really going to have to relearn that trick.

On second thought, never mind that. Sleeping that deeply was too dangerous. She was lucky he was there to watch over her. Lucky that he wasn't the type of man who'd take advantage of her.

No matter how sexy the pale curve of her throat was in the soft morning light.

Keep your mind on the road.

Right.

Still, he couldn't help but notice that asleep, she looked younger. More vulnerable. There was a quiet sense of self-sufficiency about her when she was awake, despite her delicate appearance. She'd proven her mettle by keeping up with him in the jungle. When he'd seen her blisters, he'd been triply impressed. He respected and admired her strength and the single-minded determination that had kept her going despite the pain.

He knew something about that, himself.

Emily roused from her nap almost an hour later. She rubbed her eyes and glanced out the window. "Where are we?"

"We're still on the road heading north."

"Where are those cars going?" Several vehicles had turned off onto a side road that cut across a field of cassava.

"See those buildings in the distance at two o'clock?"

She peered out the window, then nodded.

"The people in those cars probably have relatives over there."

"Oh." She lapsed into silence.

Strange how comfortable it felt to be quiet around her. Usually he worried if a woman shut up for too long. Too often it meant she was mad at him. Or plotting something he wouldn't like. But with Emily, the silence didn't make demands or hint at upcoming threats.

He liked it.

After another hour, Max pulled over. Emily helped him lower three of the five-gallon gas cans from the roof so he could fill the tank. Not long after they hit the road again, it crossed a bridge over a trickle of a river. On the other side, the quality of the road changed. The relatively even pavement gave way to smooth, well-packed dirt, then to the potholed and rutted dirt so prevalent in this part of the country.

"It's such a shock." Emily raised her camera and started snapping photos.

"What is?" Although he thought he knew.

"The change in road condition. Paved to dirt. You'd think that we'd entered a different country."

"Nah. Just a different region. One where the funding either doesn't exist to fix the roads, or where the politicians choose to use the funds for other projects." Such as building expensive homes. For themselves.

Christ. He really was turning into a bitter, cynical man. He needed to take Dietrich down and get off the continent before there was nothing left in him he'd want to face each day in the mirror.

Or that Emily would want to get to know better.

Right. Like he'd even have a chance with her if they were both back home. After all, she blamed him for the death of her friends. Hard to build trust after that.

Not that he planned to go back home any time soon. In fact, he didn't have any plans past taking Dietrich down.

"Life's so difficult here," Emily murmured. "The poverty. The inequality."

"You got that right. Which is why so many people have joined the rebels. They're hoping for a better life."

Emily snorted softly. "As if men who terrorize villages and gun down innocents are capable of creating a fair and prosperous democracy."

"Sometimes, when you're desperate, you'll grasp at any straw to get out of where you are." Dammit. What had made him say that?

She shot him a speculative glance, but to his surprise, she kept silent.

Another point in her favor. If he wasn't careful, he might end up falling for her.

Wait. What?

Impossible.

Even if her friends' deaths weren't between them, it wasn't like they had anything in common. Her whole life revolved around dance. While he didn't even know if he liked the ballet. The only time he'd attended, he'd been so thoroughly caught up in the allure of his date that every shift of her body and every breath she took had ratcheted up his arousal. By the end of the show he'd been so desperate for her that they hadn't even made it to the car. He'd found a deserted corridor and taken her in an alcove.

Shit. He couldn't even remember her name, but he sure as hell remembered the way her nails had dug into his back and how she'd urged him on with throaty moans and dirty words.

Not the kind of encounter the refined Miss Emily would welcome.

Stop thinking about sex.

See, there was a reason he focused on getting his revenge on Dietrich. It kept his mind off other, more dangerous topics. And yes, he recognized the irony of thinking that killing a major international arms dealer was safer than sex with a sheltered American woman.

Around ten o'clock that morning, Max's eyes began to drift close. "Time to stop," he announced. He pulled the Jeep over to the side of the road, then drove into the jungle until the vehicle was hidden from the other cars.

"Do you want me to drive?" Emily offered. She'd dozed off once or twice more, but for the most part had stayed awake. She'd kept his mind alert with her occasional questions about the politics and economics of the region, and had tactfully avoided asking about his work.

He was tempted to let her drive. After all, he was racing against the clock. But his body was already pulling him toward sleep and he wanted to be awake when she took her first shot at driving over these roads. Besides, she wouldn't be alert for danger like he would. So it wasn't safe to have her drive while he slept. "Nah. Let's both sack out for a few hours."

She nodded. He lowered the back seat and spread the sleeping bags out in the cargo compartment so they could lie down next to one another. Despite his exhaustion, Max wasn't sure he'd be able to sleep with Emily's seductive feminine scent tickling his nose and her warm, sexy body just inches from his. But after a few moments of fighting the urge to pull her into his arms, he fell into the abyss.

He slept for a couple hours. To his surprise, Emily was still asleep when he woke up.

Deciding to let her rest, he reached into the passenger seat for the map and spotted her camera lying on the floorboard. Curious as to how her shots came out, he picked it up. Noticing that the battery was low, he swapped it out for the one she'd left charging on the dashboard in its solar panel pouch. After removing a container of stew and fried plantains from the supplies Rene had provided, he flipped the camera on while he ate. The first photo on the LCD screen must have been from Emily's homestay. It showed her and a local woman grinning at the camera, both with native cloth wrapped around their bodies. Regretting that he hadn't personally seen such joy on Emily's face, he scrolled forward.

More people, this time without Emily present. A village. Workers at a palm oil plantation. The jungle. Another village. The jungle with a white blob in the background. A few villa—

Wait a sec.

Max scrolled back. What was it that had snagged his attention. The people?

No.

He took a good, long look at each of the photos until he came to the ones of the jungle. There. Peeking out from behind some palmetto fronds. Something white. Manmade.

Like the piece of a plane.

Emily awoke, once again, to a hand on her shoulder and someone calling her name.

"C'mon, Emily. Wake up."

She blinked, squinted against the sunlight and realized that she was lying in the cargo area of the Jeep, with Max leaning over her. He'd removed his baseball cap, and the intensity of the expression on his face had her sitting upright. *Danger.*

From Max? No. He might be at the center of much of the violence of the past few days, but he'd also saved her life. He'd stuck around to make certain she was safe when he could have just dumped her at the embassy and driven away. No matter what trouble he was mixed up in, he wouldn't hurt her. So that meant there was an external threat. "What's wrong?"

He shook his head, then grinned. "Nothing. In fact, for the first time in days, something is right." He held out her camera.

"Hey! What are you doing with that?" She reached for it, but Max kept the camera just out of her reach.

"Come outside. I need you to tell me where you took a couple of these photos. It's important."

"Why?"

Max just shook his head. "Finish waking up and go do…" He waved toward the bushes. "…whatever you need to do. We'll talk when you're finished."

Wondering what bee was up his butt, she waited until he'd walked around to the front of the Jeep before she slipped outside. A few minutes later, wishing she had coffee to truly wake her up, she joined Max. He'd spread one of the maps over the hood and frowned as he glanced between the map and her camera. A plastic bowl of bean stew and fried plantains held one side of the map down. When Max heard her approach, he thrust a spoon at her and nodded toward the food. "Eat while we talk."

Surprised that Dr. LaSalle had provided a full meal, she took a few bites, then crossed her arms over her chest and gave Max the evil eye. "Why were you going through my photos?"

He shrugged, unrepentant. "Curiosity. I wanted to see what you'd put together." He jiggled the camera. "You've got a good eye. Some of these are professional quality."

Her cheeks heated, but she wasn't going to let his praise derail her. "Thanks. So what's so important that you had to wake me up?"

Max showed her the LCD screen of the camera. The shot was of a section of jungle framing a brilliant red flowering plant. "Wait…" She turned the camera, then pointed to a spot on the right. "What's that there? That white bit?"

"I think it's part of a plane."

She studied the photo. The white object did seem to be manmade and slightly rectangular, but it could have been anything. "What makes you think that?"

Max hesitated.

"The truth, Max. Don't even think about lying to me."

When he still seemed reluctant to speak, she let out a frustrated growl. "Max, I've witnessed my friends being gunned down, have run for my life through the jungle, have missed the last flight out of the country, and have been forced to run for my life *again* from trigger-happy rebels. I think I deserve to know just what the hell is going on!"

"Emily, trust me, it's safer if you don't know. Just tell me where you took this photo and once you're safely over the border you can forget the whole thing."

She leaned forward until her nose almost touched his. "Is this photo one of the reasons Crystal was shot?"

Max stepped back until there was more than a foot between them. "I don't know. Ziegler has a personal grudge against me. But..." He glanced down at the camera. "Maybe the shooting was more strategic than I thought. Maybe he saw your friend, thought she looked like me, and shot her in a calculated move meant to stop me from finding the plane. Maybe he didn't fire in a fit of anger."

She jabbed at his chest with her fingertip. "Whatever it is you're involved in, I want to know about it. I *need* to know why Crystal and Sue died. You owe me." It was a low move, but she didn't care. She was tired of being kept in the dark. She snatched the camera. "If you don't tell me, then oops, I guess the photos are going to be erased and my memory will suddenly become faulty."

She had no idea where such tough words came from, but they had the desired effect. He glowered at her. She raised her eyebrow and stared him down.

Finally, he looked away. Gave a deep sigh. Returned his attention to her with a frown of resignation. "Tell me where you shot the photo, then I'll explain everything while we're driving. Time is short."

"Where are we?"

He raised a brow at her change of subject. "Still on the minor road. We should be coming up to the crossroads with the main north-south road soon."

"Then let's get on the road. All of those photos were taken during my homestay, so we have miles before we're anywhere near the area. You explain first, then I'll figure out where exactly I took the photos."

The corner of his mouth lifted in a rueful smile. "You're tougher than you look, Ms. Emily Iwasaki."

His words warmed her, but she refused to let him see her softening. "Well? Do we have a deal?"

He nodded. "Yes, but there's only so much I can tell you."

She started to protest, but he cut her off.

"It's for your own protection. If, God forbid, you're captured, the less you know the better. I'll tell you enough that you understand the danger we're in, but no more." He held out his hand to shake. "Do we still have a deal?"

She hesitated, then took his hand. To her shock, he pulled her in close. "I like you," he whispered as her body rested flush against him. "It's dangerous and probably stupid, but I have to know..." Before she could ask what, he lowered his mouth and kissed her.

It wasn't a polite kiss. He plundered, demanding she let him inside. With a little groan—it had been so long since she'd been kissed—she opened her lips. Mmm... He tasted delicious. The lingering taste of spices from the stew mixed with a rich, intoxicating taste that was unique to Max. Strong. Passionate. Dangerous.

Probably addictive.

This sudden flare of arousal didn't make sense. He was keeping things from her. Being around him put her in Ziegler's sights. Yet instead of backing away, she leaned into him. Because there was just something about Max's brand of danger she couldn't resist. That made her blood sing.

Max jerked away from her, breathing heavily. "Ah..." He ran his hand over his hair.

She narrowed her eyes at him. "Don't you dare apologize."

He blinked in surprise.

"Despite my outburst yesterday, I don't hate you, Max. Or didn't you notice that I kissed you back?"

"Um." He ran his hand unsteadily over his hair again.

She'd never seen him so off balance. It was kind of endearing.

"I might not fully trust you," she said, "but I know you won't hurt me."

"Good. That's good, because I wouldn't. I won't. I would never have hitched a ride with the tro-tro if I thought Ziegler would follow me and two innocent women would die."

She nodded, seeing the remorse and the grief that he probably thought he kept hidden. She felt a stab of regret that she'd lashed out at him yesterday. Yes, Ziegler had killed Crystal because of her resemblance to Max, but Emily hadn't seen any headlights behind the tro-tro to indicate that Max had been followed that night. He hadn't known he was putting anyone in immediate danger. "I believe you. Now, I think we'd better get on the road so you can start that explanation."

"So, talk," Emily said fifteen minutes later, once they'd merged onto the road.

"Here are the basics." Max's fingers tightened on the wheel, then slowly relaxed. "Ziegler, the white man who shot your friend, is the right-hand man to an international arms and intelligence dealer named Heinrich Dietrich. Dietrich is wanted by a number of different governments, but he's always eluded capture."

"See, I knew you weren't a history professor," Emily muttered.

"Not true." He gave her a smug smile. "Technically, I'm on the faculty of a small midwestern college. I've even published a couple of what you called dry treatises on the relationship between folklore and the social, political, and economic organization of today's societies. But you're right, that's not my real job."

He took a deep breath. "I used to work for the government. Not the CIA, but that's all I'm going to say. Now... You could say I'm a freelancer. Long story short, there's an underground movement working against the rebels. Some of my former coworkers have joined this group and they've asked me to help locate a plane that went down in the area near where the tro-tro picked me up."

"And you think that the white piece in my photo is part of this plane."

"Yes."

"So, what's so important about the plane that this underground group is looking for it? Isn't that the job of the local government?"

Max snorted. "Right. As if the government doesn't have enough to worry about with the rebels." He shook his head. "Even before the rebels attacked the capital, this wasn't a situation the local government could handle. According to my contact, the plane was carrying the prototype and plans to a new, powerful weapon. Dietrich has brokered the sale of the prototype to an unknown buyer. The prototype is believed to be active and capable of killing thousands and is supposed to be turned over in —" Max checked his watch. "Eight days."

"So, you were searching for this plane when you hitched the ride with the tro-tro? You escorted me all the way to the capital even though it took you away from your search?" Maybe she'd completely misjudged him.

"No. I was just trying to get to my friend in that deserted village we found. I wanted a safe place to rest and heal after being...ah...a prisoner of Ziegler's for several days."

His whole body tensed and Emily thought back to the bruises on his face when she'd first met him. It didn't take much stretch of the imagination to suspect he'd been beaten, probably even tortured.

"I knew Dietrich had a deal scheduled, but I didn't know what type of weapon was involved. Once I'd rested for a day or two, I was going to head north again and restart my investigation. I didn't find out about the plane crash until after we got to the safe house in the capital."

She stared out the window. There were several other vehicles on the road, but traffic was nowhere near as heavy as it had been leaving the capital. "Now you're stuck getting me over the border, delaying your search."

"I'm not going to abandon you, Emily," he said testily.

Not after that kiss hung unspoken between them.

"Maybe you should." Her pulse increased and she felt her stomach drop, but if this missing weapon got into the wrong hands she didn't have to be a genius to understand that innocent people would die. "Maybe we should stop at the way station and see if anyone in these other vehicles would be willing to take me over the border."

Max's jaw clenched, then relaxed. "I... I don't want to leave you in the care of strangers."

She felt another spark of warmth and a sense of connection to him. That maybe he also wasn't looking forward to separating.

"As a white lady, you'd bring danger to anyone who gave you a ride."

Oh. The warmth vanished.

"But if we can find someone willing to hide you in the back of a truck, then maybe that's best." He shrugged. "We won't know until we get there." He gestured toward the camera. "Your turn. Where'd you take the photos?"

Hiding her disappointment that his reluctance to leave her had nothing to do with liking her and not wanting to say good-bye, Emily scrolled through the pictures, using the shots with people in them as a point of reference. She compared the dates on the camera to the notes she'd made in her day planner. "Okay, it looks like the photos you're interested in were taken at a village near my homestay. It was a festival day, so we left at dawn and walked for two hours in order to get to the other village in time for the first of the activities. That day was the first time I performed the local dances in front of an audience." Her home-stay mother, Prudence, had provided Emily with a bright blue and yellow tribal costume to match her own. Emily had been so nervous about performing in front of strangers. Would they find it insulting that an Asian American girl was trying to learn their dances? Would they stare at her scars and pity her?

But her fears hadn't been realized. The women in the other village had been thrilled that the *obruni* girl was interested in learning their culture. Her scars had actually broken through the shyness of some of the women, and Emily had received plenty of advice on how best to keep the skin supple. Huh. She touched her neck. She'd been so busy running for her life that she'd forgotten about the plastic container of shea butter cream that sat at the bottom of her backpack.

Once the music had started, her nerves had vanished. She'd lost herself to the dance.

After lunch, she'd gone into the jungle to take photos, hoping to spot some exotic wildlife. Instead, if Max was right, she'd found something much more important.

"How long ago was this?"

Emily counted the days on the calendar. "Five. It was the day before Masaud arrived with the news that the Land Cruiser was out of commission and we'd have to take the tro-tro to the way station. But, if the plane crashed near my homestay village wouldn't we have heard it? Even with the festival noise or just a regular day with people talking, surely we'd have heard the whine of an engine and felt the impact when it... Oh."

"What?"

"Well, the night of the festival there were fireworks."

"Did you notice any sort of vibration, like an earthquake?"

"Er...no. I...ah..." She ducked her head and mumbled, "I got a little tipsy on palm wine. Passed out pretty much the second they showed me the pallet I'd be sleeping on."

Max chuckled, damn him. "That's cute."

"Cute?" She scowled at him. "Believe me, there was nothing cute about the headache I had the next morning."

"Hmm. If the plane crashed nearby, you're right, even with the festivities someone would have either felt the ground shake on impact or seen a fireball when the plane ignited. But maybe the plane broke up in flight." Max shrugged. "Or it went down in a different area entirely. Still, I have to investigate."

"Okay."

"How far is that village from the intersection between this road and the main road?" Max asked.

Emily spread the map across her lap and estimated the distance. "I think it's about six hundred kilometers. You take the main north-south road to a point farther north than where the tro-tro picked you up. Then there's a side road that will take you to the village." She used the pen she kept with her day planner to mark the route.

"I'm going to need to take your camera with me, so I can compare the photos to the landscape."

"Oh." She bit her lip. It wasn't so much the expensive piece of equipment she was worried about, it was losing over a week's worth of photos. But if it would save lives...

"I promise I'll be careful not to delete any of your photos."

"All right."

About an hour later, they drove around a bend in the road and found a line of cars stopped ahead of them. "Max?" She raised her camera and took a string of photos.

"Yeah, I know." He slowed their vehicle and moved it closer to the right side of the road. "Grab the binoculars from the glove box, would you?"

She set her camera on her lap, then retrieved the set of high-powered binoculars.

"Can you make out what's holding everyone up? Is it an accident? A checkpoint?"

She aimed the glasses forward and took a moment to adjust them, bracing herself against the Jeep's movement as it bounced over the ruts in the road. "We're not quite close enough to tell."

With a nod, Max pulled the Jeep into the jungle and parked just inside the tree line. "I'm going to find out what's happening. You stay here, in case it's a trap." He took the binoculars from her, then slipped out of the Jeep and eased through the trees.

She knew it was probably safer in the Jeep, yet Max had only gone a few yards before she felt the start of a panic attack. Damn him, she didn't feel safe unless he was with her. She'd rather take her chances by his side, where he could protect her with his gun, than be a sitting target in the Jeep. So before he moved out of sight, Emily slung her camera's strap over her neck and followed him. It felt good to get out of the Jeep and move, yet also scary, since she didn't know what danger lay ahead. Max threw her an angry look when she caught up with him, but she just raised her chin and glared back at him.

Finally, with an unhappy shrug, he said, "Stay close."

As they walked, they stayed far enough inside the tree line that people looking out the windows of the stopped vehicles wouldn't be able to see them clearly. Emily took more photos, liking the mystery of only being able to see glimpses of the cars through the gaps in the trees.

Max shot her an exasperated look, but wisely didn't comment.

After perhaps five minutes of walking, they heard noise. At first, Emily couldn't make it out. Then she recognized it as the rumble of large trucks. As they drew closer to the commotion, Max's tension increased. He removed his gun from its holster and carried it alongside his thigh.

Emily inched up next to him. "What is it?"

"I—"

Horns honked on the road. Engines revved. People shouted. Max grabbed her hand and pulled her to the edge of the trees. The line of cars blocked her view of what was happening at the crossroads, but whatever it was, it frightened people. Vehicles at the front of the line were trying to back up and turn around. The drivers behind them responded with honks and angry shouts out their windows. Then a man got out of one of the lead vehicles and walked back to talk to the driver behind him. The passenger in that car leaned out the window to shout at the driver behind them. Emily heard the panic in the woman's voice. Word traveled quickly down the line and soon all the cars began fighting for space to turn around.

Max cursed. He glanced from the road to Emily. He opened his mouth, a warning in his eyes. "You should go back."

"No," she whispered fiercely. "I'm not leaving you. I feel safer with you."

He shook his head. "Stubborn woman. Fine. Stay right behind me. And be prepared to run."

Walking so close that she was almost plastered against him, Emily followed Max as he moved at a diagonal through the trees. Their trajectory took them out of sight of the feeder road and toward a spot on the main road about two hundred and fifty yards north of the crossroads. When they reached the edge of the trees and looked out, Emily saw several large military trucks rolling into positions that blocked the intersection. To their right, in the direction that she and Max had been hoping to go, a dust cloud hovered above the road, kicked up by fleeing vehicles.

"Are those government trucks?" she whispered. Swallowing her fear, she edged around Max so she could take photos. He put a cautionary hand on her shoulder, which she ignored. Maybe she wasn't a photojournalist with the ability to change the world. But she bet there was some organization that would care about the plight of these people enough to be interested in her photos.

"Not government. See the yellow flags with the black dots on the doors and grills? Those are rebel trucks."

The rebels on the northern end of the crossroads fired after the fleeing vehicles, and their colleagues on the southern end followed suit, aiming for the few vehicles Emily could spot that were headed south.

Emily continued to snap photos, using the familiar weight of the camera to take her mind off the fear urging her to run as fast and as far as she could away from here.

"Shit."

"What?" Emily glanced back at the trucks forming the blockade. "Wait." One of the rebels was setting up a tripod in the back of the flat bed truck. "Is that a machine gun?" She refocused her lens and put the camera into video mode.

"Yes. Even worse, it looks like their buddies are laying dynamite." Emily looked where he pointed. Two men were walking just inside the perimeter formed by the trucks, stopping every few feet. One man buried something cylindrical in the ground, while another man strung out wire to connect the points.

"They're going to blow the intersection so no one can move past this point. But first, they're going to make sure no one tries to make a break for it by using the machine guns to shoot everyone in sight." Max turned and shoved her in front of him. She bobbled the camera and cursed under her breath, but he steadied her arm.

Urging her forward with another push at the small of her back, he ordered, "Run!"

CHAPTER EIGHT

EMILY STUMBLED FORWARD, her stomach churning with fear. Oh, God, all those people sitting in their cars, believing they'd escaped the rebels. Believing that safety was just a few more hours away.

She sobbed, thinking about the woman and her children who'd waved at her from the next vehicle on the road out of the capital. She'd lost sight of them in the initial crush. Were they out on the road in that tangle, not knowing they were about to be gunned down?

"Max, we have to warn them."

"I know."

She realized that he'd been heading toward the feeder road. When it came into sight, he let his hand drop from her back. "Stay behind this tree and don't move. It's safer if no one sees you." He pulled his baseball cap farther down on his forehead and ran up to the closest vehicle, a battered, multi-colored Datsun with its passenger side door missing.

Max waved his arms toward the intersection and shouted something. The driver poked his head out, then scrambled out of the vehicle. He reached inside, grabbed a small suitcase, then ran for the jungle. Other drivers noticed the commotion. Pretty soon, drivers of cars that weren't able to muscle their way into the jungle or force spaces between the cars behind them started abandoning their cars.

But too late. With a horrible clatter Emily would remember for the rest of her life, the machine gun fired. Max dropped to the ground. Emily screamed and threw herself behind a downed tree, just as the hail of bullets tore through the foliage to her right.

A moment later, the rebel trucks roared to life and she knew they must be moving away in preparation of setting off the dynamite. No! Max was still out on the road. She had to bring him into the relative safety of the trees.

She jumped to her feet and pushed her way through the undergrowth toward the road. "Max!" she yelled. But he didn't answer. Oh, God. He couldn't be dead. Not now. Not because he'd tried to help.

Out on the road people were crying. Shouting. Over all of it came the cry, "Dynamite. Run! They are going to blow up the intersection."

A horrific explosion splintered the air. The ground shook. Emily dropped to her belly and put her hands over her head. *Max*, a small voice inside her head wailed as debris fell on her. *Please keep Max safe.*

After what seemed like forever, the debris stopped falling. Emily shook her arms and legs to dislodge the dirt, sticks, and other stuff that had fallen on her, then slowly climbed to her feet. Next to her, a woman slowly sat up. One of the short, pouffy sleeves of her bright turquoise top was ripped and deflated, giving her a lopsided look. Emily held out her hand. The woman blinked at her in surprise, probably wondering what a white lady was doing here, then accepted Emily's help getting to her feet. After nodding her thanks, the woman brushed herself off and hurried away.

Emily picked her way as quickly as possible across the

unstable layer of dirt and debris left behind from the explosion. At the edge of the jungle she stopped and took a quick series of photos before stepping onto the road. This way there would be visual proof in case the rebels denied what they'd done.

Yeah, right. Emily Iwasaki, newborn crusader for truth and justice. She rolled her eyes.

Well, she had to do something with her life now that she couldn't dance professionally. Maybe this compulsion to document people's suffering would lead to a new career. Maybe she could use her photography to make a difference in the world.

She scanned the road for Max, but didn't see him. Off to her left, a woman lay on her back as a man tended her wounds. To her right, a man pulled two crying children out of the back of an SUV. Its hood had been crushed by a piece of falling rock. The man set the children on the ground and they clung to his legs while he removed bags of supplies from the cargo compartment. Then the small party headed into the jungle.

Emily resumed her search for Max, dodging loose chickens and goats. Each time she came across someone injured, she asked if she could help. Everyone said no.

Few people cried. No one screamed. Instead, they talked softly to one another, dealt calmly with their wounds, then drove or walked away.

But Emily's nerves were strung taut. She kept expecting the rebels to show up and open fire on the stunned people. Then she reached the huge crater that yawned in the place where the two roads had once intersected. A few dead bodies, mostly men in rebel uniforms, lay scattered around the rim. She shuddered and glanced away. Their buddies must have set the charges off too early. She checked in each direction but didn't see any rebel vehicles. Maybe they'd decided the ground was too unstable to risk coming back to check their handiwork? Maybe they figured they'd made their point and had no need to kill more people?

Whatever the reason, at least she wasn't in imminent danger of being shot.

She continued to move cautiously around the perimeter, stopping when she got to a woman with blood coating her face and holding a small girl. The woman had removed her wide cloth headband and pressed it over the girl's stomach, but blood had already soaked through the satiny yellow fabric. Emily halted. "Is there anything I can do to help?"

The woman shook her head vehemently and pulled the girl closer to her chest. "This is your fault, *obruni*. The rebels would not be attacking if they didn't want all foreigners out of the country." She spat off to the side. "You are too much trouble. If the rebels see you here we will all be killed. Go away and leave us in peace."

Emily flinched. She opened her mouth to protest, but realized there was nothing she could say. Even the truth—that she and Max had been too far back in the line of cars to have been spotted, so the rebels hadn't acted specifically to stop them—wouldn't matter. The fear and stubbornness in the woman's eyes made it clear she wanted someone to blame for her child's injury and Emily was the chosen target.

"I hope your daughter recovers quickly," Emily said quietly. Heart heavy, she continued making her way around the edge of the crater. Still no sign of Max. Dammit, where was he? Had the rebels spotted him and dragged him away, to be turned over to that Ziegler fellow? Or had Max simply wandered off, too dazed with pain to know where he was? So fuzzy in the head he didn't—

"Em!"

She turned to find Max right behind her. He was covered in dirt, with blood staining his left pant leg. She was so happy to see him that she threw herself into his arms.

He grunted, but pulled her tight to his body.

"I'm so glad you're alive," she babbled. "I saw you fall when the rebels started shooting and I thought you were dead. And then I couldn't find you near the vehicle where I'd last seen you and I worried that you were out of your head and wandering around."

Max pressed his lips to her temple. "Shh. I'm okay."

She rested against him for a while, enjoying his strength. Tremors of delayed shock shook her body and she didn't want to let him go.

"We should head back to the Jeep," Max said.

Emily nodded against his chest. His arms squeezed once, then stepped back. She stared up at him through tears of grief and relief.

"Hey," Max said, brushing a tear away. "We're going to be okay."

She just shook her head, knowing he couldn't promise that. These past few days had only reinforced the lessons she'd learned from the acid attack and from her father's emergency preparedness training. People were unpredictable. Dangerous. Bad things happened to good people for no apparent reason, so you had to be ready to fight for your survival at any time. Unable to express the tangle of emotions inside her, she reached up and slid her lips across Max's.

His breath hitched, then his arms banded around her. He pulled her snugly against him as he ravaged her mouth. Emily lifted onto tiptoe and wriggled against him, trying to get closer. The vitality of him chased away the chill from thinking he was dead. Made her realize that she cared about him more than made sense. More than was wise, certainly. Yet... It had been a long, long time since she'd been attracted to a man with this degree of urgency.

Besides, time was short. Precious. She needed to seize every moment she had with Max. She wanted...

Max staggered to the side then clutched her arm for balance.

"Oh, no!" Emily struggled to support his weight. "I'm sorry. Is it your ribs? Damn it, I shouldn't have done that I—"

"Not your fault." His grip tightened on her arms. "I...ah..." He glanced down at his thigh. "I think I'm hit."

"Oh, my God." She bent down and saw that a jagged piece of metal about two inches wide had torn through his pants and was embedded in his outer thigh. Shoving down the quick surge of panic, she thought back to the first aid classes she'd taken. "Okay. The good news is that you weren't shot. The bad news is that you've got a piece of metal sticking out of your thigh a hand's width above your knee." She raised her eyes to his. "To control the bleeding, we have to leave it in there until we get you back to the Jeep."

"Yeah. I know." He grimaced, then averted his eyes. "But... ah..." He shrugged. "The pain just kicked in. I'm not sure how well I can walk. I'm—"

"Going to need some help." She studied the uneven terrain and remembered how hard it had been to walk over it with two good legs. Still, they didn't have much choice. "Okay, lean on me." She draped his arm over her shoulders. Max found a way to balance himself so that he didn't put all of his weight on her and they headed for the slightly better footing at the side of the road.

What had been a five or ten minute walk before, now took them nearly forty-five minutes. They were both sweating and shaking by the time they finally reached the Jeep.

Emily didn't think she'd ever been so glad to see a vehicle in her life.

"Open the rear door and help me sit on the edge," Max said. "I need to disinfect and bind up the wound."

Shaking her head, she opened the cargo compartment and situated him so that his feet dangled inches above the ground. Then she reached inside and pulled out their water bottles. "Drink first."

He rolled his eyes, yet despite the lines of pain around his mouth, he gave her the ghost of a smile. After he'd finished drinking, he said, "It would be easiest to cut my pants off, but these are the only pair I have left." He studied his leg. "I think I can slip my pants over the piece of metal without jarring it too much." He reached for his belt buckle.

Emily knocked his hands aside. "I'll do it. You hold your weight up so I can slide the pants off your legs."

"You're kind of bossy, aren't you?"

She thought about it. Realized that in the past several years she'd become less likely to take charge and more used to giving full obedience to the choreographer and ballet mistress. She'd been so focused on becoming the dancer they needed, that she'd lost the habit of speaking her mind. Finally, she shrugged. "I used to be. Early on, I served as dance captain for the corps de ballet. I had to keep the rest of the dancers focused and moving together as a unit, no matter the personality conflicts or moods of the day."

"Sort of like a drill sergeant."

"Yeah."

"Well, I have to admit, I find it kinda hot."

She shot Max an exasperated look as she unbuttoned and unzipped his fly. "Seriously? You're getting all flirty now?"

"I have a beautiful woman undoing my pants, so yeah, kinda hard not to react."

"I think pain is making you giddy, Max."

But as she started to pull his pants down, the tips of her fingers grazed his growing erection. To her dismay, she blushed. "Stop it. I was doing fine until you pointed out the...ah...compromising position I'm in."

"Hate to break it to you, sweetheart, but given where your hands are, there isn't a chance in hell that I can control my body's reaction. So finish your task. Quickly." He blew out a breath and laughed. "Never thought I'd say that to a woman who had her hands over my crotch."

Emily snorted with laughter and tugged on his pants, easing

them carefully over his erection. Then she stretched the pant leg as wide as she could to lift it past the protruding piece of metal. Max tensed when her hand glanced off the metal, but didn't make a sound. She pulled the pants the rest of the way down, let the material pool around his ankles, then leaned forward. The metal had penetrated his thigh at a slight angle, as if it had been stabbed into him. Emily used an antiseptic wipe to remove the small bit of blood around the entrance wound, then she looked up. "Brace yourself."

Max gave her a tiny smile. "Just do it."

She took a deep breath, grasped the piece of metal, and yanked it out. Max flinched, but remained silent. Still, her stomach soured because she'd caused him pain.

"Okay. Penetration wound," she muttered. "There's a high risk of infection because it's hard to flush."

"That's right. Just let it bleed a bit."

Emily nodded. The blood didn't spurt, so the metal hadn't cut any major veins or arteries. That meant it was safe to let the blood flow a minute, carrying away any foreign debris.

"Here, use this to stop the bleeding." Max handed her a foil pocket. "It's gauze treated with a clotting agent."

"Cool." She swiped away the blood, tore open the pocket, then stuck a small piece of the clotting gauze over the wound. Finally, she taped a regular piece of gauze over that.

"Nice job," Max said.

She managed a weak smile. "Well, I won't be applying for a position as a doctor anywhere soon, but hopefully this will hold until we get you proper medical attention. Father would be proud."

"So what's with the intensive emergency training?"

"My father was a little boy when the Japanese in California were sent to the internment camps. By the time he and my grandparents returned home, they'd developed a deep suspicion toward the government and an obsessive need for self-reliance.

Father was raised to be prepared to take care of himself in case the government turned on us again, and he raised me and my brother the same way."

"I'm sorry."

She shrugged. "Yeah, it was hard explaining to friends growing up why I had to know where all the exits were whenever I entered an unfamiliar building, and why I kept a backpack with emergency supplies with me at all times. Then, once I was old enough, I got into a lot of fights with Father over scheduling because I couldn't take time off from ballet to spend weekends at the shooting range or driving track."

Now a successful venture capitalist, her father had enough money to pay for reliable help and a security team, and he did so. But he also made certain that the entire family kept up their emergency preparedness skills, just in case society once again decided to turn against those with different ethnic backgrounds.

Of course, their training had never occurred in the middle of the jungle with murderous rebels on the prowl.

"I'm sorry that the training caused you problems," Max said. "But at the same time, I'm selfishly glad you're able to help me."

"It's actually the first time I've used these skills in a real-life situation, but it's...satisfying. I wouldn't want to make medicine a career, but I can understand why people choose it." Remembering the pain pills and antibiotics that Dr. LaSalle had given them, Emily searched through the first aid kit until she found them.

Max accepted the antibiotic, but refused the pain pill. "It will knock me out. We're not out of danger yet. I'm staying awake and coherent until I know we're safe."

Having experienced the side effects of heavy pain medication, she didn't argue with his decision. "Anything else I need to check?"

Max glanced away. Sighed. "I might have bled through the stitches on my lower back. Knife slice."

"Max," she said, glaring at him, "are you telling me that you walked through the jungle with cracked ribs and a knife wound and didn't say anything?"

He shrugged, and she fought back the impulse to smack him upside the head. Instead, she lifted his shirt. The bandage was intact and there didn't seem to be any bleed through, so she just applied a few more pieces of tape to secure it. "You know, trying to set a record for the quantity and variety of injuries sustained is really overkill, don't you think?"

Max chuckled and some of the tenseness that had hardened his features while she worked eased. But she sensed that he was nearly out of energy.

"So," she said as brightly as she could manage, "it looks like I need to drive, doesn't it?"

"Oh, shit. Can you drive a stick?"

"Of course. Tactical driving was part of our emergency training. Although, I don't think my father had quite this scenario in mind."

He nodded and met her gaze. "Thank you. You've been amazing. I can't imagine having a better companion."

Touched more than she wanted to let on, Emily ducked her head and gathered the waste into an extra plastic bag. "So, what now? Head on as planned? Go back?"

Max pulled up his pants and rose to his feet. Emily held herself ready to catch him if he stumbled, but he put most of his weight on his good leg. "I need to find that plane. We'll keep aiming for the way station. Then we'll reassess."

"Okay." She replaced the medical supplies in the doctor's sack and tucked everything safely away. Then she slipped behind the steering wheel. She had to adjust the seat so that her feet comfortably reached the pedals, then Max gave her a few pointers on how best to navigate the jungle.

"All right. Here we go." Taking a deep breath, she eased the vehicle forward. Luckily, due to the rough terrain, she didn't need to worry about shifting out of first gear. She did, however, have to steer around bushes and trees and head slightly at an angle to her right so they'd avoid the crossroads and the crater. Compared to earlier, the jungle was now deserted. Everyone had either fled, or was out on the main road tending the wounded. She wished there was something more she could do to help.

"Max, can you call your friends in the underground and let them know what happened? Or Dr. LaSalle? Make sure that the victims get help?"

"I will, once we're out from under the trees. The satellite phone antenna needs an unobstructed view of the sky."

"Oh. Right." Adjusting her grip on the wheel, she did her best to steer them over the smoothest sections. But she hoped they reached the road soon, because wrestling this heavy vehicle with no power steering was *hard*. She wasn't sure how long her shoulder and her upper back would last before spasming.

Max watched Emily long enough to be sure she could handle the Jeep, then concentrated on ignoring the pain in his leg. When he spotted the road peeking between the trees, he ordered, "Put it in neutral and set the brake. It's doubtful that the rebels are close by—we'd have heard gunfire or seen them if they were. Still, I want you to be very careful and go check if the road is clear." He'd prefer to do the reconnaissance himself, but he didn't trust his leg to hold up. "Look for vehicles, people, or obstructions in the road. As you approach, use the bushes and trees as cover. If you see movement, freeze. The worst thing you can do is move and draw attention to yourself."

"Aye, aye, sir!"

He managed a grin, although from the worried look she shot him, she could tell he was hurting. "This isn't the Navy," he corrected. "A simple 'yes, sir' will suffice."

She rolled her eyes and saluted. "Yes, sir!"

Max lifted her hand from the gear shift. Bringing her palm to his mouth, he placed a kiss there. "You're letting your inner smart aleck out. I like it."

Her cheeks turned a faint red under the dirt covering her face. "Until recently I had to keep her tightly leashed, so watch out, there may be loads of sarcasm and other sharp statements ahead."

He winked. "I'm looking forward to it."

Emily shook her head and let herself out of the vehicle. He watched as she carefully made her way to the edge of the trees. They were far enough from the crossroads that not much debris had fallen, making the terrain easier for her to navigate. And yet... He frowned. She was still wearing those flimsy tennis shoes. Dammit, WAR needed to start stocking women's shoes and clothing at the safe houses. Emily needed sturdier shoes, but even if they found a market nearby, they couldn't risk stopping to pick up more suitable footwear.

Nevertheless, he should have at least insisted on checking her bandages earlier. He bet that trekking over the blast debris had reopened some of her blisters.

Emily paused, then stepped out onto the road. Max held his breath while she scanned both directions. According to the map, this stretch of road was a fairly straight shot, so she should have good visibility.

She gave one more look in each direction, then returned to the vehicle.

"Well?" he asked as she took her seat, released the hand brake, and took the Jeep out of neutral.

"I don't see any vehicles to the north of us, but I do see a rebel truck back at the crossroads." She glanced over at him. "So I guess I should drive parallel to the road and slightly inside the tree line for as long as I can."

"Yeah." He put his hand on her shoulder. "For someone not used to driving, you're doing great."

She gave him a wan smile. "Tell me that tomorrow when my arms are so sore from wrestling this wheel that I can barely move them."

"I'll still tell you that. I'm not kidding, you're adapting damn well. You should be proud of yourself."

Once again, she blushed. What was it about praise from him that embarrassed her? Hadn't she received praise as a ballerina? She must have, if she'd made it to the top. So there must be something about him that set her off.

"Wait." Underneath the sound of the Jeep's engine and the jungle noises coming through the open window Max heard something else. "Stop."

Emily slammed on the brakes. She must have forgotten to engage the clutch, because the engine stalled. "What?"

"Shh. Let me listen." Yeah, that was the sound of a large truck engine.

Emily must have heard it too, because her eyes met his, wide with alarm. She snatched up her camera, exited the vehicle, and hurried toward the road. "Dammit, Emily," Max muttered under his breath even though there was no way she could hear him. "Come back here."

Once again he was forced to watch as she observed whatever was happening on the road. Through the gaps between the tree trunks he thought he glimpsed a troop transport truck like the one he'd seen back at the crossroads.

Emily stood just inside the jungle until the rumble of the engine had passed. When she returned, Max waited for her to shut the door, then snatched the camera out of her hands. "What's wrong with you? Have you been infected by some sort of reckless journalist bug all of sudden? What if the rebels had spotted you?" He didn't realize that he was leaning across the console and crowding Emily against the driver's door until she placed her hand on his cheek.

"I was careful, Max."

"What do you know about careful?"

She flinched, but he was too angry to care. "You're a civilian," he snarled. "You haven't trained for years on covert techniques. You might have thought you were being careful, but what if the rebels had spotted you? Captured you? With this damn leg wound slowing me down, I wouldn't be able to get to you in time!"

"Shh. I'm okay, Max. The rebels didn't get me. I'm here." She kissed him quickly, then pulled back. "I might not be an expert like you, but I do know how to move quietly through the woods. Father made us practice, in case some day we have to sneak past guards who want to keep us prisoner."

He rested his forehead against hers, enjoying the warmth of her breath against his chin. "You scared me," he said quietly.

"I know." She pulled away and her lips curved in a small smile. "That makes us even, huh?"

He gave a shaky laugh. "Don't do that to me again."

She just shrugged and started the vehicle. "This is actually a lucky break for us. The rebels had only one truck on this side of the road when they blew up the intersection. Since that truck just passed us, it should be safe to use the road."

Max settled back into his seat. "No. Stay off the road. We're too vulnerable."

"But—"

"What if the rebels turn around and come back this way? We've already seen that they'll shoot first."

Emily gave a heavy sigh, then nodded and steered the Jeep between a couple of trees.

"Are you getting tired already? Let me drive."

"No. I'm fine. It's just going to take a really long time to get to the way station if we have to stay on this uneven terrain."

"We won't get to the way station at all if we're dead."

Emily just sighed again.

Ten minutes later, Max pointed to their right where the trees gave way to tall grasses and a field of maize. "Looks like there's a farmer's path along that field. It should be easier going."

Without a word, Emily followed his directions and eased the Jeep out of the trees and onto the small lane. Tires had worn the grass down to packed dirt, and she gave the Jeep some gas.

God, it felt good to see the world move past at a decent clip again. Made him feel less like a failure. More like he might actually be able to carry out this mission. Stop the upcoming attack.

Which reminded him, he needed to notify Rene and Kris that the rebels had destroyed the crossroads. Rene would arrange for medical assistance. And Kris would have the contacts to notify reliable people in law enforcement and the military about the damage done to the country's infrastructure.

He checked that there weren't any overhanging branches, then pulled out his sat phone.

As he hit send on the last text, Max yawned. He wanted to stay alert to any signs of danger, but the only thing keeping him from dozing off was the constant jarring of his wounds. His ribs had started throbbing a counterpoint beat to the pain in his thigh. The knife wound at his back was a constant, low ache. Even his head hurt.

But he was alive. More importantly, Emily was alive and unhurt. If they could just avoid any more encounters with the rebels, they'd be fine.

"How far until the way station?" Emily asked.

Max reached for the map and did a rough calculation of distance. Then he checked the speedometer. "At this rate, another two hours. But we don't know how far this lane extends, so if we have to drive through the jungle again we've probably got three or four more hours to go."

"Are we going to make it before nightfall?"

"I don't know. It's almost three now and sunset is around six." He glanced down at the map. "And that's assuming that the way station hasn't been turned into a temporary base for Ziegler or the rebels."

Up ahead, the lane curved out of sight around a grove of trees. "Ease to a stop," Max told her. "Then go check that the way is clear."

She nodded. This time he was prepared for the spurt of anxiety while she walked away from him. As he watched her, he had to admit that she was right. She moved gracefully through the underbrush, causing minimal disturbance. Perhaps due to a combination of survival training and dance training.

His attention was so focused on Emily that the buzzing of his phone startled him.

My friend, you just can't seem to stay out of trouble, can you? Rene's text made him smile. *Medical and other assistance is on the way to the people affected by the rebel attacks. Do you or Emily need medical attention?*

Nah, we're good, Max texted back. He'd save the story of his latest wound and how Emily had doctored him for when he next saw Rene.

Emily returned and slid into her seat. "The lane continues to our right, but I think it's going to dead-end at a village, because I heard chickens squawking."

"Okay, we'll have to cross to the other side of the main road to avoid being spotted by any nearby villagers on foot."

Emily did a few neck and arm circles, then resumed driving. The next few hours were spent alternating between driving in the jungle, along fields, and crisscrossing the road to detour around villages.

Max monitored their progress by using the GPS tracker on his watch and comparing it to the map. The sun was almost down when they reached the small turn off for Sulaiman's village.

"Turn here."

"Why?"

"I want to check if anyone has returned to my friend's village. If yes, he might be able to hide us for the night."

Emily shrugged and followed his instructions. Unfortunately, the village was just as deserted as before. Max got out of the car and did a quick reconnaissance, then Emily helped him search the village for useful supplies. They ended up with two cans of gas, a couple of jars of groundnut paste—the local equivalent of peanut butter—and a few rolls of digestive biscuits. Not exactly a feast, but it would supplement their meagre food supply.

Worried about Sulaiman, Max texted Kris and asked him to look into his friend's whereabouts.

He refused to acknowledge how easily he'd slipped back into the habit of thinking of Kris as a partner, rather than someone to be protected.

"Do you really think we'll be able to find someone at the way station willing to take me over the border?" Emily asked once they'd returned to driving alongside the main road.

"Honestly? No. With the rebels in the area, I doubt anyone will risk their life by taking on a white passenger."

"Yeah, that's what I think, too."

"So we'll keep going to the border."

"But Max, what about the plane?"

He rubbed the base of his neck. "I'll check again with my friends in the underground. See if they can't spare someone to take over the search. If not, I'll turn around and come back as soon as you're safe."

"That's all very heroic and whatnot." She shot him a look out of the corner of her eye. "But you seem to be forgetting about your leg wound. You don't even know if you can drive."

"I can drive," he grumbled. It didn't matter how much pain he was in, he'd do what needed to be done.

"Yes, but why? Maybe I should stay as your driver."

"No. It's not safe."

Emily shrugged. "It makes more sense, though."

He started to protest, but she waved him silent. "Let's not argue over it. We should almost be to the way station, right?"

He nodded.

"Are we gong to spend the night there?"

"No. We'll find a place to camp in the jungle."

"Fine. We'll revisit this topic tomorrow."

"Like I said, bossy," he muttered. But he couldn't help but smile.

CHAPTER NINE

INSIDE THE TENT that served as his command center, Dietrich studied the topographical maps spread across his desk. Areas that had already been searched for the plane's debris had been shaded faintly with a red pencil. The difficulty was that no one knew where the plane had gone down. Only the second-hand accounts of locals in this region suggested that the plane's remains were likely nearby. Yet when directly questioned, the locals proved to be remarkably unconcerned about the potential loss of life involved in a plane crash.

When asked why they hadn't investigated, the man Dietrich had personally questioned had shrugged. "Not my business. We keep to ourselves and want no trouble." He had gestured toward the thick jungle area. "Why should we waste our time searching for some mechanical bird that fell out of the sky? No one could survive."

Dietrich had figured the man was part of the area's smuggling network and that he had been lying about finding the plane. So he had offered the man an exorbitant amount of money to help him recover the contents of the plane. The man had agreed to help with the search, but so far there had been no sign of the debris.

With only eight days until the meet with the buyer, Dietrich was getting nervous. Worse, Ziegler still had not managed to recapture Max. Instead, Ziegler had reported that Max had eluded the rebels' attempts to corral him at the capital. Max had last been spotted heading north. Toward this area.

Dietrich could not allow Max to find the plane first. He—

His satellite phone rang, the signal boosted by the expensive transceiver he travelled with. "Yes?"

"I am still waiting for a report that all has been taken care of as discussed." The scrambled voice of Dietrich's sponsor was barely understandable over the weak satellite connection. "Need I remind you that you are disposable? Perhaps I need to send in a new team to take care of the problem."

"No, sir. I expect success well within our time limit." Dietrich could not afford to lose this deal. Failure would destroy his newly restored reputation. After the havoc caused by Max's team, it had taken him too many years to earn back the trust and respect of the players in the international arms market. Any additional harm to his reputation was unacceptable. "Both issues will be resolved to your complete satisfaction," he promised.

"Good. I look forward to hearing that all has been handled. It would be a pity if I had to eliminate you now that the deal is so close to fruition." With that, the man ended the call.

Dietrich stared at the phone. He did not truly believe that his men would be able to locate the plane and recover the briefcase with the plans and the prototype before the deadline. The jungle was too dense. It grew back too quickly. Even with the help of advanced detection equipment, his men still had to search the thickest jungle on foot.

Dietrich pressed his palms against the map. Liver spots marred the backs of his hands, the skin no longer as taut as it once had been. It was a fine balance keeping the men he worked for in a proper state of respect for a man old enough to be their father. He knew that in the coming years he would be attacked by those wanting to take over his business. He was prepared for that. Over the past two decades, he had accumulated a significant reserve of cash and purchased a house on a private island to which he would retire. But he was not ready to hand over the reins just yet.

He enjoyed too much the thrill of working under the radar of the authorities, and he found deep satisfaction in the manipulation and calculation involved in negotiating the best possible deal. So he would hold on to his empire as long as possible. Which, at this moment, involved following through on his promise to fulfill the upcoming deal.

Picking up the phone, he made another call. "Execute plan B," he said to the person who answered. He had not made it this far without learning to always create a backup plan. "Notify me when all is ready." He hung up.

No matter what it took, he would *not* show up empty-handed to the meet with the buyer.

WAR Headquarters
The Democratic Republic of the Ivory Coast
West Africa

"Give me details about the crossroads," Kris demanded that evening when Max finally checked in. He'd been waiting impatiently for Max's call, worried that he'd have to tell Wil that something bad had happened to his brother.

"The rebels used their trucks to block access to the intersection," Max said. "They fired on the waiting vehicles, then blasted a crater in the road with dynamite. No one is getting past the crossroads without detouring through the jungle, and most of the passenger cars don't have the muscle for jungle driving."

"Casualties?"

"Not as bad as expected. Word got out and people on our side had already started to move out of range before the rebels opened fire. Although a few rebels died because they didn't move out of the blast zone fast enough."

Kris rubbed the bridge of his nose. The leaders of the rebellion encouraged vicious, senseless violence as a way to keep people living in terror, too afraid to fight back. That allowed the rebels to hold more territory than their mostly inexperienced and undisciplined fighters warranted. Add to that a core of well-trained, well-equipped fighters who were scattered throughout the various rebel groups, and it became increasingly difficult to keep them from implementing their destructive goals.

He sighed and glanced over at the report on his desk. The rebels had emerged two years ago in West Guinea. A mercenary force had been encouraged by a shadowy group of Africans to stir up anti-government resentment and hostility left over from the civil war. Those angry locals had become the original AFA rebels. They'd quickly been augmented by a corps of African fighters who'd been trained in some of the most brutal terrorist camps in the world. These fighters had given the rebels the strength and leadership to make immediate progress toward wrestling control of the country away from the government. They'd attacked government facilities, religious institutions, and any businesses associated with foreigners until West Guinea erupted into a new civil war. The rebels had also taken control of several key resources such as oil wells, guaranteeing they had sufficient funds to keep fighting.

Eventually, the government had toppled and was replaced by a rebel-led dictatorship. Their power secure, the core force of disciplined rebel fighters had moved into the Democratic Republic of the Ivory Coast and began the same process of igniting old anger. The size and strength of the rebel forces grew, allowing them to control increasing swathes of territory.

One of the reasons Kris and his teammates from Unit 3 had joined WAR was that they'd suspected that the men who'd initiated the rebellion had more in mind than creating a unified West African state. Rumors suggested that this mystery group intended to turn the region into the newest staging ground for terrorist attacks against the United States and other Western powers.

Yet with the recent flare-ups in the Middle East and other hotspots, the U.S. and its allies had their attention elsewhere. Leaving this fight to WAR.

"Okay," Kris said, forcing his attention back to his conversation with Max. "Are you still on mission?"

"Yes. We skirted the crater. We're heading north as we speak."

"Good. Any other news?"

Max explained about the photos Emily had taken that seemed to show pieces of the downed plane. "Finally, a break," Kris said.

"Yeah."

"How far are you from the area?" He had to assume that the original timing for the sale was still in effect, leaving Max only eight more days.

"I have to get Emily over the border first. That's why I'm calling. Can you send someone else to look for the plane?"

Shit. "No. Max, I already explained. We're—"

Max cursed. Told someone to pull over. "Sorry. Gotta go. Firefight up ahead."

The line went dead. Great.

Kris set his phone back on the cradle. He was glad Wil had returned to his office in the Greater Niger Republic. The last thing the man needed was a reminder of how much danger Max was in. And Kris hadn't missed the increased tension in Max's voice. Some of it was probably due to the stress of navigating through terrain partially controlled by the rebels. But Kris suspected Max's injuries were bothering him. Hell, for all he knew, Max had been hurt again.

Yeah, much better for Wil to be back at work, no matter how dull life seemed without his presence.

With a sigh, he pulled up the current list of team assignments. He had a bad feeling that Max was going to need help sooner rather than later.

The Republic of the Volta
West Africa

MAX ENDED the call with Kristoff and stuck his phone back in its holder. From the location of the gunfire, he figured the way station was under attack.

"You didn't tell your friend about your leg," Emily chided. She steered the vehicle deeper into the trees and parked it in the shadows underneath a wide palm.

Max shrugged. "What's the point? Kristoff doesn't have any medics to send to my aid. Rene is busy taking care of the wounded down south. No one else is working nearby." He opened his door and gingerly climbed out. "Wait here. I want to see who's fighting at the way station—if it's just the rebels and the locals, or if the government has gotten involved."

Emily scowled at him, but he ignored her as he walked around the front of the Jeep. When he saw her open her door, he shook his head. Gripping the edge of the door so she couldn't get past his extended arm, he leaned forward. "Promise me you'll stay here."

A new burst of gunfire shattered the evening's calm and she flinched. "Okay. I promise."

"Thank you."

Because he understood how much courage it took for her to stay put, he bent down and kissed her. Damn, he loved how her lips cushioned his. How she tasted so sweet. He had to force himself to pull away immediately, because he really wanted to undertake a long, thorough exploration of her mouth.

Wrong time. Wrong place.

Instead, he gave her his most reassuring smile, then turned and walked closer to the fighting.

He had to push his way through tall grass and bushes, but he made decent time. Up ahead, the gunfire continued in sporadic bursts. When the vegetation began to thin, he stopped. If he hadn't been wounded, he'd have crawled forward from here. As it was, he used the binoculars to focus in on the action.

The rebels' troop transport truck blocked the entrance to the road. The rebel soldiers were pinned down in the middle of the lorry park, using one of their vehicles and what was left of the tour company's Land Cruiser as protection. The inhabitants of the way station fired at the rebels with shotguns and at least one AK-47.

Max did a quick search, but saw no sign of Ziegler.

He eased back the way he'd come.

Emily was standing outside the Jeep when he returned. Her face relaxed when she saw him and he realized that she'd been worried about him. It felt strange, but nice, to be the target of a woman's concern again. He rubbed the back of his neck. Damn, he really had been out in the jungle too long.

"What's the situation?" she asked.

He explained, then added, "We'll have to cross the road again." He glanced over at her. "I saw you rubbing your damaged shoulder. Are you good for another few hours?" Wrestling the heavy vehicle without power steering had to be taking a toll on her.

She shrugged and held out her hands. "No muscle tremors or spasms yet, so I'm okay."

"That's my girl." The words felt oddly right. Almost inevitable.

Emily raised a brow at him, the slight motion giving her such a regal air that he couldn't help but laugh.

"What?"

"You. One raised eyebrow and you went from bedraggled waif to imperious queen."

Emily stuck her nose in the air and let go of him. "Hmph."

He grabbed her hand and laced his fingers through hers. "It's cute."

She mock glared at him. "That's the best you can do?"

"Sure." He pursed his lips. "Okay, it's sexy, too. How about that?"

She rolled her eyes. "Better."

He grinned. "You're a good sport, Emily Iwasaki."

"What? Now you're British? Who says 'good sport' any more?"

"Hey, I'm a world traveler. I'll adapt whatever language I please, so long as it conveys what I need."

She opened her mouth as if to reply, but a startled parrot exploded out of the bushes next to her and she shrieked instead.

"Sorry," she immediately said. She gave him a sheepish smile. "I guess I'm a bit on edge."

"No worries. I'd be surprised if you weren't. You sure you don't want me to drive?"

She looked pointedly at his injured leg.

"Yeah, okay, that'd be my clutch leg, but still..."

She shook her head. "No. Save your strength. The way our luck has been going, you're going to need it."

Hating that she was right, he climbed back into the passenger seat.

They crossed the road without incident, then drove through tall grasses toward the jungle's edge. While the grass was easier to navigate, it also left a more noticeable trail as the Jeep flattened and otherwise displaced the grass.

Dammit, he should have created a diversion in case they were followed.

No. On second thought, he didn't want to draw the attention of the rebels away from the fight. He'd just have to watch for signs that someone was manning the transport truck. They couldn't afford to have a rebel scout spot them.

They finally reached the jungle and Emily turned into it, driving roughly parallel to the road. For someone not used to driving, let alone driving a stick shift Jeep, she impressed him with her skill. He only wished he could do something to help.

"You're an amazing woman, Emily. You're handling all of this incredibly well."

Her head rocked back in surprise at his statement. "Uh," she said. "Thanks."

He reached for her hand. "How many times do I have to say it before you'll believe it, Emily? You've got strength. The ability to still see the humor in life despite all we've been through. You haven't once thrown a hissy fit or complained about how tired you are." He placed a kiss to the middle of her palm. "Amazing."

Her cheeks reddened. "I..." She glanced away, then shrugged. "Thanks."

And...she hated being complimented. Right. Should have remembered that.

Emily pulled her hand away and pursed her lips. "Max, it's going to be full dark soon."

"Yeah, I know." He hated to ask, but, "Do you think you can keep driving after dark if I give you the night vision goggles? We really need to put more distance between us and the rebels."

She rolled her neck and flexed her fingers against the steering wheel. "I honestly don't know. I'll do my best."

"Okay." He wasn't going to say anything yet, because he didn't want to argue with her, but if they hadn't made it far enough from the way station before the light completely disappeared, then he would take over the driving. He wanted to get far, far away from the rebels.

AN HOUR after the sun disappeared beneath the horizon, Emily wore the night vision goggles as she drove without lights along the road. She'd been forced out of the jungle because the trees here grew too close together to allow the Jeep to pass.

The muscles across her back were tight and achy and her arms felt heavy as lead. She knew Max's mission to find the plane and retrieve the weapon was important, and that she needed to get over the border, but she could barely keep the Jeep on the road. If—

The vehicle bucked, then lurched to the right. "What's happening?" Emily shrieked as she fought the wheel and steered them to the side of the road. "Max?"

"It's okay, sweetheart." He put his hand on her thigh, and the heat and weight of it broke through her panic. "We've got a flat. No problem. We have a spare."

Emily sat frozen in her seat, her heart still hammering in her chest, as Max got out to take a look.

He poked his head back through the window. "Yep. Flat tire."

Emily removed the night vision goggles, then stared out at the darkness. "Max, can we *please* just stop here for the night? I'm so tired, I can't go on. I know we have the goggles, but wouldn't it be easier to change the tire tomorrow morning?"

His jaw firmed and she knew he wanted to protest. That if Max were alone, he'd keep driving until he collapsed. But if there was one thing Emily had learned during her years as a dancer, it was to recognize her limits and stop before her body shut down. "If we push on tonight, then I'm going to be too exhausted tomorrow to be of any help. Please."

She met his eyes and saw his expression soften. He stroked her cheek. "All right. But we're going to change the tire first, then find a spot wide enough so we can drive into the jungle and camp. That way, we'll be ready to make a quick getaway in the morning, if necessary."

"Thank you!" She gave him what she intended to be a grateful peck on the lips, but he leaned forward and deepened the kiss. She closed her eyes, sinking into the heat and the comfort of it. Then, before she lost her head, she pulled back. "Okay, Mr. Fix-It. Let's do this."

"You don't have to help," Max said. "I know how tired you are."

Emily crossed her arms over her chest and raised her eyebrow, since that seemed to have had a positive effect on him earlier. "So says the man who's been beaten until his ribs cracked, sliced with a knife, and speared by a piece of metal."

Max tipped his head in her direction to acknowledge her comment. He reached into the back seat and pulled out two energy bars and their water bottles. "Munch on this. We both need energy, first."

"Talk about bossy." Emily rolled her eyes, but tore off the wrapping and took a huge bite, because darn it, she was starving. The dry mix of nuts and berries tasted surprisingly good. "Where'd you get these?" She hadn't seen energy bars on sale at the local market.

He gave her a smug smile. "Special stash from that underground group. They keep road-worthy snacks available at all of their safe houses."

Emily finished her bar and washed it down with a long drink of water, then placed the used wrapper in the plastic garbage sack. Their water was running low, but since they both had advanced filters on their bottles, all they needed to do was find a stream. "Okay, I'm ready."

Max dusted off his hands and stowed their trash in the cargo compartment.

"Are your ribs up for lifting down the spare tire?" she asked, pulling on the night vision goggles and opening the panel where the tools were kept.

"Yes," he grumbled. "I'm not an invalid."

She bit her tongue instead of answering.

"Let me guess," he said as he removed the cover from the spare. "Changing a tire was included in your emergency training."

"Of course. Father made certain that everyone in the family, including Mother, could change a car's oil, other fluids, and tires." People who met her reserved, impeccably dressed father in his three-piece suits never believed that he could change a car's tire, unclog a toilet, and perform other daily maintenance. And watching her blonde, aristocratic mother don a pair of blue jeans and a ratty t-shirt to work on the car with her father had always made Emily smile.

Despite the weathered look of the Jeep, it had been very well maintained. The lug nuts on both the spare and the flat tire came off easily. As she helped Max lower the spare tire to the ground, Emily's back and shoulder muscles threatened to give out. Thankfully, the spare tire was full-sized and in good condition. It took them less than twenty minutes to change the tire. Max was just tightening the final nut when Emily saw headlights down the road in the direction of the way station.

"Max, a vehicle is headed this way."

"Shit."

Max shoved the flat tire into some bushes while Emily tossed the tools into the cargo compartment. Then she slid behind the wheel and drove with the lights off until she found a spot a few hundred yards down the road with just enough room for the Jeep to squeeze between the trees. As she navigated the obstacle course of above ground roots and thick bushes, she kept shooting glances in the rearview mirror, expecting to see headlights racing toward them. But despite their slow progress, the other vehicle wasn't in sight yet.

A couple of minutes later, Max declared, "This is good. Turn off the engine."

Not liking the spooky green tones of the night vision goggles, Emily tugged them off. The complete darkness that engulfed her sent a shiver down her spine as her eyes struggled to adjust. Through the open window, she heard the tick of the engine as it cooled. The silence caused by their passage through the jungle was soon replaced by the buzz of insects and the occasional cry of a bird. It was another five minutes before she heard the rumble of a truck engine. Even though she knew the Jeep was parked out of sight of the road, her heart still skipped a beat.

What if the rebels had some sort of night vision equipment that allowed them to see heat signatures? Should she start the Jeep? Prepare to flee? But where? Trees hemmed them in on all sides. She'd never get the Jeep started fast enough to get away if the rebels burst through the jungle.

She struggled to breathe against the rising tide of panic. What if—

Max reached over and took her hand, squeezing reassuringly. That point of contact temporarily steadied her. She squeezed back. "Max," she whispered. "What if they have heat sensing equipment?"

"Shh... The rebels aren't that sophisticated. They don't have the money for that type of stuff. Now hush."

As the wait for the truck to pass stretched on, the air pressed down on her, threatening to suffocate her. Despite Max's reassuring presence, her mind kept conjuring up grisly scenarios of what would happen if the rebels found them and she struggled not to succumb to complete panic.

The truck eventually passed by without so much as reducing speed. Yet five minutes later, her body was still poised on the edge of flight.

"Easy, Em, we're okay. They're gone." Max tugged on her hand and she went willingly into his arms.

Safety. Strength.

She snuggled against him. "How do you do it? Live with that kind of fear on a regular basis?"

She felt Max shrug underneath her cheek. "That's what my

life is like. It's normal for me. I'd definitely panic if you put me on stage in front of hundreds and asked me to dance."

Emily snickered at the image of Max in a pair of ballet tights, dancing a *pas de deux* with a semi-automatic in hand.

"Better?" Max whispered.

"Yes. Thanks."

"Good. Let's get some rest."

Emily helped Max string their mosquito nets over the open windows of the Jeep, made a quick pit stop in the bushes, then tumbled onto the sleeping bag Max had laid out for her.

She waited for sleep to claim her, but although she remained enervated, her mind refused to shut down. She kept replaying all the events of the day. "Some of the rebels at the crossroads were so young," she murmured. "Just boys. I'd heard reports from other wars in Africa, so I know the use of child soldiers is common, but still, it's a shock."

"Yeah, I know."

"Why? Why do they enjoy hurting and killing people?" She knew the question sounded naïve, but she'd never been able to understand why people resorted to violence. What made someone like Agatha, who'd seemed so docile and sweet, decide that the best way to further her career was to throw acid on Emily in hopes of taking over Emily's position? It hadn't worked out the way Agatha wanted, but what had made her think violence was the answer?

"If I could figure that out, I'd be able to stop all the bloodshed," Max said.

There was a dark edge to his voice that let her know he'd seen horrible things. Based on how he'd been abused at the hands of Ziegler, she knew he must have experienced situations that would have turned her bitter and angry. "How do you keep going without losing your own humanity?"

There was a long pause before he answered. "Sometimes you just have to lock everything away. Ignore the suffering. Ignore your conscience shouting at you to do something to help, because there's a bigger picture and what you're doing will have an effect on more people. And each time that happens, you lose a little more of your soul."

The silence that followed was heavy. She wanted to probe. To know more.

"I'm not a hero, Emily. You were right to be wary of me. I've been in Africa this past year and seen countless incidents of abuse and other acts of violence. Yet I'm not here fighting to stabilize the region. I'm not a political idealist intent on making the world a better place. My motives are entirely selfish."

She heard his body shift against his sleeping bag, then his deep exhalation. "I'm here for revenge."

CHAPTER TEN

MAX STARED INTO THE DARKNESS, unable to believe those words had come out of his mouth.

It wasn't that he'd been hiding his need for revenge against Dietrich. Kris and the rest of his former team had no illusions regarding Max's real mission. And Wil had been quite vocal in his opposition to Max's one-man quest to take Dietrich down.

No, what shocked him about what he'd just said was how reluctant he was to lose status in Emily's eyes. He might be beat-up and barely able to carry out his mission, but being with Emily reminded him that there was life outside of this narrow world he'd immersed himself in. Reminded him that people laughed and loved and went about their everyday lives without a thought to men like Dietrich whose work destroyed that peaceful world.

For Emily, Max wanted to be a hero.

Emily's soft sound of surprise reminded him that she was waiting for an explanation. "Dietrich has a side business to his arms dealing. He also deals in intelligence, if the price is high enough." He sighed and shifted on his sleeping bag to relieve pressure on his knife wound. "Okay, there's really no way to make this story short."

To Max's surprise, Emily moved in and laid her head on his chest. He draped his arm around her and she snuggled close. "We have time," she murmured. "I'm physically exhausted, but my mind won't settle down. Think of this as my bedtime story."

He snorted. "Yeah, well, I don't know that this story will relax you, but here goes." He took a deep breath. "I started my junior year of college in 2001, working on a double major in history and folklore. I hoped to get a position with a museum. Then the attacks of 9/11 happened. Like so many guys I knew, I desperately wanted to take action. In fact, a bunch of us headed into town and joined the Marines."

"You were a Marine? Really? You don't seem to have the ah... appropriate respect for authority."

Max chuckled. "Yeah. That's what my father thought. 'Max, you're always questioning. Always figuring out alternative ways to achieve a goal. You will not fit in with the military, particularly not the Marines.' But I didn't care. I wanted to be a Marine, like my younger brother Wil, who'd enlisted right out of high school."

"How'd it go?"

"For the first few years, it was fine. During basic training, I was so pumped up with patriotism that I tamped down my need to always understand why I was being asked to do something. Then I got assigned to a newly formed crisis response team and the specialized training for that kept my mind occupied. It also helped that I served under excellent commanders. Men who knew how to put my intelligence to best use. Who encouraged me to become a leader. But then my lieutenant was killed during a raid that should have been a cake walk. I helped plan the mission and everything was solid—our intel, our approach, and our execution. No way should the enemy have known we were coming and prepared an ambush. Yet they'd set up a kill zone. Fortunately, our rifleman had spooky good instincts. He insisted something was wrong, so we scaled back on our approach. His warning prevented the whole platoon from getting mowed down.

As it was, we lost the lieutenant, two other men, and took severe casualties."

"You blamed yourself."

"Yeah. Because—"

Emily put her hand over his mouth. "No, Max. I've seen how protective you are. How thoroughly you think things through. You did your best to make the mission safe for your men, right?"

"Of course, but—"

"Uh-uh. You're not to blame."

He sighed. "That's what the rest of the team said. Still, it..." His throat closed up. "It haunts me."

"Of course. You lost people you cared about. People you respected. I can't even begin to imagine the pain you dealt with." She stroked her hand down his chest and, oddly enough, he felt some of his grief ease.

"So what happened next?"

He cleared his throat. He figured Dietrich knew most of the rest, so telling Emily didn't put her at too much risk. Plus, he needed to tell her. To have her know why he'd eventually gone off on his own, so that if he died in the next couple of days she wouldn't judge him harshly. "We discovered that the weapons used by the terrorists in the ambush had been supplied by Dietrich. When we passed on the intel we were warned by our superiors to ignore it. That it was being handled by another team and any action on our part could screw up that operation. But Dietrich's name kept popping up as the arms dealer supplying the local terrorist cells, making it clear that no one was working to take him down." His heart beat faster as he remembered. "I was furious when I realized that no one was investigating the ambush. That the deaths of our teammates were being swept under the carpet."

"I'm sorry."

He shrugged and forced the roil of emotions away. "Before our team could decide what to do about our suspicions, a man approached me with an intriguing job offer. He represented a deep black ops government unit with unconventional rules." He glanced at Emily to see if she understood. At her puzzled look, he explained, "Black ops are such ultra secret operations that no one not directly involved even knows they exist. Capturing high value targets. Rescuing U.S. personnel. Destroying enemy assets. Missions that never make the news, even when they prevent thousands of deaths. The man promised that if I joined this group, not only would I have free rein to go after Dietrich, but I'd have the unit's full support. He was recruiting only the brightest, most unconventional members of the military and law enforcement."

"So you accepted."

"Yes. But every time we got close to Dietrich, he managed to escape. Either something went wrong on our end that prevented us from carrying out our mission—strange equipment failures when we'd double checked everything, failure of our backup to arrive—or we arrived and discovered that Dietrich and his men had fled. I suspected that someone on our side was sabotaging our missions in order to protect Dietrich."

Emily's hand clenched on his shirt.

"I began to doubt the competence of those in charge. Because only a handful of people knew we even existed, let alone were privy to actual mission data, it should have been simple to ferret out the traitor. He was either one of my teammates, or one of the people who gave us our missions. Unfortunately, the ones who'd founded our group had hidden themselves behind a thick layer of secrecy. Even the man who recruited me only knew them as the Consortium. Finally, my team decided to go after Dietrich without notifying anyone in command. Again, I helped plan the mission. This time, it went down without a hitch. We managed to screw up a big deal Dietrich had scheduled. Took down his buyer and captured Dietrich. His right hand man, Ziegler, was wounded but managed to get away." Max had been part of the squad in charge of clearing out the building. Sometimes he wondered if things would have been different if he'd instead been assigned to guard Dietrich.

"En route to headquarters, the convoy transporting Dietrich and the other prisoners came under attack. Several vehicles crashed and burned. Dietrich was reported dead, although his body was never recovered. Our unit's commander was killed. My gut told me that we'd been betrayed again. That someone on the secondary team—the ones responsible for taking Dietrich and the other prisoners away—had relayed the convoy's route to Dietrich's sponsor. I believed the crash had been staged and that Dietrich was alive, but without proof, our new commander didn't want to hear it."

"Did you ever figure out which man had leaked the route?"

"No. With Dietrich supposedly dead, my team was kept busy with other missions. I continued to investigate whenever I found the time, since part of my job was doing research and analyzing data."

"You were an analyst? Not a soldier?"

He shook his head. "Both. In order to be a quick-deploy unit, we were cross-trained on all aspects of a mission, from gathering intel to taking down a target with a sniper rifle. My strengths were analysis, planning, and covert infiltration. I didn't have the patience to be a good sniper, lying in the dirt all day without moving."

Emily snorted. "That, I can see."

"Smart aleck."

"So what happened next?"

"The team never clicked with our new leader. Most of us were former military and he'd come from the FBI, which has a different mental outlook. Plus, he cared a little too much about following the rules, when our team had been founded on the promise of freedom from rules. Morale quickly deteriorated. Our missions started to change. The targets weren't the clear and present danger we were used to. Several of us began to suspect that Dietrich's sponsor was trying to undermine the effectiveness of our team, yet we still couldn't break through that firewall and find out the identities of the men in the Consortium. When almost half our team was injured on a mission that felt more like political posturing than a genuine attempt to make the world a safer place, several members, including my co-leader Kristoff, quit."

"But you stayed. Why?"

"Because despite the changes, we still had the occasional success. As team leader, I'd been shielding the guys from a lot of the crap the commander threw at us. If I left, they would have been directly in the line of fire."

If he'd given up, he would've felt like a failure. His brother had continued to be promoted within the Marines. Wil was the one their father spoke of with with pride. Max... Well, his father didn't know Max's real job. His cover with Unit 3 had been as a folklore professor. He'd supposedly been traveling the world in order to draw parallels between what values a population expressed through story and the economic and political structure of their society. He hadn't been able to tell his father the truth about his work at Unit 3, so Max's lack of advancement at the university only reinforced his father's view that his oldest son had lost his ambition.

Max had consoled himself with the knowledge that his work made the world a safer place, even if his father would never be aware of the truth. Max had believed that his work mattered. Had known that he'd conducted himself with honor and integrity despite the violent world he operated in.

Then his commander had been killed and Max began to question everything about his work at Unit 3.

"You're very loyal," Emily said. "That's a good thing."

He scowled and cleared his throat. "About six months after Dietrich's supposed death, I was working in the office. I zoomed in on a digital photo as part of my research for an upcoming operation and spotted Dietrich in the background." The sense of elation that he'd been right, that the arms dealer was alive, and the anticipation of finally going after Dietrich had made his heart pound. "This was late at night and only a few night shift workers were around. Since I didn't trust my commander, I downloaded the file and took it home. I needed time to think how best to proceed. Who I could trust with this discovery."

"Taking the file was that easy?"

He snorted. "What made our team unique was that they'd recruited highly intelligent, extremely creative thinkers. Men and women labeled as mavericks by the military or law enforcement. They trained us in all aspects of covert operations and then put us into teams where we formed ironclad bonds. As the years progressed, internal security became lax. I think the higher-ups believed that our team cohesion would keep us honest. And for the most part, it worked. They hadn't counted on me realizing that our leadership was corrupt. So while it wasn't simple to take the data home with me, it wasn't as difficult as it should have been." He paused, remembering how calm he'd been despite knowing he could be arrested for what he was doing. "When I returned to the office the next morning, I discovered that the file had been deleted."

"Oh, no. Were you in danger of being found out?"

"I didn't think so. I'd been careful and erased any sign that I'd accessed the file. Still, it convinced me that I couldn't trust my superiors. But I knew that if I quit, I didn't have the resources to track Dietrich on my own. One of my former teammates had migrated to the FBI, so I set up a meeting with him. Only, he never showed. He was reported killed in a car accident the morning I was supposed to meet him."

"What did you do?"

"Destroyed all evidence that I'd contacted him. Created and hid so many backup copies of the file that it would take a long time for someone to track them all down. I returned to the office, fully expecting that a hit team would come after me. But whatever alarm my friend had triggered apparently didn't apply to me, because no one tried to kill me." He'd kept working, wondering how much longer he could pretend that everything was normal.

"Then, two days later, the base where my brother Wil was stationed in Afghanistan was attacked." And going after Dietrich had no longer been the most important thing in his life. "Wil lost both his lower legs in the explosion."

"Oh, God. I'm so sorry."

Max stroked Emily's hair. "I took leave to go to the hospital where they were treating him. When I returned, one of my contacts notified me that the security team had caught one of the militants responsible. He fingered Dietrich as the one who'd supplied both the intelligence and the weapons needed for the attack. I asked to be assigned to the multi-agency task force investigating the attack, but my commander denied my request." It had taken every ounce of Max's control not to send his fist into his commander's face that day. "I even tried going around him by reaching out directly to the agent in charge. I told him that my team had years of research on Dietrich and that I'd be happy to share if he'd let me join the task force. He responded that the earlier information about Dietrich being behind the attack had been incorrect. That Dietrich was dead and he didn't need my help."

"You didn't believe him."

"Right. I immediately turned in my resignation and have been after Dietrich ever since. Ruining his deals when I can. Trying to pin him down so I can turn him in." Kill him, if possible. To do so, Max had immersed himself in the international arms arena. Dealt with some of the most vicious low-lifes on the planet in order to get the intel he needed.

It had left him feeling dirty in a way years as a soldier hadn't.

"Retrieving the stolen weapon plans and prototype won't just damage Dietrich's reputation," he continued, "but will save lives. If rumor is correct, the group he's dealing with intends to use the prototype against an American military base or diplomatic mission somewhere in West Africa. Wil is stationed at our compound in the Greater Niger Republic."

"So getting the prototype back is a way of protecting your brother."

"Yeah."

"And you say you're not a hero." She patted his chest. He opened his mouth to protest, but she continued. "Where does that underground group fit into this?"

"Remember how I mentioned my partner, Kristoff? He and most of my former teammates formed their own private special operations group. When they realized that the situation here in West Africa has international security implications if the region becomes a future haven for terrorist groups, they joined the underground."

"Why aren't you working with them to take down Dietrich?"

"Because Dietrich's sponsor has a powerful reach. I can't risk that there will be arrest warrants taken out on Kris's team and that U.S. military and law enforcement assets will be assigned to hunt them down." He cleared his throat. "Instead of letting me go, my superiors ignored my resignation and labeled me as AWOL. This despite the fact that our contract said we could leave at any time. The only conditions were that we weren't in the middle of a mission and that we'd promise to uphold the secrecy clause after we left."

"Which is why you didn't want to approach the embassy."

"Yeah."

"And you're acting on your own in order to keep your friends safe."

"Damn straight." He would protect his family and friends at any cost. Now and always.

"But who's protecting you, Max?"

"I don't need protection. I just need Dietrich out of service. If I have to sacrifice my career to do it, I'm okay with that." In fact, he wasn't entirely certain he'd live through a confrontation with Dietrich. But as long as the bastard got what was coming to him, Max would willingly give up his life.

Emily made a sound of protest, almost as if she'd read his mind. "Shh. Enough of that," he said. "Do you think you can sleep now?"

"Are you *kidding* me? After you've told me such a tale of intrigue and betrayal?" Yet even as she spoke, she yawned.

"Put it out of your mind. We've got to get back on the road first thing in the morning. You need your rest." He moved his hand in circles over her back, hoping to soothe her to sleep.

"I'm so sorry," she murmured. "Escorting me down to the capital really screwed up your timeline, didn't it?"

"I wasn't about to leave you on your own. I'm not that much of a bastard."

"I don't think you're a bastard at all. You're a good man at heart, Max Lansing. Which is why I'm going to stick around and help you find the plane. Two of us searching will accomplish the task faster than one."

"Hell, no. I'm taking you over the border."

"Mmm...no." Emily's words slurred together. Moments later, her breathing evened out into sleep.

Good man? Him?

She was so wrong.

Day Six

WHEN MAX AWOKE the next morning, soft gray light filtered into the interior of the Jeep. Emily slept beside him with her head on his chest. Her right hand had slipped around to the side of his waist, holding him in place. He liked that she still wanted to be close to him despite him unloading his past on her last night. Liked the idea that maybe she'd been feeling a little possessive of him.

Because he sure as hell was starting to feel like she belonged to him.

Emily shifted against him, yawned, then opened her eyes. Catching him watching her, her cheeks flared hot. "I'm sorry, I must be getting heavy. Your poor ribs." She attempted to pull back, but Max tightened his arms.

"Stay," he murmured.

She froze, uncertainty and embarrassment warring in her eyes. She probably didn't realize it, but her hand had risen to cover her scars.

Max gently pried her fingers away from her neck, hating that this strong, resilient woman would in any way feel self-conscious around him. Then, holding her hand firmly enough that she couldn't tug it free, he lifted his head and placed a kiss on the center of the damaged skin.

Emily inhaled sharply.

He pulled back. "Did that hurt?"

She looked at him through wide eyes. "N-no. I..." She bit her lip and Max almost groaned. He wanted to take that plump little pillow into his own mouth and suck.

"If it didn't hurt, why did you gasp?" He kissed her scars again. "Why is your breathing faster?"

She gave a little hum of pleasure as his tongue touched a ridge of scar tissue. "I..." She gasped again. "I..." Her eyelashes fluttered as he scraped his teeth lightly along the scars.

"Yes?" he prompted.

"I...ah...yes...there...I..."

Max smiled against her skin and moved his tongue back over to the spot she liked best, licking and nipping at the skin as he tested what amount of pressure made her crazy.

"Oh...my...God..." Her fingers spasmed in his grip and her back arched just a little.

"Hmm... I'm guessing you have a few places with full or even increased sensation. Am I right?" he asked as he finished mapping out the final contour of her scars and lifted his head to plot his next move.

"Um...yeah. Most of the area is numb, but there are a few sensitive places." The heavy lidded, dazed gaze she gave him shot straight to his already hard cock. "But Max," she blinked and her eyes focused, "you're hurt. We should stop."

He let go of her hand to run his fingers over her hair. Then he gently took her head between his palms and brought her mouth to hover over his. Before their lips touched, he said, "You're so beautiful." He stroked one finger down her cheek. Even with the dirt and sweat her skin here was so smooth, so soft. "You're so damn sexy. I've been wanting your mouth on mine since the second we ended the last kiss. If you kiss me again, I won't feel a bit of pain. Promise."

He held his breath as she hesitated, hoping he hadn't judged her wrong. But then her tongue darted out to wet her lips, her eyes dropped to his mouth and he knew he'd been right. She needed to have a sense of control.

A moment later she pressed her lips to his.

The kiss started off tentatively, which didn't do a thing to stop his body from jerking as if he'd been prodded with a live wire. It took all his self-control not to haul her against him and take her mouth fast and hard. He needed her on a gut deep level he didn't understand. He needed her honesty. Needed her compassion and her courage to remind him that there was more to life than revenge.

Wanted nothing more than to lose himself in her body, absorbing her passion until he felt cleansed.

But most importantly, he needed her trust.

Emily sighed and relaxed against him. Her tongue traced the

seam of his lips, and when he opened, she began a lazy exploration of his mouth. Max held back at first, not wanting to frighten her, but when she angled her head for a deeper kiss, his control slipped. One hand settled on the back of her head, helping her find the right position so that he could delve into her mouth and taste her unique essence of innocence and grit.

His other hand roamed down her back, searching for the hem of her shirt. When he found it, he slipped underneath until his fingers met bare skin. While their mouths explored, Max stroked the silky skin of her back, walking his fingers along her spine until he met the barrier of her bra.

Emily froze and pulled back.

"I'm sorry. I didn't meant to rush—"

She sat up. Peeled her t-shirt off then her bra, leaving her bare to his gaze in the pale morning light.

His tongue stuck to the roof of his mouth and all he could do was gape at her. She was exquisite, with small, perfectly formed breasts tipped with dainty brown nipples. He could hardly reconcile this shy, yet sensual creature with the strong woman who'd handled the chaos and danger of these past few days with the strength and courage of a warrior.

Dropping her eyes and biting her lip, Emily crossed one arm over her chest so that her hand could cover the scars that extended from just under her chin to the ball of her shoulder.

"No. Shh..." It finally dawned on him what had happened to put that look of mortification on her face. She thought his silence meant he was turned off by her scars. "Don't hide yourself." He gently pulled her hand away so that he could see all of her. "You're so gorgeous you turned me speechless."

"I..." She shrugged, which caused a distracting little jiggle in her breasts. He wanted to reach up and take one in his mouth. But before he could act on that thought, she continued, "I know I'm not very well-endowed. I'm kinda skinny, too. And the scars..." Her lips twisted, as if she were fighting not to cry.

"No, Em, sweetheart, that's not it at all. God, if only you knew what you do to me." Unable to hold back any longer, he gently ran a fingertip from the start of her scars, down her neck and shoulder, then along the ivory slope of her breast. Her nipple tightened when he stroked it and his lips curled in satisfaction. Then he cupped her breast in his hand. "Your scars are simply a sign that you're strong. A survivor. That makes them beautiful. And your breasts are perfect. Just the right size for my hand. For my mouth."

As she watched his hand on her skin, her lips parted. Her breath caught.

Placing his other hand on her back, he urged her to lean forward until he could take her nipple into his mouth. At the first pull of his lips, she groaned and arched closer. God, he loved her responsiveness.

Taking her invitation, he suckled harder, working the tight little peak of her nipple with his tongue and teeth. Letting her sounds of pleasure tell him what she liked. His control slipped another notch. His erection pressed insistently against his pants. He needed to be inside her. Needed—

Emily reached out and braced her hands against his chest, inadvertently landing too close to his cracked ribs. He sucked in a sharp breath at the sudden pain.

"Max! Oh, God. I'm sorry." She sat back.

He snagged her waist with his arm and pulled her flush to his chest, the pain already forgotten. "I'm not. I was on the brink of losing control. You deserve better for our first time. That's if... Ah... I don't want to make any assumptions here." It might kill him, but he'd stop if she wanted him to. "This will only go as far as you want."

She tugged on his t-shirt. "I want you, Max. I want to feel your bare skin against mine."

His hips jerked because, damn, the thought of feeling those pert little nipples against his skin threatened to have him coming in his pants. He levered his upper body off the sleeping bag and helped her pull his t-shirt over his head.

Then Emily draped herself over his chest, rubbing her breasts against him almost shyly at first, peeking at him to see his reaction. He simply groaned and sent his hands on an exploration of her back and sides, then down over the curve of her butt. He loved molding her subtle curves with his palms, but even more he loved the growing flush of arousal on her skin as Emily slid and pressed against him, searching for the most pleasure.

Then, with a frustrated growl, she tunneled her fingers into his hair, lowered her head, and kissed him. This time her kiss was aggressive, leaving no doubt what she wanted. She took his mouth as if it belonged to her. He plunged his tongue into her, starting a fierce mating dance. Wanting to claim her as much as he wanted to be claimed by her.

When Emily slipped her fingers between them to tweak her own nipple, Max's tenuous hold over his control broke. Yanking her closer, he flipped them over so she was on bottom and took the kiss deeper. Desperate to make her understand how precious she was to him. Wanting to make certain she'd never forget him.

Emily whimpered and moved restlessly beneath him. She widened her legs, welcoming him into the place he most wanted to be. But not with clothes between them.

"Off," he demanded, tugging at her belt.

"Yours, too."

Between kisses to her mouth, face, and neck, Max managed to shove his pants and boxers down and help Emily shimmy out of both her pants and her panties. He barely caught a glimpse of her slender body before she pulled him down for another kiss, trapping his erection between them.

His hips pushed against her. There was so much he still wanted to do to her. He wanted to taste every inch of her skin. Explore and tease and linger over the special place between her legs. But the pressure inside him was building too fast, his balls already drawing up.

He braced himself on his arms and...

Shit. Condom. With a groan, he reached over and opened the first aid kit.

"What?" Emily mumbled as she licked a line from the hollow at the base of his throat up to his chin, where she sucked so hard on the thin skin beneath his jaw he knew she'd leave a mark.

The thought almost made him come. "Need. Condom."

"Umm..." She nipped at his chin.

Oh, God. Where was the damn condom? He desperately shoved aside items he didn't want until he finally felt the corner of the little packet. "Ha!"

"Give me." Emily snatched the condom. She tore it open, then, with a wicked gleam in her eyes, slowly rolled it down his length, stroking his balls as she came to the base.

"Enough!" Max pounced on her and crushed her mouth underneath his. For a split second he thought he'd done it again, scared her with his overwhelming need, because she hesitated. Then, thank God, she was kissing him back with equal ferocity. She spread her legs, dug her fingers into his buttocks, and guided him inside her.

So...damn...good. But even through the pleasure spiking his pulse he felt her tight muscles resist him. He reached deep for his last ounce of control and held still to give her time to adjust to his size. When she finally nodded, he pushed slowly forward until he was seated fully inside her. Keeping an eye on her reaction, he pulled out, then pushed back in again. She hummed in pleasure, her head arching back.

That was it. Primitive instincts took over, driving him toward the peak. Emily twisted and moaned beneath him. He'd never seen anything so erotic or so beautiful. Her fingers raked down his back. He pounded into her harder. Then harder still. Close. He was so...close. Emily spasmed around him and cried out in release. Max exploded a heartbeat later. For a perfect moment he held still, bracing himself above her, as his entire essence drained out of him. Then he collapsed on top of her.

No. Too heavy. He forced himself back up on his elbows and carefully withdrew, groaning as her muscles squeezed weakly in an attempt to hold him inside. After he disposed of the condom in their garbage baggie, he lay down beside Emily and pulled her into his arms.

She snuggled against him. "Mmm...amazing," she murmured. She pressed a soft kiss to his chest, then slipped into sleep.

"Yeah, fucking amazing." As he, too, drifted into sleep, he had the unsettling feeling that a previously cold, dark part of him had just been reborn.

CHAPTER ELEVEN

Ninety minutes later, Emily was back behind the wheel of the Jeep. They'd both slept for about an hour after that mind blowing bout of sex, then hurried through eating breakfast. It hadn't taken long before the jungle became too dense to drive through, so they'd again been forced onto the road.

Her whole body still tingled from the aftereffects of Max's loving, and she couldn't help the happiness that lifted the corners of her mouth. She didn't know what mattered most to her about what they'd done. That Max—a rough, dangerous man unlike anyone she'd ever known—had given her such pleasure, or that he'd been so completely unfazed by her scars. Aside from visits to her doctor, no one had seen her naked since the attack. In fact, she'd carefully kept as much of the scar tissue hidden as possible, knowing that seeing it upset her family and friends.

Yet Max accepted it as part of her. He saw her as beautiful despite the uneven and discolored flesh. He insisted it was just another part of her. She wished she could find the words to tell him how much that meant.

"Hey, I thought we'd moved beyond your self-consciousness." Max's fingers gently moved her hand away from her neck and

Emily frowned. She hadn't even realized she'd been touching her scars.

"I—" Not knowing what to say, she just shook her head instead.

Max pressed a quick kiss to the palm of her hand, then let her go so she could hold the wheel with both hands as she steered around a pothole. "Will you tell me about it? How you got your scars?"

Emily sighed and chewed the inside of her cheek. She wasn't surprised that he'd asked, yet she felt reluctant to bring that ugliness into the aftermath of their lovemaking. Still, Max deserved to know.

"I was a principal dancer with the Ballet of the Bay in San Francisco," she said. "They're a ballet company founded with the intent of having a culturally diverse group of dancers. Seven months ago, we were one night away from finishing a tour in Russia. But during the pre-performance warmup, one of the other dancers snapped. I still don't know what set her off. I hadn't knocked into her or stepped on her foot. I wasn't even that close to her. So I didn't see what happened. All I remember is coming out of a spin and hearing Agatha screaming. I didn't realize she was angry at me until I felt liquid hit my neck and felt a terrible burning."

She couldn't help it, her hand rubbed her scars. "The pain was worse than anything I'd ever experienced. I swear I could feel the acid eating through my skin to my muscles to my nerves, until that section went numb. That was even scarier, because even through my pain I recognized that losing feeling meant serious damage."

Her stomach churned and her breath hitched. "I don't remember much of anything beyond the sounds of my own screams. It's mostly a blur of darkness and pain. But...one of the dancers told me that they had to hold me still because I was thrashing about like a fish caught on a line."

"Jesus." Max took her hand and placed it back on the steering wheel, then began lightly stroking her scars.

The tenderness of his touch made her sniffle. Oh, no. She couldn't afford to cry. How would she see the road through the tears? To distract herself, she continued, "According to the other dancers, Agatha had grabbed a bottle of drain cleaner off the janitor's cart and thrown its contents at me. Luckily, the bottle was only partially full and I was still in motion as I finished my turn. So the acid didn't hit as large an area as she'd intended. Thanks to quick thinking on the part of one of the female dancers, they got me down on the floor and emptied everyone's water bottles over the affected area. Some of the dancers ran down to the bathrooms and returned with more water. By the time help arrived, most of the acid had been rinsed off."

Max placed a gentle kiss on her scars, then settled back in his seat. "You were lucky."

"Yeah. They rushed me to the nearest hospital."

"Tell me someone from the dance group went with you to the hospital," Max growled.

"No." Feeling the stifling fear and loneliness rise up inside her as if she was back in that cold, frightening hospital, Emily steered the Jeep over to the side of the road and parked. She crossed her arms over her chest, fighting the shakes. "According to the other dancers, they were told there was no room for anyone else in the ambulance."

"What? You had to endure the first few hours after the attack all alone?"

"Yeah. After being questioned by the authorities, the rest of the dancers flew home as planned. Except for Agatha, who'd been arrested. The remaining performances were, of course, cancelled." She shrugged, but from this distance she found it hard not to judge her fellow dancers. Someone should have fought to go with her. Someone should have realized that she'd want to see a familiar face. "I drifted in and out of consciousness, despite the drugs they gave me." She'd woken up a few times, scared and in pain and surrounded by strangers she didn't understand. "Once I was stabilized, the U.S. embassy arranged for me to be airlifted to a hospital in Moscow, where the treatment facilities were better able to handle a case like mine. The embassy also called my family to let them know what had happened and where they could meet me."

"So your colleagues left you alone, in pain, in a country where you didn't speak the language. Did you at least have a translator?"

"Not at first. That was what made the situation so scary. I had no idea what was going on. How badly I was hurt. What they were doing to me." Every time someone stepped into her room, she'd panicked. She put a hand to her chest, feeling once again the suffocating pressure and the spastic beat of her heart.

"Easy, Em. You're safe now."

Max's words brought her back to the present. "There was some big political event going on, so all of the embassy's usual translators were busy. They eventually found an available translator, but he wasn't comfortable around the hospital. He would turn his back whenever the medical team checked my wounds. And I was never certain if he was telling me the truth, or just whatever came to mind in order to get away from me faster." He'd made her feel like a freak. As if she'd been at fault for not understanding the language and for forcing him to be exposed to such unpleasantness.

A tear dripped down her cheek and Max wiped it away. "I'm sorry," he murmured. "I shouldn't have asked." He pulled her across the console and onto his lap.

"Max," she sniffled, "your leg."

"Screw my leg. Just let me hold you."

Giving in, she snuggled against him, searching for the warmth and comfort she hadn't received after the attack.

"How long did it take your parents to reach you?"

"A couple of days. My father chartered a jet immediately

upon the visas being approved. Once my parents and brother arrived at the hospital, one of them was by my bedside at all times." She rubbed her cheek against Max's t-shirt to dry her tears.

"I don't think the doctors and hospital staff knew how to handle my father." The memory of him giving orders to the shocked doctor brought a rueful smile to her lips. "He's very soft spoken and polite, but he has a will of steel. He steamrolled over the staff and the hospital's regulations without them quite realizing what he was doing. Plus, he immediately arranged for an expert translator with a stronger stomach to be present any time a staff person entered my room. As soon as it was safe to move me, my father made certain that I was transferred to the best burn care unit in the States."

"God, Em." She felt his lips touch her hair as his arms tightened around her. "I'm so sorry. I wish I could have been there for you."

That was her Max. So protective. "Thanks."

He stroked his thumb over her jawline. "What happened to your attacker?"

"Two of the male dancers restrained Agatha. They say she kicked and bit them, all the while screaming how much she hated me. How it should have been her dancing the lead. The local authorities arrested her and put her on trial. Last I heard, she was serving time in a Russian jail."

Max put his finger under her chin and raised her face so he could press a soft kiss to her lips. "You're so brave. So strong." He placed a line of kisses up her jaw and across her cheeks. "If I'd been there, I would have held you. Stayed with you. You wouldn't have been alone."

His words broke through all the lingering fear and loneliness the memories brought. Her mouth sought his for a long, searching kiss that tried to convey her gratitude. "It helps, knowing you're here with me now wanting to fight my old battles.

Because for a long time, I blamed myself. I told myself that if I'd paid more attention to Agatha's behavior I would have known she was dangerous. That if I'd understood how deeply she resented me, I could have said something to the director. Then, maybe she'd have gotten help before she snapped."

"No, sweetheart, that's not your fault. You can't go back and take responsibility for her actions. Besides, you weren't the only one she interacted with. No one else in the dance group recognized she was dangerous, right?"

She nodded.

He placed a kiss on her forehead. "Sometimes shit just happens."

"Like that ambush."

Max snorted and pulled back. "Oh, no, you don't. We're not talking about me." He stroked his hand over her hair. "Thanks for sharing, Em. As I've said before, you're a remarkable woman." He kissed her softly. "You ready to head out?"

She nodded and slid back behind the wheel. As she pulled the Jeep back on the road, she discovered that the memory of the attack was no longer a black cloud threatening to pull her under. For the first time, she understood that while the attack might have stolen her career, it had revealed that she could endure whatever life threw at her without breaking. As the last few days had proved, that was a valuable skill.

MAX STARED out the window of the Jeep two hours later, eyeing the growing clouds overhead. They were at the end of the rainy season and had been lucky so far that there'd been little rain. Hopefully, the storm would hold off until they reached the border, so they wouldn't have to struggle to drive through mud.

"Max, I still think it makes sense for me to help you find the plane. We can stop at my homestay village first. Get some supplies. Spend the night. Then head out when we're fresh to the festival village."

"No."

"But—"

"Em, we're white. The rebels are in the area. Do you really want to put your homestay family and their neighbors in danger if someone reports to the rebels that they've given us shelter?"

"But you can't afford the time to take me all the way to the border. Not with how slowly we've been moving!"

"I'm *not* going to put you in any more danger, Em. You're going to the embassy in the United African Republic even if I have to knock you out and tie you up." He'd do it, too. Anything to keep her safe.

The Jeep rounded another bend in the road and Emily slammed on the brakes.

Max cursed at the familiar sight. A crater had been blown in the road where a feeder road intersected from the left.

"Max, how are we going to get past? The trees are too close together for me to drive into the jungle."

The left side of the crater went all the way up to the edge of the tightly packed trees, leaving only enough room to walk, not drive. "I think there's enough room that we can drive along the rim to the right."

Emily shook her head. "What if the ground is unstable? We could end up falling into the hole."

"We're either going to have to risk it or leave the Jeep and head out on foot." He traced the distance between here and the border on the map. "It will take us days to walk to the border from here." Hiking that far would be no problem if he wasn't injured. But while his arousal had masked his pain this morning, after sitting in the Jeep for so long everything hurt. He'd hike if necessary, but he'd definitely slow them down.

Emily scowled at the crater. "I'm not a good enough driver to handle this."

"I'll do it." Yeah, it would aggravate his leg, but she was right, navigating the rim of the crater would be tricky. He considered unloading the gas cans from the roof, but figured the toll that would take on their already exhausted bodies would be worse than the danger to the Jeep's balance because of the extra weight. "You should get out and walk through the jungle to the other side."

She raised her eyebrows. "In case the Jeep falls in."

He shrugged. "Yeah."

"I don't want to lose you, Max."

He put his hand on her thigh. "I don't want to lose you, either. But there's no denying that this is dangerous. If I fail, you're in better physical shape to hike to the border." He gestured to his sat phone sitting on the console as it charged. "Take my phone. Here's the code to unlock the phone." After she'd correctly repeated it back to him, he continued, "If something happens to me, call Rene or Kristoff, and let them know. They'll tell you what to do next."

Emily swallowed heavily, then nodded. She kissed him fiercely, then climbed out of the Jeep. He checked the tires and walked the route he'd be driving to make certain that it was somewhat solid. It hurt to put weight on his leg, but he managed to ignore the pain. After he was satisfied that he could make it all the way around, he gave Emily a kiss and a wink, then got behind the wheel.

"Don't you dare die on me, Max Lansing!" Emily said before stepping clear.

He didn't let himself look at her through the rearview mirror. He didn't want to be distracted by her concern. He needed all of his attention focused on the task ahead.

As he'd expected, working the clutch with his injured leg sent pain shooting through him. And although he'd known that the vehicle didn't have power steering, he'd forgotten just how stiff the steering was. Dammit, no wonder Emily was so tired.

The good news was that the area he was driving over was fairly clear of debris, because most of it had slid into the crater. The bad news was that the ground wasn't completely solid beneath the tires. He kept the Jeep moving slowly forward, trying to keep as far to the right as possible so that at least his right tires were on more stable ground. He'd almost reached the safety of the other side when the earth gave way behind him. The back end slipped.

"Max!" Emily screamed.

Adrenaline surged through him as he struggled to keep the Jeep from sliding back. The front wheels were on solid ground, so he eased the Jeep forward until all four wheels hit the road. He kept driving until he figured he was far enough away to be out of danger. After taking a few deep breaths to steady his heart rate, he eased his aching body out from behind the wheel.

When he limped back to the crater, he saw that the rim he'd driven across had completely crumbled away. His pulse kicked once. Ah. Nothing like a close call to keep life interesting. He grinned across to Emily, giving her a thumbs-up. She raised her camera and snapped a photo of him. Ha. She really seemed to be taking to this photojournalist idea. Good for her. Not that he particularly wanted his life, or his death if he'd fallen into the crater, to be part of a documentary, but he loved that she seemed to have found a new passion.

She lowered the camera and gave him a relieved smile in return. Then she replaced her camera in her rucksack and walked into the jungle. The moment he lost sight of her, his heart gave another frightened kick. Great. Emily had infected him with her panic attacks. He'd been calm while he drove along the rim, but the prospect of her meeting a rebel or a jungle predator had him breaking out in a cold sweat.

That was one of the advantages of working alone. He didn't have to worry about the safety of his partners. Or the woman he—

Emily emerged from between the trees and strode up to him with a grin on her face. Fighting back the urge to hold her and not let go, he gave her a tight nod. "I need to take a quick break before we move out." He jerked his thumb toward the trees.

She looked at him and raised her brows, as if she suspected he was struggling with a riot of emotions. But she simply shrugged. "Okay."

Feeling like a coward, he took care of business and wrestled his fear under control. He'd just zipped back up when the ground shook so hard that he lost his balance and had to brace himself against a tree.

"Max! What's going on?" Emily had moved to the other side of the road to deal with her own personal needs.

"I don't know. Stay put while I check." Once the earth had quieted, he stepped onto the road. Way down, several miles closer to the border, he saw smoke and dust rising into the air.

Emily, of course, hadn't obeyed his command, but appeared at his side. "I think the rebels just dynamited another intersection," he said.

The sky chose that moment to open up, dumping warm rain on them as if they were standing under a tipped bucket. In seconds, they were both drenched to the skin. Fan-tastic. Just what they needed. "C'mon. Let's get back to the Jeep and get the hell out of here before the road becomes impassable."

Emily shot a worried glance toward the fading dust cloud in the distance, then turned and headed back toward the Jeep. They were about halfway there when the earth rumbled and the rim of the crater began to collapse inward. "Run!" he shouted.

She sprinted ahead, slipped in the growing mud, then righted herself and kept going. Max tried to keep up, but his wounded leg buckled, throwing him to his knees.

"Max! Behind you."

He checked over his shoulder. Christ. The sinkhole was swallowing the road. He scrambled forward the best he could as the ground beneath him tipped down toward the crater.

A new rumble sounded underground. The angle of the road increased. Debris hit them as it tumbled toward the mouth of the crater. A baseball sized rock slammed into Emily's shoulder. She lost her balance and started to slip toward Max.

"No!" Max braced his hands on her butt and shoved her forward. "Go," he gasped. "Go! I've got you. Aim for that piece of land with the trees straight ahead. It looks stable." Max gave her a hard enough push that momentum carried her to the edge of the jungle. Her hand latched onto a root and she used it as leverage to shimmy onto firm ground.

The earth trembled. Max's hands lost purchase on the muddy road and he slipped to the edge of the crater. At the last moment, he managed to catch hold of a vine and stop his fall. But his left foot dangled over empty space.

"Max!" Emily lunged for him.

His fingertips brushed hers and she grasped his hand. Before they could make stronger contact, the earth beneath him fell away, tearing them apart.

Max's entire lower body slipped over the edge. He snagged a protruding root and halted his descent as his belly met the edge of the crater.

Emily crawled toward him.

"No! Stay back."

"But I can help you."

He gave her a warning look. "We have no idea how stable the ground underneath you is. Your extra weight too close to me could collapse this entire area. So keep away. The phone is still in the Jeep. Remember the unlock code?"

She nodded and told it to him.

"Good. If I fall all the way in, call Rene or Kristoff, then get the hell out of here."

The earth gave out a little more beneath him and he tightened his grip on the root.

"I'm not leaving you!" She glared at him. "Tell me what to do."

That was his woman. So fierce. So loyal. "Fine. Get the rope from the cargo compartment. Tie it to the trailer hitch on the Jeep, then throw the end to me. Hurry."

She nodded and raced off.

He didn't know if she had enough time to get the rope and anchor him before the hole swallowed him. Ignoring the pain in his leg and ribs, he hauled himself forward until he could grab onto the trunk of a young tree. Refusing to look down at the growing hole, he focused instead on pulling himself closer to the more solid edge of the jungle.

He checked Emily's progress. She was just tying the rope off.

"Here!" She tossed him the other end of the rope, but it bounced off his shoulder.

"Sorry." She tried again. This time, he was ready and caught the end of it. Before he could tie it around his chest, the earth collapsed with a thunderous roar.

Max fell into the crater.

CHAPTER TWELVE

Emily screamed. "Max!"

Oh, no. No. NO.

The crater widened. The ground tumbled away in front of her, forcing her to back up. But she didn't take her eyes off the place where Max had disappeared.

She was beginning to think that the crater would just keep growing, forcing her to retreat farther along the road, when with a final shudder the earth went eerily still. In the silence, she heard the trickle of dirt inside the hole where the rain hadn't reached yet. The crater had to be at least four hundred yards across. Pebbles pinged as they tumbled down. The rain had stopped, but water dripped off the ends of leaves and runnels of water snaked into the crater.

Other than those small noises, the birds and insects were quiet. Probably scared away.

The rope she'd tied to the Jeep was taut. That was good, right? It meant Max probably had hold of the rope and was hanging down the wall of the crater, waiting for the earth to quiet before climbing out, rather than being buried under dirt and mud and unable to move.

Her rapid breathing sounded loud in the silence. But she didn't have time to calm down. She raced to the Jeep and grabbed the second rope she'd seen in the cargo compartment. After tying that to the hitch as well, she stretched out on her belly and crawled forward. After every small movement, she paused. Listened for any sign the earth had started another underground collapse. It seemed like forever before she neared the edge of the hole. But she was afraid to get too close, certain the edge would give way.

"Max? Max, can you hear me?"

Nothing.

Her stomach pitched. "Max? Answer me. Please."

Silence.

"No. I won't let you be dead. You hear me, Max Lansing?" Muttering curses in as many languages as she knew, she wriggled forward a few more inches, freezing when the edge of the crater collapsed no more than a foot in front of her.

When the ground stabilized, she called out again. "Max? Can you hear me?"

A faint response filtered out of the hole. "Here."

She whooped in joy. He was alive! The world blurred behind a curtain of tears. Swiping at her face, she blinked the moisture away. She didn't have *time* to cry.

"Pull," Max called weakly. "Jeep."

"Hang on!" She crawled away from the edge. Once she reached a safe distance, she stood up, raced to the driver's seat, and put the Jeep in gear. The tires slipped in the mud and it took her a moment to figure out how to compensate. Then she inched the vehicle forward. She didn't want to move too fast. If Max was hanging from the rope, not braced on some protrusion along the side of the crater, then his arms would be killing him. Not to mention the strain on his cracked ribs. And the fall might have torn open the wound in his back.

She needed to haul him up carefully. Slowly.

No matter how strongly her instincts insisted she had to get Max out of there *now*.

FEET RESTING ON SOME UNIDENTIFIABLE, narrow surface, Max spat another clump of dirt out of his mouth and tightened his two-handed grip on the mud-slicked rope. He shook his head, trying to dislodge the stuff covering his head, but only succeeded in getting dirt in his eyes. Damn, that hurt. He shut his tearing eyes. If only—

The rope jerked him up. He gasped at the sudden pull, then promptly coughed as dirt slipped into his mouth. When his upward motion stopped, he stuck his toes in the wall of earth in front of him and rested his head against it.

Bad idea. Water slid down the surface, turning the dirt under his cheek to mud and dissolving his foothold. Only his hold on the rope saved him from plummeting into the hole.

Great. Just what he needed, a slippery wall to climb. For once, couldn't life cut him a break?

Eyes still closed, Max hunted around with his toes until he found what felt like a rock sticking out from the side of the crater. Then he waited for the next lift.

Between the incremental pulls from Emily and his novice attempts at blind climbing, he made steady progress. But he really wished he had some idea of how far he had yet to go. Did he have feet? Inches? Yards?

Christ, he hoped the top was near. His arms were shaking, he had rope burn on his hands, and his wounded leg had pretty much gone numb. When sensation returned, he'd be in a shit-load of pain.

Yeah, like he should complain. He was just lucky to be able to feel anything. He could have been dead.

Right. Not going there.

He waited for the next tug on the rope, to time his foot

moving up. When it didn't come, his heart thumped. He spat out the remaining dirt from his mouth. "Emily?" His voice was little more than a whisper.

Dammit, he should have told her to run. Even though the tremors had stopped, that didn't mean she wasn't in danger from any rebels who'd decided to come back this way to check their handiwork. Or maybe Ziegler had finally found them. If he caught her...

"Emily!" This time, fear gave him the strength to vocalize loudly. If she was nearby, she'd hear him.

He rubbed his eyes against his arm, but that only smeared mud over his lids. He cracked open his lids, but the world was just a brown blur. Growling in frustration because he had no idea how far he was from her, he closed his eyes and shouted, "Dammit, Emily, say something. Are you okay?"

"Sorry!"

Max's body sagged. He'd never heard a sweeter word.

"I had to make adjustments to the pulley system. I'm back now."

"Don't do that again without warning me first! You nearly gave me a heart attack, thinking you'd been captured by the rebels."

"Oh..." He imagined her brows scrunching together in that cute way she had when she was surprised or confused. "Um...all right. Give me a sec to get into position. I'm not going to use the Jeep for this part. I'm going to use a pulley system to pull you out on my own. I can just see the top of your head. The good news is you don't have far to go. The bad news is this final distance will be tricky. You'll see a big root system sticking out to your right in about three or four feet. If you can aim for that, it should give you enough leverage to boost yourself up to the rim, then I'll grab you and help you the last few feet."

God, he loved her strength. Not many people would still have the energy to pull him out of this hellhole after everything Emily had been through.

He heard dirt shift as she moved away.

"Wait!" he called up.

"What?"

"I can't see. I've got dirt in my eyes. You're going to have to talk me through this."

"Oh. All right. I'll give you five more pulls, then I'll pause to come back to the edge to look down and tell you where you are. Okay?"

"Yes." No. He didn't want to lose the sound of her voice. Hadn't realized how being alone in the dark had affected him until he heard her speak. Hadn't recognized until now that the pressure in his chest was due to fear for her safety. But he had to let her do her job. "Go ahead."

"Good. Give me until the count of ten to get over to the pulley. One, one-thousand…"

Right on the count of ten, Max felt another tug on the rope. The brief rest had done him good, and he pushed off with a bit more strength than last time. He almost forgot to count the tugs, though. What he thought was five counts later, he heard Emily's voice.

"Excellent. You're just slightly above and to the left of the roots. Perhaps the length of two of your arms. Can you sidle sideways until I tell you to stop?"

Hell. At this point, he'd let go and fall if she told him he'd be okay. Moving his good leg sideways wasn't a problem. But while he'd been able to move his bad leg vertically and put some weight on it, the lateral movement caused a sharp tear of pain. He clenched his teeth and leaned his head against the dirt as he rode out the wave of agony.

"Max? What's wrong? Is it your leg?"

He had to wait until the pain subsided before he could answer. "Yeah."

"This isn't going to work, is it? You can't put weight on the leg going sideways."

"Yes. I. Can." He spat out every word. "I am getting out of this hole. Now." O-kay. That sounded a bit panicked. But dammit, the pain had thrown his sense of balance off and he didn't know how much longer he could stay oriented before dizziness caused him to fall. He was *not* going to leave Em on her own.

Taking a chance, he let go of the rope with his right hand, found a handhold in the dirt, and used what little strength remained to drag himself sideways until he touched a root.

"Good. You've reached the outer roots. Keep going."

Max inched his right hand and foot over, following Emily's concise, matter-of-fact instructions.

"Okay, now. Reach up with your right foot. There's a root about the size of your biceps sticking out at roughly knee level." Her voice painted such a clear picture, Max almost forgot that he couldn't see. And her voice calmed the part of him that was on the verge of panic.

"If you can stand on that, you should be able to reach the top."

"Is the edge stable?" he asked. He felt around for the root, then slowly hoisted himself up.

"This section of road seems to be propped up by that root system. There's another root sticking out of the ground a little bit closer to safety. I think your arms are long enough to—"

His hand eagerly closed over the bent root, eliciting a laugh. The sound of her laughter sent another spiral of dizziness through him. This was a good dizziness, though. Her laugh made him happy.

Unfortunately, it also messed with his balance and he felt himself start to pitch backward.

"Oh, no, you don't!"

The rope he held in his other hand snapped taut, stopping his momentum and pulling him up onto his toes. "Get up here, Lansing. Now."

"Yes, ma'am!"

Using what felt like the last of his strength, Max pushed and pulled himself over the edge of the crater, aware that Emily also tugged on the rope. He slowed when he made it all the way out, but she wouldn't let him rest.

"Following the wise advice of someone I know, you need to get away from the edge, Max."

He knew she was right. But goddamn, he was tired. Now that he didn't have to hold up his weight, the trembling in his arms rivaled the quake caused by the explosion.

"Come on, Max." Emily's soft, cajoling tone cut through his exhaustion. "You can do it. Just a little farther."

Those last few feet were agony. He almost passed out a couple of times. But Emily's voice kept him anchored. Like his drill instructor back in the Marines, she berated him. She seemed to understand that giving him orders would spur him to just... keep...going...

"Okay. You can rest now. I think we're far enough away."

He collapsed face down. Started to open his mouth to tell her thank you, but darkness consumed him.

EMILY STROKED Max's filthy hair back from his face. Blood from a gouge on his temple still trailed sluggishly down to his cheek. A thick smear of mud covered his eyes.

Pouring a little water on her bandana, she gently wiped the blood and dirt away. Then she took a long drink.

Now that Max was safe, the tension that had kept her alert started to ease. Fear crept in and her hands trembled.

Stop that. She had to get them both to the Jeep and off the road in case the rebels showed up.

Pushing to her feet, she jogged to the Jeep. Having learned

how to manipulate it on the muddy road, she backed up slowly until she couldn't get any closer without putting them both in danger of destabilizing the rim.

She tossed a tarp over the sleeping bags to protect them from Max's muddy clothes. Then she returned to him. "Max?" What if he didn't wake up? She wasn't strong enough to get him into the cargo compartment herself.

He opened his eyes.

Smiling in relief, she knelt beside him. "Can you help me get you into the Jeep, or should I use the tarp to drag you?"

He bent his arm, tried to lever himself up, then fell back with a grunt.

"I said help me, you idiot," she grumbled, putting her arm underneath his upper back. "Not force yourself to pass out from over exertion. Now, let's try that again."

With her support, he managed to get first onto his hands and knees, then eventually all the way to his feet. He swayed a moment, leaning so heavily on her that she stumbled forward. That brought him close enough to catch hold of the Jeep's back door handle. With that additional support, they got him into the cargo compartment and onto the tarp.

"Comfy?" she asked, tucking the tarp around him like a blanket.

"It'll do."

She smiled at him. Thankfully, aside from the gouge on his forehead, he didn't appear to have any major new wounds, although the rope burns on his palms had to sting. "God, Max, I was so scared."

"Yeah, me too." He latched onto her hand. "I'm sorry you had to rescue me, Em. Thanks."

She knew how much that had to have hurt his male pride. Knew how much she'd hated being an invalid after the acid attack. "You're welcome. But I think we're even now, since you saved my life by getting me away from the way station before

Ziegler or his companions could kill me. Now, rest. I'll get us out of here."

"Keep aiming for the border," he demanded. "It's safer." He closed his eyes on the last, barely whispered word and passed out.

Emily watched him a moment. Relief that they'd survived turned her legs to jelly. A lone tear escaped and crept down her cheek. She bent forward and kissed Max lightly on the lips, then shut the cargo compartment door.

Time to get back on the road. She sent a wary look toward the sky as she slid into her seat. Not only was rain threatening again, but the light was fading. She only had about an hour and a half until dark on a sunny day. With the cloud cover, a lot less than that.

Okay. She could do this. Aware that driving on the road was dangerous, but unable to find a clear path through the jungle, she headed north.

Several times Max groaned so loudly, she stopped to check on him. His temperature kept rising and she worried that he was fighting malaria or some other parasite she couldn't counteract. She did manage to get him to swallow some water laced with crushed aspirin and antibiotic. She wanted to strip Max of his clothes and wash both them and him, but not only didn't she have the time, she was afraid of depleting their diminishing water supply.

Each time she finishing tending to him, she found it harder to return to her seat and dredge up the energy to wrestle with the stiff steering. Particularly once the skies opened up again and the mud deepened, sucking at the tires.

Even though Max had warned against it, she kept an eye out for a village or some other place where they could stop. She couldn't keep going much—

A large truck lumbered into sight down the road. Oh, God.

Oh, God. It looked like one of the rebel troop transports. What if they spotted her? They'd start shooting. Kill her and Max.

Wishing he were awake to tell her what to do, she eased the Jeep as far over to the side of the road as possible. C'mon. C'mon. She needed a break in the trees wide enough that she could drive between. She wasn't ready to die. She had to hide. She had to—

The truck turned away and headed north.

Emily's breath whooshed out of her with dizzying speed. She put on the brake and lowered her head to the steering wheel. They were safe. For now.

It took her heart a long, long time to calm down. When she finally felt able to drive again, she saw that two more trucks had joined the first one. She still couldn't see any insignia, so she didn't know if they belonged to the government, Dietrich, or the rebels. Whoever they were, she had to get off the road in case they changed direction. Because the rain was so heavy, the ruts of her tire tracks immediately filled with water, leaving an obvious trail.

Finally, after ten minutes of searching, she located a break in the trees wide enough for the Jeep to fit through. She continued driving deep inside the shelter of the trees until she felt confident no one on the road would see them. With any luck, the tracks she'd left on the road would smooth out before anyone came looking for them. Hoping they were safe, she parked for the night and forced herself to eat a little of their nearly non-existent food supplies.

It was odd. A month ago, her biggest concern had been weathering the stares of the people at the grocery store when they saw her scars. Despite her emergency training, that girl had never been directly exposed to violence beyond Agatha's attack. She would never have imagined that soon she'd be driving through the jungle, on the run from violent rebels, and caring for a wounded, feverish man by herself.

Yes, she was scared. Who wouldn't be? Her life was in danger.

Yet at the same time, the fact that she'd gotten Max out of that crater by herself filled her with pride. She wasn't nearly as useless outside of the dance world as she'd thought. She was strong and adaptable. Maybe she *could* find another career that would fill the empty space in her soul where dance had always lived.

But what about Max?

That was the million dollar question, wasn't it? Because the thought of saying good-bye to him at the end of this adventure threatened to bring on another panic attack.

Just take it a day at a time. Don't borrow trouble.

Telling herself it would all work out, she crawled into the back, snuggled up next to Max, and fell into an uneasy sleep.

CHAPTER THIRTEEN

Day Eight

MAX JERKED BACK to consciousness and opened his eyes. Where—?

Rucksacks. Bags of supplies. Sleeping bags. Right. He was in the Jeep's cargo compartment. The surface underneath him jolted as the Jeep bumped over the rough road. Pain slammed into him the next second. His ribs, lower back, and leg all hurt, reminding him of what he'd been through. His head ached. His mouth was parchment dry and had a faintly chalky taste, as if someone had fed him medicine.

Emily. Rebels. Crater.

Hell. How long had he been out? Hours? Days? The gray, watery light made it hard to tell what time of day it was.

"Em?" he croaked. But even to his own ears the sound was barely audible.

Okay, then. He'd just have to drag his sorry ass up to the passenger compartment. And he'd get right on that once his head stopped throbbing so fiercely. After a few minutes, he attempted to raise his hand, thinking he could hold on to one of the rucksacks and pull himself upright, but although he strained to move, his body remained stubbornly stationary.

All right. He'd rest a bit more and then try again. He waited, using every technique he knew in order to ignore the pain from his various injuries, but without much success. A little voice that sounded remarkably like Rene's chastised him for pushing himself too far. Yeah, it didn't take a smug doctor to tell him that he'd used up all of his reserves. At this point he felt so weak, he wondered if he'd ever move again.

Yes. I. Will.

He tried once more to lift his hand, but the effort proved too much. Blackness engulfed him.

The next time he woke up, the Jeep wasn't moving and it was pitch dark. "Em?" His voice, though still quiet, seemed to echo in the interior. Worse, he didn't hear Emily's breathing.

Panic beat through him. "Em?" he called louder.

Still no answer.

Had Dietrich's men found her? The rebels? Was this how it was going to end? Left alone to starve to death in the back of a Jeep? While the rebels or Dietrich did God only knows what to Emily?

Failure. Always letting down the ones you love.

Hell, no. He had to sit up. Had to—

A door opened. Because they'd kept the overhead light turned off, he couldn't see who it was. "Em?" he tried again.

"Max?"

Seconds later, the cargo compartment door opened and Emily appeared in front of him. "Oh, my God, you're finally awake!"

She grinned and scrambled into the cargo compartment, then placed a quick kiss on his mouth. She pulled away too soon and sat beside him. "How are you feeling?"

He tried licking his lips so he could speak louder, but found he didn't have enough moisture in his mouth. Luckily for him, she understood.

"Right. Water." Putting her arm under his neck and shoulders, she raised his head until it rested against his rucksack, then held his water bottle to his lips. "Drink as much as you want. While you were unconscious, I found a stream and replenished our supply." She grinned at him. "I love these quick-filter bottles."

The warm, slightly flat water tasted like ambrosia. Knowing he had to take it slow, he didn't suck down the great gulps that his body demanded, instead allowing his parched tissues to soak it in gradually. When his head started to spin from being upright, he closed his eyes and turned his head away.

"Max?"

"Give me a sec. Dizzy."

"Do you want to lie back down? Are you in a lot of pain?"

"No. Not lying down. Pain not important."

Emily snorted. Max opened his eyes and saw her shaking her head in exasperation. "Max, you have cracked ribs, a knife wound, the equivalent of a stab wound in your thigh, a gouge on your forehead deep enough to worry me, and numerous other cuts, scrapes, and bruises. You've been unconscious and running a fever for the past two days. So, any macho man points you think you're earning by pretending you're fine have long since expired."

She held his gaze. Max fought the urge to squirm as the look intensified, threatening to rip out all of his darkest secrets. He didn't want Emily knowing the worst about him. That he wasn't some hero. That he stumbled along, trying to do the best he could, but always failing the ones he loved or respected.

He cleared his throat and tore his glance away. Searched for something to say to break the tension. But Emily beat him to it.

She reached forward and touched the back of her hand to his forehead. "Better." She sat back on her heels, then held up a baggie containing several bottles of pills. "I've been feeding you water laced with aspirin, your pain medication, and your antibi-otics. But now that you're awake, you can take them yourself."

He glared at the pills. No wonder his head felt muzzy. It was the pain medication. "Dammit, you know I hate pain meds. Just give me the antibiotic."

She rolled her eyes and shook three pills onto her palm. "Compromise. Two aspirins and one antibiotic. Happy?"

In answer, he swallowed the pills and washed them down with some water. Man, he felt more stable already. Amazing what effect being upright and hydrated had on his body. "Where are we? What's been going on?"

Emily glanced away. "I'll explain everything, but first we need to get moving."

Wait. Was that guilt in her voice? Dammit, what was she hiding?

"Do you want to rest some more?" she asked.

"Hell, no." He felt too helpless lying back here, cut off from seeing what was in front of them.

Emily rolled her eyes and gave him a wry smile. "Okay, then. Let's see if we can get you up front. Uh—" She bit her lip. "Do you need to...ah...answer nature's call first?"

The instant the words left her mouth, his bladder sent up an emergency flare. "Yeah. Thanks."

"All right."

She eased him out of the cargo compartment and to his horror the simple act of getting vertical made the world spin. He clutched the edge of the door and held on for dear life so he didn't face plant on the ground. When he finally felt a bit stead-ier, he admitted, "I...ah..." He cleared his throat. "I'm not going to be able to make it into the woods."

"No problem. I'll be up front. Holler if you need help."

Relieved that she understood his dilemma, he took care of business. Then Emily helped him into the passenger seat.

She pulled the night vision goggles over her eyes and put the

Jeep in gear. As the vehicle lurched forward, Max could just make out that they were in the jungle.

"So where are we?"

"We're just outside of my homestay village."

"What do you mean your homestay village? Dammit, Emily, you were supposed to head for the border."

She turned her head toward him and he knew she was glaring at him beneath the goggles. "I *did* try for the border. But that first evening I saw a bunch of those rebel troop transports down the road, so I had to hide in the jungle."

"So? You still should have headed north. God, don't you understand by now how much danger we're in?"

She gave an angry hiss before returning her attention to their path. "I tried to head north, Max. I really did. But the jungle at that point was too thick. I barely managed to find a place to enter the jungle from the road. Trying to navigate the tangle of dense bushes and close trees was a nightmare. Every time I tried to get back to the main road, I had to make so many detours that I got lost."

"Why didn't you call for help?"

She gestured angrily at the sat phone. "I couldn't get a signal under the thick canopy." She sniffed and swiped a hand under her nose. "By the time I remembered the compass on your watch, I was already so far off course I'd almost reached the road to my homestay."

"We're not stopping there."

Her shoulders jerked up. Oh, no.

"I already did. I just got back."

"Goddammit, Em!"

"What? I'm not a complete idiot. I snuck in. Prudence, my homestay mother, was the only one who saw me. She wished me luck and gave me some food." She nodded over her shoulder to the small nylon sack behind her seat. "I was only gone maybe fifteen, twenty minutes."

"What the hell were you thinking?" She could have been hurt. Captured. Or—

"You don't get it, do you?" Emily snapped. "You nearly *died*! Do you have any idea how scared I've been? How tired I am of running? Of being constantly on the verge of a panic attack because I'm afraid I'll run into a patrol of rebels and get us both killed?" She inhaled twice in rapid succession. "I'm doing the best I can, Mr. Super Soldier. I'm sorry it doesn't meet with your approval, but we were out of food. I've been so on edge that I've barely slept in days. So yes, I took the risk and asked for help."

"Christ, Em. I'm sorry. But—" Sweat trickled down his spine. If the rebels had been in the village, or worse, Dietrich's men, Emily could have been captured or killed. He could have lost her. All because he'd been unconscious.

No more.

The Jeep bucked as it left the jungle and turned onto a dirt road.

"Stop the car."

"What?" She glanced over at him.

"Stop. The car. Now."

"Why?"

"Because you don't fucking listen when I say there's danger." He reached for the wheel.

"Okay, okay. I'm stopping already. Sheesh." Emily slammed on the brakes and Max bit back a grunt as he nearly hit the dashboard.

"Get out. I'm driving."

"Max, don't be ridiculous." Emily yanked off the night vision goggles and glared at him. "You've been unconscious for over two days. You haven't had anything to eat. There's no way you're strong enough to drive."

"And you've been driving without sufficient food or rest for two days. You're making bad decisions. Ones that might get us killed."

She flinched.

"So I'm driving."

"Oh, I get it," Emily muttered. "Now that the big, bad, macho soldier is feeling better it's time for the little woman to retreat. Is this where I'm supposed to be barefoot and in the kitchen?"

"No. It's time for the *trained professional* to handle a potentially deadly situation."

"Fine. Whatever." She pushed open her door, slid sullenly out of the driver's seat, and stomped around the front of the Jeep.

Max had just put his hand on the door handle when several men holding AK-47's stepped into the road. Two of the men turned on flashlights, revealing that they were dressed in civilian clothing.

Emily froze.

Another man stepped out of the jungle, seized Emily's arm, and dragged her toward the others. As he did, he let the rifle in his other hand point to the ground. The other villagers weren't as sloppy. They pointed their weapons at Emily. None of them seem to realize yet that she wasn't alone.

Max palmed the pistol he'd stashed between his seat and the console.

"No. Wait!" Emily struggled, but the man backhanded her, then shoved her toward the other men so hard, she tripped and fell.

A wave of fury hit Max, but he forced himself to think past it.

The man snatched a fistful of Emily's hair and yanked her to her knees.

"What are you doing?" she cried. "You're Ebo, aren't you? Don't you remember me? I'm Emily. I stayed with Madame Prudence."

"I know who you are, *obruni*. The rebels will give us much reward money for you. Plus, we will take your vehicle." He raised his rifle toward Emily's head.

Max shoved open his door and pulled himself upright. The

pistol felt as heavy as a sandbag as he brought it up, braced his hand on the top of the door, and fired. The man standing above Emily fell. She screamed, but had the sense to roll toward the safety of the Jeep.

The rest of the men gaped at him in shock. Yeah, they hadn't expected Emily to have company. Or to meet lethal resistance.

Their mistake. Max fired just to the left of the nearest man, close enough that the man dropped his weapon and leapt to the side. "Let us go or I will kill another." If, as he suspected, they'd never witnessed a shooting before, his threat should be enough. "Throw your weapons onto the road and move away."

The men glared at him.

Out of the corner of his eye he saw Emily climb to her feet. "Emily, honey, are you okay? Can you drive?"

"Yes." With a quick glance at the dead man, she climbed behind the wheel.

"Start the engine and turn the headlights on. That will temporarily blind them." Max shifted his grip and fired at the feet of the man he figured for the leader. "What's your decision?" he called.

The man spat on the ground, put down his rifle, then stepped off the road. The others followed suit.

Max lowered himself into his seat. "Go!" he ordered as he shut his door and slid his window down. He leaned out and fired back toward the men to make sure they didn't pick up their weapons and return fire.

The Jeep leapt down the road.

When the men had faded from sight, Max drew his head back into the Jeep and raised his window.

"Are you okay?" he asked.

"I'm fine," she said. But her voice was subdued and she had a white knuckled grip on the steering wheel. "You killed Ebo."

"He hurt you." She had blood trickling from a cut on her lip and the shadow of a bruise on her cheek. The men were lucky he hadn't killed them all in reparation.

"I know." Her mouth turned down in an unhappy line, but at least this time she didn't yell at him for doing what he'd needed to do. "I can't believe he was willing to turn me over to the rebels. I mean…"

"He wasn't going to hand you over. He was going to kill you. He'd raised his rifle toward your head. That's why I shot to kill."

"B-but… He said he'd get money for me from the rebels."

"Of course. The rebels pay a higher bounty for dead foreigners than those turned in alive."

She paled. "That's… That's…"

He shrugged. "Reality. You can't trust anyone in this area that you haven't known for years. The villagers could probably live for weeks on the bounty they would have received for you." Max refrained from saying "I told you so." It wouldn't help.

Emily lapsed into an uneasy silence.

When Max judged they'd driven far enough away from the hostile villagers, he said, "Pull over and shut the lights off."

This time she obeyed without question and let him take the wheel.

"I'm sorry, Max," she said after she'd settled into the passenger seat and handed him the night vision goggles. "That was my fault. I should have been paying attention to my surroundings when I got out of the Jeep. I've had enough self-defense training that I shouldn't have frozen when Ebo grabbed me. But I guess I'm really not equipped to handle any of this."

Max sighed. "You're tired. Stressed. Afraid. It's difficult to make the right decisions under those conditions unless you've had extensive real life experience. That's why you need to listen to me when I tell you not to do something."

"Yes, okay, I screwed up. Can we please drop it?"

"All right." The angry, regretful silence that filled the Jeep nearly suffocated him. He maneuvered the Jeep into the jungle, heading roughly north. "Why don't you grab us some of the precious food from your homestay mother? Although for all we know, it's poisoned."

"Now you're being paranoid." She retrieved the bag from behind his seat. "I refuse to believe that Prudence had anything to do with those men accosting us."

"Don't be naïve."

"Stop being so damn suspicious. Prudence could have sounded the alarm when I knocked on her door. She didn't. But if you're too afraid to eat the food..."

Max shook his head and stared at the artificial green landscape created by the night vision goggles. How had he ended up on the wrong end of this argument? *She'd* made the mistake in judgment. *She'd* put her life at risk. Yet *she* was mad at *him*?

Emily pulled something out of the bag and bit into it. "There. The bread is safe. Okay? Now eat this."

She handed him a piece of soft, white, Western style bread smeared with groundnut paste.

He chewed cautiously at first, then with more enthusiasm as hunger hit him.

"So where are we going?" she asked once she'd fed him another three pieces.

"Far enough away that the villagers won't come after us." He glanced over at her. "Tell me more about the people you met during your homestay. Did you sense any hostility while you were there? See anything to indicate that they sympathized with the rebels? There's an underground smuggling network in this area. Based on how those villagers were armed, they're likely part of that."

"What? Smuggling?" She shook her head. "I didn't see any signs of that. They're a poor village, with no electricity. They don't even have a vehicle of their own, but share one with the villages down the road. I felt welcome. Sure, I was a bit of a novelty, but they seemed to accept me." She shrugged. "I really don't know what else to say. I spent most of my time with the women and children. I thought that was because the men weren't interested in the dance, but maybe it was also a political statement."

"Or they didn't want you learning about their smuggling activities."

"Maybe." She sighed. "You know, I wasn't even supposed to be housed there."

"Really? What happened?"

"The scheduled village pulled out. I don't know why. Our tour guide, Kofi, just handed me a revised itinerary and assured me that this village would be safe and welcoming for a foreigner. That he had friends here who would look after me."

"The other village might have decided that the rebels would eventually move into this area and they'd be at increased risk of harassment if everyone knew they'd offered shelter to a white lady."

"It sounds so mercenary stated like that."

"Emily—"

She sighed. "I know. I'm too trusting. But all this danger and intrigue is so far removed from the world I live in that it's really hard to get my mind to accept the situation."

"That's why—" He hit the brakes as he heard the sound of a helicopter. "Shit."

"Oh, the helicopter," Emily said. "Don't worry, it should pass by in ten, fifteen minutes."

"You say that as if it's happened before."

"It has. Assuming it's the same one, it's been flying overhead on and off for the past couple days. Never this late at night, though."

"And you didn't think to mention this before? Christ, Em, they could be hunting us." As far as Max knew, and his information was good as of a couple of weeks ago, Dietrich didn't own any aircraft with infrared technology, but he might have a crew out doing a visual search. "Did you notice any identifying marks? Did they hover over the Jeep?"

"No. I don't know who it belongs to," Emily said. "The first time I heard it I parked the Jeep and climbed a tree to use the binoculars. It was painted army green. So maybe it belonged to the government?"

That made sense. The rebels didn't have any air capacity and the government would want to know what the rebels had done to the roads. It would be safer for him and Emily if the helicopter belonged to the government, but he wasn't going to risk their lives on a guess.

"The helicopter spent a lot of time back by the explosion site, so I don't think it was looking for us," Emily said. "Still, I stopped each time I heard it, trying to stay unnoticed by not moving." She shrugged.

Max removed the night vision goggles and glanced over at Emily. She really had dealt with a hell of a lot since he'd passed out. Now that he had a moment to pay attention, he saw that her pant cuffs and sneakers were caked with mud. Lines of strain bracketed her mouth. Dark circles gave her eyes a sunken, haunted look and a bruise darkened her cheek where the villager had hit her.

Fierce protectiveness filled him, momentarily stealing his breath. "I'm sorry."

Her brows scrunched together. "Why?"

"For not protecting you. For being a burden instead of a help." *For being a failure.*

She shrugged. "It's not your fault you got hurt and ended up with a fever."

But if he'd been awake, he would have stopped her from going anywhere near her homestay village and she wouldn't have been hurt.

Her hand landed lightly on his forearm. He stared into her eyes and saw her lingering fear. His anger died and he sighed.

She wasn't trained for these types of situations. He had to stop expecting her to anticipate or follow orders like one of his teammates.

He reached out and cupped her jaw, careful not to touch her bruise. "I'm sorry I yelled at you, Em, but you scared me. You've got to promise you'll be more careful. Listen to me when I say there's danger."

She pulled away and crossed her arms over her chest. "Max, I understand the danger. I'm not stupid. I made the best decision I could in order to keep us both alive."

Crap. He knew better than to push her on this when she was so emotional. But the thought of anything happening to her filled him with cold terror. "You won't need to make such decisions. I'm awake now. I've got this."

The increased volume of the helicopter's noise prevented her from answering beyond narrowing her eyes at him.

Max lowered the window to listen, hoping he'd be able to tell if the bird belonged to the government or Dietrich. Unfortunately, it sounded like a Russian build. Which meant it could belong to either group. God, he couldn't believe he was going to ask this. "Em, I need you to take the night vision goggles, climb that tree," he pointed out the windshield at a tree with a medium sized trunk and plenty of low hanging branches, "and see if there are any identifying marks on the helicopter."

She shot him a look. "Are you kidding me? You just reamed me out for making bad decisions and putting my life at risk. Now you want me to leave your all-mighty protection and go climb a tree in the dark?"

He ground his teeth. "Yes. Please. I can't plan our next step if I don't know who's paying so much attention to this area."

"Wow. Bet that hurt to say, Mr. Professional." She snatched up the night vision goggles and the binoculars and opened her door.

"Yeah, you have no idea," he muttered as he watched her disappear into the night.

Twenty minutes later, with the helicopter no longer audible, Emily slid back into her seat. "I can't really tell the color because there's not enough moonlight, but it appeared to be solid black. I didn't see any markings on it."

Yeah, figured. Max started the Jeep. "What shape was it?"

"Um... Well, it wasn't the little bug-like ones that they use for the news. Its nose stuck out just a little bit—more pug than schnauzer. The length of the body looked to be the same length as the tail, which had one smaller set of rotors. Oh, and it had three wheels. One in front and two in back."

"Not bad. You've got pretty good recall."

She just shrugged. "I'm used to watching a choreographer demonstrate a series of moves only once before I have to replicate the moves. Dancers develop really good memories or else they don't advance very far."

"Nice." He slowed and turned back toward the road because the trees here grew too close together to let him drive between them. He figured they were far enough away from any village at this point to risk driving on the road, particularly since they weren't using headlights.

"So, did that help?" Emily asked.

"Yes, and no. Since you didn't see any insignia, it probably belongs to Dietrich. The government would have their national roundel—a circle with their flag's colors—visible. Any legit aircraft would have some identifying mark. Which way did it go?"

"It flew left, toward the main road."

"Did it aim straight for the road or did it move back and forth in a search pattern?"

"It kept going."

"Okay. That's good. It means we're not being hunted yet and that they're not searching for the plane on this side of the main road." Even if Dietrich knew they were in the area, he and Emily had an excellent chance of staying hidden as long as they kept to the cover of the jungle.

"What now?" Emily asked.

He wanted to keep driving, to get as close to the border as possible, but the adrenaline was wearing off and the wound in his thigh had started to throb again. "You should climb into the back and sleep. As soon as I find a safe place to pull over, I'll stop for the night."

"What? Is your reserve of superhuman strength finally giving out?"

"Em," he growled.

She exhaled heavily. "Sorry. Forget it." She leaned her head back against the seat. "Just...do whatever you have to do."

Dammit, he was getting really tired of feeling like the unreasonable one here. But he bit his tongue and focused on his driving so he wouldn't say something to make it worse.

CHAPTER FOURTEEN

Day Nine

THE NEXT MORNING, Max had just climbed out of the cargo compartment to take care of personal needs when Emily called out, "Max, the phone has a failed incoming call notification."

He gave her a wave and limped back to the Jeep. Swallowing his pride, because his leg hurt like a mother this morning, he hauled himself into the passenger seat. "Can you find us a place with a clear line of sight to the sky?"

She nodded, took a swig from her water bottle, then settled behind the wheel. "How are you feeling?"

He managed a crooked smile. "Better than yesterday. Not as good as I'll feel tomorrow."

She frowned, as if she didn't believe him. Great. Last night had destroyed her trust in him.

He cleared his throat. "So, where are we?"

She held out her wrist and he saw that she was wearing his watch. Dammit, it was already several hours past sunrise. They should have been on the move by now. Yet one look at Emily's pale, drawn face and he knew he couldn't yell at her. She'd needed sleep as much as he had.

Tamping down his frustration at their lack of progress, he unbuckled his watch from Emily's wrist and activated the GPS feature. Then he pulled out the map. Hopefully they weren't too far off course and would be able to make it to the border by the end of the day. It would be cutting it close, but if Kris still didn't have a team available to replace him, he should have time to come back and find the weapon before Dietrich's deal.

Emily braked in the middle of a small clearing. "How's this?"

He stuck his head out the window and looked up. "Should work." Afraid that his leg wouldn't hold up if he stood for long, he smacked the antenna onto the roof of the Jeep, then checked his phone. No surprise, he had a missed call from Kris.

"Where the hell have you been?" Kris demanded when the call went through.

Max gave a brief summary of the sinkhole and his injuries, relayed their current coordinates, and explained his timing regarding the embassy.

"Scratch that. Remember that wanted poster you conveniently forgot to tell me about?"

Max grimaced. "Yeah."

"Someone took it a step further. The governments of Volta and the UAR are on the lookout for you as a suspect in Emily's kidnapping."

"What?" He glanced over at Emily. "But she's fine. Didn't you contact her family?"

"We passed the word through a trusted source. I'll follow up to see if her parents actually received the message." Kris paused. "You're listed as armed and dangerous. Possibly an accomplice to Ziegler and the rebels in the deaths of the other Americans."

"Shit."

"Yeah. You know Dietrich has to be behind this. He doesn't want you escaping this time."

Max sighed and ran his hand over his hair. The last thing they needed was a trigger-happy soldier who spotted him and fired without noticing Emily in the Jeep. Like hell he was going to risk her being shot because of this bullshit. "So, what do you suggest? The border is closed to the east. Even if we entered illegally, the U.S. embassy there shut down weeks ago. The rebels are to the west, south and northwest of here. I was hoping she'd be safe in the UAR if we snuck over the border."

"Do what I assigned you to do in the first place. Find the briefcase with the weapon prototype. Then you and Emily sit tight. I'm working on clearing your name so you can cross safely over the border."

Max cursed. Yeah, they were close to the suspected crash area, but he was in no shape to go tromping around the jungle. And with armed villagers on the prowl, the idea of letting Emily go out on her own made him want to pound his fist into the nearest tree. "Kris—" he started. Then he stopped himself. What could he say? The whole freaking region was one giant danger zone. Emily wouldn't be safe until she stepped onto a plane. Complaining that it was too dangerous for her to help him look for the plane wouldn't change the facts. Remaining in this area near her homestay village might be risky, but right now it was their best option.

He blew out a breath. "Dammit. Fine. We're on it." He hung up and tossed the phone on the console.

"What's going on?" Emily asked.

Max clenched and unclenched his fists, but that small action didn't calm the warring frustration and fear inside him. "We're going after the damn prototype."

"I thought that was the plan all along."

"No, the plan was to get you safely over the border and for me to return alone. But there's been a complication."

Emily narrowed her eyes. "What?"

"I'm wanted in connection with your kidnapping."

"My *kidnapping*?" She gaped at him.

"Yeah. Apparently I'm armed and dangerous and I'm also working with Ziegler and/or the rebels."

She raised her brow. "Max, you *are* armed and dangerous. But you're not a public threat... Oh." She cleared her throat. "Er...maybe..."

"Will you get over it already? I'm trained to protect. I shot that guy last night because he hurt you and would have killed you if I hadn't." For Christ's sake, he was a soldier. What did she expect from him?

"Your reason doesn't matter to the locals. To them you *are* a threat. You killed those rebels back in your friend's deserted village and you killed Ebo. So the locals will likely believe anything negative they hear about you."

"Right. Which means we need to stay out of sight. Get you to safety. Not wander the countryside looking for the damn plane."

Emily shook her head. "You said that the prototype will be used in an attack that could kill hundreds. I'm sorry, but a little more risk on our part seems a small price to pay to save innocent lives."

MAX STARED at her like she was crazy. "You almost died last night!"

Her stomach gave a slow, twisty turn. "Yes, I know. I'm not an idiot. That terrified me." She'd come so close to being killed by someone she'd thought meant her no harm. "But Max, we're far enough away from my homestay village that it's unlikely we'll run into any of them. As long as we drive through the jungle, we can get close to the festival village without being spotted. Then I can sneak over to the village, find the path I used that day when I headed out to take pictures, and hopefully locate the piece of the plane you spotted in that photo."

"I'm not staying—"

She leaned forward, cutting him off. "Max, you're in pain. Do you think I can't recognize the signs? Your ribs and back hurt. The wound in your thigh hurts. I bet you even have a headache."

The faint tightening of the muscles around his eyes let her know her guess was correct. "Tromping through the jungle is only going to tap your dwindling energy. If we're going to find the briefcase with the prototype weapon and the plans, you need to be rested and thinking clearly. Don't be an idiot and insist on coming with me just because you think it's your job to protect me. I'm the healthy one. Let me carry my weight by doing reconnaissance."

He glared at her, but she was unimpressed. "Max, give it up. Ten to one you won't even make it fifteen minutes without keeling over. And then where will I be? How am I supposed to drag your deadweight back through the jungle to the Jeep?"

He glanced away. Crossed his arms over his chest. Scowled. "I hate being injured."

She reached out and touched his face. "I know." Understanding that she'd won, she started the Jeep.

"You'll be careful. Stay out of sight. Be quiet."

She nodded. "Of course. I have no desire to end up a prisoner of the rebels or the lunch of a jungle predator."

Max kept his silence until they'd reached a spot not far from the festival village, but not so close that their engine would be heard. Then he launched into a detailed explanation of how to conduct a search and what type of debris she might discover. When he was satisfied that she understood what she needed to do, he reminded her about stealth tactics.

"Yes, Max. I know. I do have some stealth training. And over the past few days I've learned how to adapt it for the jungle. I'll be fine."

He didn't look like he believed her, which hurt, but then he nodded. "You're right. I'm sorry. I just want you safe."

"I know." She squeezed his hand. "But it will be okay. You'll see." She reached for her backpack. "I'd better get going, so I don't lose the light."

"Take my phone with you," Max said as she collected her things, "so you can call Kristoff for help. And my watch, too. That way you can log your coordinates. Like this." He pulled his watch out and showed her how to use the GPS and compass to track her progress and save the final location. "See? I've logged in the location of the Jeep. So when you do find the area we're searching for, you'll know how to get back to me."

"Thank you." She leaned in and gave him a quick kiss. "Here, hold my watch until I get back." She slipped it off and handed it over. "Now, let me camouflage the Jeep."

With Max giving pointers, Emily used windfall branches, leaves, and the dark green mosquito nets to disguise the Jeep. Anyone walking close by would see the shape of the vehicle, but from a distance, or from the sky, the Jeep would be hidden.

As she was getting ready to leave, Max held out his gun.

"I'm not taking your gun! What if you need to defend yourself?" She took a step back.

"Don't you know how to shoot? I thought your dad was big into preparedness."

"Yes, I can shoot. That's not the point. The point is that you're injured. If the bad guys show up you can't run and hide. You need the gun more than I do."

"This isn't negotiable, Emily. Take the damn weapon or I'm coming with you. I need to know that you can protect yourself if you run into a rebel or a hostile local."

She sighed. "What about you? What if a bad guy shows up? How will you defend yourself?"

"I have a knife." He told her where to find it among his things.

When she found it, she had to admit that the matte black knife with its finely honed edge definitely had been made for combat. "I don't think this is going to do you much good against a rifle. Or a shotgun."

He shrugged. "You'd be surprised. Besides, if someone does shoot me, they'll probably come over to check if I'm alive. That gives me a chance to stab them and get away."

Her heart lurched. "Max, do you honestly think you're going to be in any condition to use the knife if you're shot? Your body will probably just shut down."

He shook his head. "Adrenaline will see me through. I'll be fine. I'm more worried about you. Promise you'll come back quickly."

"I'll do my best." She met his eyes. Saw worry and frustration and other things there she wasn't ready to address, so she turned her head. "Okay, fine. I'll take the gun." She checked it over, then slipped it into the holster Max attached to her belt.

"I'd better get going." She slid her arms into her rucksack's straps. Max had insisted that she carry some food and basic survival supplies, including the night vision goggles, in case the worst happened and she couldn't make it back before nightfall. She also had her camera. That way, if she found pieces of the plane, she could photograph them at a closer angle.

"Be careful."

"I will." Throwing Max a jaunty salute that in no way reflected the nervous butterflies dancing in her stomach, she headed off.

Half an hour later, the compass indicated that she was almost to the village. She allowed herself a brief, congratulatory smile. If anyone had told her a month ago that she'd become adept at walking through the jungle, she'd have laughed at them. But it wasn't too scary once you got to know it. Max had shown her what plants not to touch and described the poisonous snakes and insects she needed to avoid. She now navigated the undergrowth with more confidence than she'd expected.

Unfortunately, the blisters on her feet had reopened. The hours of driving had allowed them to harden, but between digging her heels in the mud to pull Max out of the crater and this trek through the jungle, she knew that if she removed her shoes she'd find her socks once again stained with blood. The more tired she became, the harder it was to ignore the pain. On the other hand, focusing on the pain kept her attention sharp whenever she started to lose focus and her thoughts drifted.

By the time the jungle opened up to reveal a small garden and a mud hut, Emily was exhausted. Keeping an eye out for jungle threats took a lot of mental energy. Needing a few minutes to recharge, she found a root she could use as a stool and helped herself to a long drink of water and a small snack. Then, somewhat reenergized, she walked back to the outskirts of the village.

Chickens pecked at the dirt in front of a sapling fence that enclosed a tiny garden. She didn't spot anyone nearby, but outside a hut closer to the center of the village, a woman hung washing on a line.

Emily stayed well back in the trees, hoping the shadows would hide her. She needed to figure out where she was in relationship to the spot where she'd exited on the festival day. The road and entrance to the village were to her right. So she faced left and closed her eyes. Brought up the memory of following Prudence and the other women into the village. They'd left the road and walked along a dirt alley that led between several huts before ending at a large, circular space in the middle of the village.

The morning of the festival there'd been dancing and singing in the center of the village. At midday, Emily had eaten lunch sitting on a bench, surrounded by children who'd peppered her with questions regarding America. Not many of them had spoken English, so one of the teenagers who'd attended the regional boarding school had served as translator. Then, while the village sat down for a worship service—a mix of Christian and animist beliefs—Emily had decided to take her camera into the jungle and explore.

Following directions from one of the village's women, she'd walked between some huts and exited past a small garden.

Emily opened her eyes and turned her head. Was this the same garden?

After some study, she decided that this spot was too close to the entrance to the village. She walked away from the road until she spotted a second garden. That one looked familiar. And yes, a few feet beyond it she came across the footpath that led from the village into the jungle.

She checked the time on Max's watch. On the festival day, she'd set her watch's alarm for fifteen minutes and had turned back only once the alarm sounded. Since she'd been afraid of getting lost, and too nervous about encountering bugs and snakes to venture into the undergrowth, she hadn't veered off the footpath.

After several minutes of walking and checking her photos for reference, she reached a dead tree that showed up in her photographs. She remembered being fascinated by the brilliantly colored fungi on its bark. Unfortunately, the tree marked a split in the path. Which way had she gone? She'd been so busy scouring the trees, hoping to catch sight of some exotic birds or animals, that she couldn't remember which path she'd taken.

She tried left. A few minutes of walking led her to a partially weeded field. Nope. She hadn't seen this spot on her previous trip. She'd just taken a few steps back the way she'd come when she heard voices. Treading carefully, she slipped between two trees, then took shelter behind a wide palm. She slipped off her rucksack and lay down on her belly. Through the leaves she could just barely see the path she'd been on.

The sound of several people talking in the local dialect grew closer.

Her heart pounded fiercely in her chest. Was this a group of rebels? What if—

A group of three women and two men came into view. The men wore stained, khaki trousers and loose, faded t-shirts. The women had tied brightly colored cloths around their waists to form skirts and also wore faded t-shirts. The men held hoes and other farming tools. The women carried shallow baskets on their heads.

All of them looked vaguely familiar, so they must have come from the festival village.

When they reached the field, the women set the empty baskets down not far from Emily. Oh, God. They were so close. If they looked up, they'd surely see her. And then what? Were they friendly? Or, like her homestay villagers, would they turn on her?

She dug her fingers into the earth as she felt the first flutterings of panic. *No.* She had to stay calm. Max wouldn't be able to save her if this situation turned dangerous. She had to think of a plan on her own.

Engrossed in their conversation, the women paid no attention to the jungle. They passed out baskets and received hoes in return, then the entire group spread out and began to weed.

Emily held herself still. But as the work continued and no one glanced in her direction, she gradually relaxed.

Okay. Now she had to figure a way to wiggle deeper into the jungle without drawing attention to herself. Then she could return to the path and continue her search. Still on her belly, she straightened her right leg, then her left. Pushed up with her hands.

One of the men in the field shouted an alarm.

Emily froze. Didn't dare to even breathe. Had they spotted her? Was she in danger?

Lowering herself back down, she twisted her neck until she could see the far end of the field. Two men reached into the branches of a thick bush and pulled out something white, roughly rectangular, and almost the length of the taller man's arm.

One of them gestured excitedly and the women hurried over.

Was that a piece of the plane? Emily felt for the binoculars attached to her pack. Max had told her that the lenses had a special anti-glare coating on them, so she felt safe using them. Glasses in hand, she brought the object into focus. Sure enough, the white object definitely appeared to be manmade. From the ragged shape, it could have been a piece torn from a falling plane.

Afraid to use her camera because it didn't have no-glare lenses, she marked the GPS location on Max's watch. The workers examined the piece for several minutes. Animated hand gestures indicated some kind of discussion. Then one of the men shrugged and they tossed the piece back into the jungle.

Emily created a rough map in her head. If, as she suspected, the white object in her photo had been taken on the other side of the fungi tree, that was east of here. Max had said that data indicated the plane had been flying east to west. So the rest of the plane probably lay somewhere to the left of where the farmers had found today's piece.

She eyed the jungle around her. Nope. Too thick. She wasn't skilled enough to move silently through that tangle of vegetation. With a sigh of resignation, she realized that she'd have to wait for the villagers to leave before she could investigate. She checked the time on her watch, but she had no idea how long it would take to fill the baskets. Or whether they had other tasks to perform once the weeding was done.

So she stayed in position as the day advanced. The temperature increased. Insects buzzed around her. Sweat beaded on her skin. Moving an inch at a time, she eased her water bottle off her backpack and took a long drink, unwilling to risk dehydration. After a few hours the helicopter flew overhead. She grimaced. Max would freak out when she didn't return after a reasonable amount of time, particularly with the helicopter still nearby. Hopefully, he was smart enough not to come searching for her. Under normal circumstances she had no doubt that Max could sneak through the jungle. Given his wounds, she suspected he wouldn't be nearly as stealthy as this situation required.

The villagers quickly filled the baskets with weeds. But

instead of taking the nearly overflowing baskets away, the women carried them to a spot not far from where the men had found the plane debris. Emily raised the binoculars again and saw a small, three-sided fire pit with concrete block walls. The villagers dumped the weeds on the ashes, then returned to the field and continued working.

Great. Looked like she'd be here all day. Emily sighed, and settled in to wait.

At some point, she dozed off. When she awoke, over an hour had passed. Her stomach rumbled, but she didn't dare unzip her pack to retrieve any food.

By the time the entire field was weeded and the uprooted weeds burned, the sun was well on its way toward the horizon. Emily almost cheered when the group finally gathered their supplies and headed back down the path.

She gave them fifteen minutes to get back to the village, then pushed to her feet. Her muscles were stiff after so many hours in one position, so she eased her body through a series of stretches. Once she could move without wincing, she ate some groundnuts and dried mango and washed them down with a huge drink of water. Then she shouldered her pack, slung her camera around her neck, and headed toward the spot where the villagers had found the plane debris. When she located the piece, which sure looked like it came from a plane, she snapped several photographs from various angles and marked the spot on the GPS.

She investigated further, moving steadily to the west and northwest of the field and found a few more pieces scattered haphazardly throughout the jungle. As she'd thought before, it appeared that these were pieces that had fallen off while the plane was still in the air.

She looked up as she walked, picturing the plane disintegrating as it fell. She imagined the panic of the courier and the desperate attempts of the pilot to forestall the crash as they—

Her right foot fell into space and her stomach pitched like a falling plane. Her dancer's reflexes kicked in and she threw her weight backward, grabbing the nearest tree before she fell head-first into a gully. Oops.

Peering down into the small gap between the thick canopy of trees growing at the bottom of the ravine, she spotted another piece of debris. She marked the GPS location, then checked the sky.

Shoot. Dusk was falling.

Still, despite the hours-long delay, she was satisfied with her work. Once again stowing her camera in her rucksack, she set the GPS toward the Jeep and hurried through the jungle.

Toward Max.

HALF AN HOUR AFTER EMILY LEFT, Max's body had simply shut down despite the worry gnawing at him. Now, after sleeping for nearly three hours and grabbing a meal from the limited supplies provided by Emily's homestay mother, he felt stronger. Not ready to take on one of Dietrich's men in hand-to-hand combat, but not invalid weak, either.

His mind sure as hell was sharper today. Unfortunately, it had already concocted a dozen different scenarios where Dietrich's men or the rebels captured Emily. He'd always sucked at waiting. If he didn't have a mental problem to chew on, then he needed physical activity to keep him busy. He had to find a way to occupy his time until Emily returned or he was going to do something stupid. Like get behind the wheel and drive after her.

Blowing out a frustrated breath, he climbed out of the Jeep.

He hobbled around the vehicle several times in each direction, testing his strength. When he felt his energy flagging, he opened the cargo compartment and organized their remaining food supplies. Shook out the sleeping bags and rearranged them. Checked the levels in the water bottles and wondered what the odds were of finding a stream. Figuring it was worth a search, he gathered up the water bottles. He'd just closed up the Jeep when he heard the helicopter.

Shit.

This time it sounded as if the chopper was traveling west to east, and at nearly top speed.

Was it Dietrich's? If so, what was he up to? Had he found the location of the plane? Is that why the helicopter was in such a hurry? Was it on its way to retrieve men to start a new search on the ground? Were he and Emily on the wrong trail?

Or did the helicopter belong to the military? Were they searching for Emily, believing he'd kidnapped her?

He waited until the helicopter passed out of earshot, then headed out to look for water. A few minutes later he found a sluggish stream and filled the water bottles. Thanks to the advanced filtration system, he was able to drink immediately. After refilling his bottle, he carried the bottles back to the Jeep.

He glanced at Emily's watch. Ugh. Only an hour and a half had passed. Great. At this rate, by the time she returned he'd be a raving lunatic.

Dammit, he should have set a time limit. Told her that unless she returned by a specific time that he'd assume she was in trouble and go looking for her. Not that he was in any shape to run through the jungle on a rescue mission.

He couldn't even take the Jeep and search for her, because what if she arrived to find him gone?

He rubbed his temples. Okay, what else could he do to occupy his time? Bracing his hand on the Jeep, he decided that a cane would come in handy.

He limped over to a nearby tree and used his knife to shape a thick branch into a workable cane. Then, walking very slowly, he found a banana tree and picked as much fruit as he could carry in the sling of his shirt. The fruit would stretch their current inventory of food.

By the time he got back to the Jeep he was drenched in sweat and shaking with exhaustion. He barely managed to set the fruit in the cargo compartment and crawl inside before he crashed.

He slept for another couple hours and awoke reenergized. He drank some water, ate a few bananas, and took another antibiotic pill. Then he slid out of the cargo compartment and frowned at the sky. The sun was going down. Where the hell was Emily? The Jeep wasn't that far from the village. She should have had plenty of time to walk there, find her photography spot, and be back by now.

Fear crept up his spine and he paced back and forth along the Jeep, balancing himself with his new cane as he tried not to think about the possibility that Emily might have been caught while he'd been sleeping. He hated to admit it, but he'd slept deeply enough not to notice any cries of triumph if the rebels or villagers had found her. If Dietrich's men had snatched her, they wouldn't have made any noise.

Dammit, this wasn't helping.

Of course, she might be delayed for a less sinister reason. Maybe she'd sprained an ankle or suffered some other injury. Even walking through the jungle now that the light had nearly faded was dangerous, as the evening brought out certain predators. But at least she had the night vision goggles. And basic medical supplies.

He really wanted to search for her, but since he didn't know what direction she'd be returning from, he was likely to miss her in the growing darkness. Argh. He beat his head lightly against the side of the Jeep. He was stuck here. God, how he hated this.

With one more angry glare at the sky, he leaned on his cane and started walking another circuit around the Jeep, determined to build up his strength and endurance so he wouldn't have to send Emily out on her own again.

Come on, sweetheart. Come back to me.

IT WAS full dark by the time Emily stumbled across the Jeep. She'd been walking so long that she'd begun to wonder if the GPS was mistaken and she'd taken a wrong turn. Or maybe she'd camouflaged the Jeep a little too well. But finally she spotted the mosquito-net-covered vehicle. She was so happy to see it that she almost wept.

The passenger side door opened. "Emily! Thank God."

She pulled the goggles off as she hurried toward Max. He enveloped her in a tight hug, but the weight of her rucksack threw them off balance and they fell against the front of the Jeep.

As soon as they were balanced again, Max pulled her against him, kissing her with fierce desperation. She dropped the goggles and ran a hand soothingly over his hair and down his back as she gentled the kiss. Then she shoved at his chest. "Let me get the backpack off, Max."

He grunted, but only gave her enough room to slide free of the straps and drop the pack to the ground before his mouth returned to plunder hers. His body pressed her against the Jeep and his erection pushed against her belly.

Her exhaustion fled as the urgency of his kisses transmitted itself to her. Heat flared, igniting nerve endings that she'd thought numbed for the night. But no. This was what she wanted. What she needed. To feel Max's body against hers. To touch her tongue to his, drinking in his uniquely addictive flavor. To run her hands over the tight muscles of his back while his hands cradled her head, holding her still as he made love to her mouth.

He made her feel beautiful. Whole.

Her fingers dipped under his shirt, finding bare skin slick with sweat. She kneaded the supple muscles beneath her fingertips and urged him closer. Slid her hands up his back until the rough texture of gauze stopped her cold.

She pulled away. "Max! Your wounds."

"Don't. Care. Need you." He took her mouth in another voracious, possessive kiss.

An unexpected wildness rose up inside her and she met his aggressiveness with a fierce possessiveness of her own. He nipped her lip. She raked him lightly with her nails. He nibbled on her scars. She closed her teeth over his earlobe.

Max's palm cupped her bare breast. She gasped as lightning shot to her core. Sneaky man. When had he opened her shirt and unfastened her bra?

Giving her a wicked smile, Max lowered his mouth and took her nipple between his lips. He suckled hard, and she grabbed his head, digging her nails into his scalp to keep him in place. "More."

He worked her breast with his mouth while his fingers lightly pinched and shaped her other breast. When he lifted his head, she whimpered in protest and twisted, trying to get closer to his heat and power. Max silenced her with a kiss. Then his fingers undid the snap on her cargo pants. She shimmied her hips, helping him push her pants and panties down her legs. He lifted her to sit on the hood of the Jeep, then, bracing himself with his hands, he knelt awkwardly between her legs.

"Max! Don't hurt—"

His mouth touched her most intimate flesh and her protest was drowned by a cry of pleasure. Her head fell back as his tongue and lips teased her, bringing her right up to the edge. "Max, I'm going to come!"

"Good. Do it." He removed one of his hands from her hips and thrust two fingers inside of her. He curled one finger against the spot that drove her crazy at the same time he lightly clamped down on her clit.

She exploded, the pleasure bursting through her and destroying all the tension of the past couple of days. She forgot who she was. Forgot the danger they were in. All that mattered was the heated pleasure that arched her back and tore a cry from her throat.

Before she'd fully recovered, Max rose to his feet. She heard the faint crinkle of a wrapper, then he thrust inside her. She gasped as her sensitive tissues protested the invasion and Max stilled. Once her body had adjusted, she nodded. He planted one hand next to her on the hood to support his body, then started a steady, gentle rhythm, peppering her face with kisses in between thrusts. His free hand stroked her throat and her breasts. Gradually the pleasure built inside her again. She started matching his thrusts. He increased the tempo and his touches became firmer. Relentless. More demanding.

The pleasure continued to ratchet up until once again the pressure became too much and she exploded. Only this time, Max was with her. She heard his satisfied roar mingle with her own exultant cry. She stroked her hand down the back of his head to his neck and along his spine. Realized that he still wore his shirt.

She heard an odd sound from the jungle and froze. "Did you hear that?" She glanced toward the trees.

"What?" He pushed away from her and withdrew.

"I don't know."

Max removed the used condom, tied it off, and set it beside her on the hood. Then his hands settled gently on her hips. "I'm glad you're back," he said quietly.

Her mouth quirked up on one side. "Yeah, I kinda gathered that."

"Smartass." He tapped her on the tip of her nose and she grinned at him. She couldn't remember when she'd last felt this lighthearted.

The sound came again. "There. Hear it? It sounds like someone's cutting wood."

"Yeah, I hear it." He stepped away from her and yanked up his pants. "Get inside the Jeep."

Obeying the urgency in his command, she slid off the hood, pulled up her panties and pants, and refastened her bra and her top. "Why? What is it?"

"That sound is called a grunt. It's a male leopard's way of warning us this is his territory."

"Oh." The leopard called out again, and this time it sounded even closer. Emily snatched up the night vision goggles from where she'd dropped them and darted toward the driver's seat. Remembering her backpack and camera, she started to turn back, but saw that Max had already tossed them into the passenger seat.

They'd just closed the doors when a shadow detached itself from the trees. Emily wanted to turn on the headlights so she could see better, but was afraid that she'd scare the big cat away. Instead, she watched the leopard through the lens on her camera.

"Wow," she breathed. The leopard strolled toward the Jeep with the aggressiveness and arrogance of a predator defending his territory. She fired off a series of shots, hoping that the windshield wasn't distorting the images too much.

The spotted cat stalked without hesitation to the side of the Jeep where she and Max had just made love. For one panicked moment Emily feared that Max had left the condom sitting there, but then she saw that the hood was empty. Wanting a better view, she crawled over to the passenger seat and put one knee between Max's legs and the other on the floor.

The leopard sniffed the side of the Jeep and the ground beneath it, then glanced up at her. Max's hand tipped her head forward. "Don't meet its eyes," he whispered.

With her head bent, she peered up at the cat through her lashes. The leopard grunted so loudly, chills slithered down her spine. After a couple more grunts, the leopard peed on the Jeep's front wheel, looked around, then leapt onto the hood. He turned his head toward Emily, staring at her through the windshield.

She cowered back and dropped her eyes. "Easy, Em. He can't get through the glass." Max touched her back between her shoulder blades. The reminder that she wasn't alone, that she was safe, pulled her back from the primitive fear she felt at the leopard's challenge.

The leopard swiped at her with his paw. His claws scraped down the windshield. Shaking his head, he backed up. Swiped at her again. When he still failed to connect with Emily, he grunted, then paced across the hood several times, his tail switching. Finally, he grunted another challenge, then peed on the hood before leaping off and stalking back into the jungle.

Emily let out a shaky laugh and clambered back to her own seat. "Oh. My. God. That was amazing. Scary, but so damn cool."

"Yeah." Max leaned over and brushed a kiss across her cheek. "I know you must be exhausted, but we need to find somewhere else to camp tonight. Just in case he comes back. I can drive."

Emily shook her head. "It's okay, I'll drive. We won't go far, right?"

"Just until we've put a little space between us. Leopards have a huge territory, but hopefully he won't bother us again if he thinks he's run us off."

"All right." As she drove, Emily told Max what the villagers had found and how she'd spotted the piece in the gully. "I think the rest of the plane is down at the bottom."

"Good work."

Max's voice sounded strained, so Emily glanced over at him. "Max? Are you okay?"

He didn't respond, just put his hand on her thigh and squeezed lightly. She thought back over what she'd said. "Max, it all worked out. The villagers didn't spot me."

His grip tightened. "That..." He shook his head. "That was too close. What if they'd been hostile? If they'd been actively searching for you?"

She didn't want to remember the fear she'd felt when she'd heard the voices. Didn't want to risk triggering a panic attack, so she tried to make light of it. "Yes, well, you've trained me well. I'm much better at sneaking through the jungle than before."

Max just shook his head.

By the time they reached the road, the energy boost Emily had experienced during their bout of lovemaking had evaporated. "Where to? I have to warn you, if you want to cover a lot of distance, then you'll have to drive. I'm on the verge of collapse."

"Pull over to the other side and find the first level place that's out of sight. We could both use a good night's sleep."

Hallelujah! For once, the man wasn't going to ask her to push her limits.

No, that was unfair. He hadn't pushed her out of spite, but necessity.

Regardless, when she finally found a place for them to spend the night, she barely had the energy to force down the food Max insisted she eat before she stretched out in the cargo compartment and fell into a deep sleep.

CHAPTER FIFTEEN

Day Ten

After sleeping late the next morning, Max watched as Emily quickly and efficiently cleaned and bandaged her bloody, blistered feet. He hated seeing the proof of the pain she was in. She'd already been hurt enough.

But like him, she had the fierce will of a warrior who kept going despite the pain. Only, Emily was very clear about how far she could push herself without negatively affecting her performance. Something he wasn't so good at. He had a tendency to work until he dropped, particularly now that he was working alone. Kris had always been good about stopping him before he hit that point.

He rolled his shoulders. Yet another reason to consider joining Kris's team when it was safe.

As Emily finished doctoring her feet, he had to admit that maybe, if he'd been paying more attention to his body's signals of exhaustion and gotten some rest, he would have noticed the guys following him that night in Ouaga. Then he wouldn't have ended up as Ziegler's prisoner.

He couldn't afford to make such a mistake with Emily's life.

Once she'd put away the medical supplies, Emily drove the Jeep as close to the ravine as possible, only stopping when the closely grown trees prevented them from moving forward. After camouflaging the Jeep, Emily led him into the jungle.

Max watched her carefully, but she moved without a limp. Unlike him. Thanks to the aid of his tree branch crutch, he was able to walk at a slow, but steady pace today, but he definitely had a hitch in his step. Yeah, between the two of them, they weren't exactly in prime shape to be playing jungle explorer.

Fifteen minutes later, Emily stopped and gestured in front of her. "There's the gully."

Max moved forward and looked down. He couldn't tell what part of the plane the white square belonged to. Roughly the size of a microwave oven and charred around the edges, it could have belonged to any manmade item.

"Not much help, is it?" Emily said.

"No. Pass me the binoculars." He searched the vegetation at the bottom of the ravine, but due to the thick canopy, didn't spot any more pieces. So he moved to his left several yards and searched again. Saw another glimpse of white in a thinner section of vegetation. "Okay, it looks like the plane headed across the ravine as it broke up."

"What would have caused the plane to break apart like that?" Emily asked.

"I can hazard a few guesses. First, weather. Turbulence from a bad storm could have put too much stress on the plane, resulting in structural failure." He shrugged. "But I don't think there have been any violent storms recently."

"None while I was at my homestay."

"Okay. A more likely scenario is a section of the plane—such as the tail or the tip of a wing—was hit by a surface-to-air missile. Maybe fired by the government, although we haven't seen any signs that they have ground troops in this area. So it's more likely that the plane was shot down by either a competitor of Dietrich's or local smugglers." He glanced over at her. "That would explain why the group from your homestay village was so well armed."

Emily flinched, but didn't jump in to defend the villagers. Progress.

"So... What?" she asked. "Someone leaked the plane's route to a group they knew would destroy the plane? Wouldn't that run the risk of the prototype activating?"

Max nodded. "You're right. We don't know exactly what the weapon does, but from the fact that the jungle hasn't been obliterated, the briefcase must have prevented the weapon from discharging." But if it had detonated—

He grasped her hand and held on tightly.

"Max?"

"If the weapon had detonated while you were at your homestay village, you might have been killed."

"Okay, that's a pretty scary thought. But it didn't happen."

Yet it was the type of outcome that Max faced all too often. Proof that his world was just too violent for her safety. And yet, he didn't want to let her go.

Not now. Not ever.

A few heartbeats later, Max forced himself to release her hand. Shit happened. He knew better than to get distracted by what-ifs. The prototype hadn't detonated. Emily was alive. All he could do was deal with whatever today threw at him.

This overwhelming fear for her safety was a direct result of working alone so long. Without the support of a team, and with him operating at less than full strength, the likelihood of failure was high. Plus, having events out of his control always set him on edge.

Yet it was more complicated than that. Caring for Emily, wanting to protect and shelter her, had brought parts of him back to life that he hadn't even noticed had been dormant. He suspected he was a better man because of it, but didn't know if he was a better soldier.

"Who would leak the plane's route if there was such a potential for disaster?" Emily asked.

"Dietrich's men both fear and respect him, so I doubt there's a traitor among his ranks. Maybe an employee at the manufacturer discovered the threat and thought this was the best way to stop it from falling into the wrong hands. Or it's possible that the buyer has a traitor among his men." He shrugged. "Of course, the plane might simply have suffered from a mechanical failure. Something that caused a small internal explosion that breached the plane's hull and caused the wind to tear the plane to pieces."

Emily glanced skeptically at the piece of debris barely visible at the bottom of the gully. "Shouldn't there be more stuff?"

Max shrugged. "We don't know how high or how fast the plane was flying. This might only be the edge of the debris field. I'm not an expert on plane crash dynamics, so I have no clue what the trail should look like. But I think debris can stretch for several miles. Plus"—he nodded toward the debris—"I bet more pieces of the plane are down there, just hidden by the thick vegetation."

Emily shot a look at him. "Max, I'm going to have to go down into the gully to investigate."

Every instinct immediately rejected that idea as too dangerous. He glanced at the nearly solid tangle of brush that started a few feet down from the rim.

"I—" she began.

He held up his hand, thinking he heard the sound of rotors. Yes. There. Faint, but growing louder. "Helicopter's coming. Quick, get deeper under cover."

Ignoring his command, Emily put her arm around his waist and hustled him farther into the jungle until they stood under the protective foliage of several trees. Max leaned his back against the trunk of the widest tree and pulled Emily flush against him.

They waited tensely while the helicopter made several passes over the area. Shit. Unlike the previous flyovers, this time it sounded as if the helicopter was moving methodically back and forth in a search pattern. Either they knew Max and Emily were here and were searching for them, or more likely, they had tracked the missing plane here.

Had Dietrich managed to get his hands on infrared technology? Were he and Em in imminent danger? Tightening his arms around Emily, he waited for the helicopter to fly away.

He kept them in position for ten minutes more, until he was certain the chopper wasn't going to make a surprise reappearance. "Okay. Let's move."

"Mmm," Emily murmured drowsily.

"Em! Are you falling asleep on me?"

She blinked up at him. "Yep. Sorry. Can't help it."

"Damn it, I'm sorry. I shouldn't have woken you so often." He'd made love to her in the Jeep twice more during the night.

She put her hand over his mouth. "Shh. It's not your fault. I could have said no." The smile she gave him was that of a well-satisfied woman. "But I didn't want to. Besides, we slept in." She pressed a kiss to his mouth. "I think I'm sluggish *because* we slept late. My body just got out of rhythm. Don't worry, once we start moving again, I'll sharpen up."

"I know you will. You're resilient like that."

Emily rewarded him with a deeper kiss. Mmm... He loved the way their mouths fit together so well. Loved that kissing her now felt like coming home. "All right," he said. "The helicopter changes things. We need to get into the gully and locate the brief-case as soon as possible." If this helicopter was equipped with thermal imaging cameras, then he and Emily were racing against the clock.

"We?" She did that eyebrow raising thing that he was coming to love.

He sighed and pressed his forehead against hers. "Okay, I give up. *We* have to find a path into the gully so that *you* can retrieve the briefcase."

"That's right."

For a long moment they remained like that, forehead to forehead, breathing one another's air. So peaceful and connected that he wished they could stay like this. Because he was terrified that if he let Emily out of his sight, something awful would happen and he'd never see her again.

She broke the spell by pulling away. Walking over to the edge of the gully, she stared down, shook her head, then walked several paces to the left. "I'm not seeing any safe path down. There's no slope here, just a sheer drop to the tops of the trees."

Max hobbled over and checked to the other side of her. He cursed. "You're right. You need a place with minimal vegetation or at least low-growing bushes you can easily break through. Some place without too many branches that could snag the rope you'll have tied around your waist. Not too steep an angle, so you won't slide all the way down. Gentle enough that you can climb back up carrying the briefcase."

"Still nothing," she called from several yards away.

"Okay. Let's split up again," Max suggested. "You go left. I'll go right. We'll meet back here in half an hour."

Unfortunately, the part of the gully that Max examined was more of the same. A straight drop from the edge through an impassable tangle of trees and bushes. When they met up again, he shook his head. "No luck. You?"

"Maybe," she said. "Come look."

The spot she led him to had a steep, but manageable slope that after a hundred yards or so ended at the crown of a large tree with branches big enough to hold Emily's weight. The slope was dotted with bushes she could use to slow her descent, but it also had enough space between the bushes for her to move freely. "We don't know what happens to the ground after that tree," he pointed out. For all they knew, the ground dropped away after that.

"I know, but I don't think we're going to find anything better." She shrugged. "Besides, worst-case scenario, the ground becomes too steep for me to walk down. I step into the tree's branches and hope I can climb safely to the bottom."

Max's stomach lurched. Without walkie talkies, they wouldn't be able to communicate once she reached the tree. Just as bad, the satellite phone wouldn't work under the thick canopy covering the gully, leaving her no way to call Kris for help.

Yet, he suspected they hadn't seen the last of the helicopter. Whether it had been searching for him and Emily or for the plane, they couldn't waste any more time. She needed to do this now.

He checked the position of the sun, then his watch. It was only ten-thirty. "You have plenty of time before the sun starts going down. Let's say that you'll return no later than five." At that point, the light would be fading, but full dark wouldn't hit until six or so.

Emily nodded.

He glanced at her feet. "Do you think you can navigate the slope with your backpack on?"

She shrugged, then eyed the slope. "Honestly, given my blisters and how tired I am, I don't think I'm up to balancing the weight of the pack on such unstable ground. Not with that steep an angle. Maybe you can use the rope to lower the pack to me after I've reached the tree?"

"Good idea." He searched for the rope while Emily slipped out of her pack and removed several non-critical items. "Make sure you take first aid supplies and the night vision goggles with you." He'd put a new battery in the goggles before they left the Jeep.

"Yes, Max." He didn't have to look over to know she was rolling her eyes.

A moment later she showed him the contents of her fanny pack. "Is this acceptable?" She'd packed her camera, one of the bags of groundnuts from her homestay mother, and a few basic medical supplies. At his nod, she fastened the bag around her waist, then checked that her water bottle sat securely within its special holder.

"All right, found the rope. Take this extra piece with you." He passed it over, then looked around for a sturdy bush. "I'll anchor you from here with this other rope. Once you reach the tree, I'll send down your rucksack."

After tying the rope to the trunk of the bush and testing it, he rummaged in his pack again. "Here, take my knife. You might need it to free the briefcase."

She grimaced. "In case I have to cut it away from the courier's body."

"Yeah." He'd already explained about the various setups for secure briefcases and that if the courier was chained to the brief-case, the chain would be unbreakable. He'd also warned her that the case would probably be booby trapped to destroy—or acti-vate—the contents if she tried to open it. "You've got the surgical gloves?"

She nodded.

Knowing he had no other choice than to let her get on with it, Max tied the rope around her waist.

"Okay," she said. "I'm ready."

"Be careful." He gave her a fierce kiss, trying to infuse good luck into her.

"I will." She threw him a jaunty wave, but he saw her under-lying tension. And exhaustion. Nerves tightened his belly. He would have given anything at this moment to be strong enough to make the trip in her place.

Hands clenched at his side, he watched as Emily sat on the edge of the steep slope, then reached forward to grab hold of the nearest bush.

"Take it slow, sweetheart."

She nodded. After pulling against the bush to test that it would hold her weight, he saw her shoulders rise then fall before she slipped off the edge and put her feet on the ground. She teetered a moment and Max leaned forward, not that he had a chance in hell of catching her if she lost her balance. But she quickly steadied herself.

She took one hesitant step. Then another.

She gave him a thumbs up before shifting her grip to another bush and Max slowly let out the breath he'd been holding. Okay. Maybe this was going to work after all.

DESCENDING the slope was partly exhilarating and partly terrifying. Emily gained momentum as she went, but managed to use the bushes to slow her progress until she reached the edge. The ground there dropped quickly away, leaving a gap of about a foot between her and the tree. Fortunately, the wide branches in front of her appeared sturdy enough to hold her weight.

She waved up at Max and untied the rope from her waist. Then she waited for him to lower her backpack. After rearranging the items that had shifted during the trip, she shrugged her shoulders through the straps. Taking a deep breath, she stepped onto the nearest branch. When it didn't break or bend too much under her weight, she moved toward the trunk and sat down. Peering through the leaves, she took a moment to plot her route. Nodding to herself, she pushed off and landed lightly on the branch below.

Twenty minutes later, she dropped from the lowest branch onto one of the tree's exposed roots, then slid down the root to the bare patch of dirt at its base. She landed on her feet and threw her arms in the air like a gymnast landing after a particularly difficult vault.

Wanting to see how far she'd come, she turned back to the

tree and looked up. And up. Whoa. She couldn't even see the top of the gully.

Ugh. Climbing back up was going to be tough.

Well, nothing she could do about that now. She sat down to rest, took a long drink of water, and ate a few groundnuts and a banana she pulled off a nearby tree. Then she logged the coordinates of the spot into the GPS and began her hunt.

After two hours of pushing through thick brush and navigating the more open areas under the heavy canopy of the trees without any sign of the plane's debris, Emily stopped for lunch and to rest her feet. She tried not to let her frustration get her down, but her lack of progress was disheartening.

Half an hour after she resumed her hunt, she finally found several pieces of the plane. She followed the trail deeper into the jungle, toward another white object peeking out from behind a flowering shrub. Birds called from the trees and insects droned. The helicopter hadn't yet made an appearance, and between the heat and the soothing background sounds, she almost forgot the looming danger. It was peaceful down here. Yet also lonely. She wished Max could have accompanied her. She missed his company. Missed the way he looked at her as if he not only liked her, but respected her.

Since the accident, people had been more likely to look at her with pity than respect. She loved that Max didn't care about her scars. That he saw her as someone strong. And she had to admit that part of her enjoyed Max's attempts to shield her from harm. She couldn't remember anyone ever doing that for her. Hardship made you stronger, so her parents encouraged her to resolve her own problems. And in the ballet world, teachers and choreographers used harsh words and grueling workouts to weed out those dancers who didn't have the heart to stick with dance no matter the cost.

Max would pamper her if he could. While she wouldn't be

comfortable with that for long, she thought it might be nice for a little bit.

Spotting another glimpse of white, she pushed through a thicket of bushes. When she reached the object, she saw that it was a mostly intact window. Farther along, she spotted the full ensemble of a seat, complete with seatbelt. She was so focused on scouring the ground for new evidence she hadn't already documented, that at first she didn't notice the low buzz in the distance. It wasn't until the roar grew closer that she stopped to listen.

Oh, crap. The helicopter.

She glanced up. At least the canopy would hide her from view. Still, she took refuge beneath the leafiest tree she could find. She hugged the tree and tried to keep her breathing as slow and even as possible, not an easy task when she worried about what would happen if the helicopter's crew noticed Max. Would they shoot him? Land and take him prisoner?

Of course, the helicopter could belong to the government instead of the rebels or Dietrich. Still, what would she do if they took Max away?

Would Max fight? No matter who was on board, he wouldn't tell them about his mission. In fact, he'd not even mention her presence in order to keep her safe.

After passing back and forth over the gully for almost ten minutes, the helicopter flew away. Emily waited another ten minutes to make certain she was truly alone before she left her hiding place.

All right. She'd better hurry. She wanted to be out of the ravine if the helicopter returned. Besides, the clouds were thickening. She didn't want to be caught in a storm.

She widened her current search area. Five minutes later, she saw a new line of debris extending back from a large tree. She quickly photographed the find, then followed the trail deeper into the wilderness.

She'd almost decided that she didn't have time to keep going if she was going to make it out before dark, when she walked around a flowering bush and saw two passenger seats on their side. One of the seats was occupied by a vaguely human shape. The body had been gnawed upon, leaving only traces of flesh visible where the man's shorts and short-sleeved shirt ended. The breeze picked up a lingering stench and wafted it her way.

Bile filled her throat, but Emily choked it down. She glanced away, waited for her stomach to settle, then looked back.

Oh, God. The corpse was missing its left arm. Worse, she saw no sign of a briefcase. She circled the body and searched the nearby bushes, but still no briefcase.

A sense of failure swamped her. Fighting back the urge to just sit down and cry, she crossed her arms over her chest. *Think. Max is counting on you.* He'd warned her that because the crash had happened more than a week ago, the local animals would likely have fed on the courier's body. Which she could see had happened. But only a large animal would have been able to carry the arm away with the briefcase dragging behind. So, she needed to look for signs of something heavy being tugged through the underbrush.

To her surprise, she found the trail quickly. After following it for several minutes, she spotted something silver up ahead in the vee of a tree. Was that the briefcase? Had a leopard dragged the arm and the briefcase up a tree? Had—

A thick odor of decay hit her. Emily gagged and pulled her bandana over her nose and mouth, inhaling the familiar scents of sweat, bug repellent, and sunscreen. A few steps later, she rounded a bush and her foot knocked against some obstacle. She glanced down. An African man lay on his back. Maggots crawled over his eyes, nose, mouth, and the torn remains of his throat.

Emily dropped to her knees and vomited into the bushes.

When she finished, she sat back on her heels. Her vision swam and dots danced in front of her. She waited for the dizziness to pass, then rinsed her mouth out.

All right. She'd stumbled across a new corpse. Maybe a local who'd spotted the briefcase and tried to retrieve it, only to be attacked by the leopard she suspected had taken the arm as its prize.

Which meant she needed to retrieve the briefcase and get out of here fast, before she suffered the same fate.

All right. You can do this.

She pushed to her feet and retied her bandana over her nose and mouth. Then she pulled on a pair of surgical gloves. Finally, keeping her eyes averted as much as possible, she sidled past the corpse to the base of the tree.

Yep, that was a silver briefcase stuck in the place where several large branches met. It was just low enough that by standing on one of the exposed roots, she was able to reach over her head and snag it by the handle. She pulled. The case was heavier than she expected and as it fell toward her, it knocked her off balance. She fell back as the security chain and what was left of the courier's arm flew toward her head. She twisted to the side, tripped over the corpse, and went sprawling. The briefcase landed with a squishy thud nearby.

Her hand landed on the dead guy's thigh. Something burst under her palm, releasing a rush of liquid. She shrieked and quickly crawled away, wiping her gloved hand on the ground. Then she glanced back to see where the briefcase had landed. It had hit the corpse's head, splattering maggots and fleshy pieces. The thigh she'd touched had split open, revealing—

She lurched forward and barely pushed the bandana away from her mouth before she convulsed, heaving her remaining stomach contents onto a fern. Once her stomach settled, she let her head hang down and waited for the dizziness to pass. Then she removed her gloves, retrieved a sanitary wipe from her fanny pack and cleaned her hands. She rinsed her mouth again, then pulled out a piece of dried mango and chewed on it. When the lingering taste of sickness had faded, she tried to stand up, but her shaky legs wouldn't hold her.

Great. How was she supposed to retrace her steps and climb out of the ravine if she felt this weak?

Come on. You can do it. Get to your feet. Don't faint. You've found the briefcase. Now get back to Max.

The mini pep talk helped. This time she managed to push to her feet. She swayed a moment, then caught her balance. After waiting to make certain she wouldn't faint, she pulled on a clean pair of latex gloves from the medical kit. Then, steeling herself, she turned around.

Resolutely keeping her eyes just on the briefcase, she followed the chain to the chewed-up mess of bone and sinew that was all that was left of the courier's arm. "All right, Max," she muttered. "I hope I'm earning extra points for this, because I am totally grossed out."

Telling herself to think of it simply as a meal for a cat, not a human body part, she located the wrist and the metal security bracelet. She cut the wrist tendons with Max's knife, then managed to twist and fold the fingers in such a way that she could pull the bracelet free. Snatching up the briefcase, she carried it into the jungle until she couldn't see or smell the dead body.

Yay! She'd done it.

She leaned back against a tree until her pulse calmed and her stomach settled. Once she felt steadier, she poured water over the bracelet and the briefcase to remove the traces of skin and fluids, cleaned them using alcohol wipes, then removed her contaminated gloves and threw them into the jungle.

She was just about ready to leave, when it occurred to her that the dead man might have family in the area. They'd want to know what had happened to him.

"Dammit." She unpacked her camera and marched back to the corpse. Once she was close enough, she marked the coordinates on the GPS and snapped several photos. Looking at the scene from behind her lens helped fight back the nausea. Then she returned to where she'd left the briefcase, picked it up, and headed back toward her exit point. As she went, she made frequent stops to hide the debris trail she'd followed. She didn't want to make it easy for the rebels or Dietrich's men to find.

Dark clouds had been building up since she left the corpse, and halfway back to the tree the heavens opened up in a downpour that obliterated visibility. Cursing at the poor timing, Emily took shelter underneath a wide overhang of branches. She was already soaked through to the skin, but at least the leaves protected her against the sting of the large raindrops. She removed her rucksack, glad that it was waterproof, and sat down with her knees up and her chin resting on her crossed arms. She stared out at the rain, feeling an odd sensation of being cut off from the world. Safe from the prying eyes of the helicopter. Safe from being tracked by an aggressive leopard.

The rhythm of the rain had almost lulled her to sleep when the wind picked up. A crack of thunder split the air. Emily's eyes opened in time to see a brilliant flash of lightning, which was followed by another clap of thunder.

O-kay. So much for the peaceful, safe storm. Worried about sitting next to the metal briefcase and under a tree during a lightning storm, Emily left her shelter and found an open space. The rain continued to fall in torrential sheets. Well, since she was going to have to wait the storm out anyway, she might as well get some benefit from it. At least the rain was warm. Wishing she had some shampoo, she unbraided her hair and let the rain soak into it. But the enjoyment of finally rinsing days worth of sweat and dust out of her hair was mitigated by the fear that struck her each time the sky flashed and thunder boomed. Still, she took advantage of the deluge to also rub down her clothes and exposed skin.

It took over an hour for the storm to pass. Emily returned to the place where she'd left her things, shrugged into her pack, and lifted the briefcase. The going was slower now as she slogged through mud and dodged tiny rivers. Humidity permeated the air, so her clothes didn't fully dry. The clouds remained overhead, bringing an early twilight.

By the time she reached her climbing tree, the light was noticeably failing. She considered staying the night at the base of the tree, but knew Max would freak out. It was almost five o'clock, so she was going to be late as it was. No sense throwing him into a full panic by not showing up at all.

Besides, although exhaustion tugged at her, she didn't think she'd be able to sleep easily down here. Not with the leopard on the loose, and not with the possibility of the helicopter returning. She wanted the safety of the Jeep. She wanted to curl up in Max's arms. To wrap herself in his safety and strength.

Sighing deeply, she fortified herself with a long drink of water, stretched her sore body until a few of the aches disappeared, then hung the night vision goggles around her neck for easy access once the light vanished.

She picked up the briefcase, hoisted it onto the first branch, and resigned herself to a long, tiring climb.

CHAPTER SIXTEEN

Where the hell was Emily?

He'd told her to be back by five o'clock and it was now pushing six.

God dammit, once she returned he was never letting her out of his sight again. His heart couldn't take it. Not only had he panicked when she'd stepped into the branches of the big tree and disappeared, but he hadn't been there to protect her when the helicopter flew overhead. The fact that it had returned less than twenty-four hours after its last pass made Max think they knew something—or someone—was here.

The good news was that the bushes overhung the slope enough so Emily's rope wouldn't be visible from above.

The bad news was that in the light of day, he'd gotten a good look at the helicopter. It was painted black, not army green, so it belonged to Dietrich. Which only increased his worry over Emily. His gut screamed that the helicopter's double flyby meant that Dietrich had switched his attention to this area. Giving weight to his theory that Dietrich had arranged to get infrared technology.

They needed to get the hell out of here before Dietrich's troops arrived.

Come on, Em. Come on.

Max hobbled for the dozenth time to the edge of the slope. Eyed the rope waiting for her return. He almost said to hell with his wounded leg and went after her. But he had to be smarter than that. First, the ground was soft and muddy after that heavy rain, making it treacherous. Plus, what if he reached the tree? Climbing down would probably reopen his wounds. Even supposing that he made it to the bottom and found Emily, at that point he'd be in no condition to climb back up. And there was no way he was going to put Emily in additional danger by forcing her to spend the night babysitting him at the bottom of the ravine.

He'd wanted to set up some sort of signal that Emily could use to prove that she was okay, but everything he'd thought of could have been spotted or heard by an enemy. So he was left to wait and worry.

He checked Emily's watch, then glanced at the sky. In a few minutes, the sun would sink out of sight. If only—

Emily's head came into view.

Max's heart soared.

Something glinted next to her in the failing light.

Hot damn. She'd found the briefcase. "That's my girl," he murmured.

Emily stepped onto the foot of the steep slope and looked up at him. "I'm sending the briefcase to you," she called, reaching for the end of the rope.

Stifling his impatience—he wanted *Emily* safe, screw the damn case—he pulled the briefcase toward him. He barely spared it a glance as he dragged it over the edge. All he cared about was releasing the knot holding the rope in place and sending the rope back to Emily.

Hauling her up the steep slope was a much slower process.

Max's ribs protested and he knew he'd be hurting tomorrow. Still, he wished he had the strength to just yank on the rope and send her flying toward him.

But eventually she scrambled over the rim of the gully. "I did it!" she crowed, grinning at him. Then she bent forward in a dancer's curtain bow.

Max tucked his cane under his arm and clapped. "You're a superstar, Em," he said.

She straightened up. "Superstar." She nodded in approval as she walked toward him. "I like it."

He chuckled. "It suits you." Balancing on his cane, he caught her up in a one-armed hug, then took her mouth in a kiss that started out full of pride, then shifted to include all the worry and longing that had plagued him during her absence.

He broke away and glanced at the sky. "Much as I hate to let you go, it's getting dark. We'd better head back to the Jeep before all the light is gone and before the helicopter returns."

With a groan, Emily picked up the briefcase.

He stared at the muddy, yet barely dented silver case. The people who'd manufactured the weapon clearly had money and access to top-level security supplies. Cases like this cost an arm and a leg.

Emily dipped her chin toward the case as they hurried back toward the Jeep. "So this is what everyone is after. Doesn't seem like it contains the key to killing hundreds of people."

"Yeah."

She looked over at him. "Now what?"

"I checked the maps while you were gone. Since the helicopter has become more active in this area, I want to head toward the minor north-south road to our east. Then we'll find a place to hole up while we wait for Kris to tell us the safest way out of the country. The underground group will take care of the briefcase once we hand it over." Now that he'd done his good deed, it was time to get Emily out of the country, find Dietrich, and end this thing.

By the time they made it back to the Jeep, they were both shuffling with exhaustion. He stowed the briefcase inside a bag that had once held food, then stuffed their sleeping bags around it to disguise the fact that something important was hidden in the middle.

"Damn, woman," he said once he was behind the wheel and driving away, night vision goggles in place. The fact that Emily hadn't even offered a token protest about him driving proved that she was at the end of her strength. "I had no idea how difficult it was to find a path through these trees. You've got some mad skills for a woman who barely drove before she got to Africa."

"I'm good at finding my path," she murmured. "I have to be able to weave through a throng of dancers without stepping on anyone's toes, knocking into anyone, or disappearing from the audience's view."

"Who knew that the perfect companion on this mission would be a ballet dancer? I'm going to have to get you to take me to a performance when we get out of here."

She snorted in disbelief, but he was too tired to argue.

"You were gone a long time, Em. Did you run into trouble?"

"You mean besides having to wait out the thunderstorm?"

"Yeah."

"Some. It took me longer than expected to find the briefcase. And...uh... You were right. The animals had been at the courier's body. I found what was left of his arm, still attached to the brief-case, partway up a tree."

"Leopard."

"Yeah, that's what I thought. Worse, a local man's body was at the base of the tree. His throat had been torn out. I think the leopard killed him."

Max suddenly had a vision of Emily being savaged by a large

cat and his heart lurched. "Jesus. You're lucky the leopard wasn't there." He could have lost her. Again.

"I know." She glanced at him out of the corner of her eye. "Do you think it's our friend from the other night?"

He shrugged. "Probably. I don't think they share territory."

She nodded. "Anyway, his body was uh...fresher. Seeing the bloated, maggot-infested corpse made me sick. Not to mention the stench." She put her hand on her belly as if even now she fought not to vomit.

He clenched his teeth. "I'm sorry."

She shrugged. "Max, it's not your fault. It had to be done."

"Still..." She'd already endured so much on this trip. She didn't deserve more trauma. "I'm sorry."

"Forget it," she answered. Then added drowsily, "I tried to make it harder for any searchers by hiding as much of the debris as I could."

His heart swelling with pride, he picked up her hand and placed a kiss on the back. "That's my girl." Even though he was driving, he didn't want to release her. He couldn't remember ever having such a craving for the simple touch of a woman's hand before.

"Grab some food, then climb into the back and try to rest," he said.

Emily's only answer was a slight snore.

He reached over and smoothed a stray lock of hair away from her face. She certainly deserved some uninterrupted sleep. It took a lot of fortitude to deal with a swollen, dead body and maggots. The fact that she'd done it despite throwing up multiple times filled him with fierce admiration. He might not agree with all of the choices she'd made these past few days, but he loved how Emily just kept going, doing her best to handle whatever life threw at her.

With a little training, she'd make a good partner.

What? Hell, no. Emily deserved a hell of a lot more than to become an operator in his shadowy world.

Yet the knowledge that he'd soon have to say good-bye to her made his chest ache. Not that he had a choice. His coming confrontation with Dietrich would be violent. Odds were good he wouldn't survive. Better to end things with Emily once she was safe than to leave her with the impression that they had a future.

Even if part of him wanted to make a relationship work with her. How, he had no idea. He didn't know if he could give up the covert ops world. And he certainly would never ask her to join him.

At the same time, the idea that Emily might go on to find another guy filled him with such possessive fury that the steering wheel creaked under his grip.

Emily murmured softly in her sleep and turned toward the window.

Tenderness filled him with an unfamiliar warmth. He might have to say good-bye, but he'd damn well enjoy every remaining minute they had together.

It didn't take long to reach the road. Max checked that the way was clear, drove out of the jungle, then stopped in the center of the muddy road where he had a clear line of sight to the sky. He shot off a quick text to Kristoff. *Success,* was all it said, but it would be enough.

That done, he maneuvered into the jungle on the opposite side of the road from the festival village. He didn't know how long it would take to hear back from Kris about their exit strategy, but he wanted to be as close to the border as possible when the call came.

Over an hour later he heard the helicopter returning.

Crap.

The sound had been partially hidden by the rattle of the Jeep, so he hadn't noticed it before now. When Max braked and peered through a gap in the trees, he saw the lights of the helicopter approaching quickly from the east. Because of the trees, Max quickly lost sight of it. But from the way the rotor sounds changed, he suspected that the helicopter was hovering near the ravine and Dietrich's soldiers were rappelling in.

Thank God they'd left when they did.

Max drove forward, keeping one ear attuned to the sounds from the helicopter. Unfortunately, the jungle soon thinned, then gave way to tilled earth. He stopped the Jeep just before the trees ended, not willing to risk exposure. He got out of the Jeep and walked a little bit to the right, until he had a better view of the sky.

Shit. Here came the helicopter. Aiming directly toward—

A fiery trail streaked across the night sky toward the helicopter. A second later, the helicopter exploded in a bright flash. What the—

Max stared in disbelief as the blazing helicopter fell to earth. Christ. Someone had shot the helicopter down with a surface-to-air missile. Guess he knew why the courier's plane had crashed.

From the trajectory, the missile had come from the other side of the road and to Max's right.

Just what he needed. The rebels or some unknown militant group were on the prowl.

He listened for signs that anyone was nearby. Heard a raucous cheer from what must be the final village along this road.

Max climbed behind the wheel and drove onto the path at the edge of the field. Luckily, the field turned back into forest before they reached the area opposite the village.

The Jeep lurched over a thick root and Emily jerked awake. "Huh? What?" She rubbed her eyes. "Where are we?"

"Just passing the last village in this region."

"Sounds like they're having a party."

"You might say that." He explained about the helicopter being shot down.

"Oh. You think the villagers are responsible? Why?"

"Maybe, they're smugglers who don't want strangers in this area. Maybe they have alliances with Dietrich's enemies." He shrugged. "Hard to say. Either way, we're steering clear."

Emily nodded.

They drove in silence until a river blocked their path, forcing them back to the road. Max considered whether speed or stealth was more important. With the villagers behind them too busy partying, and the helicopter no longer a threat, he decided to chance using the road, since they were driving without lights.

Forty-five minutes later, the road disappeared into a wall of green.

"Uh, Max?"

"Yeah, I see it." He eased the Jeep to a halt, then climbed out to take a look.

Well, that was what he'd intended. But his wounded leg buckled as he tried to put weight on it. He held onto the door to steady himself and ground his teeth as he rode out the pain. Yeah, okay, he'd known that driving would aggravate his injury. But couldn't he catch a damn break?

"Max?" Emily walked around the front of the Jeep.

"Ah... My leg..." He coughed. "It's...um...your turn to drive."

"All right." She walked over to the wall of brush in front of them, pushed against some of the leaves, then stuck her head forward. A minute later, she returned. "I think I should be able to get the Jeep in there. I can't say how long the way will be passable, but the farther we get from the village, the better, right?"

"Yeah."

"Good." She slipped her arm around his waist and helped him into the passenger's seat.

"This is hard on a man's ego," he grumbled.

"Oh, poor baby." She gave him a fleeting kiss, then strode around to the driver's side.

Well, at least she seemed to have regained some of her energy.

She settled behind the wheel and he handed her the night vision goggles. Once she had them in place, she disengaged the parking brake and drove forward.

"Here we go again," she muttered before the Jeep left the relatively stable surface of the road and lurched into the jungle.

"WHAT DO you mean the helicopter has been lost?" Dietrich pressed the phone against his ear, as if that would make the leader of his search team more coherent.

"Someone shot it out of the sky with a surface-to-air missile after it dropped us off. It exploded. There's no way anyone survived."

Dietrich pinched the bridge of his nose. Why him? This was the deal of a lifetime. More money than he had ever been offered, with promises of future deals if all went according to plan. But this past month everything had gone wrong, one thing after another. As if he had been cursed.

"Have you found any sign of the plane?" he asked.

"Not yet. It's still dark. Even with night vision goggles, the ravine's terrain is treacherous. We're going to have to wait until dawn to enter."

Dietrich bit back a curse. He had thought they had finally received a break. He had paid an exorbitant fee in order to obtain two refurbished Soviet helicopters with radar and infrared equipment. They had been delivered just this morning and his crew had spent the rest of the day vetting one helicopter and preparing it for this evening's flight. Not only had infrared revealed debris on the ground in an area far on the other side of the main road, possibly from his missing plane, but there had been two heat signatures nearby. The presence of human beings could simply mean that some of the locals from the nearby village had found the debris. Given his luck, it was more probable that Max had outsmarted him and found the plane first.

But no. The crew had reported two heat signatures and Max now worked alone.

Regardless, he could not allow Max or anyone else to gain possession of the briefcase. So Dietrich had authorized his men to rappel in and investigate.

"Do not forget," Dietrich said. "This matter is urgent. You will receive a bonus for the quick retrieval of the object or for the capture of any foreigners in the area."

"I understand. However, the other half of my team was on the helicopter when it went down. The plan was to drop that team closer to the heat signatures, which were on the move. Now eight of my men are dead."

So. His soldiers had been killed. By the locals? Or by Max? Either way, the loss was both inconvenient and costly. He paid his men outrageous salaries to handle such problems quickly and with lethal force. The risk was understood, yet his commander would still have to waste time recruiting and training replacements.

Another cost to lay at Max's feet.

After receiving his commander's assurances that he would report back once his team had entered the ravine, Dietrich ended the call. He would have to send out a second team in order to chase down the heat signatures. Fortunately, he had a backup helicopter, but mobilizing another crew would take time. He did not know if the second helicopter would arrive soon enough to stop Max, or whoever was on the ground, from locating the prototype first.

That assumed that the plane had truly crashed there.

He sighed and glanced around his tent. He had only recently set up camp here, on the edge of the area his men had most recently been searching. Unfortunately, the debris they had located had proved to be the remains of an old bus. Not the plane carrying the courier and his precious cargo.

Now he had to wonder if the same party that had shot down

his helicopter tonight had also shot down the courier's plane. He knew that none of the rebel groups he dealt with would dare to do so. However, it was possible that some of the locals were ignorant enough to see both the plane and the helicopter as threats. After all, as Max's escape had proven, the smuggling network in this area was quite complex.

It was also conceivable that the government had troops nearby. However, that particular strip of jungle was sparsely populated and the only reason the government would be in the area would be to search for his plane. Dietrich had been very, very careful to pay the pilot enough so he would take all maneuvers to avoid being detected by the government. So, if government troops were on the ground, it meant some of the villagers had witnessed the plane's crash and reported it.

He turned to the rebel commander standing next to him. "Tell me again about the area surrounding the ravine."

The man shrugged. "Few villages. Very primitive. No electricity. No telephones. No running water."

Which meant that if someone had notified the government of the plane, they would have had to leave the area and place a call at the closest city. Not enough time had passed to allow such a delay in reporting and then the activation of forces. So, that likely eliminated the government as the source for bringing the plane down. Since he suspected the same person or group had shot down his helicopter...

"Where do the loyalties of the people in this area lie? With the government or with the rebels?"

The man shrugged. "This I cannot know. I am not from this place."

Dietrich drilled him with a stare. "Then find someone who *can* give me the information I seek. I need to understand what type of threat we are facing before we pack up this camp and move."

The man squirmed. He clearly did not want to believe that

anyone had the authority to give him orders. Yet underneath his lust for power lay a weak-willed man. He liked to strut and throw his power around, but he had no head for war. He was entirely ruled by his juvenile emotions and often erupted in vicious outbursts that lost him the respect of his men.

Dietrich held the rebel's gaze unwaveringly, until the man glanced down. "Yes, sir," the man mumbled. He turned and fled the tent. Once outside, he began shouting orders in the local language, no doubt trying to boost his confidence.

Fool.

While the West African men who had started the rebellion were intelligent and disciplined, in order to quickly build up their army they had encouraged all people to join their organization. The result was that in many areas, unsuitable men had formed gangs of thugs and called themselves members of the rebellion. The man who had just exited did not realize that the rebel leaders were simply using him to consolidate their power. Once the rebellion was well-established and in control of the region, Dietrich fully expected the rebel leadership to purge their ranks of men such as this one. A man who could not see beyond his need for revenge for petty injustices.

Ultimately, the success or failure of this local group did not concern Dietrich. He simply wanted the money promised him. But first, he must retrieve the briefcase.

One of his lieutenants poked his head into the tent. "Sir, I understand that you want us to give up searching in this location and move to an area on the other side of the road."

"Yes."

The man stepped into the tent. "May I remind you that the rebels have dynamited the crossroads? We will have to clear a safe passage around the destruction in order to access the road."

Dietrich swore out loud. His lieutenant gave him a look full of sympathy. This was another headache the unruly rebels were causing him. "Very well. See that it gets done."

"Sir." The man nodded sharply, turned on his heel and left.

The tent flap had no sooner swung closed than another of his lieutenants entered, dragging a local man by the arm. "Sir. This man lives on the other side of the road. He should be able to provide you with the information you require about the villages near the ravine."

He shoved the man forward.

Dietrich gestured with his chin and his lieutenant took up guard position at the door.

Half an hour later, Dietrich released the man. Unfortunately, because the man had been helping to remove brush from the debris here, he was not up-to-date on today's events on the other side of the road. This being an area without cell phone or even landline service, gossip relied on face-to-face contact. However, the man had been able to provide useful background information.

Dietrich paced around the small tent, trying to decide how best to use this new information. So. He had been correct. According to the local man, most of the villages in this region were part of a smuggling ring. They handled specialty goods brought over the border and sold them to buyers in the local markets. In order to protect their business interests, they had formed a local militia. The man claimed the militia was well-armed. That they had stolen a box of weapons meant for the rebels. Not, luckily for them, any weapons that Dietrich had sold. Otherwise, he would have had to destroy them all.

It being probable that their stolen weapons included a surface-to-air missile, these smugglers were the most likely candidates for having shot his helicopter down. Such an aggressive act could not go unpunished. His men would need to track down the guilty party. Then Dietrich would arrange for suitable retaliation.

In the meantime, he needed to start packing.

WAR Headquarters
The Democratic Republic of the Ivory Coast
West Africa

"ANY NEWS OF MAX?" Wil asked that night when Kristoff answered his phone.

Kris closed his eyes and rubbed the back of his neck. "Wil—"

"Don't even think about it, Kris. I know you want to protect me, but he's my brother. I know he can be reckless. I know he's got a martyr complex a mile wide. What's going to hurt worse than learning he's finally managed to get himself killed is finding out you didn't tell me just how much trouble he was in."

Dammit, he shouldn't have answered the phone. He didn't want to have this conversation.

Yet the need to hear Wil's voice, to feel just that little sense of connection, mattered more. It was the only thing that had kept him going today as WAR raced to put out fire after fire. Because once again, the region teetered on the brink of total chaos.

He sighed. "As far as I know, Max is still alive. He texted me a while ago to let me know that he'd found the briefcase."

"So why don't you sound happy?"

Kris stared at the regional map, wishing so much of it wasn't covered in red flags. "Tonight, we finally got a satellite view of the region where Max is. The image showed a refurbished Soviet era Mil M-8 helicopter canvassing the area. We've identified it as one of two helicopters recently purchased by a shell company of Dietrich's. Worse, we believe it's equipped with FLIR."

Wil cursed. "Max can't hide from thermal imaging and he's in no shape to fight off Dietrich's trained soldiers."

"Right." Kris shuffled the papers on his desk. "If it's any consolation, rumor has it that Dietrich wants Max alive. So it's unlikely the helicopter will fire on Max and Emily unless it's merely to disable their vehicle."

"What the fuck? He still has the girl with him?"

"Yeah. But it's not his fault. They've had a string of bad luck, and without an extraction team available to go after her, they're still together. But hey, at least he hasn't been arrested for kidnapping her."

"Not funny."

"Sorry."

"All right." Wil blew out a breath. "If Dietrich doesn't want Max killed on sight, that at least buys us some time." But he didn't sound any happier than Kris felt.

"I've issued new orders to MacKay's team," Kris said. "Once they finish their current operation, I'm sending them after Max."

"You run that by Azumah?"

"What do you think?" The head of WAR had a very narrow view of how he wanted his operators to be utilized. And rescuing a rogue element like Max wasn't included.

Wil chuckled, and Kris's heart lurched. He wanted to reach through the phone, grab the sound, and hold it close. Not even a full laugh, it still erased all the stress from the tough decisions he'd been forced to make today. He squeezed his eyes closed again. Christ. He really had it bad.

"Thanks, Kris. I'll cover for you if Azumah causes trouble." Being the U.S. military's unofficial liaison with WAR gave Wil some leverage with Azumah.

"I don't think it will come to that. As long as Max has the briefcase, I can justify sending men after him." He'd do it regardless of the fallout. No matter what he said, Max was part of his team. Kris didn't leave teammates behind.

Plus, Max was Wil's brother. For that alone, Kris would do anything to help. Regardless of whether Max wanted it or Azumah approved it.

Not that Kris didn't understand Azumah's hesitation. He did. WAR didn't have an extensive stable of soldiers. At least sixty percent of its membership consisted of concerned civilians like Rene—doctors, journalists, politicians, and financiers. People working to spread information and money that allowed citizens to oppose both the rebels and those members of their own governments who believed supporting the rebels would be of personal benefit.

Azumah had recruited a few disillusioned soldiers from the region's official armies, but he had to be careful who he accepted into WAR's ranks. Men without the proper attitude would only cause WAR to dissolve from the inside out. Soldiers looking to join needed more than just a passionate drive to wrest control from the rebels and regain freedom for their people. Potential members had to be willing to make sacrifices. Take orders. Work well with others. Understand that membership in WAR was not a route to personal wealth or power.

That was partly where Kris and his team came in. Not only did they carry out missions, but they also trained the incoming soldiers and molded them into a disciplined fighting force. Unfortunately, to date they only had about two companies of fully functional soldiers, and with the increased rebel presence their resources were spread thin.

"Thanks, Kris. Let me know if there's anything I can do to help."

Tell me that you feel this attraction, too. Tell me I'm not alone. The need for such a sign was so intense, Kris's voice came out huskier than usual. "My pleasure."

His other line rang.

"Sorry, Wil. I've got to take another call. I promise to check in the next time I hear from Max."

"Thanks."

Kris stared at the phone, feeling a sense of loss as he replaced the receiver. Shaking his head, his picked up the second line. "Hello?"

It was one of his newer lieutenants reporting on the successful drive to oust the rebels from one of the country's regional capitals. After taking the man's preliminary report, Kris hung up and changed the flag on the map from red to green. Finally, for the first time in weeks, WAR had a tangible success. That team would be busy for the next day or so rounding up the last stragglers of the rebel army, helping release and evacuate prisoners, and establishing order so that normal daily activities could resume, but their primary objective had been achieved.

The recent influx of foreign soldiers was having a noticeable effect on WAR's ability to achieve its military goals. Some of the newcomers were probably only temporary allies—they needed WAR's help in righting wrongs that had been done while serving in West Africa—but Kris didn't care. As long as they stayed focused while carrying out an assigned mission, he'd exploit their abilities in order to achieve WAR's objectives.

Right now, that meant stopping the rebels from gaining more power. Retrieving the weapon before Dietrich turned it over to the rebels' buyer was one more victory in the attempt to stop West Africa from succumbing to anarchy.

CHAPTER SEVENTEEN

The Republic of the Volta
West Africa

THE NEXT MORNING, Max held onto the stability handle as Emily expertly swerved the Jeep around another pothole. They'd made it without incident to the minor north-south road last night, then driven another half hour before pulling over to sleep. Kris had called at dawn, telling them to meet a contact of his at the next village. The man would help get them safely over the border.

Kris had also warned that sources claimed Dietrich had purchased two Mil Mi-8s with thermal imaging capabilities, which meant the jungle would no longer provide a secure hiding place. In return, Max had told Kris his suspicion that one of the helicopters had been shot down last night.

Now, after two hours of slow, yet uneventful driving in the morning drizzle with no sign of any helicopters, Max thought they might actually make it to safety.

Emily straightened the Jeep and gave it gas. The tires slipped a bit on the muddy surface, but she handled the skid like a pro. "You really—"

Max squinted at the side view mirror. He thought he'd seen... Yeah, there. "Shit."

"What?"

"We've got a helicopter coming in from the southwest. Pull over." The fact that the helicopter wasn't coming from the direction of the capital, but from the crash site, didn't bode well.

Emily did as he said, then glanced over at the jungle and bit her lip. "There's not enough cover over the road to hide the Jeep, and the spaces between the trees are too narrow for us to drive into the jungle."

"I know. The thermal imaging will detect the engine's heat anyway." Max grabbed the maps and other items from the console and the glove box, then reached for the door handle. "That's why you're going to hide in the jungle while I lead them away."

"No! Max, I'm not leaving you."

"Yes, you are." Leaning heavily on his makeshift cane, he hobbled back to the cargo compartment. He stuffed everything essential into Emily's pack, including the phone and its charger, then thrust it at her.

Emily clutched at his arm. "Max. What are you planning?"

He closed his eyes and rested his cheek against her temple. Knowing that she cared for him made what he was about to do worth it. "Em, we can't outrun them and I can't move fast enough on foot to escape. One of us has to stay alive and free to get the briefcase to the underground movement. That's you." He stepped back and handed her the Mylar blanket from his pack. "Find a thick system of above ground roots. Hide deep inside. Get as close to the tree trunk as you can. Put your backpack in front of you, then the briefcase, and drape this blanket over you. It will help diminish your heat signature. This drizzle and fog will also reduce the thermal camera's effectiveness. Once it's quiet again, call Kristoff. He'll send his contact down here to help you. Don't come after me. I need you safe."

She took a deep, shuddering inhale. "Max, please don't ask me to do this. I—"

He took her chin in his fingers, turned her face toward him, and kissed her. The salt on her lips from her tears made his heart ache. "I—"

The sound of the helicopter grew louder.

Emily flinched.

"Quick, take the pistol." Max snapped the holster to her belt. He pressed the briefcase into her arms. "Go. Now."

He gave her one last, quick kiss, then turned her around and pushed her away from him. She threw a frightened look over her shoulder. "Don't you dare die on me, Max Lansing. I love you."

His heart soared. Strength flooded him. He met her eyes. "I love you, too. Now go!"

With one last glance, she turned and fled.

He watched for a second to make certain the jungle showed no sign of her passage, then climbed behind the wheel and drove north as fast as the Jeep and the muddy road allowed. Minutes later, the helicopter appeared over the nearest trees. It spotted him and turned to follow. When the helicopter fired at the road behind him, Max swerved to the left, slammed on the brakes, snagged his cane, and climbed out.

Hobbling as fast as he could, he pushed his way past wet branches into the jungle.

The helicopter arrived, its rotor wash ruffling the tops of the trees. It made one, two, three passes over the jungle before gunfire erupted back where he'd left the Jeep. Didn't the shooters know no one was inside? Or were they simply destroying what they thought was his best chance at making a speedy escape?

The sound of the helicopter changed. It was hovering. Probably dropping soldiers.

Max continued limping along, choosing the most difficult path. No sense in making this easy for his pursuers. Still, it took longer than he'd expected before men burst out of the jungle behind him. "Halt!"

Max slowly turned around. Keeping one hand on his cane, he raised the other over his head. Now he understood what had taken them so long. These weren't the ragtag, undisciplined rebel soldiers that had accompanied Ziegler at the way station. These were Dietrich's private troops. Which meant they'd carefully canvassed every foot of the jungle between their entry point and this spot instead of rushing in haphazardly like the rebels.

A man stepped out from behind the row of soldiers.

Ah, shit.

"Hello, Max," Ziegler said. His eyes roamed from Max's upraised hand to the end of his cane jammed into the jungle soil.

Max tensed. Did Ziegler hate him enough to order him killed in front of all these witnesses, despite Dietrich's order to the contrary? Because Dietrich would want Max held for questioning about the briefcase. Never mind settling their personal feud.

But Ziegler just gave an evil chuckle. "You have an annoying resiliency, Herr Lansing. After all we have done, you should be dead by now."

Max raised his brow. "Yeah, well, can't say that I'm sorry to disappoint you." He made certain to show no fear and no pain when he met Ziegler's icy blue eyes.

"I will never understand why Dietrich has been so patient with you. He should have ordered you killed months ago."

"Like you tried to do at that way station, instead killing an innocent girl?"

Ziegler's eyes narrowed. "Ah, so you were close enough to see that, were you? A pity you didn't step forward to save her. It would have prevented so many other deaths."

Max didn't comment. He wouldn't succumb to Ziegler's mind games. He knew Ziegler wanted Max to be weakened by guilt over the deaths. But Rene, Kristoff, and Emily were right. Ziegler and his rebel buddies had done the killing. There'd been no warning. No chance for Max to give himself up. The deaths *weren't* his fault.

So Max kept his head held high and his gaze locked with Ziegler's. Finally, Ziegler signaled with his hand. "Take him."

Max felt movement behind him. Before he could turn, something hard connected with his skull and the world went black.

EMILY LIFTED her head from her bent knees. According to Max's watch, it had been over an hour since he'd left her to play martyr. She'd heard shooting not long after he left and it had taken all her willpower not to go rushing after him. Yet Max had trusted her with the briefcase. She needed to prove to him that she wasn't impulsive and emotional. That she could think strategically and follow directions.

Her decision to stay put had been justified when the helicopter began to fly back and forth over the area. Probably searching for her. Thankfully, the Mylar blanket seemed to have done the trick. Or maybe it was the thunderstorm that hit forty-five minutes ago. Whatever the reason, the helicopter passed right overhead. Then, fifteen minutes ago, the sounds of the helicopter had faded. The rain stopped and the jungle settled back into its usual rhythm. Insects buzzed. Birds called. A snake slithered past her foot, completely ignoring her. Trusting that the critters knew it was safe, she slowly unclenched her body and crawled out of her hiding place.

Grief, fear, and anger had long since hollowed her out, and she climbed to her feet with a blessed sense of numbness. So detached that it might have been a stranger brushing leaves and mud off the blanket, folding it and packing it in her rucksack. But the numbness vanished when she went to pick up the briefcase.

Max had given himself up to Dietrich's men because of this

damned case. He'd willingly allowed himself to be put in a position to be tortured again so she could get to safety.

Clamping her hands over her mouth to hold back the sound, Emily dropped to her knees and screamed in rage. When her throat was raw, she pounded her fists over and over against the unyielding surface of the briefcase. It wasn't fair. She'd finally found a man who loved her. Who accepted her as she was and encouraged her to draw on her inner strength. Yet Dietrich might have already killed Max. Might—

A sharp bite of pain in her hands brought reality crashing back. She sat back on her heels and wiped the tears from her cheeks. She couldn't help Max, couldn't do *anything* if she damaged herself in a fit of temper.

A wave of exhaustion and despair hit her and she swayed.

No. Unacceptable. She had to stay strong. She had to get help for Max.

She grabbed a quick drink of water and some dried mango. Giving her rucksack the evil eye—if she never again had to feel its weight bearing down on her sore shoulders that would be fine with her—she lifted it and slipped her arms through the straps. Then she picked up the briefcase and headed toward the road. Once there, she checked that no one was around, then poked her head out and studied the road's surface. Nope. She didn't see any telltale human footprints in the mud to indicate that Dietrich's soldiers had brought Max this way. There were just the usual footprints of small jungle creatures and birds and what she thought were the nearly washed away tire tracks of the Jeep.

Okay. She'd follow the road in the direction Max had been heading. Ducking back inside the jungle, she kept to the protection of the trees as she walked. When she found a spot where the trees thinned enough to allow a somewhat clear line of sight to the sky, she pulled out the sat phone. After raising the phone's antennae, she called the number for Kristoff.

"Max, you bastard," an American voice snapped, "what is it now?"

"Um... This isn't Max, sir. He's been captured."

"Ah, f—" The man cleared his throat. "Sorry. My name is Kristoff. You're Emily?"

"Yes, sir."

"Details, please."

She explained about Max's decision to play decoy while she hid. That she believed Max had been captured. She refused to give voice to the possibility that he was dead, in case speaking the words made it true.

"But you didn't set eyes on the helicopter or the soldiers?"

"No, sir. The helicopter was just a silhouette against the clouds when I left the road. But Max thought it was one of Dietrich's. With thermal imaging."

"Okay. Are you someplace safe?"

She shrugged, then answered, "I don't know. I'm in the jungle just off the road. The helicopter left the area about twenty-five minutes ago. I don't see or hear any soldiers. I haven't even spotted our Jeep yet." She kept walking, picking her way across the soggy ground. "I'm heading north, aiming for the rendezvous point with your contact."

"Forget that. Our man didn't check in last night, so it's not safe for you to continue. I want you to head deeper into the jungle and find a place to hide. Then text me the coordinates and stay put until I can free up a team to extract you."

Out of the corner of her eye, she saw metal glinting in the ray of sunshine peeking out from the threatening clouds. Was that —? She moved closer to the road. Yes.

Their Jeep sat at the edge of the jungle on the opposite side of the road. It had been shot full of holes and had four flat tires. Okay. She wouldn't be driving away. Scanning to check that no one was nearby, she saw fresh ruts in the center of the road that had filled with water. She darted across to the ruined Jeep and crouched beside it. Waterlogged footprints surrounded the Jeep, then led into the jungle. A bit farther up the road, the footprints emerged from the jungle and stopped at a set of deep tire tracks.

Just as if a group of soldiers had been picked up by a large truck. Her spirits lifted.

The sun disappeared behind the clouds and thunder rumbled in the distance.

"With all due respect sir, no. I'm not going to hide in the jungle," Emily said.

"Excuse me?"

"I just found our Jeep and there's a bunch of footprints and tire tracks in the muddy road. I'll bury the briefcase and send you those coordinates later. I need to follow the tracks before the storm that's threatening wipes them out." The sun made one more valiant attempt to break free of the clouds, but was immediately swallowed up.

"Emily—"

"Look, sir, I'm not suggesting that I try to rescue him. I know I'm just an inexperienced civilian." The words tasted bitter in her mouth. "But I'm not leaving Max alone out there. I've become quite adept at moving through the jungle. I can find out where they're holding him. Text you those coordinates so your team can rescue Max first. The briefcase won't be going anywhere."

There was a long pause. "You...surprise me, Emily. That's still a risky endeavor."

"So? I love him. I'm not leaving him to be tortured and killed."

"O-kay." This time she heard admiration in his voice. Along with a tinge of amusement. "But you have to promise to text me your coordinates every hour, so that we can keep track of you. As long as you can see the tracks from inside the tree line, stay under cover. And use that Mylar blanket to hide your heat signature the second you hear a helicopter again. Something tells me that Max will have my skin if anything happens to you."

"Agreed. I don't have any wish to join Max in captivity."

"Right. If you don't need anything else, I'll see about that rescue team."

She managed a faint smile. "No, I think that'll do it for now. I'll text you the coordinates once I've buried the briefcase."

"Good luck, Emily."

"Thank you, sir." She disconnected the call and slipped the phone into her pocket. She hoped the sun reemerged sometime soon, because the phone was almost out of power and without a vehicle to plug into, she'd have to use Max's solar travel charger.

"All right. Let's do this." With a sharp nod to give herself confidence, she headed deeper into the jungle, looking for a place to stash the briefcase.

MAX WOKE up with a splitting headache and found himself chained to stakes stuck in the dirt inside a tent. No surprise there. Ziegler wasn't the most original jailor.

This time, they'd stripped him of all clothing and his watch. Leaving him no way to check how long he'd been unconscious. Plus, without his belt and his shoes he wouldn't be able to retrieve his hidden weapons and tools in order to escape. Rolling his head from side to side—which ratcheted his headache from painful to excruciating—he saw that the tent was empty. Outside, he heard what sounded like guys hammering on metal tent stakes.

So. He was being held in a camp in progress. Not a lot of help. He didn't even know what country he was in.

Besides, what he really wanted to know was if Emily was safe. The fear that maybe Ziegler had captured her, too, and she was staked out in a nearby tent made cold sweat trickle down his brow.

No. He had to believe she was free. That was the only way to keep his head in the game.

He tried to sit up, but the world whirled around him and he

flopped back down, waiting for the dizziness to pass. It took him three times before he managed to sit up with a determined heave. He choked back a groan, but damn, that hurt. Ziegler's men obviously hadn't cared if Max got knocked around during transport. Even parts of his body that shouldn't hurt, hurt.

So much for instantly freeing himself, then escaping. At this point, not only wasn't he at maximum strength, but the iron chains running from the stakes to the manacles on his wrists and ankles weren't long enough to let him stand up. He had just enough play in the chains to lay his wrists across his bent knees.

All right. First thing. Regain his strength.

Second. Break out of here.

Third. Scope out the camp for Dietrich's tent.

If there was no sign of Dietrich, he'd disappear into the jungle and wait for the man to show up. Then Max would find a way to take him down.

Uh-huh. Right.

He eyed the manacles. If he had a thin piece of metal, he could pick the locks. He eyed the ground closest to him, but saw no convenient piece of metal sticking up.

Okay. For now, unlocking the manacles was out. He'd just have to wait and watch for an opportunity to get the tools he needed. In the meantime, if his previous captivity was any indication, he'd better mentally prepare for a shitload of pain.

You wouldn't be in this predicament if you'd asked for help in the beginning. The annoying voice in his head sounded an awful lot like Kristoff.

"No freaking kidding," he muttered. But he still held fast to the belief that keeping his distance had protected Kris and the rest of the team from Dietrich's sponsor.

While having backup made sense, Max didn't regret what he'd done. If he ended up dying here, so be it. At least he wouldn't be taking anyone else down with him. And he'd have the satisfaction of knowing that he'd done everything possible to stop Dietrich from hurting anyone else.

As long as Ziegler and Dietrich didn't have Emily, all was good.

Please, let Emily be free.

CHAPTER EIGHTEEN

Day Eleven

THE NEXT MORNING, Emily's stomach growled as she stared through the lens of her camera at the camp she'd found yesterday. Most of the tents were up now, and the organized chaos of yesterday's construction had calmed. The black-and-white logo on the uniforms of the men had been proof that the camp belonged to Dietrich even before she'd spotted Ziegler.

But although she'd been watching the men since dawn, she still didn't understand why they'd chosen this place to set up what appeared to be a semi-permanent camp. Yes, it was far enough away from the road to be hidden from people passing by. Still, why here? Why not back at the ravine near the plane crash?

Across the camp, Ziegler exited from the tent where she believed Max was being held. She'd snapped so many photos of Ziegler that once she got home she knew his face would feature in her nightmares for years to come. If she'd seen him on the street she'd never have suspected that he was a cold-blooded murderer. She still thought he looked like a middle-aged banker. He wore a neat business suit that set him apart from the uniforms of the guards. Of average height and weight, he was neither particularly handsome or particularly ugly.

She snapped another photo. His smug expression made her stomach churn with anger. Suspecting that he'd just been torturing Max, she wanted to march across the camp and shoot him.

But then Dietrich's men would kill her, leaving Max at their mercy. So she bided her time. Once Max was free, Kristoff and the others would make Ziegler pay for everything he'd done.

A guard patrolled a few hundred yards from her tree. Emily checked her watch. She'd been in this spot for nearly an hour. Time to move to another one of her observation posts. She—

The sat phone buzzed against her hip, startling her so much that she almost dropped her camera. She tightened her grip and bit back a curse, eyeing the soldier to make certain he hadn't heard the phone vibrating. When he continued on as if nothing had happened, she slowly let out her breath. Once her heart rate had returned to normal, she scooted back on her tree branch and sidled around until the trunk was between her and the camp. Then she carefully, quietly, climbed down the tree and walked several minutes until she was well out of earshot. Only then did she search for a place where she'd get strong enough reception to put through a call.

"Emily, where the hell have you been?" Kristoff demanded. "You were supposed to check in last night."

"I know, sir. I'm sorry. But the phone died not long after I texted you the briefcase's coordinates. There wasn't enough light to activate the solar charger until this morning."

"Are you safe?"

"Er..."

Kristoff's aggravated sigh reminded her so much of Max, that she teared up. "Emily, what have you done?"

"I'm not in any immediate danger. But I am outside of the camp where I think they're holding Max."

"Christ, Emily. You're taking a risk."

"I know, but I've spotted Ziegler. If he's here, surely Max is, too."

"Yes, that's probably true. Describe the camp's setup."

Struggling to keep the discouragement out of her voice, she answered, "There are two dozen men in camp at the moment, with more arriving every hour." How would Kristoff's team manage to rescue Max with so many armed men nearby? "All of the men wear black uniforms with a black-and-white logo on the pocket. An hour ago, a large truck drove up bearing several crates. A team of men unloaded the crates, then set about raising a large tent made out of white canvas with the group's insignia on the door flap. The logo is also displayed on the flag flying on the tent's pointed roof. Once the tent was in place, the men carried the crates inside."

"Good work. If they're setting up a semi-permanent base, this is probably the spot where the deal is going down. What's their perimeter security like?"

"The soldiers don't seem to think this remote spot poses any risk beyond the occasional wild animal, because I've only seen them patrolling at the very edge of camp. They seem more concerned about someone approaching from the direction of the road."

"Are you taking precautions not to be spotted?"

"Yes. I'm observing them from up in the trees and I've been switching my location every hour. I'm also keeping away from the side of camp closest to the road."

"All right. Text me your coordinates. Unfortunately, I still haven't heard from the man who was supposed to meet you, and the team I was trying to free up to extract you came under fire during a mission. Their helicopter is out of service. We're working on another way for them to reach you, but it will take time. So stay safe. In fact, now that I know where Max is, I want you to move far away from the camp."

"I—" Wait. What was that? She strained to hear.

The roar of an engine came from the direction of the road. Excited shouts and barked commands from inside the camp suggested the arrival of an important visitor. "Sorry, sir, I have to go," she said hastily. "There's a commotion back at camp." Without waiting for his reply, she disconnected and hurried to the closest tree that would give her a good view of the goings-on. Once she'd climbed high enough to see clearly into the camp, she pulled out her camera.

A moment later, a small convoy drove into the clearing in front of the tents. The open-topped Jeep in the lead had two men standing in the back, each holding an automatic rifle. Several dust-covered black Land Rovers followed the Jeep.

The camp's soldiers formed two receiving lines around the edges of the clearing as men piled out of the arriving vehicles and set up their own perimeter guard.

An older white man wearing a lightweight suit stepped out. Thick gray hair swung just below his jaw, giving him a metrosexual look. Dark sunglasses hid his eyes. From the way every man in the clearing snapped to attention, she didn't have to be a genius to figure out his identity.

Dietrich.

Which meant that the luxury tent the men had erected earlier belonged to him.

Emily continued to take photos as the group greeted Dietrich and he was escorted to his tent, but her mind raced. Fear tore through her veins. Max couldn't wait for Kristoff's men to rescue him. Once Dietrich realized that Max couldn't give him the location of the briefcase, he wouldn't have any reason to keep Max alive.

She chewed on her lip. What could she do?

After several minutes of staring at the camp, which now bustled with more activity than before, she decided to chance calling Kristoff back.

As soon as he answered, she explained the situation. "We need to help Max now."

Emily heard someone in the background ask Kristoff for an update. He relayed the information, then asked, "How many men do you see outside of the tents? Where are the guards standing?"

The other person told Kristoff to ask additional questions. "What are the rest of the men doing?" Kristoff continued. "What's the arrangement of the tents? Where's the food tent? Is there an obvious supply of water?"

She described the camp in as much detail as possible, then added, "It looks like they're preparing for some large gathering. Maybe lunch or dinner with Dietrich and all the men."

"Okay." He conferred with whoever was there in the room with him. "Tell me again about the water supply."

"Hold on, let me change to another location. I'll call you back." Sensing where the conversation was going, Emily slipped out of her tree and snuck through the jungle until she reached the stream to the left of the camp. She found a spot up another tree that gave the phone a signal, and dialed Kristoff.

"I'm at the stream now," she explained when he'd answered. "There are twelve, fifty-gallon plastic barrels set up in a line along the riverbank. You know, those big blue barrels that people here use to store the water they pull from their wells." Her home-stay family had used one. "Hoses run from the barrels to a pump in the middle of the stream. Each barrel has a spigot that the guards use to fill up the smaller containers they carry back to camp."

"Sounds like a custom filtration system. Are the lids on the containers locked?"

She used the binoculars to zoom in. "It doesn't look like it from here."

"Right. Give us a minute." Kristoff's words were followed by the heavy silence of an activated mute function.

Emily peered out from the bushes. A thorn caught on her

sleeve and she stilled in order to free herself. That's when she noticed the heavy black seeds on the bush.

Richard slapped his little sister's hand away from the bush. "Do not eat seeds. Even small taste make you very sick."

Emily stared at the round seeds inches away from her nose, certain these were the same ones Richard, a boy in her homestay village, had said were poisonous. And he'd said something else. Something about the taste. Yes. Not bad, he'd said, admitting he'd gotten sick from eating a seed when he was little. So sick he'd almost died.

When Kristoff came back on the line, Emily excitedly relayed the information about the seeds. "I could crush the seeds and put them in the water. With the bushes growing close, I'm sure I can sneak over to the containers. No one seems to be paying any attention to this area of camp."

"And then what? You're just going to stroll into camp and waltz out with Max? You don't even know if he can walk."

Emily understood the frustration in Kristoff's voice, but she refused to give up. "Yes. Why not? If all the men are sick, who's going to stop me?"

"Some soldier who didn't drink any water, that's who. And what if Max drinks the tainted water?"

"That's a chance we have to take. Although, since I haven't seen anyone bring him food or water since I arrived, dehydration is more of a threat." She'd deal with that after she got him free. "What else are we going to do? You're God knows how many miles away. You're the one who told me to check the water supply. If this wasn't what you intended, then what's your grand plan?"

Kristoff let out a long sigh. "No, you're right. I'm sorry. My extraction team was supposed to handle this, not you. I'm just worried about your safety."

"Trust me, I know how dangerous this plan is. I'm scared to death of being caught. But we can't wait. Dietrich will kill Max soon."

Emily heard the other voice in the background telling Kristoff to let it go. That the risk was necessary. "Yes," Emily said. "Listen to whoever's there with you, Kristoff. I have to do this."

"I—" Kristoff swore.

"All right, Emily," a new voice said. She sensed a barely leashed anger underneath the man's authoritative tone. "You're a go. Tell me more about these seeds."

"Sir?"

"Nah, don't sir me. I'm Wil. Max's brother."

"Oh." Maybe that wasn't anger she heard. Maybe it was fear.

"Kris tells me you're in love with my idiot brother, so you and I are practically family."

Oddly warmed by his comment, Emily relayed everything she remembered about the seeds.

"Working with the seeds will be dangerous," Wil warned. "Here's what you need to do..."

"HERR ZIEGLER, I am disappointed in you. This is no way to treat a guest."

Dietrich's hated voice roused Max from his stupor. Crap. The big man was here and Max was no closer to getting himself free. Well, that wasn't entirely true. Because Max was too weak to do anything but lie here, fighting to stay conscious, Ziegler had removed all but one of the manacles.

Max struggled to raise his head from the pool of vomit and blood next to him, and caught Dietrich's moue of distaste as he took in Max's bloody, filthy appearance. *That's right, asshole, look what your buddy has done to me.*

After ordering his men to use tent stakes to beat him, Ziegler had personally kicked the crap out of Max. He was pretty sure that not only had the blows deepened the current cracks in his ribs, but had damaged another one or two. As if that hadn't been enough, then Ziegler had gone to work with his needles.

"He is withholding information, Herr Dietrich. I wished to have details of the briefcase's location ready upon your arrival."

Ignoring the agony in his bloody hands, Max seized hold of the nearest stake and pulled himself to a seated position. Pain speared through him. He ignored it. He would not pass out in front of Dietrich and he would not lie back down. "Never...asked me...briefcase..." No, Ziegler had just gleefully started in on the torture without saying a word to Max.

Dietrich frowned, then turned his back on Max. "Johann!" he called.

Johann Strauss, Dietrich's captain of the guard, poked his head into the tent. "Yes, sir?"

"See that our guest is cleaned up and his wounds treated. Then escort him to my tent."

"Yes, sir." The man moved toward Max.

Ziegler made a choked protest, but Dietrich waved him off. "Herr Ziegler, your personal vendetta against Max has become a liability. Did I, or did I not, tell you that Max was not to be harmed? That I wanted him to be in prime condition when I questioned him?

"Yes, but—"

"No." Dietrich pointed at Ziegler. "I have had enough of your insubordination. The correct answer was, 'Yes, sir.' The fact that you continually ignore my orders is inexcusable."

Ziegler stared calmly back at Dietrich before finally bowing his head. "I apologize, sir. It will not happen again."

"Of course not. I will not allow it." Dietrich pulled a silenced pistol from his pocket and shot Ziegler once in the chest, then once between the eyes.

Max stared in shock as Ziegler toppled to the ground.

Dietrich turned toward Max. "I apologize for the mistreatment you have suffered at the hand of my colleague, Herr Lansing. When you are feeling more yourself, you and I shall talk."

Turning on his heel, Dietrich walked out.

What the fuck? Max didn't realize he'd spoken out loud until Johann said, "You heard the boss, let's get you cleaned up." He called for help and two more soldiers entered. The tent was so small, the men barely had room to maneuver.

Johann ordered one of the men to undo the remaining manacle.

Damn. A perfect opportunity to break free, and he could barely—

Johann and the other man lifted Max off the ground.

Agony. Darkness. Oblivion.

CHAPTER NINETEEN

WITH SURGICAL GLOVES protecting her hands, Emily gathered another handful of poisonous seeds and placed them in the plastic baggie she'd found among the medical supplies. The bushes she needed only grew here along the river, and after her call with Kristoff and Wil she'd started collecting seeds. Water dripped down her chin from the persistent drizzle that had started half an hour ago. Eyeing the nearly full baggie, she figured this last batch of seeds was enough. Now she could—

Hearing men's voices, she quickly backed deeper into the bushes, then dropped to her knees and set the baggie aside. Hooking her right index finger inside the wristband of her left glove, she rolled the glove outside in as she pulled it off, following Wil's instructions on how to avoid getting the seed's oil on her skin. Once both gloves were safely off, with their uncontaminated interiors now on the outside, she placed them into a spare baggie she was using for trash.

Two men exited the camp, carrying Max on a stretcher. They strode to the river's edge and dumped the stretcher on the bank. Almost every inch of Max's naked body was covered in blood, dirt, and bruises, yet he didn't so much as groan at the impact. He just lay there, unmoving.

Dead?

Emily's heart constricted. She shoved one of her fists against her mouth to stifle her screams. No. Oh, no. Max couldn't be dead. Not now, when she was so close to enacting her rescue plan. Tears cascaded down her face.

Acting on automatic pilot, she pulled out her camera and snapped off photos to use as proof of what had been done.

A moment later, a stout, older white man holding a large medical bag joined the group on the riverbank. At a nod from the doctor, the men lifted the stretcher, then set it into the river downstream from the water filtration system. Max moaned and turned his head as the cold river washed over him.

Emily nearly cried out in relief. He was alive!

Her hands shook as she put the camera in video mode. She wanted this abuse documented so that none of these men could deny the abuse Max had suffered. Because she was going to make those responsible pay.

Emily touched Max's pistol and debated shooting the men. No. The sound of shots would only draw attention from the other guards. Max didn't appear able to walk, and dragging the stretcher back to her home tree would leave a distinctive trail that would lead Dietrich's men right to her.

Besides, despite her fury, she didn't think she could coldly shoot these men. No matter what they'd done to Max, her mind shied away from the idea of pulling the trigger while their backs were turned. It would be too similar to how Crystal and Sue had died.

After the doctor cut away Max's stained bandages, he washed away the blood and dirt from Max's front. Then the men turned Max over and one man held Max's face above the water as the doctor cleaned his back.

Emily didn't understand what was going on. Max had received a severe beating, but now these men were caring for Max as if he were one of their own. She didn't remember Max saying anything about Dietrich's spiritual beliefs. Were the men preparing Max for some bizarre religious ritual? Were they going to sacrifice him?

Could her imagination get any more fanciful? But why else would they—

The doctor pulled a knife out of his bag. The men steadied Max.

Emily's fingers closed over the grip of the pistol. She opened her mouth to shout a protest, but snapped it closed when the doctor simply cut Max's hair close to his scalp.

Very weird. Was she right about this leading up to a religious ritual?

After the last hank of Max's hair had fallen into the river, the doctor scrubbed the stubble with a bright blue solution. Finally, he rinsed it away, then examined Max's scalp. Was he checking for some sort of infestation? The thought made Emily scratch her own scalp.

Once the doctor had finished, the men moved Max out of the water. Now that the surface coating of blood was gone, some of Emily's fear subsided. Yes, Max was badly hurt, but the number and severity of his cuts weren't as high as she'd thought.

After one of the men dried Max off, the doctor examined the worst of his injuries and applied iodine to the cuts. Max groaned and opened his eyes. Then he tried to fight free.

The doctor put his hand on Max's chest and leaned close, saying something in Max's ear. Max immediately quieted. But Emily noticed that Max studied his captors and his surroundings as they worked on him. Good. He appeared to be mentally sharp.

The doctor resumed dabbing iodine on Max's cuts and scrapes. Then he pulled out a small kit from his medical bag and removed a needle and thread. He sewed closed the wound in Max's thigh and added a few stitches to the ones Dr. LaSalle had used to close the knife slice across Max's lower back. Finally, the doctor bandaged Max's cuts.

After replacing his tools in his bag, the doctor pulled out a pair of loose local pants and a batik tunic top and the men helped him dress Max. Then they carried Max back to camp. Emily followed only long enough to observe them carrying him to Dietrich's tent, before she slipped back to the stash of seeds she'd left at the river.

All right. Max was alive, for now. Her plan was still a go.

Which meant it was time to prepare the poison.

MAX WISHED he knew what the hell Dietrich was up to. Still reeling over the fact that Dietrich had killed Ziegler, Max stared in amazement at the luxurious interior of the tent. There was a guard outside the entrance, but other than that, he'd been left here alone and unrestrained.

Not that in his current condition he could walk far, but still...

He shook his head. Never in a million years would he have thought that Dietrich would order his men to wash him and tend to his wounds. He ran his hand over his head. They'd even shorn his hair. Because of lice or other vermin?

Once they'd brought him here, he'd been given clean water to drink and weak broth. To his relief, he hadn't immediately thrown up, and he hadn't developed any other symptoms, so he hadn't been drugged or poisoned.

What the fuck was going on?

Gritting his teeth, he tried again to stand. A few minutes ago, he'd pushed to his feet and nearly passed out from dizziness. But this time the whirling of the room settled down after a few heartbeats. He dared to move his bare right foot forward across the thick woven carpet covering the tent floor. Put some weight on his foot.

He didn't collapse in agony. Good. Nothing broken on that side.

The wound in his thigh had been reopened by a well-placed kick from the toe of Ziegler's loafer, but the doctor had done a good job of stitching it closed. He'd even applied a topical analgesic so Max didn't feel too much pain.

He took another hesitant step. Then another.

By his internal clock, he estimated that it took him ten minutes to walk one complete circuit of the tent's interior. Okay. He wasn't going to run any marathons, but if necessary, he might be able to walk out of here.

He plopped onto the chair behind Dietrich's desk with a sigh of relief. While he felt one hundred percent more human now that he was clean and hydrated, what he really needed was a week of sleep and a couple of steak dinners.

Max studied his surroundings. The carpets on the floor displayed a repeating pattern of Dietrich's black-and-white logo. Two sturdy chairs and a desk took up the center of the tent, all made from intricately carved ebony that would make them heavy bastards to carry.

A narrow bed in a matching base sat to the right, piled high with batik pillows in a variety of rainbow colors.

Huh. Not what he would have expected from the grim, ever-so-proper Dietrich.

Max examined the desk, hoping to find some details about the upcoming deal. Such as the exact location. Or the name of the buyer. But not a single sheet of paper littered the surface. The only adornments were an ornate silver lantern on one corner and a wooden pencil cup on the other. Dietrich obviously didn't expect any resistance from Max, because he'd left pens and pencils in the cup. Hell, Max could even use the lantern as a weapon.

He searched the desk, but found nothing but a few empty file folders and two metal paper clips. Okay, so he hadn't really expected Dietrich to leave incriminating evidence lying around. The man was too intelligent. With a mental shrug, Max took the paperclips, one pen, and one pencil and stuck them in the pocket of his tunic.

He hobbled over to a large steamer trunk, but it contained nothing but clothing.

Figured.

"Find anything interesting?"

Max startled and would have fallen if he hadn't been gripping the raised lid of the heavy trunk. Taking a steadying breath, he turned to find Dietrich smiling at him from the entrance.

Max straightened. He studied the man he'd only observed from a distance. The life of an international arms dealer agreed with Dietrich. He'd removed his trademark fedora and his thick gray hair, slightly on the long side for a man of his generation, paired with his slight tan gave him the appearance of a movie tycoon. Faint age lines spread out from his thundercloud gray eyes. But for the most part, Dietrich's face, neck, and throat were unlined. No doubt due to cosmetic surgery.

His sixty-plus years showed only in the liver spots on his hands.

Dietrich walked into the tent and placed a map on his desk. He sat down and indicated for Max to take the visitor's chair.

It took all of Max's will to walk over to the chair without limping or swaying, but he managed it.

Determined not to be the first to break the silence, Max waited for Dietrich to speak.

The man studied him for a long while. "How are you feeling? I apologize for your mistreatment at Herr Ziegler's hands."

"Yeah, I know you wanted to keep that little honor for yourself."

Max had the satisfaction of watching Dietrich's mouth tighten. But the man quickly got his emotions under control. "Max, Max," he chided. "You have been nothing but a thorn in my side since that day outside of Fallujah all those years ago. Of course I wish to settle our score. Not only have you and your teammates cost me much money, but you nearly destroyed my career."

"Your tough luck for selling weapons to people who kill thousands of innocents."

Dietrich gave a delicate shrug. "But all thoughts of retribution must wait. You know what information I need from you."

"Why don't you spell it out for me? Just to make certain there's no misunderstanding."

Dietrich shook his head in disappointment. "Where is the briefcase you retrieved from my downed plane?"

"What makes you think I have this briefcase?"

"My men found the crash site. They located the courier's arm. Someone had cut the man's tendons with a knife and removed the security bracelet connecting him to the briefcase he had been bringing to me. My men are quite convinced that the locals had no knowledge of the briefcase." Dietrich spread his hands. "So that leaves you and the white girl the locals claim was with you when you killed one of their men."

Max's pulse spiked. No way did Dietrich have Emily as prisoner. If he did, he'd have the briefcase. Which meant she was safe. For now. "To be honest, yes, we did retrieve your briefcase."

Dietrich's eyes flared with triumph.

"But the girl and I split a while back." He shrugged nonchalantly, as if he didn't care about Emily. "She took the briefcase and headed into the jungle. I have no clue where she is or what she's done with the case."

Dietrich gave him a lengthy, probing look. He tilted his head back, steepled his fingers under his chin, and stared at the ceiling of the tent. Several minutes later, he returned his cold gaze to Max. "I find that I believe you. That is most unfortunate. It means that you are no longer of use to me." He stood, so Max did the same.

"You're going to kill me?"

"Oh, no. That would be far too easy." Dietrich gave him a faint smile. "I want you to suffer not just pain but humiliation, Maximilian Lansing. I want you to feel despair. Therefore, I believe that I shall offer you to my buyer as compensation for providing him with the original prototype, rather than the improved one that you have so inconveniently stolen from me."

Max's heart sank. Great. All that effort, all that risk to Emily's life, had been for nothing. The deal was still going to happen. The buyer would get a powerful weapon to test against a target of his choice. Dietrich would get his money.

No. There had to be a way to stop the deal. And his best chance of escaping was if Dietrich thought Max was too weak to leave. With that in mind, he let his body sag. "Our little chat has been great," he wheezed, "but the room's kinda spinning." To emphasize his point, he listed to the right.

"Yes, of course. I apologize. For a man who was so close to dying, you have shown incredible strength by sitting up for so long. I will have you escorted back to your tent."

Max flinched at the thought of returning to that dark, filthy prison.

"No, no," Dietrich reassured him. "Not the place where I found you. I have had a more pleasant tent prepared for you. My buyer will want you in good condition."

No way in hell would Max let them turn him over to the buyer and send him to the labor or slave markets.

Dietrich called out in German and Johann stepped into the tent.

"Please escort—" Dietrich began, then he glanced over at Max. "Are you able to walk? Or would you prefer a stretcher?"

Max barely held back his growl. "I might..." Dammit, he hated showing weakness. But he truly needed to conserve his strength and playing the invalid worked in his favor. He dropped his gaze to the floor and cleared his throat. "A stretcher, please."

CHAPTER TWENTY

Max's new prison tent barely had room for his cot. The guards had carried him in, laid him down, and manacled his right wrist to the cot's metal frame before leaving him alone. That had been several hours ago. No one had been by to check on him since or even to bring him food or water. From the sounds of the camp, Dietrich had called his men together for a meal. Or maybe an inspirational speech.

Whatever. The absence of more guards worked in his favor.

Max twisted the lock pick he'd formed using the paperclips. The tumblers of the manacle's lock finally clicked and the cuff fell open. Stupid of them not to have searched him, but then he supposed they figured he was too weak to walk out of here.

He circled his wrist to restore full circulation. Then—careful to make as little noise as possible—he broke off two of the cot's wooden cross supports that ran underneath the mattress. Using strips torn from the blanket, he bound the supports together to form a makeshift cane. It wouldn't hold up for long once he hit the rough floor of the jungle, but all he needed was to get out of camp. He'd make a new cane once he was out of immediate danger.

Satisfied that the cane was the right height, he took a series of practice walks. From the cot to the door. Back. Again.

He had to rest frequently, being careful to only sit on the edge of the cot where there was still horizontal support. About an hour later, he heard retching from the guard outside the door, then a thump.

Max rose and hobbled over to the door. He peeked out the tent flap.

The setting sun speared through heavy clouds to cast deep shadows across the dirt lanes between the tents. In front of the tent, the guard lay in a heap next to a steaming pile of vomit. Several tents away, two men slumped to the ground, retching and clutching their stomachs. A black plastic plate full of stew and rice tumbled to the dirt beside them. Water slipped from a fallen cup and pooled on the moist earth. On the other side of camp, a man called out an alarm.

All right. Either the food or the water was contaminated. Good thing he hadn't eaten recently.

Max stepped out of the tent and paused. While the loose pants he wore were dark enough to fool a casual glance, his purple and white batik shirt marked him as different. So, supporting himself on his good leg and leaning heavily on his cane, he knelt down and removed the guard's uniform shirt. After switching shirts, he stuck the man's cap on his head and slung the man's HK417 assault rifle over his shoulder. Then he eyed the guard's feet and compared the size to his own. Close enough.

Max put the man's boots on. They were slightly loose, so he'd probably end up with blisters, but better that than tear up the soles of his feet walking through the jungle. Satisfied, he stood up.

Now. Which way to go? He couldn't see the jungle, only more tents.

Hmm... Right sounded good.

He started walking.

A figure rounded the corner of the tent behind him. Max ducked his head and kept hobbling, but dammit, his cane was a dead giveaway.

"Max, stop! You're going the wrong way." The whispered command had him spinning around so fast he overbalanced.

Emily, wearing the uniform of one of Dietrich's soldiers, rushed in to support him. "Quickly. This way."

"Wha— How?"

"Later."

Emily led him through the maze of tents. The scent of vomit permeated the camp. Men lay bonelessly where they'd fallen. Plates and cups littered the ground. A couple of men raised their heads and glared at him and Emily, but none managed to get to their feet to stop them. "What the hell did you do?"

"Put the powder of some poisonous seeds in the water," Emily explained, tugging on his waist to steer him down a narrow alley between two tents. The alley ended at a clearing with several parked Jeeps and Land Rovers. "It took me an hour to grind enough seeds to get a sufficient amount of powder that I felt confident it would take out the whole camp."

"Where'd you put it?"

"In the water containers they left by the river. I slipped the powder into the containers just before dinner."

Smart, but dangerous. "You didn't get any of the powder on your skin, did you? Or breathe it in?"

She rolled her eyes. "No, Max. I'm not a complete idiot. Wil talked me through what precautions to take. I—"

"What? You talked to my *brother*?"

"Yes. I'll explain later. The important part is that I used a pair of surgical gloves to protect my hands and covered my nose and mouth with a bandana, then disposed of everything properly."

"Okay, that's good." Still, he didn't want to think about the danger she'd been in. Not only while adding the powder, but also while stealing the uniform.

Just as they reached the edge of the parking area, Max heard the roar of several vehicles approaching. "Cars coming!"

Emily must have heard the vehicles too, because she peeked into the nearest tent, then pulled him inside. Along two of the walls, empty boxes and crates were stacked neatly inside one another. A couple of automotive toolkits sat to their right.

Balancing on his cane, Max slid back the flap to the tent just far enough to let him and Emily watch what was happening.

A convoy of six Toyota Land Cruisers and two Hummers drove into the car park. They stopped and disgorged about two dozen security men, all dark skinned Africans. The men took one look at Dietrich's unconscious guards and the pools of vomit next to them and immediately retreated to stand by their vehicles. After conferring with someone in the lead Hummer, four men broke away and headed into the camp.

Emily tugged on Max's sleeve. *Buyer*, she mouthed, lifting her eyebrows in question.

He nodded. By his calculations, the deal was supposed to take place tomorrow. Either his info was wrong, or the buyer was early. Or he'd lost a day being unconscious.

Several minutes later, the buyer's men reappeared, holding a limp, pale Dietrich between them. As they approached the buyer's vehicles, Dietrich heaved. The men dropped him and backpedaled as he threw up.

Max grinned. Ah. Finally, a measure of justice.

When Dietrich had recovered, the men hauled him to his feet and dragged him over to the main Hummer. Once again they spoke with someone inside, then Dietrich was transferred to the cargo compartment of one of the Land Cruisers. The buyer's men climbed back into their respective vehicles and the convoy left.

"We have to follow them," Max said. "There's a second prototype."

"Are you freaking kidding me?" Emily snarled as she led him into the car park and toward a Land Rover on the far side.

"Trust me, I wish I wasn't. Dietrich wanted the briefcase we found because it contains the plans and prototype for a more recent, improved weapon. But he has an earlier prototype ready to pass on to the buyer as a backup plan. We still have to make sure that the deal doesn't go through."

Emily growled in frustration and indicated for him to get into the Land Rover's passenger seat. As he complied, he noticed that her rucksack already sat on the back seat. So. She'd really planned this out. Smart.

"Okay, give me a minute to get this thing started," she said, ducking under the steering column.

"Damn, woman. You can hotwire a car? Now I know I'm in love."

Emily chuckled. "All part of the survival skills Father taught us."

"I really want to meet your father."

"Um..." The engine roared to life. Emily shimmied into the driver's seat, executed a fast three-point turn, then sped out of the parking area.

Max grinned as she deftly avoided a tree stump, then increased speed. "Look at your driving," he said. "Just like a kickass movie heroine." He took her hand and kissed it. "*My* kickass heroine. I love it." He paused. "I—"

A Hummer turned off the road and headed right toward them.

EMILY SLAMMED on the brakes and jammed the Land Rover into reverse. Oh, God. They'd been so close to getting away.

"Shit," Max said as the Hummer roared toward them.

Emily floored it, speeding backward just as the man in the passenger seat of the Hummer opened his window and fired at them.

"Duck!" Max shoved her head down a second before the Land

Rover's windshield burst into thousands of tiny pieces. Emily felt stinging along her bare arms and face, but was too concerned with keeping the Land Rover straight to worry about it. Using the side view mirror, she aimed for a particular tree. Just before they reached it, she sat up and yanked the wheel hard to the left. They spun away from the road, bullets thudding into the Land Rover's sides as the back end slid across the carpet of mud and wet leaves. Emily shifted into first, straightened the car's trajectory, and made a beeline for the thicker protection of the jungle.

"Oohrah!" Max shouted. "Where'd you learn to drive like that?"

She zoomed around the trees. "From my cousin. He's into the drifting scene in Japan and he gave me a few lessons when the dance company was in town."

"Well, damn. You can drive my escape vehicle any time you—"

With a roar, the Hummer rammed between two slender trees behind them. The trees bent, then the Hummer muscled through.

"*Merde!*" The rearview mirror had been destroyed by the bullets, so Emily peeked in the side view mirror to keep track of their pursuers. The Hummer was bigger and sturdier than their Land Rover and the driver didn't seem to care about little piddling obstacles such as trees. He just plowed ahead, while his passenger continued to spray them with bullets. "Max, they're gaining on us."

"Don't panic. We're more maneuverable than they are. Use that advantage now." He raised the rifle he'd taken from Dietrich's camp and sent a burst of fire toward the Hummer.

"Great," he grumbled.

"What?"

"They're armored."

"Hold on." Emily swerved to the left just before a thick section of buttressed roots. Then she turned back the way they'd come, passing the Hummer racing in the other direction before making a sharp right into a gap between the trees.

She heard the Hummer slam on its brakes. Then the sound of gunfire. Bullets tore through the trees around them and a few more bullets hit the Land Rover.

Red lights flashed on the dash. "Max! I've got both the check engine and low oil lights on. Plus, the gas gauge has plummeted."

"Keep driving as long as you can. Aim toward the road." Max showed her their location on the GPS.

"Okay."

Unfortunately, the terrain soon became very dense and difficult to drive through. While she hoped that meant that the Hummer would also have trouble navigating, she suspected that once they picked up her trail they'd simply muscle over the low-lying vegetation. Emily did her best to drive along the path of least resistance, trying to put less stress on the Land Rover. She kept a wary eye on the gauges as the vehicle slowly lost momentum, until finally the engine coughed, sputtered, and died.

Merde, merde, merde. Emily glanced over at Max. "Are you going to be okay walking?"

He shrugged, grabbed his cane, and shoved open his door. "Don't have much choice."

Emily slung her backpack over her shoulder, put her arm around Max's waist, and together they fast hobbled into the jungle. With the light failing, it was hard to see where they were going and she didn't have the chance to pull out the night vision goggles. They hadn't gone very far before she heard the sound of the Hummer. It slammed into the Land Rover, then its engine growled. Emily threw a frightened glance over her shoulder and saw the Hummer's headlights breaking through the jungle's dim twilight.

An instant later, the lights abruptly cut off. The vehicle's doors opened, slammed shut, then an eerie silence fell over the jungle. Great. The men probably had night vision goggles. The fact that she couldn't hear them move through the underbrush meant they were well trained.

"Emily—" Max glanced down at her. She saw the determination in his eyes and knew he was going to suggest that they split up.

"No," she whispered fiercely, tightening her grip on his waist. "I didn't rescue you just to have you play martyr again. We're in this together. I'm not leaving you, so deal with it and get your butt in gear."

He shifted his weight and nodded toward a thick above ground root system. "I was going to suggest that we ambush them. We need their vehicle in order to continue following Dietrich and the buyer."

"Oh." She hesitated, then asked, "Are you going to kill them?"

"What? No. I know you think I'm trigger-happy, but I'm not some heartless killer. They're not holding a weapon on you, so they're not enough of a threat to kill. But I will disable them. Now, give me the night vision goggles and the pistol." He handed her the automatic rifle. "Keep this and get behind the tree."

She did as he asked, adjusting her position until she found a spot that allowed her to peer out between two of the roots and watch Max.

He waited until both men had walked past his position. Then he put his arm around the neck of the rear guy and slammed the butt of the pistol into his temple. Max took him down to the ground, so when the second man turned to shoot, Max wasn't where he'd expected. Max shot the man in the leg. The man bit back a scream and lunged toward Max.

Emily came out from behind her tree as Max and the downed guard fought. There wasn't anything she could do to help Max, so she used a loose section of vine to tie up the unconscious man. Then she used his bandana to gag him. By the time she was finished, Max had knocked out the other guy.

Chest heaving, he glanced over at her, then the trussed up guard. "Good...work," he gasped.

"Are you okay?" She rushed over but when she offered to pull him to his feet, he shook his head. "Just give me...a minute. Gotta catch my breath. Finish the other guy."

Emily tied up the second guard. Then she confiscated their weapons, their night vision goggles, and their car keys. The small insignia on their uniforms proclaimed them to be Dietrich's men. Had they been out on patrol when she poisoned the camp? Or were they a backup team called in when most everyone fell sick?

Guard neutralized, she walked over to Max. This time he let her help him to his feet. She could tell from the way he moved that he was in pain, but didn't comment.

"Need a new cane," he muttered as he slowly eased his weight away from her. He pointed to a thick branch lying on the ground at the base of the tree and Emily handed it to him. He tested it, then grunted. "It'll do. Let's go."

Emily winced when they reached the Land Rover. The Hummer had slammed into the rear of the Land Rover, crumpling its back end without leaving any noticeable damage to the Hummer. She helped Max into the passenger seat of the Hummer, put her rucksack on the back seat, then took off toward the road.

The Hummer wasn't as maneuverable as the Land Rover, but she enjoyed the sense of invincibility it gave her.

"What now?"

"Drive north. That's the direction the convoy was heading. Hopefully, we'll see their taillights to confirm they're still on the road."

She grimaced. "The odds aren't good that we're going to catch them, Max."

"We don't have to catch them. They're going to stop at some point. Dietrich didn't have the second prototype with him when the buyer's men dragged him out of camp. Which means they'll either send someone back to Dietrich's camp to get it or call Dietrich's men and hope that someone is feeling strong enough to bring the prototype to them."

"So we just have to keep on their trail and we'll find the buyer's camp."

Max didn't answer her. He was too busy fiddling with the electronics on the dashboard.

"What are you doing?" she asked.

He nodded at the LCD screen. "I think Dietrich installed a fleet tracking system. Which means his men can see where we are."

As they bumped along the root-riddled ground just inside the protection of the trees, Max muttered a curse under his breath. "Ah, to hell with it." He rummaged in the glove box. Emily glanced over and saw him remove an all-in-one portable tool.

Max opened the screwdriver, pried the LCD screen away from the dash and hacked at the insides. Sparks flew. He growled at the mess he'd made, reached deeper into the dashboard, and yanked out a handful of wires. He sliced across them with the tool's knife, then sagged back in his seat.

"Did you kill the big, bad tracking device oh mighty hunter?" Emily asked, biting back a smile.

"You bet your sweet ass I did."

She wanted to reach out and pat his leg, but even though the Hummer had power steering, it still took both hands to keep it steady. Instead, she batted her eyelashes and said in a high-pitched, breathy voice, "My hero."

Max just snorted.

THE RAIN STARTED UP AGAIN, hitting the Hummer's roof with a driving rhythm despite the leaves overhead. Still, the rain created a sense of intimacy inside the vehicle that Max found soothing.

"Tell me what's been going on since I left you," he said.

"Where's the briefcase? Why did you follow me?"

"Why did I—?" She muttered what he assumed was a curse or three in Japanese. "I—" She slowed the Hummer to a halt. "Max, look."

Light filtered through the trees ahead of them. "What'd I tell you," he said. "I bet that's them." He reached behind him for Emily's pack, groaning at the pain.

"Wait. What do you need? I'll get it. Don't irritate your ribs."

"The binoculars. I'm going to investigate." He shot her a glare. "You will stay here."

She sighed and reached into the back seat. "Yes, Max."

"Wait. What was that? Did you actually agree with me? Can I hear that again?"

Rolling her eyes, Emily pulled out the binoculars and slapped them into his hands.

Max gave her a quick kiss. "While I'm gone, you can check for an external tracking device." He explained what to look for and where.

"Oh joy, I get to crawl under the car in the rain."

"It's a tough job, sugar, but..."

She rolled her eyes and reached for her door handle as Max let himself out into the rain.

It didn't take him long to reach the spot where the buyer's men were setting up camp. Like Dietrich, they'd brought a few tents, although theirs were smaller. Men were in the process of raising the tents when Max took up position behind a tree. A few minutes later, two guards hustled a man wearing a trench coat out of one of the Hummers. They held an umbrella over his head until he disappeared into the largest tent. Probably the buyer.

Not long after that, one of the guards dragged Dietrich out of the Land Cruiser and threw him inside a four-person tent.

As the rest of the tents went up, the guards unloaded equipment from the vehicles. Based on the frowns and angry hand gestures, some of the men weren't happy to be setting up camp in the rain and dark. Unprofessional of them. Say what you like about Dietrich, his guards were well-disciplined and didn't tolerate such grumbling.

The buyer's men moved their vehicles to form a perimeter around the tents, then strung a series of wires outside the circle of vehicles. Probably an alarm system. Yet they apparently didn't expect serious trouble tonight, because they only stationed two men to guard the encampment. One inside each of the Hummers.

Yeah. Not impressing him, here.

So far, all the men he'd seen were wearing the buyer's uniforms. But between Dietrich being kidnapped and the fact that the two men Max and Emily had disabled would fail to make any scheduled check-in, he figured Dietrich's men were bound to show up at some point.

Once the camp had settled down, Max headed back to Emily.

"It doesn't look like they're going anywhere tonight," he said once he'd explained the situation to her. "They're close enough to the edge of the jungle that if we move to the other side of the road, directly opposite, we should have good eyes on them. Did you find anything?"

"Yeah." Emily nodded and started the Hummer. "Just one, in the engine compartment, stuck against the firewall. I crushed it like you told me to and buried the pieces in the woods."

"Thank you."

The point opposite the camp where they took up their new position not only provided him and Emily protection from observers in the camp, but also had a wide tree they could climb to get a better view. Assuming he could haul his ass up there given his wounds. The fight had set his ribs to throbbing and might have broken open the stitches in his thigh.

He sighed. "I need you to do some reconnaissance. Check that no one is moving around in the camp. Then you'll need to play doctor again."

She studied him, then nodded. "I figured you'd taken more damage during the fight." Leaning forward, she kissed him on his cheek. "Thank you for asking for help, rather than hiding the fact that you're hurting."

As she slipped outside, he realized that it felt right sharing the work with her. That they'd moved into that rare state of partnership he'd experienced with very few people. He trusted that she'd take care of herself and get the information they needed. While the panic he used to feel when she left his sight was still present, it was a fraction of its previous strength.

"They still appear to be hunkered down for the night," Emily said when she returned a few minutes later.

"Okay. We'll need to check on them every half an hour." He handed her a peeled banana. She threw him a grateful smile before biting into it.

Once she was done eating, Emily changed his bandages. He'd been right, the stitches had broken open, so she used the last of their clotting gauze to stop the bleeding. Leaning back against the seat after he'd been patched up, Max rested for a long moment. Then he indicated for Emily to pass him the sat phone. "There's a break in the trees behind us, so I should be able to get reception. Let me check in with Kris. See if he can send a team to take over."

Emily shook her head. "Kristoff isn't going to be able to help. Not right away." She chewed on her bottom lip a moment, then explained why Kris couldn't send backup.

Max shrugged off his disappointment. "I'll still call him. Give him an update. See if he has any idea when the extraction team might be available. Then we'll keep an eye on the buyer and Dietrich and do our best to stop them from completing the deal."

Emily glanced at the phone in her hand. "Uh-oh. The battery's dead. Sorry. I was on the phone a lot with Kristoff and Wil planning your rescue. I must have used up all the juice." She twisted so she could access her rucksack in the back seat. "I think you put the car charger in my pack, right?"

"Yeah." Figured Kris would be out of touch.

Emily grunted in satisfaction. "Found it." She settled back in her seat, then plugged the charger into the power outlet.

"So," Max said. "Did you say that *Wil* guided you on how to poison the water supply? How'd you end up talking to him? Just how pissed was he?"

Instead of answering, Emily's face crumpled. "God, Max, I've been worried sick about you. I saw them carry you out on that stretcher and I thought... I thought..."

Tears filled her eyes. "I'm sorry," she said, sniffling.

"Shh. It's all right, sweetheart." Max reached for her. She snuggled against him. Yes. This is where he wanted her. Safe in his arms again.

He pressed his cheek to her hair. "I told you not to come after me. Why didn't you listen?"

"Are you nuts?" She pulled back, her eyes shooting sparks. "I love you. I'd never abandon you!"

Her fierce loyalty broke something open deep inside of him. Hot, burning joy welled up and obliterated all his doubts and fears. He kissed her passionately, trying to express everything he couldn't put into words.

God, he'd missed her so much. Knowing she was safe was the only thing that had kept him from losing his mind. Having her with him now, her mouth opening to welcome him inside, felt like coming home. He took the kiss deeper, needing to taste all of her. Wishing he could absorb her into his skin so he'd always have her with him.

A loud clap of thunder startled them apart. Emily gave a shaky laugh, but he could see how tense she was by the rigidity of her shoulders. "It's almost over," he said. "Hang in there just a little longer, hon."

Sighing, Emily stared out the windshield. The corner of her mouth curled down. "I'm so tired and hungry."

The dejection in her voice broke his heart.

"I was really looking forward to getting out of the jungle." She crossed her arms over her chest. "Sleeping on a real bed. Taking a hot shower and eating some onigiri."

"I promise, once we're out of here I'll buy you all the rice balls you want. And we will get out of here. No matter what."

She just gave a half-hearted shrug.

"C'mon, don't lose that kickass spirit now. I know you're scared and exhausted, but you're doing a fantastic job. Honestly, I don't know many civilians who would have held up as well as you have."

He tilted her face toward him and looked into her eyes. He still didn't understand why she had such a deep-seated belief that she wasn't capable outside the dance world. "When I look at you, I see a woman who has a core of inner strength that allows her to keep going even when she'd rather lie down and give up." He reinforced his words by taking his still damp sleeve and cleaning dirt off a small portion of her face, then placing a kiss on the cleaned area. "I see a woman confident enough, and loyal enough, to take on an entire camp full of professional soldiers in order to rescue me." Another section of skin revealed. Another kiss.

Emily's eyes remained on his, her expression so intent, he couldn't tear his gaze away. "I see a woman who adapts. Who has kept her sense of humor. Who knuckles down and does what she needs to do without complaint." With her face clean, he cupped her cheeks in his palms. "I see the woman I love."

He took her mouth in a kiss that he intended to keep tender. But once she opened her lips and he delved inside, he couldn't stop the kiss from turning carnal. He groaned. "God, I want—"

Lightning flashed, turning the world outside the Hummer silver. Emily squeaked and pulled back.

Max gave a rueful laugh and rolled his eyes to the heavens. "Okay," he muttered. "I get the point. Stay focused."

"Sorry," she murmured. "I'm a little on edge."

"That's okay. Tell me more about how you found me and what you did to the water supply."

As she talked, Max's respect for her grew. She'd handled herself as well as any soldier.

"Do you think Ziegler will bring his men and try to rescue Dietrich?" she asked.

"No. Ziegler's dead. Dietrich killed him."

"What?" She swiveled her head to stare at him.

"Yep. Shocked the hell out of me, too. But Dietrich was angry that Ziegler continued to disobey his orders. So he shot Ziegler right in front of me."

"Oh. Well. Good riddance. Too bad I didn't get a chance to do it myself."

He laughed. "I have to agree with you on that, but did you hear what you said? You've become bloodthirsty, sweetheart."

She stuck her chin up. "He hurt you."

"Yes, he did. But I survived. Thanks to you." He kissed her. "You've got the heart of a warrior, Em. But it's much better that you don't have his death on your conscience. That's a line I hope you never have to cross. I like you just the way you are."

She blushed and gave an embarrassed shrug.

"Uh-uh. Don't ever hide from me." He kissed her again, letting his mouth express the depth of his love and his pride in her.

When they broke apart, she'd lost that embarrassed look. She cleared her throat. "So. Ah... Now what?"

"Now you crawl into the back and sleep. I'll stand guard." He glanced at the dashboard. Almost forty minutes had passed since she'd returned from her sneak and peek. "Once the thunder stops, I'll head out again."

"Are you sure you don't want me to take first watch? After all, you were starved and dehydrated. Plus, you're hurting again."

He cupped her cheek in his hand. "No. You're exhausted. Have you gotten any sleep since I last saw you?"

She shrugged and glanced away. "A little. Sleeping in a tree while it's raining isn't particularly restful. Besides, I was too scared."

He pressed a soft kiss to her temple. "Which is why you're going to sleep now. I've been unconscious or otherwise lying down for most of the past day. Between the treatment from Dietrich's doctor and you fixing me up tonight, my injuries aren't hurting enough to distract me."

Emily made a strangled sound.

"What?"

"I couldn't figure out why the doctor was bathing you and dressing your wounds. I thought maybe he was preparing you for some bizarre religious ritual à la *Raiders of the Lost Ark*."

"Nah. Dietrich just has odd views on hospitality. Plus—" No, better not to tell her that part.

But Emily had caught his self-censorship and leveled a look at him. "Plus what?"

He shrugged, but she punched him in the shoulder. "After all I've been through, the least I deserve is a little honesty, Max Lansing."

"Oh, ouch." He mock winced and rubbed his shoulder. Carefully watching her reaction, he explained, "Dietrich was going to turn me over to his buyer."

Emily's brow furrowed. "So what... That he could torture you?"

"Er..." Sometimes he forgot how little exposure she'd had to the darker realities of this part of the world. "No. So he could sell me into the...ah...labor or sex markets."

"What?"

"The rebels have been selling foreigners and prominent West African officials who oppose them into slavery. Short of death, they find the humiliation of being a slave to be a fitting punishment for not supporting their cause."

"That's..."

"Yeah, I know."

"Well, I have you now and I'm not letting Dietrich or the buyer get their hands on you." Emily leaned over and gave him a quick kiss. "And I can take my turn at watch. You need rest in order to heal."

He shook his head. "You're our driver and scout. Our food and water gatherer. You need to be sharp. As well-rested as possible." And he needed to feel useful, if just in a small way.

She studied him a moment, before nodding. "Okay. Thank you." She gave him a soft kiss, then crawled into the back.

Damn, but he loved this woman.

THREE HOURS after he'd started observation, with the rain gone and a half moon peeking out from behind the clouds, Max shifted position on the thick, low-hanging branch of a tree just off the road. Headlights appeared as pinpricks to his left, then gradually increased in size to reveal a convoy of two black Land Rovers and two black Hummers.

As the vehicles pulled into the buyer's camp, guards exited the tents, weapons ready. The men who climbed out of the vehicles all wore Dietrich's black uniforms with the small black-and-white logo on their pockets. Max expected a fight, but instead, the buyer's men greeted Dietrich's men politely. At a gesture from one of the buyer's men, Johann ducked into the tent holding his boss. Other guards began unloading materials from the Land Rovers. Several began erecting a new tent.

The buyer's men watched the proceedings for a few minutes, then retreated into their own tents, leaving only two guards to keep an eye on the newcomers.

Max didn't spot anything that looked like a second briefcase. Instead, Dietrich's men transferred food, clothing, and furnishings from the vehicles. One guard set up a portable shower near the edge of the jungle and it wasn't long before Johann and another man escorted Dietrich to the bathing area. Other men began cooking a meal.

Max rolled his eyes. Ah... All the comforts of home.

Two hours later, the camp had once again settled into quiet.

Max shifted position. Damn, but this spot was uncomfortable. His butt was numb. He would have preferred to lie on his stomach, but his wounded leg couldn't tolerate the pressure. He had a hell of a lot of respect for Emily being able to stay in a tree for hours while she'd watched Dietrich's camp.

He was itchy to take action. Any action.

Yeah, okay, so patience still wasn't one of his virtues.

God, he couldn't wait until his leg was healed and he could walk on his own. *If you can walk again without a limp,* a niggling voice warned.

Nope. He refused to go there. Refused to give life to the doubts that whispered his wound had taken so much abuse he'd done permanent damage to his leg. Because he fully intended to hold Emily in his arms and dance with her at their wedding.

Whoa. Wedding?

He glanced back at the Hummer. He'd never thought about a long-term relationship, never mind marriage, before. Considering the type of work he did, it had seemed unfair to burden a woman with his extended absences and his inability to tell her where he was going or when he'd be back. Besides, Emily didn't even know what she wanted to do with her life. But the same voice that warned him about his leg also insisted that he'd be a fool to let her go. That coming home to Emily was something worth fighting for.

It was the first time in months he'd wanted something beyond revenge and basic survival.

So, yeah. Wedding. Not that there was any rush, or anything. He had time to get used to the idea himself. Then to convince Emily that a life with him wouldn't be so bad.

That she wouldn't have to prop him up forever.

CHAPTER TWENTY-ONE

Day Twelve

"Emily. Emily, c'mon sweetheart, you've got to wake up."

Emily moaned and slapped at the hand that was shaking her shoulder. "Just fell asleep," she mumbled. "Go 'way."

"Uh, no, you've been asleep for hours. It's dawn and the bad guys are awake and getting ready to head out. I need you alert and ready to follow them."

She opened her eyes and glared at Max. "Are you serious?"

"Absolutely."

Grumbling under her breath, she sat up. She checked her watch and saw that it was six in the morning. She'd actually slept for almost ten hours. "All right, I'm up." She slipped out of the cargo compartment. "How much time do we have?"

Max had retreated a few hundred yards into the jungle, where she could just barely see him watching the activity through the binoculars. "Can't say for sure. Probably at least fifteen minutes. They're finishing up breakfast."

"Okay." She did a few quick stretches and pliés to wake herself up, then popped a handful of groundnuts into her mouth and snagged one of the last two bananas. They were almost out of food again.

While she waited for Max's signal to start the Hummer, Emily thought about what he'd said yesterday about her strength. The warm glow from his praise still filled her, yet at the same time, a tiny part of her refused to let go of the worry. What good would being adaptable in the jungle do her once she was back in the States? Yes, she'd discovered that she had the strength to carry on despite overwhelming odds, but the only thing she'd ever wanted to do was dance professionally. Not teach. Lacking another consuming passion, she still didn't know what she would do with her life. Maybe photography would continue to interest her once she got home, maybe not. At this point it just made her sick to her stomach that there was so much misery to document.

She sighed. Or maybe she was feeling a bit despondent because no matter what progress she and Max made, there was always one more obstacle to overcome. More injuries. More pain. More fear.

She rolled her eyes and squashed her pity party. She needed to focus on the job at hand. Stopping the transfer of the second weapon.

Right. Because she and Max were such effective superheroes.

"They're packing up," Max called out, just loud enough for her to hear. He stepped out from the trees. "Let's go."

He looked haggard. His face was pale, with dark circles under his eyes and lines of strain showing at his eyes. "Did you get any sleep last night?"

"Some. I dozed off and on."

That wasn't nearly enough to help him heal. But he had that stubborn look in his eyes that said she'd better not comment, so all she said was, "Okay. There's a banana and some groundnuts left."

She climbed behind the wheel and eased toward the road. Once the convoy of vehicles abandoned the other camp she followed, staying as usual just inside the tree line. "Are there more vehicles now than last night?"

"Yeah. Dietrich's men arrived a few hours after you fell asleep."

"Oh, no. Did they already complete the sale?"

"Nope. As far as I can tell, they spent the night in their separate tents. I checked every hour and didn't see any signs of activity."

"So, where do you think they're going?"

"I haven't seen anything to indicate they have the second prototype with them. So I bet they're going to retrieve it."

"Is that why we're heading back toward Dietrich's camp?"

"Probably." Max rubbed between his eyes. "If I were Dietrich, I'd have stashed it near enough to camp to be easily accessible when the buyer showed up. He likely only trusted a few people with the location, so that he could send someone to fetch it when the negotiations with the buyer were finished."

"Only he didn't expect to be poisoned, then dragged out of camp by the buyer."

"Exactly. Unless..."

She waited for him to continue, but he just stared out at the passing jungle. "Unless what?" she prompted.

"Unless he plans on giving the buyer a demonstration."

"Well, that's a scary thought. Do you know if the prototype can be used more than once, or is it like a bomb, only a one-shot wonder?"

"Haven't a clue." Max rubbed between his eyes again. She wondered if he had a headache, or maybe even a mild concussion. "I was only told that it was experimental and could wipe out an entire population center."

"Would Kristoff know?"

"Maybe." Max picked up his phone from where it was charging on the console. "But we won't be able to call him until we have a clearer line of sight, because this isn't getting a strong enough signal."

"Oh. Right."

Ten minutes later, the convoy pulled into the jungle on the other side of the road.

"Keep driving past them," Max said. "When I tell you, cross the road and enter their side of the jungle. Then we'll sneak in to observe."

Hearing the steel in Max's voice, Emily didn't bother protesting that he was too injured and should stay in the vehicle. Besides, he had experience with this type of situation. He'd be able to figure out a plan to stop the deal better than she could.

Once they were in a good position on the other side of the road, Max had her park the Hummer. "Gather all your stuff, in case someone finds this vehicle and we can't use it again."

She nodded and shoved the few remaining food supplies into her pack. "What about the phone?"

Max unplugged it and clipped it to his waist. He put the charger into his pants pocket. "After we've scoped the situation out, I'll find a spot to call Kris."

"Okay."

"Don't worry, we're just going to observe. We'll be safe enough."

Emily waited until Max had turned his back to roll her eyes. He was limping and leaning heavily on his makeshift cane. Despite having a good night's sleep, she felt sluggish and bone tired. Which meant they were prone to make mistakes. Mentally crossing her fingers for luck, she followed Max through the jungle.

HALF AN HOUR LATER, Max adjusted the focus on the binoculars. He and Emily occupied observation posts on neighboring branches in a giant tree. Emily had switched out the full memory card in her camera for a new extra-capacity one. She was taking video of the activity down below, while he watched through the binoculars. Dietrich—once again his impeccably dressed self complete with trademark fedora—Johann, and one of Dietrich's soldiers stood in a clearing. Behind them loomed a buttressed root system that must be well over six feet tall because it dwarfed Johann, the tallest man present. Three other men formed a separate group a few feet away—a man with light brown skin wearing an incongruous black suit and a bowler hat who Max figured was the buyer, and two African guards wearing jungle camouflage uniforms that marked them as the buyer's guards. One of the guards carried a briefcase that Max assumed held the money.

The number of visible men was far lower than what Max had observed last night at the camp. Some of the men would be guarding the vehicles, but Max suspected the rest were hiding nearby. Not knowing exactly where they were made him twitchy. That was the only reason he'd allowed Emily to share his observation tree. He didn't want her alone in case one of the missing guards spotted her.

With a graceful hand gesture, Dietrich motioned for Johann to duck underneath the roots. The rest of the group kept their attention warily on each other.

It wasn't more than a minute before Johann emerged from underneath the roots, carrying a briefcase identical to the one Emily had retrieved. He brushed off the lingering dirt and leaves and held it up for the buyer's inspection. At the buyer's nod, Dietrich snapped his fingers and two men walked forward from the direction of the road. One man carried a small folding table, which he set up on a small patch of relatively flat ground. The other man carried two folding chairs, which he set up on opposite sides of the table. Then Johann set the case on the table. Dietrich strode forward and, with a dramatic flourish worthy of a stage magician, he unfastened the latches on the briefcase.

Dietrich pulled back the briefcase's lid to reveal several file folders and a square, metal device about the size of a large mango. The buyer leaned forward to take a look. He thumbed through the folders, turned the device around several times, then set everything back in the case.

Had he noticed that this wasn't the newer prototype? His expression didn't change, but Max thought his body had stiffened slightly.

Dietrich closed the lid and picked up the case. He indicated for the buyer to put his case on the table. Instead, the buyer nodded at his guards.

Max tensed.

The buyer's guards drew their weapons as four of their comrades stepped out of the jungle. At the same time, all of Dietrich's men pulled out their weapons, and a number of Dietrich's men also stepped out of the jungle. The two groups of men stared at one another.

Hello, Mexican standoff.

The buyer said something to Dietrich. Dietrich shook his head and gave a one-shouldered shrug. The buyer shouted and took a step forward. Johann stepped between the buyer and his boss, gesturing angrily.

Max reached out and touched Emily's arm. Any second, someone was going to snap and start shooting. He and Emily could be hit by a stray bullet. He motioned for her to sneak down the back of the tree. Once she was safely on the ground, he followed suit. Then he led her through the jungle in the direction of the vehicles. If they could disable the vehicles and put a call to Kris through in time, the WAR team might be able to nab Dietrich, the buyer, and the weapon.

Max pulled Emily to a halt at the edge of the clearing. Four men guarded the vehicles. Two each from Dietrich and the buyer.

Gunfire erupted from the meeting place. The guards glanced at one another, then ran toward the fight. A moment later, two more men tore out of the bushes near the road and also ran toward the firefight.

Excellent.

Max gestured for Emily to wait while he cautiously stepped into the clearing. There was no cry of alarm, so he started checking vehicles. Aha! He found a massive tool kit in the second vehicle. After removing a pair of wire cutters, he motioned Emily over. "Since they're still shooting at one another, we have time to cut the brake lines of as many vehicles as we can. Do you know where the brake lines are?" He would prefer to do the sabotage himself, but no way would his wounded leg and ribs tolerate him crawling across the uneven jungle floor.

Emily nodded and took the wire cutters from him.

"Work fast." He pressed a quick kiss to her mouth. "I'm going to load one of the Hummers with supplies so we can use it for our getaway."

She darted over to the first vehicle, dropped to the ground and slid easily underneath.

Once he lost sight of her, Max removed the keys left in the ignitions. Being suspicious types, the drivers must have expected to need a quick escape. Better for him.

He decided to take the nearest Hummer as their getaway vehicle. He tossed Emily's backpack inside, then checked out the cargo compartment. Max whistled silently as he ran his gaze over the cases of weapons and ammo. He opened one box that contained a variety of high-end European combat knives. Another box held Heckler & Koch G36 assault rifles and Glock 9 mm pistols. "Damn, these boys mean business," he murmured. And not just the ordinary rebel kind of trouble. The rebels mainly bought cheaper AK-47s and were happy with them. No, this cargo hinted at that core of better funded, better trained soldiers he'd heard rumors of.

Just who was this buyer? Kris hadn't provided details, but a hell of a lot of targeted damage could be done with this level of sophisticated weaponry. He'd bet these rifles were also going to be used in support of the upcoming attack.

Had Dietrich sold both the prototype and these weapons to the buyer?

After checking over his shoulder on Emily's progress, Max unzipped one of the cloth rifle bags on the back seat, keeping attended for any sound of approaching danger. "Holy Shit." He ran his hand reverently over the CheyTac M200. It was a top-of-the-line sniper rifle for a highly trained, experienced shooter. No way did the rebels have anyone with the skill to properly handle this baby. Hell, Max was an excellent shot with years of combat experience, and even he wouldn't be able to use the rifle to its full capacity.

Not to mention that the rifle cost a fortune.

Well, their bad luck. Max was taking their expensive cargo. He zipped the rifle bag closed and set it on the floor of the passenger seat. Added a few combat knives, a couple grenades, and two G36s with extra ammo to the passenger's area. Loaded magazines into two of the Glocks, then stuck one pistol and a couple of spare magazines in the map holder on the driver's door and the same on the passenger's side door. Just in case they needed to fight on the run.

A loud boom sounded from the direction of the deal. Men shouted. Branches cracked, indicating someone had broken away from the fighting and was headed their way.

"Em! Stop. We're going to have company. Let's go." Max hauled himself into the driver's seat and started the Hummer.

Emily popped up from beneath one of the Land Rovers on the far side of the clearing and raced toward him.

As Max drew near, he leaned over and flung open the passenger side door.

Several of Dietrich's guards burst out of the jungle. The man in the lead saw Emily and fired. She screamed, pitched forward, then lay unmoving.

Blood spread across her right upper back. "Emily!"

The shooter shifted his aim and fired at Max as two of his buddies darted forward, hooked their hands under Emily's arms, and dragged her over to one of Dietrich's Land Rovers. Max grabbed the Glock and shot the man aiming at him, but couldn't fire at Emily's captors because they held her like a shield.

Another group of guards exited the jungle and opened fire.

Shit.

Bullets tore into the interior of the vehicle before Max managed to slam the passenger door closed. More bullets thudded into the vehicle's exterior, but didn't penetrate. Armored. Good to know. He slammed his foot on the accelerator and the Hummer leaped forward. He had to rescue Emily before—

The men across the clearing threw Emily into the back of the Land Rover. "No!" He was almost there. Almost—

One of Dietrich's Hummers cut him off, trapping him against one of the buyer's Land Cruisers.

Max reversed and swerved around the Land Cruiser, but ended up playing dodge with the other Hummer until he finally faked them out and raced past them.

But while he'd been maneuvering, the Land Rover holding Emily had sped into reverse. It slowed as Dietrich ran out of the jungle holding the briefcase with the second prototype. The passenger side door opened.

Max couldn't take a shot because Dietrich's guards were keeping him under heavy fire. But he raced toward the Land Rover as fast as he could, zigging and zagging around the buyer's stationary vehicles. Behind Dietrich, Johann, who held the buyer's briefcase, jumped into one of Dietrich's Hummers.

Just before Dietrich climbed inside the Land Rover, he glanced into the back seat at Emily. With an evil smile, he gave Max a mocking nod. Then he ducked inside and the Land Rover raced toward the road.

Agony tore through Max's chest as he chased after them.

They might as well have tied a chain to his heart, attached it to their bumper, and yanked it out as they drove away. That pain wouldn't be any worse.

Max blinked to clear the moisture from his vision.

Shots fired behind him. A quick glance in the rearview mirror showed more of Dietrich's men running into the clearing. They fired at Max, then piled into Dietrich's remaining vehicles and joined the chase. Just before the jungle blocked his view, Max saw the buyer's men reach the clearing. Guess Dietrich's guys hadn't managed to kill everyone after all.

Keeping Dietrich's vehicles in view, Max drove out of the jungle and turned left onto the road. To his surprise, the other vehicles seemed content to stay ahead of him without shooting. Which made him suspect Dietrich wanted to lead Max to a spot where his team could better ambush him without the buyer's men interfering. Or else Dietrich hoped to outrun Max, leaving him to despair in the dust.

Hearing a crunch of metal behind him, Max glanced back. The second of Dietrich's Hummers and one of the buyer's Land Cruisers lay on their sides on the road. They must have tried to slow to make the sharp turn north, discovered their brakes were out, and flipped. As he watched, another vehicle crashed into the back of the Land Cruiser.

Good for Emily, she'd managed to disable several vehicles before being kidnapped.

God, even that thought made his heart ache.

Bullets slammed into the rear of his vehicle. Who—?

He checked his mirror again. Well, damn. One of Dietrich's Land Rovers and one of the buyer's Land Cruisers must still have working brakes, because they were tearing after Max while alternating between shooting at him and shooting at each other.

The buyer's vehicle sideswiped the Land Rover, but Dietrich's man managed to keep it on the road. Then the Land Rover tried to run the Land Cruiser off the road.

Max pulled away from the tussling vehicles and focused on the vehicles he was chasing. By staying in the rear position, the Hummer provided protection for Dietrich's Land Rover. Max couldn't use the grenades for fear of causing the Hummer to rear end the Land Rover.

He wouldn't risk that Emily would be shot in a crash.

An explosion went off behind him and he momentarily lost control of the Hummer. After he'd wrestled the vehicle straight again, he checked the rearview mirror. The buyer's Land Rover sat in the middle of the road, engulfed in flames. Looked like Dietrich's men had tossed a grenade. If so, it hadn't work out so well. As he watched, the Land Rover swerved across the road and crashed into a tree.

Okay. Two more down. Max gave his Hummer more gas.

The jungle on either side of the road gradually thinned, then gave way to maize fields. Unfortunately, Dietrich's vehicles had drawn farther ahead. Max pushed his speed as fast as the Hummer would go, but the vehicles were evenly matched and he didn't make much progress.

Dietrich must have decided that he was done playing with Max, because the back window of the Hummer lowered to reveal an RPG launcher.

Oh, shit.

Max swerved into the field as Dietrich's man fired. The grenade exploded in the road several hundred feet away. Still, the force of the blast hit the Hummer like a punch from a giant fist. The impact threw Max so hard against the steering wheel that he saw double.

No. Can't...pass...out... Have...to get...to Emily...

After a few shakes of his head and a lot of blinking, the world returned to focus. Ignoring the pain in his head and ribs, Max checked that all the critical lights on the dashboard showed the Hummer was still operational, then resumed driving. He skirted the shallow crater left by the grenade and returned to the road.

But he'd lost so much time, he could barely make out the other vehicles ahead of him.

He tamped down a flare of panic. There was no choice but to keep going. He was not giving up on Emily.

Several minutes later, he realized that the humming in his ears wasn't a side effect from the blast. A helicopter was approaching. Goddammit, if he didn't act fast, Dietrich and his men would airlift Emily out of here.

He'd promised he'd keep her safe, and he'd failed.

Jagged needles of pain tore into his heart. He licked his lips and tasted blood. And tears.

Well, why the hell not? He loved Emily. Dietrich had her and would hurt her. Maybe even kill her.

The odds of getting Emily back were near to impossible. But those odds had never stopped him before. He had a couple of grenades. The assault rifles. Plus the CheyTac, which had better range and power.

As a plan formed in his mind, Max checked the signal strength on the sat phone. Good to go.

His hands shook as he picked up the phone. His vision swam in and out of focus and the pain in his head pounded with such intensity, it could have split granite. He braked. Closed his eyes and gathered his senses.

Then he dialed Kristoff.

"Hello?" His friend's voice sounded half-wary, half-pissed.

It had never sounded so welcome.

"Kris, it's Max. I need your help."

CHAPTER TWENTY-TWO

WHEN EMILY WOKE up she didn't know where she was. Then the bouncing, jarring movement and the sound of an engine clued her in that she was in a vehicle. But what—?

Oh, no. Cutting the brake lines. Running. Pain.

She'd been shot.

Max!

Was he alive? Dead? Alive but a prisoner?

She tried to sit up. Pain tore through her shoulder. She gasped and opened her eyes.

Two sets of legs hung off a car's seat in front of her. A large, black, military style boot nudged her shoulder. She looked up and saw a white man wearing one of Dietrich's uniforms staring down at her. He had a pistol holstered at his waist and a rifle on his lap. He gave her a chilling smile, then looked away.

The man sitting next to him could have been his twin. He had the same closely shorn hair and black uniform. Both men radiated tension. Competence.

"The woman is awake, Herr Dietrich," the man closest to her said.

"So. You are the young woman who has become Maximilian's

companion." The cultured voice spoke with a faint accent. German? She couldn't tell.

Barely moving her head, she stared up into the emotionless gray eyes of Dietrich, who had turned to address her from the front passenger seat. You wouldn't know from looking at him that he'd just escaped a gun battle in the jungle. He'd combed out his hair and cleaned his face and hands. A sharp contrast to the bloodstained, dusty men guarding her.

"I do apologize for my man shooting you. The heat of battle, you understand."

Emily remained silent.

Dietrich's eyes twinkled at her in amusement. "Too afraid to speak? I assure you, we mean you no harm. You are simply leverage in case Max decides to cause trouble for us."

Max was alive!

"If you require proof, you will notice that my man has treated and bandaged your shoulder. This should prevent excessive blood loss, allowing you ample time to reach a medical facility. Once we are safely away."

Emily focused on her shoulder, not wanting to move in case it caused more pain. Yes, she felt something pressing against her skin that might be a bandage. She gave Dietrich a slight nod of acknowledgment. The man certainly had an odd habit of tending to the wounds of his prisoners.

"Of course, my buyer's reinforcements might arrive before you get very far." Dietrich gave an elegant shrug. "A delicate girl like you would bring him a high price in the right market."

Emily pretended as if she were dancing the role of an arrogant queen and didn't let any of her fear show on her face.

"Ah, that does not scare you? Perhaps you believe Max will rescue you?" Dietrich's smile was condescending. "Only time will tell, hmm?" With that, he turned to face forward again.

The truth was, Emily knew Max would do whatever he could to rescue her. Only... He was just one man and he wasn't at full strength. If she wanted to make it out alive, she had to help herself.

The guards were too close for her to try anything now. Still, she'd wait and watch and hope for an opportunity to exploit. Because if she'd learned anything from this ordeal, it was that she was adaptable. More creative and smart than she'd given herself credit for. And while she still wasn't certain if she wanted to make a new career in photography, she wanted to live so she could make a difference in the world. So she could become a positive force, counterbalancing the harm caused by Dietrich and the rebels.

And she wanted a future with Max.

Ignoring the pain in her shoulder and the fear of what the men might do to her, she focused on gathering as much information about her surroundings and her captors as possible. Because she intended to escape at the first opportunity.

WAR Headquarters
The Democratic Republic of the Ivory Coast
West Africa

"Who was that?"

Kristoff's shoulders jerked in surprise and he spun around. "Dammit, Wil. What are you doing here?"

Max's brother stood in the doorway, giving him the teasing smirk that always made Kris want to kiss him.

Too soon. Much too soon. Besides, we're in the middle of a crisis.

Wil shrugged and moved into the room. His new protheses must have settled in, because he moved without a limp. "Let me guess, Emily rescued Max but the situation went south and now they're in deeper trouble than before. Right?"

Kris sighed. "Yes." Wil had been called back to base after talking Emily through the process of grinding up the seeds and putting the poison in the water supply. This was the first time they'd spoken since.

"Typical Max," Wil growled. "So how bad is it?"

Kris shook his head. "No."

Wil halted. Raised his brows in the same you-and-what-army-are-gonna-make-me look that Max got. "No? I don't believe I've asked a question."

Dammit, he did not need to be dealing with the Lansing stubbornness right now. "No, you can't help. We've got it covered."

"Kristoff, dammit, I told you to stop protecting me!" Wil took a threatening step toward him, moving into Kris's personal space. Now that he could walk again, he topped Kris by a couple of inches. It was a strange feeling, looking up to meet that fierce gaze, when Kris had been used to tilting his head down all those weeks when Wil had been confined to his wheelchair.

This new position felt almost submissive. And didn't it figure, his dick twitched at the idea of being dominated by Wil.

Hoping none of his thoughts showed on his face, Kris turned to straighten some papers on his desk.

Wil stayed in place a moment, then backed up.

Huh. Maybe Wil had sensed the tension, too. Maybe Kris wasn't alone in this after all.

Yeah, right. Wishful thinking.

"What did Max say?" Wil demanded.

Right. Max. Dietrich. Trouble.

Kris bit back his sigh. "Dietrich has a second briefcase with another prototype. The buyer tried a double cross. There was a firefight. Long story short, Dietrich's men snatched Emily. Max is barely conscious, but determined to ride to the rescue."

"So let's go."

Kris shook his head. "Even if we had a helicopter gassed up and waiting to take off, it would still take a team nearly two hours to get there. We'd be too late."

Wil swore viciously and Kris turned around. His heart ached

at the helplessness in Wil's eyes. Because he knew the man wanted the same thing he did—to be able to swoop in and save both Max and Emily. "But there's some hope," Kris added. "MacKay's team is already on its way. They think they're rescuing Max from Dietrich's camp. I just need to redirect them." He hesitated, then added, "I don't know if they'll make it in time, but you know those guys. They'll bust their balls to get there."

Wil spun and slammed his fist against the wall. He stood a moment with his head bowed and his body vibrating with tension.

Heart pounding with what Kris had to admit was mostly arousal—an angry, dominant Wil fired him up—he dialed MacKay.

"Lachlan? It's Kris. Change of plans. Max is on the move. Here are his latest coordinates."

Wil turned to face Kris. "You tell him I don't care what laws his team breaks," he said loud enough for Lachlan to hear. "They goddamn better bring my brother back alive."

"You hear that, Lach? Yeah. Hurry."

The Republic of the Volta
West Africa

MAX DROVE after Dietrich and Emily until the maize fields gave way to tilled, unplanted land. Dietrich's vehicles were so far ahead of him, they were barely visible as they travelled around a wide curve in the road. Knowing he'd never catch them at this rate, Max cut across the field, aiming to rejoin the road once it straightened out.

His plan worked. He bounced onto the road about a quarter mile behind the vehicles.

Just then, an old Soviet model helicopter roared across the

field from his left. It flew to the middle of the road not far ahead of Dietrich's vehicles, and landed.

Max cursed.

The other vehicles put on a burst of speed and raced toward the helicopter. When they were close, the vehicles turned and parked with their driver's windows toward Max, forming a blockade. Men jumped out the far doors. Dietrich ran through the rotor wash toward the helicopter, one hand holding his fedora in place, the other holding the prototype's briefcase. Johann ran at Dietrich's right, holding the other briefcase. To Dietrich's left, one guard dragged a kicking, screaming Emily toward the helicopter while four other guards ran behind them as a shield.

That left only the drivers inside the vehicles.

No sooner had he thought it, than the driver's windows on the Land Rover and the other Hummer rolled down and the drivers began firing at Max.

Max drove a serpentine, aiming for the spot where the Land Rover's front bumper almost touched the Hummer's back bumper. He rammed the vehicles at their intersection, bursting through on the other side to see that Dietrich had almost reached the helicopter.

"Oh no, you don't, you bastard."

Max spun the Hummer to the left so that his flank was toward the shooters. Then he grabbed the CheyTac and climbed over to the passenger seat. He put one knee on the floor and one knee on the seat. He lowered the window and braced his forearms on the door. He fired at the helicopter pilot, gritting his teeth as the rifle's recoil jarred his damaged ribs.

The shot had been hurried, but it had the effect he wanted. The helicopter jerked to the side, then flew erratically away before crashing onto the field.

Johann pulled Dietrich to the ground and the other guards took up defensive positions, firing at Max.

He ducked back inside and raised his window. Swapped the

CheyTac out for one of the G36's. As he ammo'd up, the driver of the Land Rover behind him pulled his head out of his ass and drove around Max, moving into a position that blocked Dietrich and Johann from Max's line of sight, but leaving Emily, her captor, and two guards exposed. Those guards fired at Max's Hummer, but the bullets didn't penetrate all the way through the light armor or the bullet-resistant windshield. Max knew that if enough rounds hit the glass, some bullets would eventually break through. But for now he had—

The other Hummer slammed at an angle into the rear bumper of his vehicle, sending Max's Hummer into a spin. Max was thrown sideways from the passenger seat across the console. The gear shift slammed into his cracked ribs. Pain burst through him. He lost his grip on the rifle and it tumbled to the floor. The other Hummer slammed into his vehicle again.

Agony swamped Max. Spots swirled across his eyes. *Ah shit, not again.*

He clenched his teeth and clung to consciousness by a hair.

Emily's screaming reoriented him. He forced his body to ignore the pain and hauled himself upright. Seeing one of Dietrich's men approaching, Max reached down to the weapons he'd stashed. He unsheathed a combat knife and palmed it just as Dietrich's man yanked open the passenger door. As the man pulled him out of the vehicle, Max stabbed him in the gut. The man released him and fell back a step. Max pulled his knife free, turned it around, then slammed the hilt into the wound he'd just made. The man collapsed to the ground, clutching his stomach. Max kicked him in the head to knock him out, then snatched up the man's Uzi.

He raised the rifle, then turned his head toward Emily's screams. Saw that she was kicking and flailing against her captor's hold. When the man tightened his elbow around her neck, she gouged his hand with her nails even as the man cut off her air.

The man turned so that Max could see the pistol he held to Emily's head. "Don't try anything or I'll shoot."

Max glared at the man. Dammit, he couldn't fire. The man was a pro. He held Emily in such a way that all of his vulnerable points were hidden behind her body. There was nothing Max could do but watch helplessly, once again, as the man dragged Emily toward the other Hummer, which had stopped to Max's left. The Land Rover and Dietrich were now to his right. Smart move. Max could fire at Dietrich's group, but then the guard would kill Emily. He could wait for a chance to take down Emily's captor, but the second Max made a move, the men around Dietrich would fire.

Max growled in frustration. The man holding Emily smirked and tightened his elbow around her throat. She gasped, clutching at his hand. After a moment, the man eased up on the pressure and she sagged in his grip.

Her eyes met his, blazing with emotion. So fierce. So determined. So full of love.

He would *not* let Dietrich hurt her. He would die first.

"Step away from the vehicle, Maximilian," Dietrich called from behind the open door of the Land Rover. His head, shoulders and lower legs were exposed, but as long as the guard held a weapon to Emily's head, Max couldn't fire.

"Let us discuss the resolution to this situation like civilized gentlemen," Dietrich added. "Put down your weapons and surrender peacefully."

"Only if you release the girl. She needs medical attention and has nothing to do with this."

"Patience, Max. First, your weapons."

Max vibrated with frustration. With the need to act.

But he wouldn't risk Emily's life.

So he put the Uzi on the roof and slid it out of reach.

"Now the knife with which you so coldly cut down my man."

Max hesitated, then put the bloody knife on the roof and

nudged it out of reach. Dietrich nodded approval. "See, I always knew you could be reasonable."

Max snorted. Right. Kris and Wil would bust a gut laughing if they heard that statement.

At a signal from Dietrich, one of his guards marched over while keeping his HK417 trained on Max. "Move slowly," the man said. "Keep your hands where I can see them."

Max nearly laughed. He was barely staying vertical thanks to his white knuckled grip on the door. His hands wouldn't be going anywhere.

The guard glanced into the Hummer. "He has multiple weapons inside," he called out.

Two more guards moved in. One gathered up the CheyTac and the other loose rifles, while the second man lifted the injured guard and carried him away.

The guard nearest Max prodded him. Hoping to mask his vulnerability, Max attempted to edge around the door. The world spun. He bowed his head, fighting back dizziness. He could not, *would* not, pass out now.

Not when Emily's life depended on him. He was *not* going to fail this time.

The guard poked him with his rifle. "Stop stalling. Move."

Max raised his head and glared at the man. "Are you freaking kidding me?"

The guard's eyes narrowed.

"Dietrich, tell this moron that I can't walk on my own. I'm barely managing to stay upright with the help of this door."

Dietrich tsked, then explained to the guard in German that Max had been severely injured and therefore was no threat now that he was unarmed. Still regarding Max suspiciously, the guard nevertheless lowered his weapon and stepped back.

It would have been the perfect opening. If Max had a second weapon close to hand. But with the rifles gone, the nearest weapon was the pistol he'd stuck in the other door's map holder. Impossible to reach without getting himself shot.

Even if Max wasn't under guard, the man holding Emily had his finger on the trigger of the pistol pressed to her temple. Max wouldn't risk her life by going for a weapon. So, putting on his most nonchalant expression, he called out, "We're going to have to talk like this, Dietrich, unless you want to come over here."

Dietrich gave him a mocking smile. "I do not think so."

"All right, then. What do you want?"

"What I really want, is not in your power to give me. Not any longer."

Ah, fuck. He'd been counting on Dietrich still wanting the location of the original briefcase. Feeling a sense of doom, he waited for Dietrich to elaborate.

"You will tell your friends at WAR to give me and my men safe passage out of the country."

Max jerked. How did Dietrich know about WAR? Let alone that Max had a connection to them?

Shit. Did WAR have a traitor? Or had one of their partners been less than discreet?

"In addition, you will also send me all of the intelligence you have gathered about me over the years. I can't have you turning that data over to the authorities, should you find someone who believes you." He smirked. "Only then will I have my man release your girl, unharmed."

Max glanced over and saw to his horror that the man holding Emily now held a knife to her throat instead of a pistol.

"If you deviate in any way from our agreement, then my man will carve up the lovely lady. Something to match the scars she already has, yes?"

CHAPTER TWENTY-THREE

Max swallowed back bile at the thought of that knife so much as nicking Emily's skin. "That's not the act of a gentleman, Dietrich."

His nemesis gave an elegant shrug. "What can I say? This is a cutthroat world." He chuckled at his own pun. "I did not rise to be one of the best in my profession by serving tea and cookies."

No, the man was one of the most ruthless bastards Max had ever come up against. And he had Emily. Who, Max could see, was losing energy. Dammit, he was out of time.

He fought not to let his fear show as he stared at Dietrich and tried to figure a way to free her. The late afternoon sun at his back threw shadows across the tilled earth. Dietrich and his men were looking into the sun as they watched him. Could he use that to his advantage?

While he struggled to come up with a plan, Max decided to play dumb. "What's this WAR you mentioned?" he called.

"Do not stall, Max. You and I both know that in addition to weapons, I deal in information. I know what Azumah is up to. I know that several of your former teammates from Unit 3, led by Kristoff Wren, have joined with WAR to fight the rebels. And I know that before you went rogue you gathered a file of incriminating evidence against me. I want your promise that all I have been asked will be granted. Do I have your agreement?"

Max hesitated.

"I grow impatient, Maximilian. Perhaps you need some persuasion?" Dietrich motioned toward the man holding Emily.

The man turned her head to the side. Emily whimpered as he lowered the knife.

"No!"

Dietrich barked at the man to stop. "Yes, Max?"

"Fine. You win. I'll call WAR and tell them to let you leave the country."

"And the data?"

"Yes, damn you. You'll get it. There's no need to hurt the girl."

Max saw a flash of light above the tree line on the other side of the field. Crap. It looked like a second helicopter. Did Dietrich have a whole friggin' fleet out there?

No wonder the man had been so chatty. He'd been stalling until his ride arrived. And in the process, he'd manipulated Max into confirming his association with WAR. Kris was going to kick his ass. If Max survived.

Dietrich nodded at the man holding Emily. The guard shifted his grip, pulling her onto her toes as he walked backward toward the Hummer. *Bad move, buddy.* The man might have thought he was putting Emily at a disadvantage, but Max knew that years of dancing ballet would give her an edge.

If she still had enough energy to fight. Her struggles had weakened.

He looked for an opportunity to act. Even though the new position of Emily's body left the guard's lower legs exposed, it was too narrow a target for Max in his current, shaky condition. He'd just have to watch for the guard to make another mistake, providing him with a bigger target and a reason to risk diving for the Glock in the other door's map holder.

"Call your contact at WAR now," Dietrich ordered. "And put it on speakerphone."

The guard on his right moved in. "Where's your phone?"

Luckily, the collision with the other Hummer had knocked the sat phone out of sight. "I locked it in the glove box. So I need to get the keys." Max pointed to where they dangled from the ignition.

The guard nodded, but kept his rifle aimed at Max's head. Max moved slowly, exaggerating his injuries. He sat down in the passenger seat, reached over, and deliberately fumbled the keys as he pulled them out. The sound of the helicopter grew louder and everyone's heads went up. Max took advantage of the distraction to drop the keys onto the floor under the steering wheel.

Cursing as if he hadn't meant to do that, Max leaned down to retrieve them, angling his body so the guard couldn't see him reach for the hidden Glock. He misjudged the distance and his ribs connected with the gear shift. God*damn*, but that hurt. The world spun.

No! Forget the pain. Focus on your task. Save Emily.

He took a deep breath.

The sound of the helicopter's rotors was a faint hum that grew louder by the minute.

Dietrich shouted orders to his men.

Time slowed.

Max's fingers closed around the pistol and he yanked it free. With the guard distracted by Dietrich's shouted instructions, Max shot him in the chest. Before the guard fell, Max switched his focus out the open driver's door to Emily and her captor.

Emily had also made use of the distraction. Her captor held her slightly toward his right hip, with his right arm hooked around her upper chest and his left hand holding the knife to her throat under her chin. Still on tiptoe, Emily's left leg rose in a quick kick that hit the man's left elbow. She leaned away as the kick drove the knife up and back. Instead of cutting her, the knife sliced across her captor's cheek. He loosened his hold. Emily wedged her hands in between the man's elbow and her throat, then pushed out to force him to release her.

She dropped to the ground and rolled away.

Yes! That was his kickass ballerina.

Max fired at the man who'd been holding her. Shot the man twice, and the driver who'd gotten out to offer support once, before Dietrich noticed and his men opened fire. Not at him, but at—

"Emily!"

He turned in time to see her dive inside the other Hummer and slam the door shut behind her.

Thank God. She was safe.

Max aimed at the group surrounding Dietrich, but they'd all ducked into the Land Rover. His pistol wasn't going to do him much good against the armor covering the other vehicle. Max slipped into the cargo compartment of the Hummer as Dietrich's men laid down fire.

As he waited the round out, he pulled a G36 out of one of the boxes Dietrich's men had failed to remove. He quickly loaded it, crawled into the front seat, and started shooting out the side window.

There must have been a weapon inside the other Hummer, because Emily was also shooting at Dietrich's men. Damn, his woman was amazing.

But instead of returning fire, Dietrich and his men drove away.

Fuck. Thanks to the number of bullets it had taken, his windshield was a cloudy mess. Peering through a narrow strip of relatively clear glass at the far left side, Max drove after Dietrich. A second later, an explosion knocked Dietrich's Land Rover onto its side.

Emily stood behind the open door of her Hummer, getting ready to throw another grenade. Hooah! Just call her Ballet

Rambo Girl. Max tightened his grip on the steering wheel as another explosion rocked the vehicle.

Through the dust, Max saw Dietrich and his men crawl out of the Land Rover. His guards immediately started shooting at Emily, but she once again ducked inside her Hummer in the nick of time.

All right. Change of plans. "Let's see how you like this," he muttered. He slammed his foot on the gas pedal and aimed for Dietrich's Land Rover, which still balanced on its side.

Dietrich's men realized too late what he intended. They brought their weapons around, but the Hummer hit their vehicle broadside before they could fire. The Land Rover toppled back onto all four wheels, trapping the men underneath.

Before he ran anyone over—he wanted Dietrich and his men alive for questioning—Max hit the brakes and put the Hummer into reverse. Then he drove around the damaged Land Rover. Dietrich lay on the ground a few feet away. Johann knelt by his boss, holding a handkerchief to Dietrich's head.

Max pulled into position where he had a clear shot at Dietrich.

Another of Dietrich's guards crawled out from underneath the Land Rover, his bloody hand clutching his weapon.

Max raised the window on his door—the reinforced glass was still intact and would give him some protection—opened the door to use as a shield, then hauled himself to his feet. Bracing his hips against the door, he aimed his rifle at Dietrich, but spoke to the guard. "Drop your weapon, lie face down, and put your hands on the back of your head."

Emily's Hummer raced past him and came to a stop in a perfect flanking maneuver with the side of her vehicle closest to the group. She poked a rifle out of the passenger's window and held it steady on the injured guard, using the lower half of her partially raised window as protection.

After glancing over at Dietrich, the guard followed Max's orders.

Johann helped Dietrich sit up. Dietrich glanced behind him at the black shadow that was the approaching helicopter, then smirked at Max. "It appears, Maximilian, that although you hold the upper hand at this moment, once again I shall best you. My backup helicopter has arrived."

A guard Max hadn't noticed before crawled out from the other side of the Land Rover and lurched toward Emily's Hummer, firing. Max pivoted and pulled the trigger, but his damn weapon jammed. As Emily ducked back inside and rolled up the window, Max turned his rifle to the side and racked the slide twice to eject the jammed shell casing.

The guard kept firing at Emily's vehicle, but his bullets didn't fully penetrate the light armor or the reinforced glass. Running up to the vehicle, the grabbed the door handle and tried to pull it open, but Emily had locked it.

The Hummer lurched into reverse and careened backward across the field. The guard grabbed onto the side mirror, and was dragged along as Emily zigged and zagged trying to throw him off.

Max chambered a new round, raised his rifle, then jumped back into the driver's seat barely in time to avoid having his feet shot up. The injured guard had taken advantage of his temporary distraction, retrieved his weapon, and fired.

Max stuck his head and shoulders out just long enough to shoot the injured guard and the man hanging on to Emily's vehicle. Then he took aim at Dietrich. "Nobody move."

Dietrich smiled at him and nodded toward the approaching helicopter.

But that didn't sound like a Soviet chopper. Sure enough, when Max glanced up he saw an unmarked Black Hawk. He bit back a smile. Dietrich didn't own any Black Hawks.

The helicopter came in fast, turned its flank, hovered, then opened its bay door.

"Max Lansing, you sorry son of a bitch," the familiar Texas twang of Marcus Jones boomed out from the helicopter's PA system. "I thought this was a rescue mission. Where the hell's the firefight?"

Max gave WAR's best pilot a one-fingered salute and a grin as a team of six men in black assault gear jumped out of the helicopter and rushed over to secure Dietrich and the guards. The look on Dietrich's face was priceless. God, he wished Emily had her camera—

Oh no. She'd been racing away. He turned to look for her just as her Hummer came racing back and screeched to a halt beside his. She must have noticed that help had arrived.

A grin broke out on her face as she hopped out and ran toward him.

Max fumbled with his door. Christ. Why couldn't his damn body work for once? But his fingers were suddenly clumsy.

Then Emily was there, yanking open the door and throwing herself into his arms.

"You're safe." She covered his face with kisses.

He pulled her against him. "Your shoulder. Shot. Doctor." Dammit, why couldn't he get his thoughts out?

"It hurts, but I'm okay." She glanced toward the helicopter. "That's Kristoff's team?"

He nodded.

"Oh, thank God. We're both safe. Max, I was so scared!"

He put his hands to either side of her face and kissed her. Damn, she tasted good. But why was the world slipping sideways?

"Max?"

His vision tunneled. "Love...you..."

"Max!"

His world went dark.

CHAPTER TWENTY-FOUR

Day Seventeen
Undisclosed Hospital, New York City
United States

EMILY PACED across the waiting room in an exclusive hospital in New York City. Dr. LaSalle and a surgeon working with WAR had decided that the damage to Max's leg was so severe it required a specialist. Not only had it become infected, but in addition to extensive nerve and muscle damage, there'd been some fracturing of the bone due to the kicks from Ziegler's steel-toed loafers. So after he'd been stabilized, and with Emily's father calling in some favors, Max had been transferred here from WAR's small clinic in The Democratic Republic of the Ivory Coast.

"You shouldn't be putting weight on those feet."

Emily turned as Max's brother Wil strode into the room. Thanks to top-of-the-line prostheses, you wouldn't know from watching him walk that he'd lost both his lower legs.

She shrugged and met his disapproving blue eyes. "I was a

ballet dancer," she said, dismissing his comment with a wave of her hand. "I'm used to having beat up feet."

Wil glanced pointedly at the special booties she was wearing. "Broken, infected blisters. Multiple lacerations." He glanced up and started ticking points off on his fingers. "Gunshot wound to the shoulder that required minor surgery. Bruises. Insect bites. Dehydration and malnutrition. Orders are for you to rest. To take your antibiotics and heal." He crossed his arms over his chest and raised his eyebrows. "Have I missed anything?"

She shook her head. With his military buzz cut and the lines of strain etched into his face, Wil looked sterner than Max. Less likely to laugh. Just her luck that with Max in and out of surgery since their arrival, Wil had decided to step in as her keeper.

Well, she was too worried about whether the doctors would be able to repair Max's leg to appreciate Wil's brotherly concern. So she met his stare without flinching. "There's no way I can stay in my tiny room until I know Max is going to be okay." They'd been notified a while ago that Max had been moved to post-surgery recovery, but hospital protocol prohibited them from visiting him until he'd been moved to his regular room. Because his surgeon had been immediately called away to another patient, they hadn't heard yet if Max would regain full use of his leg.

"I'd go crazy in my room." Not to mention that she was still edgy. Jumping at every tiny noise. At least the waiting room had a television in the corner to distract her, plus the occasional passerby to snag her attention. And here she could see who was walking down the hallway, unlike being trapped in her room where she never knew if the footsteps indicated danger or not.

Wil scowled at her, the expression so much like Max's that she had to look away. He sighed and put his hand on her undamaged shoulder. "Look, I understand waiting is hard for you. It's no piece of cake for me, either." He gave a rueful laugh. "Guess now I know how my family felt when I was in and out of the operating room. But wearing yourself out with worry isn't helping Max. When he wakes up he'll want to see that you're healthy and happy. And frankly, you still look like shit."

She choked in astonishment and raised her eyebrows. "Wil, you seriously need to work on your motivational speeches. Does that kind of harsh talk work with your soldiers?"

"Nah, Marines are tougher than that," he said. "You're getting the soft sell."

"Be still my heart." She sighed and ran a hand over her hair, tucking the few stray strands back into her bun. Wil was right. Always slender, she'd lost weight she couldn't afford to lose during her time in the jungle. So she *did* sort of resemble a cadaver more than a healthy woman. Yet food didn't interest her. A typical response when she was stressed.

She'd probably look a little better if she could sleep. But she didn't want to take the sleeping pill they'd prescribed for her. She wanted to be able to go to Max's side as soon as he was cleared for visitors, not be lost in an artificially deep sleep.

Besides, while it had been four days since the WAR helicopter had taken them away from the field where they'd confronted Dietrich and his men, Emily still hadn't been able to shake the sense of urgency riding her. Whenever she did manage a few hours of sleep, she had nightmares about being chased. About Max being shot and her holding his bloody body while he died.

She shivered and ran her hands up and down her arms. Then winced, because that pulled at her shoulder wound.

"Hey." Wil took her hands, rubbing them between his own. "Max is going to be okay. My brother is as stubborn as they come. And if they do have to take his leg..." Wil shrugged. "I can help him work through it."

Emily sighed and squeezed Wil's fingers. "I'm sorry. I must seem terribly self-centered to you."

He shook his head. "No. You're not." He nailed her with a look. "Don't think I haven't noticed how jumpy you are. Take it from someone who's been there, don't hold your thoughts and feelings inside. As soon as you're ready, we'll get you access to professionals who can help you work through this experience."

Until he'd spoken, she hadn't realized how much she'd needed someone else to understand why she was still so on edge. "Thanks," she whispered, fighting back tears.

"You're welcome." Wil pulled her into a hug, carefully not touching her wounded shoulder.

"I really hate hospitals," she said against his chest.

He made a sound of disgust. "Yeah, me too. And my poor parents. First me, now Max."

Emily pushed away. "Oh, God," she choked out. "My parents are going to be here in a few hours." They were arriving on the same flight as Max's mom and dad. "The hospital staff aren't going to know what hit them once my dad is on scene."

"Is he bossy? Argumentative? Refuses to take no for an answer?"

She nodded.

"Sounds like Max when I was in the hospital. According to my parents, he treated the staff as if they were recruits in his unit, only there to do his bidding and make my life easier." The corner of his mouth lifted. "I have to say one thing about my brother, he's ferociously loyal. And protective."

She gave him a crooked smile. "Yeah, I've noticed."

Wil sobered. "Don't let him push you away, Emily. He might try, thinking he needs to protect you. But don't fall for that bull-shit. You love him. He loves you. More, he needs you. He needs to let the people who care for him back into his life."

"You know that even with Dietrich in custody, Max is still going to want to protect you and the others from Dietrich's spon-sor," she warned.

"Screw that. He's had enough time to play lone martyr. I fully intend to be a part of his life again. Kristoff and the rest of Max's former teammates feel the same way. Are you with us?"

She hesitated. "I'm not sure there's a place for me in Max's future." Seeing the question in Wil's eyes, she glanced away. "I don't even know what I want to do with my life." Only one thing was certain. She was done wallowing in pity because her career as a principal ballet dancer was over. Her scars weren't the big deal that she'd thought they were. With careful adherence to her physical therapy regimen, this latest damage to her shoulder shouldn't further decrease her mobility. There were other forms of dance or physical activity that she could participate in. Learning the African dances and running through the jungle had proven that.

So, maybe she'd choose to branch out in the dance world. Or maybe she'd decide to follow-up with her photography. Advocate for those affected by war. The point was, she had options she hadn't recognized before.

Speaking of her photography, "Have you heard anything about the photos I took?"

Wil nodded. "My source says they're being used as evidence against Dietrich and his men. Excellent work." He met her eyes. "If you're wondering about the future, I think WAR would be interested in utilizing your photography skills."

"Oh." She frowned. "You're that close to them?"

Some indefinable emotion crossed Wil's face. "Yeah, I've been working closely with Kris and the rest of Max's former team from Unit 3."

"Thanks. Even if I figure out what I want to do with my life, that doesn't mean Max will let me in."

"That's why I'm talking to you now. Don't let him get away with that crap. If you love him, fight for him. That's our plan. From now on, it's going to be a full court press." He gave her a wicked smile. "Max doesn't stand a chance. So, are you with us on Campaign Max?"

Emily laughed and held out her hand. "I'm in."

"Excellent." Instead of taking her hand, Wil pulled her into another hug.

Max's surgeon strode into the waiting room. "Sorry for the delay. I have good news."

Emily rushed over to him. "He's okay?"

"Yes. We were able to repair Max's leg. He might lose some sensation, but other than that, he should regain full use of his leg."

Emily clutched at Wil's arm, so dizzy with elation that she thought she'd faint. "Can we see him?"

"They're just now moving him from recovery to his room, but—"

A gurney rattled down the corridor. Max's voice, faint but querulous, argued with the nurse walking beside him.

The surgeon shook his head and gave a rueful smile. "Max is a stubborn, stubborn man. He shouldn't even be awake yet. Given his level of determination, I expect he'll be pushing the limits of his recovery at every opportunity." He speared first Wil, then Emily with a stern glance. "You two will have your hands full, but I'm counting on you to make certain he doesn't re-injure the leg."

Wil gave an evil smile and rubbed his hands together. "I'm looking forward to it."

Emily didn't even realize she'd moved until she was beside Max, looking down into his pale, beat up face. "Max, honey, are you already causing trouble?"

His eyes met hers, full of such intense love that her heart soared. "I—"

She leaned forward and kissed him. The familiar taste of him, the softness of his lips beneath hers, broke the barricade she'd erected to hold back her emotions. Tears dripped onto his face.

"Hey," he said weakly. "Hey, now. Don't cry, Em. I'm okay. We made it." He frowned. "You're okay, right? Your shoulder isn't permanently damaged?"

She sniffled. "I'm fine, Max."

He tried to raise his hand, but the nurse held him down.

"Don't move, Max," Emily chided. "Just be quiet and listen to the nurses. You need to rest. To heal. I'll be right here."

"Come closer."

"Huh?"

"I want to tell you something."

"O-kay." She leaned down.

Max put his mouth against her ear. "I am so incredibly proud of you. You're amazingly fierce. Strong. Such a fighter." His tongue traced the shell of her ear. "You turn me on."

She glanced at the nurse. "Ma-ax!"

He gave her an innocent look, but his words were anything but. "Think about you and me and a bed. Imagine all the things I can do to you. Dream about everything you want to do to me. I promise, when we get out of here, we're going to explore every single one of those fantasies. Every. Single. One. I'm going to start by working you with my tongue until you're begging for release, then I'll send you screaming over the edge."

Heat filled her cheeks. "You're going to pay for this, Max Lansing," she whispered. "Just you wait."

"Oh yeah, baby, I'm counting on it."

Emily cleared her throat and gestured behind her. "Ah... Your brother is here." She hoped no one could tell from her expression what Max had been saying to her, but the heat in her cheeks probably gave her away. Thank God her parents weren't here yet. Her eagle-eyed father would know immediately what Max had been saying and would want to know Max's intentions.

At least she was spared that humiliation for the moment. Besides, she didn't want her family intruding on her time with Max. This was about her, her newfound strength, and the love she held for this amazing man. Showing her father that she was no longer the depressed, purposeless woman she'd been when she left the United States could wait for another day.

Wil walked over. "I know it goes against your nature, Max, but for once in your goddamn life obey orders without questioning everything. The doctors really do know what they're talking about, and you'll heal faster if you just do as they say. Once you're in a wheelchair, I'm gonna give you some pointers, then I'm gonna kick your ass at wheelchair basketball. And since I hate using the chair, you better recognize how fucking generous I'm being."

Max narrowed his eyes. "You're on."

"Enough of that," the female nurse said. "Mr. Lansing, we're taking you back to your room now. Once there you will rest, or we won't let your girlfriend or your family in to visit. Do you understand?"

Max rolled his eyes. "Yes, ma'am."

"Love you," Emily said, placing a quick kiss on his forehead before they wheeled him away.

"Good to see you're okay, bro," Wil said.

"Love you both," Max said groggily. "Later." His eyes closed as the nurses pushed the gurney down the hall.

Emily wiped her eyes and saw Wil surreptitiously do the same. She blew her nose and cleared her throat.

"Okay," Wil said. "You owe me a rematch on that game of Parcheesi. Let's go."

With one last look in the direction Max had gone, she summoned up a watery smile and headed down to the game room, feeling lighter than she had in days.

Three Months Later
Rental House, Chesapeake Bay
United States

MAX SAT on the enclosed porch, wrapping up a discussion with Wil and Kris via Skype.

"Thanks to Emily's photos, we've tentatively identified Dietrich's buyer as Jonathan Morenga," Kris said from his office at

WAR's headquarters. "Mixed race, born in Nigeria before the revolution. Known to support groups with radical, pan-African leanings. Currently believed to be working for the African Freedom Army."

While most of Morenga's men had been killed by Dietrich's guards, Morenga himself had escaped. "Any idea where he disappeared to?" Max asked.

"Negative. We've got word out to our informants to let us know if they hear anything."

"Right. Wil?" His brother was back at his office at the U.S. compound in the Greater Niger Republic.

"The weapon prototypes have been turned over to the Department of Defense's research division," Wil said. "If they've figured out what the weapon does, they're keeping silent about it."

"Typical," Max snorted.

"Yeah."

"As far as we know, AFA has not yet lined up another weapon, so they've had to call off their planned attack," Kris added. "Again, our informants will keep us apprised of the situation."

Max glanced out the window to where Emily was playing on the beach with the next door neighbor's dog. Her shoulder had healed well, although Max still had the occasional nightmare where she died from the shot, just like her friend Crystal. "Any sign of Dietrich's sponsor?" Dietrich had died of an alleged heart attack a month after being taken into custody. Max suspected Dietrich's sponsor had arranged for his death.

"Not a clue. Dietrich didn't say a word before he died," Wil said.

"Of course not, that would have been too easy," Max grumbled.

"But we have confirmed that you're no longer considered AWOL from Unit 3. Technically, they would have accepted you back—"

"Over my dead body," Max said.

"Yeah, well, your record is clean. You now have an official honorable discharge. And all charges that you kidnapped Emily have been dropped."

"Thanks, bro." Max cleared his throat.

"Before you ask, no. We don't know yet who leaked WAR's existence to Dietrich," Wil said. "But we think it came from my side, not from within WAR."

"Wil—"

"No, I don't blame myself. Dietrich's sponsor has already proved he has access to the most classified areas of the military. Why not my base, too?"

Max raised an eyebrow. His brother might know it wasn't his fault, but that didn't erase the bitterness from his voice. After all, an insider had leaked the plans of Wil's previous base, setting off the chain of events that had led to the attack. Still, Max tried to ease the tension by joking "Why should you be exempt? Join the club."

Wil snorted, then gave Max a small nod of acknowledgment.

"All right, enough small talk," Kris said. "Are you and Emily in or not?"

Emily had finished playing with the dog and now stood on the porch steps, kicking sand off her feet. She'd finally put on some weight and lost the constant wariness that had stuck with her for weeks, resulting in a number of panic attacks. In addition to her physical therapy, she'd worked with a PTSD expert to reduce her anxiety and now only rarely had an attack.

He was so proud of her, his chest ached.

She stepped inside and he motioned her over.

She glanced at the computer, shook her head, then started to inch toward the kitchen door.

"Don't go. Kris wants to know if we're accepting his job offer."

"Oh." She walked over and put her hand on his shoulder.

Just that simple touch sent his body into overdrive. Needing to feel her warm skin under his, he put his hand on top of hers. As he'd promised, the moment his body had been strong enough, he'd taken her to bed and started fulfilling all their sexual fantasies.

Emily glanced from the computer screen to Max.

"Why don't you tell him," Max said.

She shrugged, then directed her attention to the image of Kris. "Yes. We accept."

Both Kris and Wil whooped.

Emily shared an amused glance with Max. The agreement was that Max would resume his cover of being a professor working on a book. Only this time, Emily would accompany him as the photographer for his research. In reality, they'd document abuses by the rebels, gather intel, and coordinate activities with WAR's civilian supporters such as Rene. They'd also work with Wil in his position of unofficial liaison between WAR and the U.S. military.

Fifteen minutes later, they'd finalized the logistics for the transition to their new life. The plan was for Max and Emily to move to West Africa in six months. Max needed to wait until the doctors had cleared him for heavy activity, which would probably take another month. Then he had to get back up to combat fitness. Although Emily's work would be mostly as an observer, due to the danger in the region she would undergo training to enhance her current skills and qualify her as a low-level operator. She'd also work with her psychiatrist on techniques she could use in the field to avoid future panic attacks. Once they'd said good-bye to Kris and Wil, Max shut off the computer.

He stood up and pulled Emily into his arms, right where she belonged. Then he took her mouth in a deep kiss. "I thought they'd never shut up," he murmured as he switched to planting kisses all over her face.

Emily laughed. "Face it, you love their attention. You missed being part of a team, didn't you?"

He sighed and rested his forehead against hers. "Yeah. It feels good to know that someone has my back." It humbled him knowing that Wil and Kris had never given up on him, despite his attempt to freeze them out of his life. "I'm a lucky guy."

"You are. I like them. And," she snuggled against him, "unless I'm wrong, Kristoff more than likes Wil. I think he has a major crush on your brother."

"Yeah, I noticed that, too."

"Do you think Wil knows it? He's harder to read than Kristoff."

Max nibbled on her ear. "Oh, Wil's definitely noticed. And he's interested. But wary after his previous lover died in the attack against the base. Plus, he's still adjusting to his new job and life without his lower legs. It'll take him a while to decide whether to get involved with Kris."

"Well, they seem like a good fit. I hope they end up together." Emily arched her neck and Max took her invitation, kissing his way from her ear to her collarbone and back again.

"Wil knows I'll back him no matter what."

"Mmm... He's lucky to have you as a brother."

Max just shrugged and took her mouth in a longer, deeper kiss.

"So," he began when he came up for air. He ran his hands down her back to her butt and stroked over the curves she'd recently put on once she'd started eating again. "How about heading to West Africa as my wife?"

She raised laughing eyes to him. "Max Lansing, is that the best you can do for a proposal?"

"What? I love you. You love me. Marriage is a natural next step." One he'd never thought he'd take. Or be so eager for. But he wanted this so badly, he'd actually approached her terrifying father—he held very old-fashioned views regarding his daughter's love life—for permission. Max figured since her dad had eventually said yes, odds were in his favor here.

Shaking her head, Emily briefly touched her lips to his. "You're one in a million, Max Lansing, but you do lack what my parents would call the finer social skills."

"What? Did I do something wrong? Your dad said it was okay."

"You talked to my dad?" She choked back laughter. "I bet that was intense."

"Yeah. So you have to say yes, as compensation for enduring the interrogation he put me through."

Shaking her head and smiling, she kissed him again, this time teasing him with a featherlight brush of her tongue. "You are completely unconventional and one of a kind, Max."

Uh-oh. That didn't sound good. Was she thinking of saying no? He'd been so sure...

She took his face in her hands and stared into his eyes. "Yes, I'll marry you."

Max threw his head back and shouted in joy. Then he scooped her up and carried her inside. "I believe we're up to fantasy number thirty-nine," he murmured as he set her on the bed and began to strip her of her clothes.

When she was naked, Emily sprawled on her back, unashamedly letting him see her scars as she raised her arms to him. "I don't remember that one," she said.

He shed his clothes and covered her body with his. "Let me remind you." He whispered in her ear exactly what he was going to do to her and what he wanted her to do in return.

She laughed in delight and ran her hands down his back.

Max lowered his mouth to hers. Felt that now familiar sensation of coming home.

Yes. He'd finally found his place in the world. He belonged here, in the arms of this amazing woman.

And for the first time in years, he looked to the future with hope.

Thank you for reading *WAR: Disruption*. The WAR series has been a long time in the making, ever since the days when I lived in West Africa. I'm so excited to finally share these characters with you!

Max wasn't too happy with me, but I had a lot of fun putting him through hell.

Does the acid attack against Emily sound familiar? The idea was triggered by the acid attack in January 2013 against the Bolshoi Ballet Theater's artistic director, Sergei Filin.

Finally, if you enjoyed reading *Disruption*, please consider recommending it to family, friends, and anyone else you think might be interested in Max and Emily's adventures. Leaving a review on the retail store where you purchased it or on Goodreads will also help other readers discover *Disruption*.

Thank you for your support!

The adventures of the WAR team that came in at the end of this book continue in *WAR: Intrusion*, the second book in the WAR series.

Happy reading!

Vanessa

ACKNOWLEDGMENTS

There were so many points during the creation of this book when I needed outside assistance. Whether it was help brainstorming the plot and character development, providing feedback on the blurb and cover, being a resource for accurate details, or listening to me complain (as I do every book) that this is the demon book from hell and my characters hate me, the people listed below are partly responsible for this book reaching publication. Since many people helped in more than one of the above areas, I'm simply going to list them all in alphabetical order.

With hugs and gratitude to: anonymae, Beth, Cyndi, Grace, Kristin, Mic, Poppy, Rachael, Sophie, Susan, and Virna.

A special thanks to the members of the Crime Scene Questions for Writers Yahoo! Group for answering my research questions. You're an invaluable resource.

Thanks also to my editing/proofreading team of Angela, Theresa, and Valerie, and to Frauke, my awesome cover designer.

Most of all, a huge thank-you to my family for supporting me in this crazy endeavor.

ABOUT THE AUTHOR

Photo by Gigi Pandian

I confess. I spend way too much time thinking up ways to torture my characters. As a worst-case scenario thinker, I channel my persistently dark what-if questions into writing romantic thrillers that combine intense emotion with action-packed plots.

I'm best known for The Surgical Strike Unit series about a privately run special operations group. My new series, WAR, is set in West Africa, where I lived for a time.

When I'm not writing, listening to music, or playing puzzle games on my mobile device, I help writers learn Scrivener and take long hikes in the nearby hills.

JOIN THE KIERDEVILS

Receive snippets-of-life stories, writing updates, sneak peeks, and other exclusive content such as *The SSU/WAR Bonus Pack* when you join the KierDevils newsletter.

www.vanessakier.com/kierdevils